PHANTOMS
FROM THE FILES OF THE
OFFICE OF PARANORMAL RESEARCH
BOOK 1

Terence West

FALLEN ANGELS
FROM THE FILES OF THE
OFFICE OF PARANORMAL RESEARCH
BOOK 1

Dedication

This book is for Donna, who always made sure my nightlight was plugged in and my closet door was securely shut. Thanks Mom.

Chapter 1

The clock read 12:50, but that meant little to him. At his age he had, at best, a vague conception of time. Rolling onto his back, he jostled his little legs and kicked off the covers. It was warm tonight, even for him. Looking to his left, he stared at his fluffy brown teddy bear. It had fallen from a sitting position to a crumpled mess next to his pillow. Reaching over, he snatched up the stuffed animal and held it tightly in his arms. Charlie Grant would turn eight years old tomorrow.

Charlie was small for his age. The other kids he played with were much taller than he was. As he lay quietly in bed, he wondered if he would ever grow up. He touched a small scratch on his left cheek and winced. He would show those other kids once he grew up. He knew the cut was an accident, but they didn't have to laugh at him. He didn't mean to cry, it just hurt so much. Next time, he would remember to be much more careful as he slid into second base. Running his hand over his messy blonde hair, he tried to think about something else.

Looking over at the nightstand next to his bed, he began to reach for his glass of water, but stopped. It was empty. Pushing his bear aside, Charlie swung his feet over the edge of the bed. He wasn't supposed to be up right now. It was way past his bedtime. He didn't want to make his parents mad, but he really needed a drink. Sliding off the edge of the bed, he snatched the empty glass from his nightstand and began to walk toward the door.

He stopped. Something didn't feel right. His wide innocent eyes quickly scanned his room. It was the smallest room in the house, but his parents assured him it was just his size. To his left, there was a small window that looked out onto the front yard of their two story house, and in front of him, he could see his toy box, still heaped with action figures from the previous day's adventures. To his right was the closet. Always closed at night. Always.

A small round nightlight was plugged into the outlet next to his door. He didn't really like the light. It always seemed to cast strange shadows across the room; mean outlines of things he didn't like, but Charlie was brave. Clenching the glass tightly in his small clammy hands, he pulled his attention away from the shadows and walked briskly to get some water. His heart began to pound. It felt like something was watching him. Charlie froze. The room seemed to become still almost instantly. He could hear his heart pounding in his chest, but then came another sound. A sound so terrifying, it shook him to his very bones. Slowly turning his eyes to the right, he could see his closet door slowly opening. It creaked and groaned as its old hinges rubbed against each other. In an act of sheer will, Charlie slowly craned his head to look at the closet. The door had been partially opened and was starting to close again. Looking into the closet, Charlie could only see darkness, but then terror gripped him. He wasn't sure how, but before he could even register the thought to run, he was already out of his room and charging toward his parents. Bursting out of the room, Charlie dropped the glass to the floor and dove head first into his parents' bed. The bed shook hard, then stopped.

Charlie's father shot straight up out of bed. Groggy and dazed, he looked frantically around the room. His boxers were hanging down slightly exposing the small gut he had been cultivating over the past few months. Rubbing his hands over his eyes to wipe the sleep from them, he looked down to see Charlie cocooning himself in his blankets. He let out a soft sigh of relief, then sat down on the edge of the bed. "Charlie," he said softly. He could hear his only son breathing heavily, almost frantically. "Charlie," he added a little more sternly. Reaching over slowly, he pulled the blankets away from Charlie's face. He recoiled slightly when he saw the fear in his eyes. "What's the matter, boy?"

"What's going on?" his wife asked as she sat up in bed.

"Mom, Dad," Charlie began as he started to catch his breath, "can I sleep with you tonight?"

Dylan Grant looked over at his wife and smiled. This was not the first time this had happened. He rubbed his thick brown beard as a smile emerged on his face. Dylan was a tall and well-built man. He had medium length dark brown hair that hung to the middle of his neck. It was naturally wavy, which drove his wife crazy. He was closing in on his thirty-fifth birthday, but he didn't feel it. In his mind, he was just a big kid. "I don't know. Cynthia, what do you think?"

Cynthia waved her hand in the air as she scooted back down in bed. "Why can't you sleep in your own room, Charlie?" She was much more petite than Dylan. Measuring only five foot three inches, her forehead barely reached Dylan's chin when they stood next to each other. She had long blonde hair and what Dylan referred to as "sky blue eyes". She used to be afraid to age, but even now, at thirty-two, she was one of the most beautiful women around.

"There's a monster in the closet," Charlie admitted sheepishly, not wanting his parents to know he was scared. After all, he was a big boy now.

Dylan ran his large hand over his son's hair. "I've got an idea."

"What, Dad?"

"Let's go find that monster and flush him out!" Dylan stood and walked across the room toward his golf bag. Hastily looking over the silver clubs, he grabbed a wedge out of the bag.

Charlie started to shake his head. "That's not a good idea, Dad."

"Why not?" Dylan asked, holding the club tightly in his hands. "Your old man's a pro at this. I bet you didn't know that back in college your dad majored in monster hunting."

Cynthia chuckled. "Stop making things up, honey."

Dylan shook his head. "No, it's true," he said with a laugh. "While other kids went out for the football team, I went out for monster hunting."

"Stop egging Charlie on and take him back to bed." Cynthia pulled the covers up tightly to her chin. She had to be up in less than five hours to be at work. She had a major meeting she had to be well rested for.

Dylan knelt down in front of Charlie. "Your mom never was a believer," he said in a whisper.

Charlie laughed. His dad was his hero. They

10

did everything together. Tomorrow was going to be extra special for him. His dad was taking the day off from work to take Charlie to his first major league baseball game. He had even promised to show Charlie how to run the scorebook. Sitting up in bed, Charlie scooted toward the edge and hopped off. When he was with his father, they were invincible.

"Are you ready to go get that monster?" Dylan asked as if he was taking the family out for ice cream.

Charlie nodded his head. "Yeah."

"Then what are we doing standing around here for? Let's go."

Dylan started for the door with Charlie closely in tow. Once in the hall, Dylan glanced across at Charlie's room. The door was still wide open and an empty glass was lying in the middle of the floor. Dylan looked down at his son. "Did you leave that glass there, Charlie?"

Charlie nodded.

"I'm going to let it go for the moment, but as soon as we get that monster, I want you to pick that up and put it where it belongs, okay?"

"Okay, Dad."

Turning back toward Charlie's door, Dylan lifted the club in front of him. It was his sword and he was headed to slay the dragon to bring peace back to the kingdom, or at least a good night's sleep. Taking another step, he stopped. Something wasn't right. Looking down the hall to his left, he caught a glimpse of a dark form moving past the window. "What the hell was that?" he asked himself. Reaching behind himself, he patted Charlie on the head. "Stay here for a minute, okay?"

Charlie looked up at his dad. He was transfixed, staring unblinking at the window at the end of the hall. "Dad?"

"It's okay," Dylan assured him without turning his attention away from the window, "I just want to go look at something. Stay here." Without another word, Dylan began to walk slowly down the hall, his bare feet sinking into the thick carpeting.

Charlie looked at his dad, then returned his attention to his room. He glared into the darkened space. *What happened to my nightlight?* He began to feel his heart pound in his chest again as he heard a soft rustling noise coming from within. Turning around, he ran back into his parent's room and dove back under the covers with this mother.

Dylan stopped. Turning around, his eyes widened. There was no sign of Charlie. "Son?" The golf club momentarily loosened in his hands. "Charlie!" he said again. An odd sensation passed over him. He felt as if he was being watched. Spinning around, he saw a pair of burning red eyes outside the window peering in at him. Dylan's mouth fell agape as he stared.

The window shattered inward sending shards of glass sailing past Dylan. One of the larger pieces sliced through his upper arm. Blood instantly began to seep from the wound. Slapping his hand on it, Dylan began to stumble backwards through the hall. He kept his vision trained on the red orbs still outside his window, barely noticing the crunch of glass under his bare feet. All at once, the eyes blinked once and a dark object flung itself in through the shattered glass. There was no sound from the creature, only the howl of the wind outside. The dark form undulated and transformed as it moved down the hallway toward Dylan, its form finally settling on something vaguely human. Dylan could swear he was looking at a man standing before him wearing a large flowing black cape, although he could make out no detail in the creature, only darkness and those burning red eyes.

"You will not escape," the being hissed in a low, angry voice.

"Leave me alone!" Dylan cried as he moved faster. "Cynthia!" he cried out. "Cynthia, call 911!" Dylan looked down at his hands and stopped. He gripped the golf club tightly. Taking a deep breath, he lunged forward at the being and swung with all his might, but connected with nothing. The blade of the club sliced right through the middle of the creature without any effect. The force of the swing threw Dylan off balance and he tumbled to the floor. Looking up, he saw he was lying at the feet of the being.

Turning his head to the right, he peered into Charlie's room. To his horror, a second pair of red eyes appeared. "Shit," he muttered under his breath. Pushing himself off the floor, he tried to run for his room, but was cut off by the first shadow. The creature lifted what looked like an arm and pointed it toward him. Four thin tendrils of darkness shot from the hand like coiled snakes and wrapped themselves around Dylan's neck. Reaching up, Dylan tried to tear them off, but they were like steel. Gasping for air, he watched as the second pair of red eyes emerged from Charlie's room and moved toward him. This one was also in the form of a human. He didn't appear three dimensional in nature, rather flat. Its billowing darkness reached out and began to wrap around Dylan. It felt cold and evil. The darkness began to engulf him as it slowly moved up his body.

The second shadow echoed the first's sentiment. "You will not escape." Dylan felt his eyelids becoming heavy. The oxygen was being cut off to his brain; he was dying of asphyxia. A horrid smile crossed the faces of the two shadows as Dylan took his final breath. Retracting the darkness, the two of them ripped Dylan in half. Red blood splattered against the wall in a horrible pattern as his torso fell next to his legs. Reaching down, one of the shadows slid its fingers forcefully into Dylan's chest. It wrapped the darkness around his still beating heart and ripped it from the man's chest. The creature held it above its head to examine. Once satisfied they had what they came for, the two creatures slowly moved toward Dylan's bedroom and entered.

Charlie looked out from beneath the covers at the two pairs of burning red eyes in the darkness of the room. Reaching over, he shook his mom's shoulder in an attempt to wake her up. "Mom," Charlie said frantically. "What is it now, Charlie?" Cynthia asked, still half asleep.

Charlie swallowed hard as he stared at the eyes. "The Shadow People are here," he whispered.

***

The large office was lavishly decorated. The walls were painted a creamy shade of white that emanated warmth. Pictures dominated a majority of the space, as well as several tall filing cabinets and book shelves. Trophies collected from all over the world sat quietly observing the day-to-day routine. A large brown wooden desk sat to one side with two dark, plush seats in front of it, while a large, round conference table occupied a substantial section of the floor. A huge window behind the desk was letting the soft rays of morning light spill into the room. Two men sat inside, one in an expensive leather chair behind the desk, the other in one of the chairs facing it. Both men were swathed in the usual business attire of suits and ties.

The one behind the desk swiveled his chair around to face the other man in his office. Lifting a small tan folder off his desk, he leaned back in his chair and flipped it open. Adjusting his wire-framed glasses, he began to peruse the pages inside.

"Mr. Bishop," the man began in a light tone, "I assume you know why you've been called in here."

Nick Bishop adjusted his dark gray tie and sat forward in his seat. Folding his hands together, he propped his elbows up on his knees. He was a young man with short, messy dark hair and piercing blue eyes. He was clean-shaven with the exception of a small patch of hair on his chin below his lips. His black suit was hanging loosely off his thin, muscular frame. "I do, Chairman Weiss," he answered in a firm voice.

Thomas Weiss set the folder down on his desk and rubbed his bearded chin. He was sometimes called "the Old Man" of the firm because of his gray hair, but in actuality, he wasn't even close to being the oldest member there. "Why did you want to join the Office of Paranormal Investigation?"

Weiss asked after a moment.

Bishop pointed to the yellow folder, "It's all there in my files."

"Yes," Weiss said with a nod, "it is, but I want to hear it from you."

"Is there a problem with my application, sir?" Bishop asked.

A smile crossed Weiss' face. "A little defensive, aren't we?"

"I'm sorry." Bishop looked away from Weiss as he ran his hand through his hair. "This is very important to me."

"I can see that." Weiss pulled off his glasses and set them down next to the folder. He rubbed the bridge of his nose with his finger and thumb, massaging the two small red indentations caused by the glasses. Looking back up at Bishop, he started to run his fingers over his beard again. "I just want to know a little more about who Nick Bishop is," Weiss confessed. "I do this with all the new recruits."

Bishop breathed a sigh of relief and slipped back into his seat. "I'm sorry, Chairman," he said again. "You wanted to know why I want to join the Office of Paranormal Investigation?"

Weiss nodded.

"I guess to use a popular phrase, I am a 'believer'," Bishop said with a smile. "I just want to know this kind of stuff is real."

"What," Weiss hated to use the word, "'Stuff'?"

"The paranormal." Bishop sat forward again. "I know these occurrences are happening, and I want to be part of the organization that proves it. I want

16

to take the paranormal out of the domain of science fiction and tabloid magazines, and shout to the world that this is real."

"Those are very high ideals, Mr. Bishop, and something we here at the OPR haven't been able to do in thirty years." Weiss lifted his glasses off the desk and slipped them back on.

Bishop shook his head, "But, sir, I've read some of the OPR's files. You have documented proof of the paranormal. How can the scientific community not recognize that?"

"Easily," Weiss stated with a bit of disdain in his voice. "Unless something can be repeated or quantified under laboratory conditions, scientists won't accept the findings." Weiss leaned forward on his desk. "When I started this organization, I had the very same ideals you have right now. I was hell bent to prove to the entire world this kind of phenomenon was real, but over the years, this company's, as well as my own, ideals have changed. We're not here to change the world, Mr. Bishop, just to study it." He lifted a small blue coffee mug from the side of his desk and took a sip from the warm liquid inside. "We've become the guardians at the gate, so to speak. We have the knowledge, and when the scientific community finally accepts the idea, they'll have to come to us."

"So what is the OPR's mission?"

"The same as it has always been, to collect information, to find the truth," Weiss said as he set the mug aside. "That hasn't changed." He flipped open the yellow folder again. "It says here you were recruited by the CIA, but dropped out a week before you graduated. Why?"

17

"The Agency just wasn't for me."

"It says here you were among the top of your class."

Bishop nodded, "I can't quite justify my actions. I just came to a point where I knew I was on the wrong path. I wasn't cut out to be a part of the intelligence community. I just didn't fit in.

"Fair enough," Weiss replied. Flipping over a page in the folder, Weiss stopped. "You have a medical condition?"

Bishop ran his hand over his chin. "I wouldn't really call it a medical condition, sir, but yes, I am a chronic insomniac. I assure you it won't interfere with my job performance."

"Very good," Weiss said with a smile. "Let's make sure it doesn't." Closing the folder, he lifted it up and slid it into a drawer on his desk. Leaning back in his chair, he looked over his new recruit. "You don't have a background in science, do you?"

Bishop shook his head. "I don't. I've taken science classes in college, but nothing serious. Why?"

"The OPR is mainly a scientific agency, Mr. Bishop. Most of our members have degrees in various science related fields."

Bishop smiled, "I thought you were just ghost hunters."

"We are," Weiss admitted, "but we chase the supernatural with science and hard evidence. Your lack of a solid scientific background could be a hindrance."

"But my FBI training should more than make up for that," Bishop argued. "I've been trained to correctly interrogate suspects and witnesses, and I

18

have an eye for detail. I may not be an egghead, but my experience as an investigator will be invaluable."

Weiss laughed out loud. "Good answer." Opening the top drawer of his desk, Weiss pulled out a small, stapled packet of papers. Standing up, he tossed them across to Bishop. "In that packet, you'll find all your tax information, as well as medical and insurance forms. Fill them out and have them back to my secretary by tomorrow morning."

"I'm hired?"

Weiss nodded. "Head over to photography after you leave. We need to get IDs made for you."

Bishop stood up and extended a hand toward Weiss. "Thank you, Chairman Weiss. You won't regret this decision."

Weiss shook Bishop's hand firmly. "I hope not." Sitting back down, Weiss removed a small stack of papers from his inbox on his desk. Tapping them on the desk to straighten them, he handed them to Bishop. "Here's the information on your first assignment. I want you to study them thoroughly tonight, then report to office three-thirteen in the morning to meet your partners."

Chapter 2

The red and blue flashing lights were casting an eerie glow over the front of the brick home. Various police officers and investigators were moving about their duties. Yellow strands of police tape were littered around the area, blocking access to the media and the public.

Amidst the bustle of the busy crime scene, a lone detective stood next to his battered green sedan drinking a cup of coffee. A large man, he was wearing a long tan trench coat, an off-white dress shirt with a red tie and a pair of gray slacks. The white shirt had various stains scattered over it, while his shoes were generally untied. He wore a dark gray fedora over his thinning black hair that partially hid his rough face in shadow. A three day beard was growing on his chin he had no intention of shaving, while dark bags hung under his eyes from a lack of sleep.

"Detective Enbaugh!" An officer shouted from across the yard.

Jack Enbaugh looked up and tilted his fedora back on his head. Setting his paper coffee cup down on the hood of his car, he began to weave his way through the crime scene toward the front of the house. For an overweight man, he was relatively light on his feet. Stopping at the front door, Enbaugh looked at the young officer. "What is it, officer?"

The young officer in his black uniform pulled off his hat and held it uncomfortably in his hands. "Coroner wants to know if he can start removing the bodies."

Enbaugh took a deep breath and thought for a moment. "Move them." The young officer nodded, then walked back into the house. Turning, Enbaugh looked over the front yard. It was still wet from last night's rain. Turning his face skyward, he looked at the dark clouds looming overhead. It was officially the hurricane season here in Stone Brook, Florida. The weatherman on the radio this morning confirmed that a possible hurricane was forming off the southern coast. It was still too early to tell, but it looked like it was preparing to head on shore.

Enbaugh had lived and worked in Stone Brook for most of his life. He had been born in California, but his parents relocated to Florida when he was just a child. Stone Brook was a small town of about fifty thousand people located on the coast of the Gulf of Mexico, just slightly north of the cities of Tampa and St. Petersburg. He had been protecting the population here for close to fifteen years now. He liked it here. The town was big enough to have its share of trouble, but it was still free of the large city problems.

"Detective?" a voice asked from behind him.

Spinning around, Enbaugh saw three men pushing gurneys toward him through the house. Each one had a body resting atop it with a plain white sheet thrown over it.

"Can we get you to move?" the first man asked.

Enbaugh nodded and stepped aside. The first gurney made its way over the doorjamb and onto the cement walkway, followed closely by the second and third. The man pushing the third gurney stopped and looked down. The front wheel had gotten jammed between the railing and the

21

sidewalk.

"Hold on," he said to the others. "Let me see if I can get this loosened."

"Come on, Joey," the first man announced. "We're on a tight schedule here. Just pull it out of there and let's go."

Joey knelt down next to the wheel and began to tug on it. Letting out a sigh of exhaustion, he wrapped his hands firmly around the wheel and gave one final tug. The wheel shot loose and sent the gurney toppling to the ground. The body of Cynthia Grant rolled onto the sidewalk in plain sight of everyone. She had been decapitated and her body mutilated.

Enbaugh swore under his breath. Grabbing the sheet off the ground, he quickly laid it over the remains. "What the hell is wrong with you?" Enbaugh asked Joey angrily.

"I was just trying to—"

"Look over there." Enbaugh pointed to a small crowd that had gathered outside the yellow police tape. Several members of the media were standing there with cameras rolling. "We don't want this to show up on the ten o'clock news."

Joey shook his head. "I'm sorry, I didn't mean to…."

"Look," Enbaugh said quietly, "it's our job to protect these people from the crazies out there, and sometimes that even means protecting them from the knowledge something horrible happened. Do you understand?"

Joey nodded. "Sorry, Detective."

"Go grab your two buddies and get this cleaned up, and do not remove this sheet again," instructed

Enbaugh. Standing up, he watched Joey run over to the waiting ambulance. Looking down at the sheet, he could see the two separate lumps beneath. A chill ran down his spine. He had never witnessed anything this gruesome during all his years on the force. He had certainly read about this kind of thing, but never seen it first-hand. Just another reason he liked living in Stone Brook.

Stepping over the body, Enbaugh made his way into the Grant's house. The living room was very large and well furnished. Dylan Grant, the husband, was a doctor in this area, and a well-respected one, while his wife, Cynthia, was employed by a small advertising firm. Everyone knew the Grants had money, and by looking at their home décor, it was obvious.

Enbaugh had already been here for three hours. He had been called out here at eight a.m. to investigate. Apparently, Cynthia's employer had expected her at work two hours earlier and had been trying to call her all morning. He had told officers that Cynthia was never late. As luck would have it, one of the officers on the force was a close friend of the family and was delivering a birthday present to the Grant's son, Charlie, so he looked in on the family. That's when he found them.

Enbaugh began his usual routine at a crime scene. Pulling a pair of latex gloves out of the pocket of his trench coat, he snapped them on. Slowly, he began to move over the living room. He needed to know if anything was missing. Robbery was his first guess when he arrived this morning, although nothing appeared to be missing. Enbaugh knelt down next to a small wooden coffee table located between two brown leather couches. A small layer of dust had settled on the table. This would make his job easier. He would be able to tell if anything had been moved or taken due to the dust. It would leave a clearly detectable clean spot if an item was taken. He scanned the table and found nothing.

Standing up, he quickly glanced over the rest of the living room. Everything seemed to be in its place. He noticed a small plastic cube on the fireplace mantle. Taking a step toward it, he smiled at the contents. "Wow," he said under his breath.

"Jack?"

Enbaugh spun around. "Montoya."

Detective Caroline Montoya was slowly walking down the stairs into the living room. Half Enbaugh's age, she was his partner. Her long blonde hair was tied up behind her head showing off her slender face and neck. Long dark eyelashes hung seductively over her green eyes, while her lips were painted a deep red. She was wearing all black this morning, from her long trench coat, to the blouse and skirt which hung just above her ankles. "What are you doing?" she asked Enbaugh in a soft voice.

Enbaugh smiled. "Just doing a cursory check around the house. I wanted to see if anything was missing." They had been partners for six years now. Montoya had transferred to the Stone Brook Police Department after a three year stint as part of the Miami law enforcement community. "Come take a look at this."

Montoya walked slowly down the stairs and into the living room. "What am I looking at?"

Enbaugh pointed to the plastic cube on the mantle. "It's a baseball."

"Wow," Montoya said sarcastically. "That's really neat."

"No, look at it. It's been signed by Mark McGuire, and it has the number '62' written under the signature."

"Which means what?" Montoya asked.

Enbaugh laughed. "You have no culture. This was McGuire's sixty-second home run during the 2000 season. You know, the year he hit the record breaking seventy homers?"

"That's absolutely fascinating," Montoya said with a yawn.

"You're missing the point," Enbaugh scolded her. "Last year, one of these home run balls went up for auction and sold for in the neighborhood of sixty thousand dollars. This is a very expensive piece of baseball memorabilia."

"So if it's still here…." Montoya started.

"We're probably not looking at a robbery," Enbaugh finished.

"Still not very conclusive," Montoya argued. "Maybe the thief just didn't know much about baseball."

"It's just a theory in progress." Enbaugh snapped off his rubber gloves. "Did you find anything upstairs?"

Montoya shook her head, "Just a lot of bloodstains." She turned around to look at the stairs. "It's strange though, only that one second floor window was broken."

"Did the boys from forensics examine the ground beneath that window for signs a ladder had

25

been used?"

Montoya nodded. "They couldn't find any evidence that one had been used. The usual signs of smashed patches of grass or indentations weren't present."

Enbaugh thought for a moment. "Is there any other way to get up to that window?"

"It's basically a sheer wall. There are no pipes or storm drains on that side of the house. No latticework over there either."

"So why'd the killer use the second floor window?" Enbaugh wondered. He turned back around to take another look at the autographed baseball, but it was gone. Only a small square clean spot remained on the mantle. "What the hell? Did you take the baseball, Montoya?"

Montoya looked confused. "No, I've been standing here in front of you the whole time and there's no one else in the room."

Enbaugh glanced around the living room. A worried look crossed his face. "How the hell?" He began to walk across the living room. The plastic cube was sitting on the top of one of the brown leather couches. "How did it get over here?"

Enbaugh began to reach for it, when it shot off like a rocket across the room. It impacted a mirror hanging in front of the staircase, shattering it on contact. The cube and shards of glass fell to the floor in a heap. Enbaugh spun around to look at Montoya. "Did you see that?"

Montoya was already heading for the door. "I didn't see anything." Enbaugh quickly started to chase Montoya. "Wait a minute!" He grabbed her by the shoulder and spun her around just outside the

26

front door. "You can't tell me that you didn't see that."

"Why did you throw the ball into the mirror, Jack?" Montoya asked quietly. "I didn't," Enbaugh said quietly.

***

Bishop found himself marveling at the sheer size of the building. He had a little time before his photos were taken yesterday to wander around the OPR headquarters, but he hadn't seen even half of the office in that time. Looking down at his watch, he noted he still had almost ten minutes before he had to meet his new partners this morning. *Good thing, I'm going to need all that time to find the office.* Adjusting his tie, he pulled his black leather jacket around himself. He had decided on a white shirt and a pair of black slacks this morning. After reading over most of the OPR's policies last night, he never came across a dress code, so he decided to wear what he felt comfortable in.

The OPR Headquarters was built in the heart of downtown Washington D.C. Bishop had been informed that when standing on the roof, you could look down into the White House's backyard, although he hadn't put that theory to the test...yet. It was a massive twelve story building constructed entirely of concrete and glass. Each floor contained offices, labs and small research sections. The main research facility, however, was located in the basement of the building. Weiss had enclosed all the case files in a room that could probably survive a direct nuclear assault. It was claimed the OPR's files were more tightly guarded than the Constitution itself.

Bishop glanced along the walls as he passed. In a normal office, you would find awards and plaques, as well as a painting or photo of the crusty owner, but not at the OPR. The photos on the wall varied from the bizarre to the downright macabre. Each framed photo had its own story to tell, from spiritual photography to exorcism. One particular image caught Bishop's attention. It was a photo of a wrecked car on the highway. The front end had been completely smashed into the passenger's compartment making it look more like a tuna can than a car. Bishop's eyes were drawn to the front of the vehicle, there you could clearly see a large white semi-translucent object, which appeared to be hovering slightly over it. It had the basic human form, but no discernable features. He leaned over and began to read the small gold plaque beneath it.

"This was the car of fifty-seven year old Elaine Ram. The front of her car was crushed when it collided with a semi heading in the opposite direction. A claims adjuster for Elaine's insurance company took the photo only hours after the accident. She claims it shows definitive proof of Elaine's guardian angel."

Bishop stood up and looked at the photo again. "That's very interesting."

"What's interesting?" a female voice asked from behind him.

Bishop spun around startled. "You scared me," he said with a smile. "Sorry." The woman was leaning against the frame of a nearby office door.

She had long brown hair with startling green

eyes. Over her long slender frame, she was wearing a black skirt, white t-shirt and long black leather jacket that hung just past her hips. A pair of black pumps rounded out her outfit. "Just comes with the territory, I guess." She walked slowly from the doorway toward Bishop. "Are you new here?"

Bishop nodded. All his prayers had been answered. Here, standing in front of him, was a beautiful woman who believed in the paranormal. He tilted his head back for a moment and said a silent "thank you" to God. "My name's Nick Bishop."

"Nice to meet you, Nick. My name's Dawn, Dawn Lassiter," she reached out and shook Bishop's hand gracefully.

Bishop snuck a peek at her left hand, and said another silent "thanks". She wasn't wearing a wedding ring. He knew he had to make conversation.

There was no way he was going to let this brief encounter end. "I was just looking at some of the photos here in the hall. There's some truly incredible phenomenon captured here."

"Yes," Dawn said slowly, "but there's a reason they're hanging here and not down in the 'vault'." She crossed her slender arms and looked at the photo in front of them. "Tell me why."

Bishop thought for a moment as he scanned over the photo. *This would be simple*. "These are obviously copies of the originals."

Dawn laughed. "Guess again, sport, these are the real photos." Bishop looked at the photo again. "I don't know why."

A smirk crossed Dawn's face. "Have to teach

you rookies everything," she muttered. "Look here," she pointed at the car. "You see what's left of the windshield?"

Bishop nodded, "Yeah."

"There's no reflection in it. Look at the ground around the car. Light from the quote, unquote 'apparition' is spilling all over it. If that's the case, why isn't there a reflection of the ghost in the windshield?"

Bishop shook his head. "It's at the wrong angle. From their vantage point, the photographer wouldn't have seen the ghost's reflection."

Dawn's smirk quickly faded. "Okay, hot shot, take a look at this." She ran her finger around the edge of the ghost. "You can tell this photo has been digitally manipulated. Upon close inspection, you can see the ghost's 'aura' becomes pixilated as you near the edge."

Bishop leaned close to the photo. "That's very curious. You can see it." He looked up at Dawn, "You're right."

"Of course I am," Dawn replied confidently.

A moment of silence passed between the two. Bishop felt it was his obligation to continue the conversation. "I hate to be too forward," Bishop turned and leaned on the wall, "but how would you like to have dinner with me tonight?" he asked, turning on his charm. "I know this great little Italian restaurant downtown. We could have dinner, go dancing and then…who knows?"

Dawn patted Bishop's shoulder. "You're just so cute," she pinched his cheeks, "like a little puppy dog."

"So is that a 'yes'?" Bishop asked proudly.

Dawn laughed. "I don't think so, Mr. Bishop."

Dejected, Bishop glanced down at his watch and his eyes widened. "Shoot, I'm late. Can you tell me where office three-thirteen is?"

Dawn pointed over her shoulder. "It's right there." Bishop began to walk away, "Are you sure?"

"Pretty sure. That's my office."

Bishop felt his heart sink. Spinning around, he looked at Dawn. "Look, I'm sorry about hitting on you. I didn't know you were my partner." He was trying to salvage the situation.

Dawn waived her hand, as if pushing that behind her. "Water under the bridge, Mr. Bishop." She stopped and stood next to him, "But if my husband finds out, there's going to be trouble."

Bishop felt his jaw drop open. "I didn't know you were married, you're not wearing a wedding ring. I'm so sorry."

Dawn held up her left hand and a wicked smile crossed her face. "Gotcha." She began to laugh as she walked into the office.

Bishop cursed under his breath. Not only had he been shot down, but he had been had as well.

"Are you coming, Mr. Bishop?" Dawn yelled from inside the office. Bishop looked at the photo again, then turned to follow Dawn. Crossing into the office, he stared in awe. It was a large room with two desks sitting face to face in the center. Large floor to ceiling windows were on the far wall, allowing light to spill into the room. Several large bookshelves had been arranged against another wall. Each one contained artifacts from previous investigations. The wall adjacent to the door was covered with corkboard, which, in turn, was littered with small photographs and white, lined index cards explaining them. On the wall to Bishop's left, hung a huge map of the United States. Red and black pushpins had been placed everywhere they had investigated a case. The map was beginning to fill up. To his right, he could see a small area partially separated by black filing cabinets. He counted at least twenty that ringed the small area.

Dawn had walked into the room and slid into a small gray chair behind the first desk. She lifted a small yellow notepad out of her drawer and began to quickly scrawl something across it. "Cane?" she asked without looking up.

A trim, older man emerged from the circle of filing cabinets with an open manila folder in his hand. He was dressed in a pair of black trousers and a black leather jacket that hung just above his knees. A black vest covered the dark blue shirt and tie he was wearing. He had a thin goatee beginning to gray, with neatly combed brown hair and a pair of rectangular glasses sitting just below the bridge of his nose. Bishop could see the edge of a dark black tattoo peeking out from his shirt collar as it stretched onto his neck. Cane stopped and looked up at Bishop. "So," he said to no one with a proper British accent, "this is our new recruit."

Bishop took one step toward Cane and extended his hand. "My name's Nick Bishop, and you are…?"

The man didn't return Bishop's gesture. "I am Cane."

Bishop slowly drew his hand back and stuffed it into his pant pocket. "I—" Cane pointed to a chair next to his desk. "Please, sit down."

Bishop complied quickly. He knew this man was twenty years his elder, but Cane was still very daunting.

"I have one speech," Cane said as he continued to scan the file he had in his hands, "so listen carefully." He flipped the folder shut and tossed it onto his desk. Crossing his hands in front of him, Cane glared at Bishop with his gray eyes. "We are not 'ghost hunters', or 'ghost busters'. We do not 'chase' ghosts, nor do we 'eliminate' them. We are paranormal investigators and we take that title very seriously. First and foremost, we are researchers. Don't ever forget that and we'll get along just fine." A crooked smile crossed his face.

Bishop nodded slowly. He felt as if his teacher was talking down to him. Bishop began to open his mouth to speak, but one glance from Cane stopped him.

Cane pointed to Dawn, "Dawn is going to give you your instructions." Cane lifted his folder off his desk and retreated back into the ring of cabinets.

Bishop leaned close to Dawn. "Did I do something to offend him?"

Dawn shook her head, "No, he's like that with everyone. Get on his good side and he's as loyal as a dog, but piss him off, and he'll be your worst enemy."

"How do you put up with that?"

Dawn laughed. "Cane is my best friend." She tore a page off her notebook and handed it to Bishop. "This is your task list for this morning. Get this done quickly, because we're leaving for Florida this afternoon."

Bishop accepted the list and scanned over it.

"Find research material and get you guys coffee?" he asked angrily. "I'm your partner, not your gofer!"

Dawn patted him on the shoulder. "Everyone has to start at the bottom, Mr. Bishop." Dawn snickered to herself as she stood up. She moved across the office to join Cane.

Bishop leaned back in his chair and let out a long sigh. Folding the paper in half, he stuffed it into his jacket pocket. Lifting himself out of the chair, he walked slowly out of the office, muttering under his breath.

Chapter 3

Detective Enbaugh felt apprehensive while he stood at the front door of the Grants' former home. He didn't like it here, not after what happened earlier this morning. A small metal awning was providing a bit of relief from the weather, but not much. Nothing remained in the Grants' yard except a few errant strands of yellow police tape and even they had almost all blown away. A few stray tire tracks could be seen in the wet soil of the front lawn, but it was quiet now. Only his battered car occupied a space on the curb in front of the house. He watched as a crumpled piece of newspaper tumbled across the green grass, then was swept up into the wind and carried away.

He looked up at the gray sky. Rain was falling and.it was coming down hard. The clouds seemed to be in fast forward as they sailed across the sky. The weatherman said this morning this was a tropical storm hitting the coast. It was probably the remnants of Hurricane Jennifer that struck about a week earlier. It was October Twenty-ninth. Very near the end of hurricane season in the south. Enbaugh watched the tree limbs bend and shake in the winds. He hoped it was the end. This small town couldn't handle another hurricane.

Enbaugh remembered the one that struck three years ago. It was called Hurricane Lisa. Enbaugh wondered why they always named hurricanes after women. Several off-color jokes immediately popped into his head. A crooked smile crossed his face, but he pushed it down. He had to remain serious, had to remain focused.

A small black car pulled into the concrete driveway and stopped. The driver's side door popped open, but no one stepped out. The windshield wipers, which looked to have been on high speed, stopped in the middle of the window as the car was turned off. Reaching into his tan trench coat, Enbaugh removed a large black umbrella he had been holding under his arm. Undoing the Velcro strap that held it closed, he snapped the umbrella open and took a step off the front stoop. He felt a quick burst of wind whip up around him. He grabbed onto his hat and held the umbrella tightly in his hand. "Ms. Frieze?" he asked loudly over the howl of the wind. Taking another step toward the car, he could see an elderly woman sitting in the front seat.

She looked up at him. Her face was long and gaunt. Jagged wrinkles crisscrossed her face from years of living, and her once deep blue eyes were now a light shade of gray. Her white hair was cut short around her face, leaving only a few wispy strands falling onto her neck. She was wearing a long black coat, a dark colored skirt that hung to her ankles and a white blouse with a gold and silver broach on the collar. Reaching over to the passenger's seat, she lifted a long black cane and pushed it out the door. Turning in the seat, she dropped her feet out and placed them firmly on the ground. Reaching up, she clutched the doorframe with her almost skeletal hands and pulled herself out of the car. Grabbing the cane from its resting spot, she moved it to her right hand.

Enbaugh lowered the umbrella to cover her from the elements. "Ms. Frieze?" he asked again, this time much softer.

The old woman nodded. "I'm Rachelle Frieze," she replied in a soft, frail voice. "You must be Detective Enbaugh."

"That's correct, ma'am." Enbaugh placed his hand Rachelle's shoulder. "Can I help you inside?"

Rachelle reached up and brushed Enbaugh's hand away. "I can do it myself," she said angrily. "I may look old and weak, but I can still get around just fine."

Enbaugh took a step back. "Yes, ma'am." A smile crept over his scruffy, pudgy face. *I hope I still have that much piss and vinegar in me when I'm her age.*

The two walked carefully over the wet cement as they approached the front door. Enbaugh's smile quickly faded when he looked up at the house. A shiver ran down his spine. He read his silver, ten-dollar watch. It was closing in on two-thirty in the afternoon, but the overcast sky made it appear a lot later. As they approached the front door, Enbaugh saw two strips of yellow tape fastened to the doorframe just below a plastic cut-out of a jack-o'-lantern. Large black letters ran across them that read:

CRIME SCENE. DO NOT CROSS.

Reaching into the pocket of his trench coat, he removed a small silver knife and snapped it open. Enbaugh pressed his left hand against the frame of the door as he slowly sliced through the yellow tape. Closing the blade, he deposited the knife in his pocket. He looked over at Rachelle. She was standing patiently, her cane at her side. Enbaugh wrapped his meaty paws around the gold doorknob and twisted it. The heavy wooden door groaned in protest as he pushed it open.

Enbaugh stared into the darkened house. It was calm inside, almost serene. With a deep breath, Enbaugh stepped inside, followed by Rachelle. The two walked into the living room. Enbaugh could still see the glimmering remains of the mirror that had broken that very morning.

Rachelle hobbled across the room toward the broken mirror. Slowly leaning over, she picked up the translucent cube that still held the autographed baseball. The cube had a large crack that ran down two of its sides. Rachelle shook her head slowly. "These were two of Dylan and Cynthia's prized possessions. When Dylan caught this baseball, he talked about it for months. I think it was one of his crowning achievements in life, and this mirror...." she let her voice trail off.

"What is it, Ms. Frieze?" Enbaugh asked sympathetically. He didn't want to admit he might have had a hand in their destruction.

Rachelle ran her old hand along the painted aluminum frame. "I gave this mirror to Cynthia on her thirtieth birthday. She was feeling old, you see," she said as she turned to Enbaugh. "I wanted to prove to her that there was still a vibrant, young woman staring back at her every day in the mirror." Rachelle lowered her gaze. "She told me never a day past that she didn't stop and look at herself in that mirror before she left for work and think of how beautiful she was."

"Ms. Frieze," Enbaugh started, "We can do this

another time. We just need you to look through the house to see if anything's missing. It's not imperative that we do it today."

"No," Rachelle said, wiping a tear from her eye. "Cynthia always relied on me for my strength, Detective. Why should that be any different now?"

"I just had your best interests in mind, ma'am." Enbaugh walked around one of the leather couches, letting his fingers slide along it. Glancing around the living room, he spotted a small white lamp seated on a nearby coffee table. He reached under the lampshade and gently toggled the light on. A pleasant white glow filled the room. He turned back to Rachelle. She was still standing next to the mirror with her hand resting on the cool metal frame. He knew she needed time to mourn the loss of her family. He couldn't understand why she wanted to proceed with the inventory so soon. "We can begin whenever you're ready, Ms. Frieze."

Rachelle turned to look at Enbaugh. "If you don't mind, I'd like to have a moment alone."

Enbaugh nodded. Turning, he looked past the living room into the dining room. There was a small door that adjoined the kitchen on the far wall next to a tall cabinet that contained all of the Grant's best china. "I'll be in the kitchen if you need me, Ms. Frieze."

Rachelle mustered a smile. "Thank you, Mr. Enbaugh."

Enbaugh tilted his fedora forward on his head so his eyes were shadowed. Walking into the dining room, he moved past the large rectangular wooden dining table and pushed into the kitchen.

Walking away from the broken mirror,

Rachelle made her way into the living room. She used her cane to steady herself as she sank down into one of the large, leather couches. While still clutching the cube with one hand, Rachelle pressed the other to her mouth. She could feel the pain inside. The heartache, the loss, the emptiness, it was all inside her. Yesterday, she had a daughter, a son-in-law and a beautiful grandchild. Today, she was alone.

Tears began to roll down her leathery cheeks. Today was Charlie's eighth birthday. She loved him so. Reaching into her coat, she removed a small yellow envelope and placed it in her lap. It was his birthday card. She had enclosed one hundred dollars inside. She knew he had wanted a new baseball bat and mitt. She didn't know exactly which one to buy, so she thought giving him the money and taking him shopping would be the best way to do it. She wiped the tears off of her face with her hand.

"Grandma?"

Rachelle sat straight up on the couch as a chill ran down her spine. "Charlie?" she asked quietly, unsure of what she had just heard. She quickly scanned the living room, but found nothing. She shook her head. "The stress is getting to me," she mumbled.

"Help me, Grandma."

Rachelle stood up and spun around. Her eyes quickly focused on a bright light emanating from the top of the stairs. "Charlie?" she asked again. Grabbing her cane, she began to walk slowly across the living room. The click of her shoes against the hard wood floors was the only sound she could hear. As she walked across the broken shards of glass, she ran her hand along the thick wooden banister. Rachelle stopped when she reached the bottom of the stairs. "Is that you, Charlie?"

Looking up, she saw a soft blue light. It was spilling down onto the staircase as it rippled through the air. Rachelle swore she was looking into a pool of water. Fear gripped her body. Looking around the banister into the dining room, she wondered if she should go and get Enbaugh. Turning back toward the staircase, she began to hear the muted sobs of a child. Her motherly instincts overcame her. Rachelle steadied herself against the rail as she started to move up the stairs. One foot after the other, she slowly walked up.

A dark form streaked across the hallway in front of her. Rachelle stopped. Her hand was gripped firmly around the railing to her left. She opened her mouth to speak, but couldn't get the words to pass her lips. Swallowing hard, she took another step. "Charlie," she asked quietly, "is that you?" The sobs slowly mutated into the low rumble of laughter. The hairs on the back of Rachelle's neck stood straight up at the sound. It was an evil laugh. "Detective Enbaugh!" she called out frantically.

The blue light quickly faded and was replaced by darkness. It seemed to flow through the emptiness, choking it. Then a pair of red eyes appeared at the top of the stairs. They seemed to stare right through her. Now terrified, Rachelle spun around on the steps and began to move awkwardly toward the bottom with her cane. Her old legs became tangled and she began to topple. Her body hit the stairs with a sickening crunch. She rolled down uncontrollably. Finally hitting the bottom, Rachelle tried to roll herself onto her back amidst the broken glass of the mirror. She knew she had broken several ribs and one of her hips.

Crooking her head to look back up the stairs, she saw a dark mass hovering toward her. It had no form, but its two red eyes remained fixed near the top. "You will not escape," the being said menacingly with a laugh.

Rachelle watched in agony as the form floated above her. She couldn't move and was too frightened to cry out. Wisps of darkness began to arch out of the form toward Rachelle. They slithered slowly, almost erratically, as they neared her body. The being's red eyes hardened. They became no more than horrible slits in the mass. With the speed of a striking cobra, the wisps wrapped themselves around Rachelle's body. They felt ice cold against her skin. Slowly, the form began to lift her off the floor. Her head fell limply backwards, allowing her to see she was now at least seven feet off the ground. The wisps suddenly hardened around her. Pain shot up her body as they pressed against her broken ribs. Rachelle cried out. The being's eyes widened, then hardened again. Rachelle could almost sense it was enjoying her suffering. Two wisps snaked around her neck and began to constrict. She found herself unable to scream.

***

Walking around the solid white kitchen, Enbaugh ran his finger along the counter. There was no dust, no food crumbs and no water spots. *Did these people ever use this lavish kitchen?* A rack of pots and pans hung above a small wooden island in the center of the kitchen. A small metal basket of fruit accompanied the pots. Reaching up into the basket, Enbaugh removed a red apple. Rubbing it against his shirt, he took a large bite.

Moving across the room, Enbaugh checked the knobs on the stove. He wanted to make sure they were off. Opening the oven door, he spied a pink cardboard box inside. While holding the apple in his mouth, Enbaugh carefully removed the box. He let out a sigh when he gazed inside through the clear plastic window. It was a birthday cake. Setting it on the island, he flipped open the top. He couldn't tell what kind of cake it was through the layer of white frosting, but the words "Happy 8th Birthday Charlie" were scrawled lovingly across it in blue frosting. Setting the apple on the counter, Enbaugh closed the box and lifted it up. Holding it carefully, he walked across the kitchen toward the silver fridge. He grabbed the black handle on the door and carefully pulled it open. Spotting an empty area on the second shelf, Enbaugh carefully slid the cake inside.

Enbaugh stopped. Did he just hear a scream? Closing the refrigerator, he moved around the small island in the center of the kitchen toward the door. Reaching into his trench coat, he pulled his black pistol and cradled it in his hand. He reached down and slid his other hand around the handle. Twisting it to the left, Enbaugh pushed on the door, but it didn't move. Enbaugh twisted the knob in the opposite direction and pushed again. The door wouldn't budge.

"What the hell?" Enbaugh said out loud. Turning to the side, Enbaugh slammed his shoulder into the door. He felt the door give a little, but not open. He slammed himself against it again, then again. "Fuck it," he said finally. He took a step back from the door. He fired his weapon at the lock three times. The crack of the pistol echoed around the empty kitchen. Lifting his leg, Enbaugh kicked the door just below the handle, but it remained closed. He heard a disembodied laugh echo through the room.

***

Rachelle looked pleadingly at the form above her. She didn't know what it wanted, or why it was here. She began to pray for compassion. The being twisted hard, breaking her neck. It felt her essence drain out of her. Pleasure rippled through the shadow. It twisted Rachelle's head again so it was facing backward, then removed all the wisps. Her body fell to the floor in a broken heap.

***

Enbaugh spun around. The lights began to dim in the kitchen. Holding the pistol grip tightly, he turned back toward the door. He rushed headlong at it, this time, breaking through. The wooden frame splintered into a hundred pieces as the door flew open. Without taking a moment to look back, Enbaugh rushed through the dining room and into the living room. "Ms. Frieze?"

Enbaugh scanned the room. His eyes focused

44

on a dark mass at the foot of the stairs. He froze. The mass looked like a cloud of pure darkness. He blinked his eyes twice to make sure he wasn't seeing things. He watched in horror as the mass began to disappear, revealing the body of Rachelle below it. Enbaugh holstered his gun and ran toward her. Kneeling down, he glanced over her disfigured body. Her torso had been cracked open from the base of her neck to just below her abdomen. Jagged edges of her ribs jutted out from the torn flesh and her intestines had been partially uncoiled and now laid in a heap next to her. Amidst a sea of blood that was pooling in her chest cavity, he could clearly see her lungs, her stomach, and her…wait, something was missing. "Shit," he muttered under his breath. Reaching into his jacket pocket, he removed a small black radio. He hit the transmit button with his thumb. "This is Detective Jack Enbaugh," he shouted. "I'm at the Grant House and I need backup right now! Repeat, I need backup at the Grant House right now!"

Looking up the stairs, he saw a pair of burning red eyes hovering motionless in the darkness. Pulling his weapon, he fired up at the eyes. The dark form dissipated as the bullets whizzed through it. Enbaugh lifted his bulky frame off the floor and took several steps back. Turning to his left, he spotted a second pair of red eyes staring at him from the dining room. "What the fuck?" Spinning around, Enbaugh raced for the front door. He grabbed the handle and threw the heavy wooden door open. Dashing outside into the rain, he stopped and turned around. The door slammed shut behind him. Enbaugh began to slowly backpedal. He wasn't

taking his eyes off that house. Not until backup
arrived.

46

Chapter 4

Bishop winced at the horrific sight. The three investigators had gathered around a small projection screen in their office. Cane was standing in the rear controlling the slide projector, while Dawn and Bishop were seated at the desks in front. The office was pitch black, except for the images on the screen. Only the hum of the projector's cooling fan filled the room.

"These are crime scene photos we downloaded from the Stone Brook Police Department's main frame," explained Cane unemotionally. He tapped a button on the small black remote he held in his hand. The image on the screen in front of them faded to the next photo. "This *was* Dylan Grant."

Bishop looked at the body in the photo. It had been torn in half at the midsection. The feet were aligned sickeningly toward the man's head while the torso had been cracked open like a melon. He felt a wave of nausea pass through him but quickly swallowed hard to fight it. "What did this?" he asked as he took a deep breath.

Cane tapped the button again. "We don't know." That of a small boy replaced the image of Dylan's body. He was twisted grotesquely at the waist, allowing his feet to point up while he was face-down on the bed. "This was a normal family in Florida."

"Any signs this points to some kind of occult ritual?" Dawn wondered as she stared unblinking at the photos.

"Not that the Stone Brook Police Department could find," Cane replied after a moment, "but both parent's hearts had been removed."

"Surgically?" Dawn queried.

"No," Cane said quickly, "more like ripped out of their chests."

"What about the boy?" Bishop asked.

"His heart was still in his chest when they found him," Cane answered quietly. "It's odd they would take both of the parent's hearts, and not the boy's," he said half to himself. "That has to mean something."

"Whoever did this had to be incredibly strong," Bishop conjectured. "That boy's body is twisted a full one hundred and eighty degrees."

"Whoever, or *whatever*, Mr. Bishop," Cane quickly corrected him. He lifted his fingers and rubbed them over the edge of his mustache.

"Did the police reports list anything odd?" Dawn wondered. "You mean besides the hearts being removed?"

Dawn nodded.

"Not that I could find," Cane admitted. "I combed through every scrap of paper they had on this investigation."

"When did this happen?" Bishop asked.

Cane leaned over and began to thumb through a stack of papers he had on the desk next to him. "Late last night," he answered.

Bishop rubbed his clean-shaven chin. "How did we find out about this so quickly?"

"We have very reliable sources all over the country," Dawn said, finally taking her eyes off the photo. "Over the years, the OPR has built up quite an extensive network. Mostly due to the efforts of Cane and Chairman Weiss."

Cane scoffed. "Thanks to me."

Dawn turned to look at Cane. "It's been almost thirty years, Cane. Don't you think you should that go?"

A devious smile crossed Cane's face. "When you get to be my age, sometimes all you have left to hold on to are the grudges."

"Is there something I should know here?" Bishop asked innocently. "No," Dawn and Cane replied in unison.

Cane looked up at the projection screen. "Back to the debriefing." He tapped his control again. The image quickly flipped to a satellite view of Florida.

A large swirling cloud mass was hanging just off the western coast. "What you're looking at is Tropical Storm Katrina. Meteorologists expect this tropical storm to turn into a full blown hurricane in the next twenty-four hours."

"Where's Stone Brook?" Dawn asked.

Cane walked up to the screen and pointed to an area directly in Katrina's path. "Right here."

"We're going to wait until the storm passes to go investigate, right?" Bishop asked nervously.

"Afraid not, Mr. Bishop," Cane replied with a smile. "I hope you packed an overnight bag, because we're leaving in an hour."

Bishop leaned back in his chair. "This isn't exactly how I wanted to start my career with the OPR," he declared.

"Theories?" Dawn asked after a moment of silence. Cane shook his head. "None at present."

Dawn tapped her long fingernails against her front teeth. "Does this area have a history of paranormal activity?"

"Not that we've been able to find yet." Cane returned to his position next to the projector. "The records department is still trying to dig up anything they can find on Stone Brook." Cane flipped a switch on the body of the projector shutting it off. He then walked across the office and clicked on the office lights.

Dawn rubbed her hands through her hair, "So we're going in blind." She thought for a moment. "Do we have a contact at the SBPD?"

Cane nodded. "A Detective Enbaugh." He glanced down at his watch. "Tick, tick," he said quickly. "We better get moving if we want to catch our plane." Cane scooped up the pile of papers on the desk and held them under his arm. Turning, he walked out of the office.

Dawn and Bishop rose slowly from their seats. Bishop looked across at Dawn. "Have you ever been in a hurricane before?"

Dawn shook her head. "This is why I love working at the OPR. Always new experiences."

***

"For *Ghost Chasers, Inc.*, I'm Rivers Gallows," the host said in a firm voice directly into the camera. "Remember, the next paranormal experience could be yours." A serious expression crossed Gallows' face as he stood still. The lights on the small set dimmed.

"We're clear, Mr. Gallows," a disembodied voice said off camera.

"About damned time," Gallows grunted. His body posture changed as he reached into his black leather jacket pocket. The serious look on his face mutated into that of exhaustion. "How many takes was that? Ten? Fifteen?" he asked in a dark tone. Pulling out a pack of cigarettes, he lifted open the box top and pulled one out. Depositing the pack back into his pocket, he removed a small gold lighter.

"You can't smoke in here, Mr. Gallows."

Gallows looked at the crew behind the camera. "Hey, when you're the star of this show, you can tell me to do whatever you want." Gallows lifted the lighter to his cigarette and took a long drag. He slowly exhaled the smoke in the direction of the crew. "Until then, you can fuck off." He reached up and loosened the tie around his neck, then undid the top button of his dark shirt.

Gallows was a tall and well-built man. He weighed in at about two hundred pounds, but most of that was muscle. He had short red hair combed neatly across his head and dark, piercing green eyes. His face was the classic oval shape with a chiseled chin. He looked as if he should be starring in the next big action movie out of Hollywood instead of hosting a show on the supernatural. Gallows ran his hand down his leather jacket and unbuttoned it. He was wearing a pair of dark slacks, a deep red shirt and matching tie under his jacket.

"Mr. Gallows, are you ready to shoot the next segment?" the director asked from behind the camera.

Gallows rolled his cigarette between his fingers as he stared menacingly at the director. "I think we're done for today, Jimmy."

The director, a small, thin man wearing a blue

51

baseball cap and white t- shirt, stood and marched toward Gallows. He stood a full foot shorter than Gallows. "We're already a full day behind because of you, Gallows." He pulled off his hat and tossed it angrily on the floor, "And my fucking name's not Jimmy!"

"Timmy?" Gallows asked as he took a puff off his cigarette.

"Jesus-h-tap-dancing-Christ!" the director shouted in vain. Tossing his clipboard on the floor, he walked off the set.

"Billy?" Gallows asked again. Turning, a smug look crossed his face. "I guess we're done for the day."

The crew began to shuffle slowly off the set, shaking their heads. A lone man stood near the back of the sound stage. He walked slowly across the set toward Gallows. "What the hell is wrong with you?"

"Walter!" Gallows exclaimed. "How are you?"

Walter James stepped into the lights and stopped. He was a thin man of about forty, wearing a dark gray blazer, a white polo shirt and a pair of blue jeans. "Don't give me that shit," Walter said angrily. "Are you trying to throw your career away?"

Gallows wrapped his arm around Walter's shoulder. "You're my agent, right?"

"Yeah," Walter answered suspiciously.

Gallows began to walk toward the stage exit. "I pay you eleven percent of whatever I make, right?"

"Yes."

Gallows stopped and stared at Walter. "Then why the fuck am I working on some show about

52

ghosts, when I could be making movies?"

"Honestly?"

Gallows nodded. "I want the truth."

Walter stuffed his hands into his pockets. "Most casting directors think you're a prima donna, and directors just don't want to work with you. You've shot your career in the foot with this attitude of yours."

"What attitude?" Gallows asked.

"Don't give me that shit, Rivers," Walter snapped. "You know exactly what I'm talking about. This ego of yours is keeping you out of work. Even the producers of this show are getting tired of it. Word around here is that you've already got one foot out the door. Hell, we probably won't even get Danny to come back and direct the rest of this episode."

"Danny," Gallows said to himself. "I knew I was close." He dropped his cigarette and crushed it out. "Look," he tapped Walter on the chest. "If the producers of this show want to get rid of me, then fuck 'em. They can watch their show tank without me. I'll walk right now, Walter."

"I don't think that's a good idea," Walter cautioned him. "Why not?" Gallows asked angrily.

"Because this show is all you've got left." Walter let the words sink in for a moment before he continued. "If you walk, then pack your goddamned bags, because you're heading home to Iowa." Walter turned and began to walk away.

Gallows stood in silence for a moment. "Walter!" he shouted across the stage. He watched Walter open the door and walk into the bright California afternoon. The door closed slowly behind him. Gallows ran his hand through his red hair. "Christ," he muttered under his breath. The creak of another door startled him. He spun around.

"Mr. Gallows?" A young man asked. "Yes?"

The young man nervously stopped a few feet away from Gallows. "The producer want to see you immediately."

***

The interior of Enbaugh's office was cold and musty. The walls had the tell-tale dark blotches of water stains over their already dingy brown color. Broken ceiling tiles from the roof lay in a disorderly pile in the far corner, swept there by a lazy janitor. The ceiling fan, a noisy contraption that could very well predate modern man, chugged overhead.

Enbaugh sat in his padded brown wooden chair behind his small metal desk. The desk, which occupied almost a quarter of the space in this cramped office, was strewn with old reports which had never been filed and half empty Styrofoam cups of diet cola. An ancient black blotter sat in the middle of the mess.

Enbaugh reached across and grabbed one of the cups. Lifting it to his nose, he took a quick sniff, then after he was satisfied it wouldn't kill him, took a long sip. Crushing the cup in his hand, he tossed it to the hard wood floor and watched it skip and roll until it reached its final resting place near the door. He closed his eyes and leaned back. They were haunting, the glowing red eyes he had seen earlier that day. No matter what thought he picked to occupy his mind, they were still there, burned into the very fabric of his consciousness.

Shaking his head, he sat up and looked toward the window. Rain was pelting the weathered glass panes. He took some comfort in the sound of it, its almost rhythmic dance as it hit and then slid down. They had seen nothing but dark gray clouds and rain for the past week here in northern Florida, which in itself wasn't unusual for this time of year, but this storm seemed particularly bad. Enbaugh couldn't explain why. It had an evil element to it. He couldn't put his finger on it.

A knock at the door pulled him out of his trance. Blinking twice, he looked away from the window toward his open door. A soft smile crossed his face. "What's up, Montoya?"

Montoya was leaning against the brown trim of the doorframe, her hands buried in her pockets. Her black trench coat was gone, leaving only her black blouse and slacks. The brown leather holster for her weapon was attached neatly to her belt. "Can we talk?"

Enbaugh nodded. He could already tell there was something on her mind. "What's the matter?"

Montoya slid into a waiting chair in front of Enbaugh's desk. She fidgeted uncomfortably for a moment before finally coming to rest with her legs crossed. She brushed a stray lock of blonde hair away from her face as she looked at her partner. "What happened out there?"

"What do you mean?" Enbaugh replied, playing the fool. He didn't want to talk about it.

"What do I mean?" she asked awestruck. "I mean why the hell do we have another member of the Grant family lying in our freezer downstairs?"

55

"Look," Enbaugh said, rubbing the back of his neck, "I don't want to talk about it."

"I don't give a shit what you want, Jack," Montoya snapped. "We've got four dead people on our hands. All of them died within twenty-four hours of each other in the same place!" Montoya uncrossed her legs and sat forward, "And the only answer I have is a pair of red eyes. What the hell is going on here, Jack?"

"I—"

"Have you been hitting the bottle again?"

"Fuck you." A dark scowl crossed Enbaugh's face. "I have been clean and sober for six years now."

"Then what the hell aren't you telling me?" Montoya pleaded. "Nothing!" Enbaugh sent a stack of papers crashing to the floor as he sprung up. Walking around the desk, he pushed his office door closed and leaned up against it. Most of the older offices in the building weren't equipped with locks. "That's what I saw! Those fucking red eyes in the darkness."

Montoya stood up to face Enbaugh. "I think you're a good cop, Jack, don't get me wrong, but I think your losing your Goddamned mind! Don't you sell me some bullshit about glowing eyes in the darkness, tell me what really happened!"

"Christ o'mighty!" Enbaugh shouted. "I've told you the truth three times now. Why won't you believe me?"

"You're full of shit, Jack." Montoya pushed past Enbaugh and grabbed the door handle. Throwing open the door, she stood with her back to him. "A person killed and mutilated an entire family on our watch, and they're still out there. Doesn't that mean anything to you?" She walked away before Enbaugh had a chance to answer.

Enbaugh took a few steps across his office, then stopped. Lashing out, he knocked the rest of the papers and trash from his desk. Standing tall, he took a deep breath into his nicotine stained lungs and tried to relax.

"Detective?"

Enbaugh spun around to see a shapely young brunette woman standing in his doorway. He instantly recognized her as one of the receptionists, Julie he thought. "Yes?"

"Captain Thomas wanted me to inform you that you have guests on the way," she said in a sweet voice.

"I don't understand," Enbaugh admitted.

"The Office of Paranormal Research is paying the town of Stone Brook a visit and you are to extend every courtesy to them."

Enbaugh slammed the butt of his hand against his desk.

Chapter 5

"How long have we known each other, Rivers?" Stephen Edwards asked rhetorically. Stephen was the Executive Producer of *Ghost Chasers, Inc.* He had been there since the very first day of shooting, and even well before that. He was a middle-aged man with a thin graying beard and a receding hairline that was retreating faster than the Germans did when they tried to invade Russia during the winter. He was a thin man and his body was beginning to show the wear and tear of stress. "Long enough to know your fucking name isn't Rivers," he said with a laugh.

Rivers smiled uncomfortably. He was sitting in a plush leather chair opposite Stephen. His hands were folded neatly in his lap. Rivers liked Stephen's office. It looked like you would expect it to look. Framed posters from his various projects littered the white walls, while a row of shelving behind his glass desk held the sundry awards he had won, or bought, depending on who you asked. He nodded at Stephen.

Stephen leaned back in his black padded chair and steepled his hands in front of his face. He stared at Rivers for a long moment before moving. "Let me ask you this," he said thoughtfully, "why do you see fit to run most of our directors off the set?"

Rivers thought for a moment. Even though he outweighed Stephen by at least seventy pounds, Stephen had a commanding presence about him. "I don't intentionally do anything to—"

"Bullshit!" Stephen shot forward in his seat. "You're a fucking raving egomaniac! You think you're too good for this show." Standing up, Stephen pointed to the door. "If you're so fucking wonderful, Gallows, then get the fuck out of my office. You can obviously find better work than I'm offering you, so go." Stephen sank back into his chair. He was a master tactician. All he had to do now was wait for the result he wanted or start looking for a new host, but he believed the former to be more likely.

Rivers sat in the chair for a long moment. He was speechless. His mighty ego had been sent tumbling to the ground and now, the only thought on his mind was how to salvage *some* of his dignity without seeming weak. "I don't think you should talk to me like that, Stephen." Rivers cringed as soon as the words left his lips.

"You fucking pussy," Stephen roared. "Get out of my office. I don't want to see you on this set ever again." He leaned over and lifted the telephone receiver up to his ear. He quickly punched in a four digit code. "Yeah," he said finally into the phone, "get me casting."

Rivers, insulted and belittled, stood and began to march toward the door. He wasn't going to take Stephen's shit anymore. He would find a new job, and then he would rub that little fucker's face in…. Rivers stopped. He suddenly remembered his agent's words from before. Maybe he was right; maybe this *was* all he was capable of. Rivers swallowed his pride and turned around. "Stephen," he said solemnly, "man, I'm really sorry."

Stephen's face brightened. He immediately hung up the phone. He was tired of listening to the dial tone anyway. He stood and walked across the room toward Rivers. Stretching out a hand, he patted Rivers firmly on the shoulder. "I'm proud of you, Riv. It takes a big man to admit when he's wrong."

"I just get a little full of myself at times," Rivers admitted like a beaten child.

"I know," Stephen said sympathetically. He motioned for Gallows to sit down. Stephen moved around his desk and slid back into his plush chair. "Let's talk, shall we?"

Rivers nodded silently.

"First of all," Stephen said as he shuffled a stack of random papers on his desk, "if you ever do that to another of my directors, I am going to make sure you are blacklisted in this town, is that understood?"

Rivers slumped down in the chair. "Yeah."

"Second," a wide smile crossed Stephen face, "I've been mulling an idea around that I think is going to take this show all the way to the top, and a situation has just arisen that will blend perfectly with that."

Rivers perked up. "Ready?" Stephen asked. Rivers nodded.

Stephen held his hands in front of him, palms facing out, "I call it 'Paranormal Reality Television'." He waited for effect. "What do you think?" Rivers nodded his head and placed his index finger on his chin. "I like it," he admitted after a moment of mulling.

The smile faded from Stephen' face. "You don't get it, do you?" Rivers let out an audible sigh. "No."

Stephen leaned back in his chair. "Most reality

shows take people and stick them in places, make them do things they wouldn't usually do. The Australian Outback for eight weeks?" Stephen scoffed, "Only if you're a fucking kangaroo. I want to take people and put them in situations they *would* face in normal life, and living in a haunted house is one of those."

Rivers became intrigued. "So we send a bunch of schmucks into a house and tape it?"

"A *haunted* house," Stephen reiterated.

"So we get a tape full of these people being freaked out. What's the big deal?"

"That *is* the big deal. Human emotion in its most raw form is fear and it's absolutely mesmerizing to watch. Let me give you the big picture," Stephen smiled, "allow me to put all the pieces of the puzzle in their correct locations." He stood up and walked across his office and began to pace out of habit. "*Ghost Chasers, Inc.* is a televised paranormal news magazine. We cover all the strange shit that goes on in the world in a basically standard news format. We interview witnesses, talk to presumed abductees, show locations, and so on and so forth." Stephen began gesturing with his hands. "It's all very matter-of-fact in presentation, and that was fine for a while. We drew in viewers just by sheer curiosity and by presenting the most complete picture of an event that we could, but that's not enough now. We need something new, and this is it."

Stephen stopped and looked at Rivers. "We'll be able to throw down with the big 'reality shows' currently dominating the airwaves."

Rivers was sold. "Great, when do we start?"

"*You* start today."

"Me?"

"Think of it as attrition to me," Stephen said with a smile. "I've already booked you on the ten o'clock flight out of LAX."

"Destination?" Rivers asked. "Stone Brook, Florida."

"Never heard of it."

"It was the site last night of a vicious triple murder," Stephen admitted with glee. "One of the detectives at the local precinct filed a report this afternoon that had some very bizarre shit in it."

"Like what?"

"Like a pair of fucking red glowing eyes!"

Rivers felt his stomach become unsettled, "And you want me to take a bunch of people into this place?" Rivers swallowed hard. "What does the local law enforcement think of this idea?"

"They can think whatever they want. I have the Mayor of Stone Brook on my side. He thinks this is a great idea."

"Is this guy some kind of fucking ghoul? Why would he want his town presented on national television as a place where triple homicides happen?"

Stephen laughed as he rubbed his beard. "Press is press, good or bad, and if we can prove this place is actually haunted, he thinks it'll put them on the map. Might even make the town a bit of a tourist attraction. Make them the *new* Amityville."

Rivers was silent for a moment. "Isn't there some kind of serious storm brewing right now in Florida?"

"Tropical storm Katrina," Stephen said.

"Won't that be dangerous to fly into?"

"Oh, come on, Rivers, grow a pair, for God's sake," Stephen snapped. "Just think of it as making your experience all the more real, plus the storm will add a real flavor to the piece." Stephen checked the gold watch on his wrist. "You have exactly five hours to go home, get packed and meet the crew at LAX. You better get going."

"Who's directing this episode?" Rivers asked against his better judgment. "I've assigned Chloe."

"Chloe Andrews?" Rivers asked. "One and the same."

"You know Chloe and I don't get along, Stephen," Rivers whined. Stephen laughed. "Just because you couldn't keep the warhead in your pants with Chloe doesn't mean she isn't a great director. Tough it out."

Rivers stood and looked at Stephen. He could swear his pride had oozed out of him at least five minutes ago and was hiding somewhere in the corner. He extended an open hand to Stephen. "Thanks for giving me another shot. Most producers wouldn't do that."

Stephen shook his hand in return. "I know."

***

The flight from Washington D.C. to Stone Brook had been, to say the least, bumpy so far. The "fasten seatbelts" sign had gone off shortly after take-off, then clicked back on about twenty minutes later. It seemed tropical storm Katrina was wreaking havoc up and down the entire eastern seaboard.

Bishop leaned back in his seat and propped his

hands behind his head. He looked around the small cabin, which was mostly empty. Two rows of dark blue seats were packed along the edges, while a small strip of carpet separated them. Bishop counted around ten people scattered about. He was near the rear of the cabin, while Dawn and Cane had each claimed a row in front of him. Cane had immediately stretched out over the two seats, despite the complaints of the stewardesses. Dawn, meanwhile, was working diligently at her laptop. She glanced up only occasionally, and then usually just to ask for another drink. Bishop was getting the feeling Dawn didn't like to fly.

Sitting forward, Bishop peered through the small porthole next to him. Early in the flight, the pilot had to increase their altitude due to the storm. Now only a dark sheet of clouds could be seen below them, along with the occasional blue flash of lightning. Above them, Bishop could see a beautiful ocean of stars uninterrupted by clouds. They had reached the airport in time to catch their flight, only it wasn't on time. It had been delayed for several hours while the air traffic controllers waited for a break in the storm. Bishop thought for a moment. He couldn't remember the last time he had witnessed such a severe storm front.

Glancing across the seats, Bishop noticed Dawn had pushed her laptop into the seat next to her. He quickly unbuckled himself and slid across the aisle. He caught sight of a stewardess emerging from the dark curtain that separated the cabin and the cockpit and quickly dropped into the seat next to Dawn. She slowly craned her head to the left to look at Bishop. She was wearing a small pair of prescription reading glasses.

"What are you doing?" Dawn asked, her speech slightly slurred. "I wanted to talk to you."

"About what?"

Bishop shrugged. "Anything," he admitted. "You've been with the OPR long enough that you must've seen some bizarre things."

"Yep," Dawn replied as she slapped Bishop on the leg, "I have seen some crazy shit."

"Like what?" Bishop smiled.

"Like this one time, I saw this…this," she searched for the word, "thing."

"Best leave it alone. She's drunk."

Bishop saw Cane sitting up with his back to the cabin wall. His eyes were just barely visible over the back of the seats. "How many has she had?"

Cane laughed. "It's not about quantity with her. She just can't hold her liquor."

"Cane," Bishop said tentatively, "can I ask you a question?" Without any hesitation, Cane agreed. "Of course."

"Why did you join the OPR?"

"That's a long story," Cane admitted, "And we've only about an hour left in this flight."

"Why do you stay with the OPR then?"

"Just full of questions, aren't we, Mr. Bishop?" Cane laughed. "I'll submit my resume to you when we get back."

"No," Bishop said. He was slightly perturbed Cane wasn't taking any of his questions seriously. "*Seriously*, I want to know what you find appealing about working for the OPR."

"Having career doubts on your first day of work? That's not a good sign." Cane looked over

65

the top of the seat to see the resentment on Bishop's face. "Just teasing," Cane reassured him. He looked down at his rugged hands, "I'm not as young as I used to be, but then again, who is?" Cane laughed at his own joke. "There's not a lot I could do anymore. I've been a ghost hunter most of my life. I don't think I'm qualified to do anything else."

"You could always learn a new trade," Bishop offered. Cane shook his head and pointed to himself, "Old dog."

"Is that the only reason you're still with the OPR?"

"No," Cane paused and then smiled, "I love this shit."

A bright bolt of lightning crashed through the clouds just below the plane. The flash startled Bishop. He looked over at Dawn. She had crashed. Her head was leaning awkwardly to one side as she lightly snored. "Dawn's out cold."

"You may as well try and get some sleep too. It's going to be a long day tomorrow."

Bishop scooted forward in his seat. "What exactly is our game plan when we arrive at the site?"

"What's the fun in knowing?" Cane asked. "Wait until tomorrow and be surprised!"

Bishop slumped back into his seat. He thought about a witty retort for a moment, but decided against it. He had been taught partners were the people that helped you, the ones who informed you, but these two were just being a pain in the ass. He felt the thud of Dawn's head as it fell on his shoulder. Shaking his head, he turned to look out the window.

Chapter 6

The front door to the apartment flew open and a young woman skittered inside. She grabbed the door handle and began to force the door shut against the wind. Finally succeeding, the young woman began to pull off her raincoat and sneakers. She dropped them both lazily next to the door and ventured into the living room. She shook her head once to get rid of the rain soaking her hair. She tapped her girlfriend on the shoulder as she walked past.

"Did you hear what happened to the Grants?" Kelley asked.

Joanne Stone looked up from her book to acknowledge Kelly. She was curled up in a large plush maroon chair wearing a pair of tattered sweat pants and an old tank top set off by a gold heart-shaped locket. Her curly brown hair was pulled up away from her neck. She pulled off her glasses, "To whom?" The chair was nestled in the far corner of the eclectic living room. On the far side sat a dated nineteen inch television/VCR combo with a mass of black videos surrounding it. It was cramped, but cosy.

Kelley Windel had just walked into their small two bedroom apartment from work. She was still dressed in the green nurse's uniform from the hospital. She ran her hand through her short blonde hair and plopped down on the old gray couch that faced Joanne.

The light sounds of classical music were filtering through the apartment from Joanne's bedroom.

"You know Dr. Grant that I worked with?" Kelley asked.

"The name rings a bell, but I can't quite place him," Joanne admitted. "He was the tall guy with dark hair that was the patient's favorite."

Okay," Joanne said slowly, "I remember now." She closed her book and set it on the table next to her. "What happened?"

"He and his family were found murdered this morning," Kelley said gravely. "I heard he had been completely eviscerated, while his wife had been decapitated."

"Didn't they have a son?"

Kelley nodded. "I used to babysit their son, Charlie, when he was younger."

"Was he home when it happened?" Joanne asked.

"Afraid so. Apparently, they found him dead next to the body of his mother."

"Dear God," Joanne muttered. "Did the police catch the guy who did it?"

"The word at the hospital is they didn't," Kelley answered gravely.

Joanne let out a long sigh, "That means some psycho is running loose on the streets tonight," Joanne said more to herself than Kelley. She quickly stood and walked toward the front door. Pressing hard against it to make sure it was securely closed, Joanne flipped the latch on the deadbolt.

Kelley lifted herself off the couch and walked slowly across the living room. She reached out and pulled Joanne into her arms. "I don't think we have to worry about anything, Jo."

"Why not?" Joanne asked as she laid her head

against Kelley's chest. "This nut could be anywhere."

"Tell you what," Kelley said after a moment, "I have some vacation time saved up. I think we should get out of town for a week or so. What do you think?"

Joanne looked up at her lover's face with a smile. "I think that's a wonderful idea. Let's leave tomorrow."

Kelley craned her neck and kissed Joanne gently on the forehead. "Sure, we'll pack up in the morning."

"Where do you want to go?"

Kelley shrugged. "How about Miami?"

"I don't really like it there. There's too many...."

A sharp noise cut her off. Both women stood silently as they listened. "What the hell was that?" Kelley asked after a minute.

"I don't know."

Both women were on edge. They could feel their hearts thumping in their chests while adrenaline pumped through their veins.

"Probably nothing," Joanne reasoned. "This damn storm probably knocked open a shutter or something."

"You're probably right," Kelley agreed. She slowly slipped out of Joanne's embrace, "But I think I should go look, just in case something's broken."

"Be careful," Joanne cautioned.

Kelley took Joanne by the hand, "Why don't you come with me?"

"Safety in numbers?"

"Yes," Kelley said with a mischievous smile, "But the bedroom's back there, too."

Joanne laughed loudly. "Tramp."

Kelley ran her hand across Joanne's face, "Slut."

"Such affectionate nicknames we have for each other," Joanne confessed. "Yeah, but you know I love you."

Joanne pressed her hand against Kelley's. "I love you, too."

The two forgot about the noise for a moment, as they were lost in each other's eyes. Hand in hand, the two slowly moved through the living room and into the connecting hallway. Reaching toward the wall, Joanne felt around clumsily for the light switch. Her hand brushed across it, then she flipped it on. The small hallway, barely large enough for one person, let alone two, was flooded with a soft white light. The two quickly made a visual inventory of the pictures on the walls. Nothing appeared to have fallen or was broken.

They looked up ahead of them. The hallway had a small bathroom at the end, with two doors on either side that led into the two bedrooms. They stopped when they reached the bathroom. To the left was their bedroom, a hole in the wall with only enough room for a bed and a nightstand. On their right was their computer room. They had set up a small desk and two tall bookcases. An older gray computer sat idly on the desk, it's colorful screen saver flashing in the darkness.

Kelley glanced over at Joanne. "I'll take the computer room, you take the bedroom."

Joanne nodded. "Hurry."

70

Kelley turned to her right and walked into the computer room. She reached for the light switch on the wall and clicked it. She glanced around the still darkened room and then clicked the switch again. "Bulb's burned out," she announced. Looking around the small room, she could see nothing out of place and the window appeared to be tightly shut. She walked a few steps across the room and placed her hands on the window. She checked the latch with her fingers. It was locked. "Anything?" She yelled across the hall.

"Nothing over here," Joanne yelled back.

Kelley peered out the window to the ground three floors behind her. The wind outside was playing havoc with the trees, tossing them about like they were just saplings. The streets were oddly empty. A lone streetlight at the intersection was blinking a steady yellow light. Kelley shifted her gaze to the apartment complex across the street. A few lights in the building were still on, but a majority of it was dark. She glimpsed something odd on the rooftop. A dark form weaving back and forth as it approached the ledge. It was very difficult to make out against the dark sky behind it, but it didn't look right. It wasn't moving like a person, or even an animal for that matter. A flash of lightning broke through the sky illuminating everything for a brief second. Kelley fixed her eyes on the form across the way. It seemed to be proportioned like a human, but something still seemed off. It suddenly stopped, apparently aware it was being watched. Kelley saw two quick red flashes, then it was gone. She stood staring at the rooftop for a long time before pulling herself away. Turning, she began to walk toward her bedroom. "Joanne?"

No reply.

Kelley stopped when she reached the hallway. The bedroom door was closed. "Joanne, are you all right?" She took the few steps across the hall and stopped. She pressed her ear up against the door and listened. There was nothing but silence. Kelley reached down and wrapped her slender hands around the silver handle and began to twist it. It was unlocked.

Tossing the door open, Kelley stepped inside expecting the worst. Instead, she saw Joanne lying seductively on the bed. A small flickering candle on the nightstand was casting long beautiful shadows across Joanne's shapely, naked body.

Joanne motioned with her fingers. "Come here."

Kelley reached down and undid the tie on her pants. They fell to the floor in a pile. Reaching up, she pulled off her shirt in one quick motion. Sliding her hand behind her back, Kelley unsnapped her bra and slowly let it slip off her shoulders. Sliding her hands unhurriedly down her body, Kelly began to pull off her panties. Now fully unclothed, Kelley crawled onto the bed toward Joanne.

The two began to wrap around each other, legs and arms intertwining as they kissed passionately. As the candle began to fade, neither of them noticed the pair of burning red eyes watching them from the corner.

***

Detectives Enbaugh and Montoya stood quietly

72

amidst the scheduled insanity of the Stone Brook Airport. It was a small terminal that would easily fit inside Miami's International Airport, but it was all they had. There was a large main lobby in the middle of the terminal with several rows of off red plastic chairs running through it. On the far side, several small booths lined the walls containing car rental agencies and magazine stands. On the other wall were the obligatory airline counters with their smiling, bleached blonde, ascot wearing flight attendants. A family of tourists was just entering the terminal through the row of metal detectors. They made their way through the people toward the luggage conveyor. Enbaugh watched with amusement as the father began to curse when he found his leather suitcase scratched. Enbaugh laughed to himself as he turned to his partner.

"Where the hell are these fucking guys?" Enbaugh asked.

Montoya had sank into one of the off red seats next to Enbaugh. Her legs were crossed and her long black trench coat was laid neatly over them. "How should I know?" She checked her wristwatch, "Their plane should've landed over an hour ago."

"I'm giving them fifteen more minutes, then I'm out of here," Enbaugh stated.

Montoya shook her head. "The Captain said we had to extend every courtesy to them. I don't think ditching them at the airport would be very 'courteous'."

"Who cares?" Enbaugh asked with a shrug. "We don't need the goddamned Ghostbusters on this case." He turned and began to ominously eye the snack counter. "Whatever this is, we can solve it."

"Did you not say you saw some kind of glowing eyes in that house?"

"Probably some fucker in a pair of night-vision goggles. You know those things glow when they're turned on," Enbaugh rationalized.

"Probably," Montoya snickered. Looking away from Enbaugh, she saw another plane begin to pull toward the terminal. She reached up and tugged on his dirty trench coat, "I think our boys have just arrived."

Enbaugh spun around. "Shit. I was hoping they wouldn't make it."

"I know," Montoya said as she stood up. She patted her partner on the back as if he were a child. "Remember to play nice, Jack."

Enbaugh muttered grumpily under his breath. "If they impede my investigation in any way, they're gone. No questions asked."

"Give it up, Jack," Montoya said as they began to walk toward the boarding ramp. "Don't mess this up and piss off the captain again. You're already on thin ice as it is."

Enbaugh had no retort. The two detectives stood silently in front of the large windows. He knew he wasn't in the best of positions, but Enbaugh didn't care. This was his investigation. This was his crime to solve.

They watched as the scant number of passengers quickly moved single file out of the plane beneath the ominous dark sky. Behind it, both detectives could see the black storm clouds hovering over their little town. There had been a small break in the storm, probably the only reason this plane was allowed to land. Enbaugh wondered why the airport was even still open during this mess. The last of the passengers strode onto the tarmac and began to make their way toward the terminal. A group of three was talking amongst themselves as they walked inside. Enbaugh was startled at their appearance. He hoped these weren't the people he was waiting for.

An older man dressed in black walked up to Enbaugh and Montoya and stopped. "Are you from the SBPD?" he asked tentatively.

Enbaugh sighed and nodded. "I'm Detective Jack Enbaugh, and this is my partner, Detective Caroline Montoya."

The older man extended his hand to Enbaugh. "Nice to meet you, Detective. May I call you Jack?"

Enbaugh refused to shake the man's hand. "No."

"Okay," Cane said slowly, retracting his hand. "My name's Zachary Cane," he pointed behind him, "and this is my team. We're with the Office of Paranormal Investigation."

"I gathered as much," Enbaugh said spitefully. "Look," Enbaugh said as he took a step closer to Cane, "You stay out of my way, I'll stay out of yours. Got that?"

"Fair enough," Cane said with a nod. "We're here to help you, Detective, not to be a hindrance."

A smile flashed across Enbaugh's face, but was gone as quickly as it appeared. "Good to know that you understand your place, Mr. Cane."

Cane nodded. "We're here as guests of the city of Stone Brook and the Stone Brook Police Department. I don't want to screw that up." Cane

75

cast a quick glance back at Dawn and Bishop. Dawn had a wide-eyed look of disbelief on her face. Cane ignored her for the moment. "Now if you don't mind, Detective, my colleagues and I would like to get a look at the crime scene."

Enbaugh nodded. "We were heading there anyway." He tapped Montoya on the shoulder, "We'll wait for you outside while you round up your baggage."

Cane smiled. "Thanks, Detective." He watched quietly as Enbaugh and Montoya turned and walked out of the terminal.

Dawn grabbed Cane by the shoulder and spun him around. "What the fuck was that?"

Cane laughed. "You can catch more flies with sugar—"

"Shut up," Dawn snapped. "He was talking down to you, to us, like we're a bunch of children he has to babysit."

"I realize that, Dawn."

"Then why did you let him?" She asked.

"Unfortunately, we need the police, they *don't* need us. We need to have access to their files, crime scene photos and autopsy reports," Cane stated. "We can't afford to piss them off." He looked back at Bishop, who was standing quietly behind them. "Getting all this?"

"Of course," Bishop said with a nod. "Access to local law enforcement is essential for any good investigation."

Cane grinned. "Very good, now go get our baggage."

***

76

Chloe Andrews looked over the cabin of the small jet the production company had rented for them. There were just two rows of white seats along the thin center aisle. Members of the crew had dispersed themselves as much as possible. Spotting her target, she adjusted the dark blue skirt she was wearing and straightened her white blouse. She pushed her long, wavy brown hair away from her face and began to walk down the aisle.

"Rivers, we need to talk."

Rivers looked up to see Chloe standing above him. "I've heard that a lot lately." He was sitting with an issue of *Cosmo* in his lap and a whole pack of nicotine gum in his mouth. He was chewing loudly as he looked at Chloe. He knew it bothered her when he chewed with his mouth open. He was making a conscious effort to open it as wide as he could.

Chloe slid down into the seat across from him. "We need to talk about the shoot. I think it's best if we're on the same page when we arrive."

Rivers chomped louder on his gum. "Sounds like a plan, boss."

Chloe stared at Rivers angrily. "Close your damned mouth when you chew! You look like a pig, Riv."

Coyly, Rivers smiled. "I'm sorry, I didn't realize I was doing it."

"You're such an asshole."

Rivers smiled broadly. "Thank you."

"Now, can we talk business?" Chloe asked.

"Whatever you want. You're the director."

Chloe stared at Rivers for a moment. She

couldn't believe he was acting like this. She shook the thought; she had to power through it. This was her job after all. "I thought we could start with a few exterior shots of the house, then we could move inside to you. I envision you hosting this show from the living room surrounded by your Ghost Chaser teammates."

"Teammates?" Rivers asked.

"We've brought in world-renowned psychic Sam Peters, and a young Wicca practitioner named Morgan LeFay."

"To do…?"

Chloe smiled. "That's the beauty. These people claim to be able to communicate with spirits." She leaned back in her seat, confidence oozing from her.

"Sam Peters," Rivers said to himself. "Hey," he said, snapping his fingers, "Isn't that the guy who used to go on Letterman and bend spoons with his mind?"

Chloe shot him a cross glare. "Don't be ridiculous." Rivers shrugged, "I was just wondering."

"Look," Chloe said after a moment in a quiet voice, "I realize you're still upset with me for breaking up with you, but the fact remains that we have to work together. Can we at least try and be civil?" She paused, "Besides, from what I read about this place, this could be one of the best episodes of *Ghost Chasers, Inc.* that we've ever produced." Chloe smiled. "I smell an Emmy."

Rivers stared contently at Chloe across the aisle. "If you remember correctly, I dumped you."

"You're so full of shit," Chloe said, adjusting the thin, wire rimmed glasses on her face. "If I…."

she let her thought trail off. "I'm not going to let you suck me back in, Rivers. Our relationship is over. I'm sorry we have to work together, but that's just the way it is. Either you get over yourself, or I have a little talk with Stephen."

"Is that a threat?" Rivers asked surprised.

"You bet your ass it is." Chloe leaned forward, "And I *will* follow through on it."

Rivers was taken aback. "Since when did you grow a spine?"

Chloe stood up in a huff. "Fuck off." She marched to the back of the cabin and slumped down into a seat.

Rivers leaned back in his chair and quietly giggled to himself. Pulling another piece of nicotine gum out of his pocket, he stuffed it into his mouth. He lifted his magazine and began to read again. *This could be more fun than I thought.*

Chapter 7

Kelley was wrapped in a tan hospital blanket as she cowered in the corner. A long splash of red blood was covering the right side of her face. She was naked except for the blanket, but at this point, she didn't care. She could be on fire and wouldn't feel any less comfortable. She was slowly rocking back and forth and muttering to herself.

The flash of blue and red alternating lights in her apartment was unnerving her. Most of the furniture in their living room had been moved out of the way to allow the ambulance gurney access. She looked up to see the gurney and two EMTs exiting her bedroom. The white sheet covering Joanne's body was starting to absorb some of her blood, changing it into a sickening maroon color.

Kelley had seen this many times at the hospital and had been trained to overcome it, but it was still gruesome. Usually, she didn't know the person under the sheet, but this time, it was different. This time, it was someone she loved.

She felt a lone tear run down her bloodstained cheek. Quickly wiping it away, she took a deep breath. She didn't want to cry. Not now.

Two officers dressed in black emerged from the hallway and approached her. They were both dressed in the black uniforms of the SBPD, but they had clear plastic covering their hats and long black vinyl trench coats on. The first officer knelt down next to Kelley. "What happened here?" he asked as he tilted his hat back on his head.

Kelley remained quiet. She knew if she opened her mouth, she would scream.

"Miss," the officer said politely, "can you tell us what happened here?" Kelley stayed quiet.

The other officer looked at Kelley. "Were you the one who called 911?" Kelley looked up at the dark-skinned man and nodded.

"That's good," the man said, "That's good. Now, can you tell us what happened to your roommate?"

Kelley inhaled an uneven breath. "She wasn't my roommate," she said quietly. "She was my girlfriend."

"I'm sorry," the officer said. "I didn't know."

"Everything's going to be okay." The officer in front of her placed his hand on her exposed knee to try and calm her.

Kelly recoiled in terror. "Don't touch me!" Kelley screamed.

"Whoa," the officer said as he pulled away. "I didn't mean anything by it." He looked up at his partner. "Maybe we need to have the EMTs take a look at her."

The other officer sighed. "That's probably our best bet right now. She's not in any condition to tell us anything."

Kelley watched as the officer in front of her stood up and began to walk away. She wrapped the tan wool blanket tightly around her body and lowered her head. She knew the police were just trying to do their job, they were just trying to help her, but she couldn't bring herself to cooperate. Not after what she had just been through. A shiver ran down her spine as a wave of nausea settled in the pit of her stomach. Dropping to her hands and knees, she felt the contents of her stomach surging up her esophagus. She vomited again and again. Each time her muscles seized, holding her in that unnatural position.

She fell back against the wall, her naked body trembling and her abdomen aching from the vomiting. She was exhausted. She knew sleep would make her physically feel better, but that was the last thing she wanted to do right now. She couldn't even bring herself to blink; lest she see those eyes again, those evil red eyes.

***

The rain had begun to fall again as they arrived at the Grant House. Mighty bolts of lightning arced across the charcoal gray sky in magnificent, but brief, dances. The wind had also picked up. Smaller trees were bending in submission while larger ones tried to remain firm. Katrina had mutated from a tropical storm to a full-blown hurricane that was just resting off the western coast of Florida. Residents were being advised to seek shelter or evacuate the area.

Enbaugh brought his beat-up blue car to a screeching stop in the driveway, followed by the black SUV the OPR had rented at the airport. He kicked the automatic transmission into park and popped open the door. Stepping out into the rain, he pulled his trench coat more closely around himself and pushed his fedora tightly on his head. He watched as the three members of the OPR exited their vehicle and walked toward him.

"This is the place," Enbaugh said loudly over the howling wind.

"I get the feeling you're not accompanying us inside, Detective," Dawn observed.

Enbaugh shook his head. "Nothing could get me back into that house." He reached into his jacket pocket and removed a small white business card. "Here's my number. When you're done, give me a call and I'll come and get you."

Cane graciously accepted the card. "Thank you, Detective. We will be in contact."

Enbaugh spun around and retreated to the dryness of his car. Shifting the car back into gear, he pulled quickly out of the driveway and took off. Bishop and Dawn stood amazed in the pounding rain.

"You think he doesn't like this place?" Bishop asked sarcastically. "I sense that," Dawn smiled.

Cane began walking back to their vehicle. "Let's start unloading the equipment. I'm anxious to see what's inside." He stopped behind the black SUV and lifted the gate. He looked at the two silver trunks and assorted bags. "Bishop," he shouted, "help me with this first trunk."

Bishop glanced at the trunk. It was made of polished silver metal with rivets running along all its edges. It looked like it would survive almost anything. Two handles were recessed into either side of the case. Cane grabbed the ones facing him and began to slide the case out of the back. Bishop reached around and snatched the other handle and helped Cane pull it the rest of the way out.

"Jesus," Bishop said while holding the trunk handle with both hands. "How much does this stuff weigh?"

Cane looked at the trunk, "A rough estimate?

Probably around two hundred pounds of equipment in here." Cane looked back at Dawn. "Grab bags three and five and bring them in, will you?"

Dawn nodded and started to sort through the black duffel bags arranged next to the second trunk.

"Let's get this inside," Cane instructed them.

Bishop and Cane walked the heavy silver trunk along the sidewalk toward the house. The rain, mixed with small pellet-sized hail, was pounding their bodies. The two pushed against the wind as they stumbled toward the house. Cane glanced behind to see Dawn trudging along with the two black bags slung over her shoulders. Her long hair was being whipped about.

Turning back around, he glanced up at the house looming in front of them. It seemed like a very ordinary house, one like he would find in any suburb, but there was something ominous about it. Cane shook his head. He knew he was letting outside factors play on his subconscious. He needed to keep his mind clear and rational. The feeling was still there, though. An odd sense of dread permeated the house. Cane imagined a huge neon sign blinking "stay out" on the door.

Reaching the front door, Bishop grabbed the handle and twisted it open. He and Cane walked slowly into the darkened house and set the trunk down. Dawn followed them into the house and set her bags down. Shutting the door behind her, she began to wring the water out of her hair.

Bishop let out a sigh of relief. "Damn, that thing's heavy. What's in there?"

"Everything a good ghost hunter needs." Cane pulled off his sopping wet coat and deposited it in a heap on the floor. Kneeling down, he popped the two metal latches on the front of the trunk and flipped open the lid revealing a plethora of electronic equipment stowed neatly in separate compartments. He grabbed a clipboard and pen out of the trunk. "Time?" he asked.

Dawn checked her watch, "One-thirty-seven pm, eastern standard time."

Cane noted the time on the clipboard, along with the names of the investigators. "All right, we're logged, let's begin." He began to pull several pieces of equipment out of the trunk one by one. He handed Bishop and Dawn two small rectangular objects, as well as a flashlight.

"What are these?" Bishop asked, looking at the odd device in his hands. Cane pointed to the first one, "That one is an Electromagnetic Field Meter, or EMF Meter for short. It measures changes in a location's magnetic field. The second one is a Thermal Scanner. We use that to measure and catalogue 'cold spots'."

Bishop pressed the power button on the EMF Meter. The small silver device sprung to life, the needle inside the clear plastic window began jumping wildly. "Is it supposed to do that?"

Cane leaned over and looked at his meter. "No," he responded unemotionally. He pointed at Dawn. "She's carrying a Motion Sensor as well as a small voice activated tape recorder. If there are any noises, that little baby will pick them up, and the Motion Sensor can sometimes lead us to the activity."

Cane reached back into the trunk and removed three small black headsets. He placed one on

85

Bishop's and Dawn's heads, and then adjusted their mics. Sliding the third onto his own head, he leaned over and lifted a small silver video camera out of the trunk. "Are we ready?"

Bishop and Dawn both nodded at Cane.

Slipping the camera's strap over his hand, he tapped the red record button with his thumb. "Let's start with the first floor, then move up to the second. I don't want to miss anything."

The three began to quietly fan out through the living room. Bishop walked around the large black leather couches toward the fireplace as Dawn moved toward the shattered pieces of glass in front of the stairs. Cane, looking through the viewfinder, moved carefully into the dining room.

Dawn looked over the mirror. "Seven years bad luck."

Bishop lifted the EMF Meter toward the fireplace. The thin needle jumped again. "Cane, I'm getting some wild readings in this room." He thought for a moment, "Could these be caused by the lightning storm outside?"

"It's possible," Cane answered from the dining room, "but not likely. Unless the lightning was right on top of us, we shouldn't be getting any interference."

"Then what do these readings mean?" Bishop asked.

"Could mean you're reading a ghost," Cane replied as he moved further into the dining room. "Most researchers, like myself, believe ghosts manifest themselves through energy. When they move, they let off high amounts of electromagnetic discharge. Check the spot with your Thermal

Scanner."

Bishop sat the EMF on the fireplace's mantle and reached for his Scanner. After turning it on, he held it near the fireplace. "This is weird," he said, looking at the scanner's digital display.

"What've you got?" Dawn asked from across the room.

"The room is right around seventy-eight degrees, but when I sweep the scanner toward the fireplace, the temperature drops substantially." Bishop checked the readings again, "I'm getting a reading of fifty-nine point four right now."

Dawn quickly walked across the living room toward Bishop. She was careful not to disturb any of the glass on the floor around the shattered mirror. She stopped next to Bishop and read his scanner over his shoulder. "Maybe your thermal is malfunctioning."

"Possible," Bishop conceded.

"Let me check mine." Dawn lifted her scanner and swept it through the area. "I'm getting the same exact readings," she said after a moment. She dropped the scanner into the pocket of her jacket and held out her hand. "That's extraordinary," she admitted. "Put your hand over here, Bishop."

Bishop complied. "That is wild," he said with a smile. "There's a column of cold air that runs from the floor up." He pushed his other hand into the column, "It feels like it's circular." He swept his hand out of the column, then back in. "We've definitely found one of your 'cold spots', Cane."

"Catalogue it," they heard Cane yell from across the room.

Dawn removed her hand and fished a small

notebook out of her pocket. She hastily noted the place, time and type of event. "Before we leave," she said as she slid the notepad back into her pocket, "we need to check this area again." She held up her scanner, "It's strange, the temperature isn't even fluctuating…wait a minute."

Bishop ripped his hand away from the column. "Son of a bitch!" he shouted as he shook his hands. "It grew exceptionally hot very quickly."

Dawn nodded. "I watched the reading shoot up from fifty-nine to one hundred and twelve in less than a second."

"Why didn't you say something?" Bishop asked, cradling his red hand. "It felt like I had my hand in a pot of boiling water!"

"Sorry," Dawn replied as she noted the reading. "They don't usually do that. Let me take a look at your hand."

Bishop gingerly held out his hand, "Be careful."

"It looks like," Dawn started, "you have first degree burns. That's incredible." Dawn carefully turned over Bishop's hand. "We'll get you some gauze from the first-aid kit when we're finished in here."

Bishop nodded. "Thanks."

"Dawn, Bishop," they heard Cane's voice over their headsets, "Can you come into the kitchen with your equipment?"

Dawn reached up and keyed the mic, "We're on our way."

The two moved quickly through the dark dining room toward the swinging kitchen door. Bishop noticed as he passed that the door handle had been shot off. Once inside, they saw Cane standing motionless in front of the tall white refrigerator.

Dawn moved worriedly toward her partner. "What's wrong, Cane?" Cane pointed to the pink box on the second shelf. "Open it."

Dawn knelt down in front of the pink box. Carefully grabbing the edge with her slender fingers, she pulled the top open. Her eyes suddenly widened as a gasp escaped her lips. "Good Lord!"

Bishop moved quickly around the island to get a look inside the box. He stopped cold in his tracks when he saw the contents. The pink box was filled with mashed birthday cake and a bloody human heart. One side of the cake, which was still intact, had the words "you will not escape" scrawled messily in the white frosting.

Cane lifted the camera and began to film again. "Get an EMF reading." Dawn lifted the small silver device and held it toward the box. The needle immediately swung to the far right-hand side. "This is really hot," she said as she stood up.

"You mean the ghosts did this?" Bishop asked in horror. "It appears that way, Mr. Bishop," Cane responded.

"What are we dealing with?" Bishop asked, suddenly feeling very uncomfortable.

Cane hit the stop button on the camera and lowered it to his side. "At this point, I have no idea."

"A poltergeist?" Dawn suggested after regaining her composure.

"I don't think I could even hazard a guess," Cane replied. "We've seen a lot of signs of supernatural activity, but no actual events as of yet."

"Next move?" Bishop asked hesitantly. When he was training with the CIA, they had taught him how to deal with violent crime scenes, but his training was failing him now.

Cane thought for a moment. "I think we should check upstairs. I really want to get some readings from where the Grant family was killed."

"Let me bandage Bishop's hand first," Dawn said. "Plus, I think we all need to get out of this house for a minute."

Cane looked over at Bishop, "Agreed."

Chapter 8

"Sam Peters?" a woman asked.

Sam Peters spun around to see the young woman standing before him. She was tall and thin with long, straight, jet-black hair that hung past her shoulders. She couldn't be more than twenty-three, but her dark eyes held lifetimes of wisdom. Sam knew instantly she had an old soul. She was dressed in a long, black, tight-fitting gown which brushed the floor when she walked. Her complexion was very pale and looked even lighter with her dark eye shadow and lipstick highlighting her well-defined face. *Jesus, I'm standing in front of Morticia Addams.* "Can I help you?"

Sam was a man of medium height and build. He had a thick mustache growing on his upper lip, and wavy gray hair just past his cheeks in length. He was in his mid-thirties, but he looked a lot older. He was wearing a sherbet colored Henley with a pair of blue jeans and white sneakers. The top three buttons of his shirt were undone, allowing a wisp of gray chest hair to peek out. He had held many professions during his life, a carpenter, a schoolteacher, a deep-sea fisherman and a writer, but he was primarily a psychic.

The two were standing in the middle of Tampa's international airport. It was mostly quiet, mainly due to the hurricane steadily moving on shore. Rumor around the airport was all flights were about to be cancelled and all traffic would be diverted to a different location. Various palm trees and pink and blue neon lights littered the walls of the terminal in an effort to give visitors that

"Miami" look while still in the airport. The white tiling and stucco walls were a nice touch.

"I read your book on the 'Brairfield Haunting'," the young woman stated. "I think that's one of the best documented hauntings I've ever heard of, and you did a fantastic job of portraying it in your book."

"Thank you," Sam said almost glowing. He loved praise, but then again, what writer doesn't? "What's your name?"

"People call me Morgan," the young woman replied. "I'm a witch." Sam was a bit startled by her honesty. "Wiccan, I hope."

Morgan smiled devilishly, "Mostly, but you can't have the light without the dark."

"Good point," Sam said with a laugh. He wasn't sure why, but he was very at ease with this woman. "What can I do for you today, Morgan?"

"I just wanted to meet you before the others arrived," Morgan admitted. "I wanted to have a chance to talk with you before we were swept up with filming."

"How do you know about the shoot?" Sam asked.

"I'm part of it," Morgan replied with a smile.

"In what capacity?" Sam wondered.

"After I read your book, I decided to use my particular talents for more useful purposes." Morgan held out her hand with her open palm up. She quickly snapped her fingers and produced a black business card. "Neat trick, huh?"

Sam accepted the card and read the silver embossed print aloud. "Morgan LeFay, Ghost Hunter." He slipped the card into the pocket of his

92

jeans. "It takes more to be a ghost hunter than just a snazzy business card, Morgan."

"I'm well aware of that," Morgan said with a smile. "I have investigated paranormal activity in ten states, as well as having a degree in parapsychology. I'm extremely well versed in the paranormal."

"Very good," Sam smiled.

"That's why I jumped at the chance to be on this episode of *Ghost Chasers, Inc.* I wanted to work with a master hunter." Morgan took a step closer to Sam. "You are a legend in our field."

"Legend," Sam said, rolling the word pleasantly around his mouth. "That's a very strong word to be tossing around."

"I mean it." Morgan ran her hand down Sam's arm softly. "For me, it's like being a composer and getting to study at the feet of Beethoven."

"I appreciate the compliment," Sam said politely, "But I'm just a man. I'm by no means comparable to Beethoven."

"Sam? Morgan?"

Both Sam and Morgan turned to see a large group approaching them. Chloe Andrews walked up with her hand extended. "My name's Chloe Andrews, and I'm the director of this segment of Ghost Chasers."

Sam reached out and shook Chloe's hand. "Pleasure to meet you, Chloe." Chloe turned to Morgan. "Morgan?"

Morgan nodded and shook Chloe's hand. "Pleasure."

Chloe turned and motioned toward her group. "This is my crew." She waved to the left. "This is my cameraman, Trent."

Trent was a twenty-something guy with frosted brown hair wearing a black shirt with a pair of khaki cargo pants. His left ear was pierced and he had two visible black tattoos on his forearms.

"This is our sound tech, Chris," Chloe continued.

Chris was black and just a hair taller than Trent. His dark hair was shaved close to his head. He was wearing a black jacket and a pair of blue jeans. He had a large duffel bag slung over his left shoulder.

Chloe moved on, "This is our grip, Jackson."

Jackson stood just short of Chris. His long, wavy blonde hair hung in waves around his slim face. He had a better build than either Chris or Trent and was wearing a white button-up shirt with a pair of black Dockers and a clunky pair of black boots. Jackson nodded at Morgan and Sam.

Chloe pointed to a young woman behind Jackson. "This is our producer, Carrie Lang."

Carrie's long red hair was tied up in a ponytail behind her head exposing her radiant green eyes. She was wearing a gray t-shirt with a long black skirt and a pair of tall high heels. She was strikingly beautiful, and appeared to be in her mid-thirties. As with most redheads, her skin was a creamy white.

"This," Chloe said, pointing to the last member of her crew, "is our host, Rivers Gallows."

Rivers stepped forward and looked over Sam and Morgan. Pulling a cigarette from his jacket pocket, he slid it into his mouth and lit it. After a long drag, he exhaled the smoke into their faces. "You stay out of my way, and I'll stay out of yours." With that, he marched passed them, leaving the group behind.

Morgan turned to look at Rivers as he walked away. "What's his problem?" Chloe laughed. "He's in a good mood today."

Sam glanced down at his watch. It was nearly two in the afternoon. "Are we going to get started today, or wait until tomorrow?"

"Weather permitting," Carrie said. "We plan on filming some background footage tomorrow morning, but we don't go live until tomorrow night. We want to have a production meeting tonight."

Sam smiled. "Wonderful. Have you booked accommodations for Morgan and me?"

Carrie nodded. She reached into her small leather bag and produced two envelopes. "I've put you both up at the Brenton. It's one of Florida's premiere hotels."

"Thank you," Sam said. "I think if it's all right with everyone, I'd like to go check-in to my room and get cleaned up."

Chloe nodded. "That was our agenda as well." She glanced down at her wristwatch. "Let's meet at the Brenton's Bar in, say, four hours?"

"Sounds good," Sam said. He turned to Morgan, "Do you need a ride?"

Morgan shook her head, "No, I drove here. I'll follow you to the hotel in my car."

"Good," Chloe said. "I better go catch up to Rivers."

Morgan turned to Sam. "I'll meet you out in the parking lot in a second, I have to use the little girls' room." Sam smiled. "Don't get lost."

Morgan began to walk through the empty terminal. "I won't."

Morgan's mind was brimming with excitement. Today, she had gotten a job on television and met one of her idols. This day couldn't possibly get any better. *Not bad for a girl who was voted "most likely to end up a prostitute" in high school...* She stopped for a moment as the hairs on the back of her neck stood up. An odd sensation had just passed through her. She felt like she was being watched. Spinning around, she glanced around the terminal. It was empty except for a few baggage handlers and a stray flight attendant or two, and none of them were paying any attention to her. She unconsciously reached up and wrapped her fingers around the clear crystal she had hanging around her neck and began to rub it with her thumb. She glanced toward the large windows to her right. She could see nothing through them except the dark gray clouds looming outside.

"My mind's playing tricks on me," she muttered to herself. Turning back around, she continued her journey to the bathroom. Walking through a small alcove, she saw the door to the women's restroom and pushed through it.

The long room was wall-to-wall white tile. The stalls were painted a lime green, while the sinks were ringed in the same color of tile. Art deco lights hung on the walls and were backlit with red. *Very festive,* Morgan chuckled to herself. Moving to the first sink, she lifted the handle on the silver tap. Warm water immediately began to spray out. Morgan jumped back in an effort to remain dry. Standing to one side, she pushed the handle down until the water was flowing normally from the spigot. Dipping her hands under it, she let the warm water run over them. She felt sticky from the drive here. She knew she would be at the hotel soon and that she would be able to take a shower, but she couldn't take it anymore. She hated it when her hands felt unclean. She knew she was a little obsessive-compulsive in that department. Shutting off the water, she reached for a paper towel.

She stopped. The sensation hit her again. She couldn't explain it, but she had the oddest feeling that someone was watching her. Turning around, she looked over the stalls. All the doors were closed except for the last one, which hung partially open.

"Hello?" she asked. Her voice echoed in the emptiness. "Is anyone in here?" She stood quietly for a moment, listening for the tell-tale signs of another human presence, but heard nothing but the dull hum of the fan in the ceiling.

Dropping down to the floor, Morgan reached hastily into the small black bag she had slung over her shoulder. She fished out a red piece of chalk and held it tightly between her fingers. Glancing around the bathroom one more time, she leaned over and drew a circle around herself. She crossed the lines and created a pentagram. In the center of the pentagram, she hastily scribbled the image of an eye. Dropping the piece of chalk, she stood and grabbed her crystal.

She closed her eyes and tilted her head back. "This is a spell of protection," she said out loud. "It will protect me from whoever, or whatever, you are. No harm may come to the person standing in the circle until the spell has worn off." She swallowed hard and repeated the words eight more times silently to herself. She hated rushing spells. That

97

had a tendency of rendering them ineffective. She hoped this case would be different.

Taking a deep breath, Morgan opened her eyes. She slowly looked around the bathroom. It was empty. Letting go of her crystal, she charged for the door. Throwing it open, she ran through the doorway and back into the main terminal. It was also empty. All the baggage handlers and attendants had gone. There was no one as far as she could see. Her heart began to race as the hairs on the back of her neck stood up again. Slowly turning to her left, Morgan spotted a dark form lurking behind one of the nearby palm trees. It wasn't human as far as she could tell. It had no solid mass, just darkness, as if a patch of black ink had been thrown on a white canvas. The mass undulated as it slowly left its perch behind the tree.

Morgan stumbled backwards. She had never seen anything like this before. The mass moved slowly toward her, then stopped about three feet from her. It's form mutated into that of a large animal that stood on all fours. It looked like a jungle cat, but Morgan couldn't be sure. It had no details, just darkness.

The cat turned its head toward her, revealing its glowing, almond-shaped eyes. The eyes hardened into slits as they glanced over her. The beast began to pace back and forth in front of her, all the while maintaining its three feet of separation.

"The spell must have worked," Morgan muttered. She slowly began to walk through the terminal, the shadow echoing her every move.

"You will not escape," the shadow growled.

Morgan recoiled in horror at the being's almost

human voice. She quickly began to pick up her pace, and soon, hit a dead run down through the terminal. She had no idea of how long her spell of protection would last, but she knew she didn't want to be here when it ran out. The shadow was easily keeping pace with her, its glowing red eyes burning into her back.

"Leave me alone!" Morgan screamed. She was pumping her legs as hard as she could as she rounded a corner. Not looking ahead of her, Morgan hit something and went skittering to the floor. Her crystal broke, sending shards flying in every direction.

"Morgan?"

Morgan looked up, fully expecting the beast to be standing over her. Instead, she found Sam lifting himself off the floor. Jumping up, Morgan spun to look behind her. There was nothing but an empty corridor. Turning around, she threw her arms around Sam's neck. "Thank God!"

Sam was confused. "What the hell is going on?"

"Let's get out of here," Morgan pleaded. "Please."

"Okay, we're going," Sam assured her.

The two began to move through the terminal toward the exit. As the doors slid shut behind them, the shadow crept out from a corner and stood silently over the remains of Morgan's crystal. Now in human form, the phantom crushed the remainder of it with its foot. Looking up at the exit, a horrible smile crossed its face.

***

Hail was pelting the roof of their vehicle, making it difficult to hear each other. The stones had grown in size from a pea to almost a golf ball within the seconds they had been in the vehicle. They had left the house a few minutes before and retreated to the safety of their Blazer. Cane sat quietly in the front seat, twisting the edge of his mustache with his fingers while Dawn and Bishop were in the back. Dawn was slowly wrapping gauze around Bishop's hand in slow, deliberate circles. She knew he needed medical attention to treat the burns on his hand, but she also knew Cane wasn't ready to leave yet.

"How's the patient?" Cane asked without turning around. His gaze was transfixed on the house in front of him.

Dawn sighed. "It looks like he has first degree burns on his hand, Cane. We need to get him to a hospital."

"We're not leaving yet," Cane said quietly.

A massive hailstone slammed into the windshield of the SUV sending cracks webbing across the entire window. Cane threw his arms across his face to protect himself against fragments of glass. A second softball-sized hailstone erupted through the window, crushing it in like a flimsy piece of aluminum. The stone finally came to rest in the center console next to Cane.

"Abandon ship!" Cane yelled. He clumsily reached down for the handle and threw open the door. Lifting his arm over his head, he jumped out of the car and began to tear across the driveway toward the house. He tried in vain to dodge the hailstones. A large chunk of ice drilled him square in the shoulders, dropping him to the ground. Cane moaned as he tried to lift himself off the ground.

Dawn and Bishop leapt out of the vehicle just as a bolt of lightning crossed the sky and touched down in an empty lot across from the Grant House. Sparks and flames erupted from the small grove of trees that stood there.

"Jesus," Bishop said out loud, "did you see that?"

"Run, dip shit!" Dawn screamed as she headed toward Cane.

Bishop turned around to see a second flash of light in front of him. "Oh shit," he said under his breath.

The lightning arced down in front of the house, then curved up, and then down again into the trunk of a nearby tree. Bishop watched as the bolt split it in two in an instant. The mighty tree began to topple toward the ground, and Bishop realized he was in its path.

Turning toward the house, Bishop sprinted away from the SUV. No longer feeling the impact of the hail, he pushed his body hard toward his partners.

Without even stopping, Bishop shoved Dawn toward the front door and scooped Cane off the sidewalk. He began to drag the older man by the shoulders toward the door as Dawn skittered to a stop on the stoop. Bishop spun around to see the tree fall into the middle of their SUV, shredding it. The metal of the vehicle offered no resistance to the tree. Grabbing the door handle with his bandaged hand, Bishop winced as pain shot up his arm. Twisting hard, he threw the door open. Dawn was first inside, followed closely by Bishop and Cane.

Bishop laid Cane gently on his back just inside the door, and dropped down next to him. "Are you okay?" Bishop pressed his fingers against Cane's throat to check his pulse.

Cane grabbed Bishop's fingers and pushed them away. "Yes, I'm fine," Cane replied. "Now stop touching me."

"That's the gratitude I get for helping you?" Bishop asked.

"I'll give you a bloody treat once we get home," Cane said sarcastically. "Dick." Bishop said as he lifted himself off the floor. He slowly turned toward Dawn. She was leaning against the back of one of the leather couches in the living room trying to catch her breath. She was cradling her head in her hands. "Are you okay, Dawn?"

Dawn slowly lifted her head. A trickle of blood was running down from her scalp. "I'm fine."

Bishop took an uneasy step toward her. "No you're not. You're bleeding."

"It's nothing," Dawn shrugged. "A piece of hail hit me on the way in. Just a minor contusion."

Bishop pressed his hands to her head and leaned it forward. He slowly moved her long hair out of the way so he could see the cut. There was a small bloody gash just above her forehead. "You may need stitches."

Dawn shook her head. "Just get me a dry cloth to hold against it. If I apply pressure, the bleeding will stop."

Bishop started to open his mouth to argue, but a quick stern glance from Dawn stopped him. "Okay, I'll go find a rag or something."

Dawn watched Bishop head into the dining room and toward the kitchen. She pressed her fingers against the cut and then looked at them. A fair amount of blood was smeared on her fingertips. She quickly wiped them on her pants, and then looked over at Cane. He had lifted himself into a sitting position and was trying to rub the sore spot on his back. "What the fuck is wrong with you?" Dawn asked.

"What?" Cane replied innocently.

"Are you just a stuffy old English bastard, or what?"

"What the hell are you talking about?" Cane wondered.

"I mean, why are you treating Bishop like shit?" Dawn slowly lifted herself off the back of the couch and walked toward Cane. "He's been nothing but helpful so far, and all you've done is ride his ass."

"Why shouldn't I?" Cane stood up to face Dawn. "Do you realize we've been through five partners this year alone? When is Weiss going to stop sending us these over-privileged brats that wash out within a week?"

"Maybe they wouldn't quit the program so quickly if you weren't such an asshole to them. Did you ever stop to think some of these people may have been great investigators if you'd only given them half a chance?"

Cane laughed. "Those kids weren't investigators." He turned away from Dawn. "They were people who had seen one too many ghost movies. They weren't serious about the craft, and neither is Bishop."

Dawn grabbed Cane by the shoulder and spun him around. "How do you fucking know? You didn't even try to let them prove themselves!"

"I started this organization with Weiss! I know what makes a good investigator and what doesn't!" Cane roared.

Dawn took a step back from Cane. "You self-centered old bastard. That's what this is all about, isn't it?"

"What, pray tell?" Cane asked angrily. "What great insight have you just gained into my psyche? Please tell me Ms. I have degrees in psychology and parapsychology."

"You've finally given up, haven't you?" Dawn asked quietly. "You don't care about the OPR anymore, or the cases we investigate. You've become an old, bitter man. You still can't get past the fact Weiss runs the company now, can you?"

"Why should I?" Cane yelled. "He stole it from me!"

"He did nothing of the sort," Dawn corrected him. "When Weiss decided to incorporate the OPR, he offered you a seat on the board and you refused! You thought by taking the position, you wouldn't be able to investigate anymore."

"That's bullshit," Cane said.

"I was there, remember?" Dawn put her hand on Cane's shoulder. "When you declined the seat, Weiss began to run the company himself without consulting you, didn't he?"

Cane nodded. "He never asked me."

"Why should he?" Dawn wondered. "He was chairman. He didn't need the approval of one of his investigators." Dawn let her hand slip off his shoulder. "You did this to yourself, and now you're taking it out on the world."

"I—"

Bishop emerged from the kitchen with a small cloth in his hands. "I found...." he let his sentence trail off when he saw Dawn and Cane. "Did I interrupt something?"

Cane pulled away from Dawn. "No."

Dawn shook her head. She turned toward Bishop. "Thanks for getting that for me, Bish."

Bishop smiled. "It was no problem." He handed Dawn the small white cloth.

Dawn folded the cloth in half and pressed it against the cut on her head.

She felt the sting of pain under the pressure. She winced for a moment, but knew she had to keep it tightly pressed to her wound. Dawn looked around the room. She spotted a tall classic wooden radio standing in the corner. "I wonder if the local stations are still broadcasting." She moved around the couches toward the radio. Reaching down, she gently twisted the first light brown knob.

The radio was shaped like a cathedral with a high arched top. The brown and black woven mesh speaker in front looked like tall stained glass windows, and the dial looked like the front entrance. The dial immediately lit up, and the speaker squawked to life. There was nothing but static. Dawn began to slowly twist the second knob, searching for a station amidst the snow. She stopped and began to twist the dial in the opposite direction. Almost at once, she stumbled onto human voices. All three moved into the living room and hovered quietly around the radio.

Bishop couldn't help but wonder if this was what it was like before television was introduced. Families and friends huddled around a small wooden radio listening for weather and news and their favorite programs. He enjoyed radio much more than he did television. There was a station back home that played classic radio theater on the weekends. He almost never missed one if he had the chance. You were much more inclined to use your imagination with radio. You had to imagine the adventures of your favorite superhero, and follow along very carefully so as to not miss a clue during the mysteries. Bishop let his mind wander as he listened to the disembodied voices filter through the speaker.

"...Airports are closed at this time," the steady male voice reported. *"The Department of Transportation and the Highway Patrol are reporting that visibility is extremely low, and people should avoid travel at all cost. Once again, Hurricane Katrina has gone from a tropical storm to a full-blown hurricane as of this afternoon. She's expected to come on shore in the next hour. Authorities are asking you to close and lock all windows and doors, and use your emergency preparedness kits. You should have a small radio, a flashlight, extra batteries, and blankets—"*

"We're stuck here," announced Dawn. "It appears that way," Cane agreed.

They heard the news personality shuffle the papers in his hands. *"Sorry, kids, it looks like Halloween may be cancelled this year. There's more news coming up at the top of the hour. You're listening to Stone Brook's adult contemporary alternative, ninety-one point three, W-R-"*

Dawn clicked off the radio. "I am not staying here." Bishop smiled, "We can have a pajama party."

"My pajamas are in the Blazer," Dawn admitted, "As well as the rest of our clothes."

Cane looked over at the two trunks next to the door, "At least we still have our equipment." He walked across the living room and began to pace. "After what happened to the Grants, I think it would be a very bad idea for us to stay here tonight."

"Agreed," Dawn said, "But where are we going to go? I doubt very much the taxis are still out and about in this storm. I got the idea from the radio report that most of the streets have been closed down except for emergency vehicles."

All three were startled when the power blinked off. "Damn," Cane muttered under his breath.

"Wait!" Bishop shouted. "I've got it!"

Dawn and Bishop both turned to look at Bishop. "Well," Cane said impatiently, "are you going to share, or do we have to read your mind?"

"You said only emergency vehicles are still operating, right?" Dawn nodded, "That was just an educated guess, but probably."

"We have three injured people, right?" Bishop asked.

"None of us are that bad...." Cane stopped. "I get it! Call an ambulance!"

"Right!" Bishop smiled. "I'm sure the hospitals have emergency generators for times like these."

Dawn stood. "I'll call 911."

Chapter 9

The Brenton Hotel was beautifully decorated. The walls were a creamy white trimmed with dark brown wood. The floor was marble, etched with tiny gray veins that spider webbed through it. The cathedral ceiling of the lobby had several gold chandeliers strung from it, and the registration desk was solid mahogany. Huge plants seemed to adorn every free space, and almost looked to be taking over the place.

A bank of elevators stood on the right side of the room, just past the registration desk, while the opposite wall contained several large archways leading to the hotel's conference rooms and dining hall. A grand staircase ran up the center of the floor to the second story. A beautiful balcony, edged with gold iron fencing, ran the length of the room and led to even more conference rooms and the second floor restaurant and bar.

"I'm not working in these conditions!" Rivers yelled as he tossed his glass across the room. The glass hit the wall just behind Chloe and shattered.

Chloe didn't flinch. "There's no arguing, Rivers. We go live in less than twenty-four hours." She brushed a few strands of her brown hair behind her ear and crossed her slender arms, "And you will be ready." She had changed into a pair of black pants and a tight red long sleeved shirt. Her hair was pulled up, revealing her slender neck.

Rivers stood from his seat at the Brenton's bar and staggered across the floor toward Chloe. He was drunk and she knew it. He straightened his dark gray sport jacket over his white golf shirt. He reached over and tried to steady himself against the back of a nearby chair, but slipped and toppled to the ground.

Chloe sighed and reached down to grab his hand. Rivers batted her angrily away. "I can do it myself."

Chloe knelt down in front of him. "Then you better fucking get up right now, you piece of shit. Do you realize how big of an ass you're making of yourself?" Chloe took a deep breath. She didn't realize she was this angry. "You're a nationally syndicated TV host, and right now you're drunk, and laying face-down in a hotel bar. How do you think that's going to reflect on our show, let alone your career?"

Rivers rolled onto his back and looked up at Chloe with glassy eyes. "What are you on about now?"

"Bastard. You haven't even been listening." Chloe stood up in a huff and walked toward the bar.

Rivers stared up at the ceiling as the world began to spin around him. "Can someone help me up?" He stammered. "I think I'm gonna puke."

Chloe stopped in front of the rest of the crew and dropped her head. "Chris, can you take Rivers up to his room?"

Chris stood and nodded. "This isn't your fault, Chloe." He patted her on the shoulder and moved toward Rivers. Reaching down, he pulled the drunken man easily off the floor. "Time to go nighty-night," he told Rivers as they walked out of the bar.

Chloe looked up to face the rest of the crew. They were all seated at a small, round table in the middle of the bar. To their left were two large red felt pool tables. A long green light hung parallel over each. To their right, stood the bar. It was a long black chunk of plastic that ran the length of the room. The cliché rectangular mirror hung behind the bar flanked by two tall shelves filled with alcohol bottles. The floor was nothing more than black carpeting, while dim neon strips ringed the walls and the bar. Chloe couldn't believe this place was actually part of the Brenton. It seemed so…skuzzy.

"I'm really sorry," Chloe said at last. "This is bad, even for Rivers." Trent was sitting to Chloe's left. He placed his hand on her back. "So Rivers is an asshole. Who cares?"

Jackson nodded. He had his blonde hair tied up in a small ponytail. "Yeah, fuck him. We don't need him anyway."

Carrie was playing with the ice left in the bottom of her glass. She lifted the glass to her mouth and dumped the ice inside. She sucked off a bit of the drink's residual flavor and began to crunch them with her teeth. "Unfortunately," she said after swallowing what was left of the ice, "We do."

"Do what?" Jackson asked.

"Need Rivers," Chloe answered. "This isn't just some taped segment that he can add a voice-over to in post. We are hosting this entire show live from Grant House on Halloween!"

"And that requires a host," Carrie added. She was twirling her curly red hair with her fingers. She looked up over Chloe's shoulder. "There's our two crazies," she said just loud enough for the group to

110

hear.

Chloe spun around in her chair to see Sam and Morgan enter the bar. Sam was dressed in a white t-shirt with a pair of blue jeans and light brown boots. Morgan was decked out in black. She had on a long black skirt that hung to her ankles, a loosely crocheted sweater that you could see her bra through, and a pair of clunky black boots. Her black hair hung straight down around her slim face.

"Sorry we're a little late," Morgan said as they approached the group. "I wanted to take a shower."

"Okay," Chloe said slowly, "but why does that make Sam late?"

"I didn't want to walk here alone, so I made him wait." Morgan answered. "We left the airport four hours ago," Chloe said sternly. She had no patience for tardy people, especially in the film industry. "How long do you need to take a shower, Morgan?"

"We were talking," Sam replied, with an almost guilty look on his face. "Let's leave it at that. Besides, we're only ten minutes late."

"All right," Chloe said finally. "Let's get this production meeting underway." She motioned for the two to join her at the table. "As most of you know, this will be the first, in hopefully a series, of live episodes of *Ghost Chasers, Inc.* We'll go live at seven pm eastern standard time tomorrow on October Thirty-first."

"How are we going to coordinate this with the studio?" Trent asked. Chloe nodded. "The local TV station has rented us one of their satellite trucks for the day. Everything, including the live segments, will be managed from our control room back in

111

California."

"What about delay?" Jackson asked, referring to the satellite delay.

"That shouldn't be a problem," Chloe replied. "Since our host is here, and not back in the studio, we won't have to worry about the lag time between the two. The studio has already produced our custom intro and outro, so all Rivers has to do is remember the out-qs."

"Sounds easy," Trent remarked. "Are we going to use pre-recorded segments during the show?"

Chloe nodded. "Carrie has a list of those."

Carrie lifted a small notebook off the table and flipped it open. "We're going to do a history of Stone Brook and the Grant house first. We'll tape that tomorrow morning and send a feedback to the studio so they can edit it." She ran her bright red nails down over the page, "then we'll have a segment on 'Project Stargate' that was taped two weeks ago."

Jackson smiled. "I love that movie."

"Not the movie, you idiot," Carrie quickly corrected him, "the military project involving psychics and remote viewing."

Jackson shot Carrie an angry glance.

"We also have another segment on previous haunted houses we've investigated, a short one on the history of this wretched holiday, and one final segment on the vampire that supposedly lived in Highgate Cemetery in England." Carrie put her notepad down. "Basically, your run-of-the-mill Halloween episode."

"But this year, we have a new twist," Chloe said with a devious smile. She thought for a

112

moment, "Let's move the Halloween segment to the end and flip- flop the ghost, vampire and Stargate segments."

Carrie nodded and made the appropriate corrections on her notepad. "I think that's a good idea."

"Chloe," Sam said tentatively, "can you tell me exactly what our role will be?" Sam asked.

"You'll be there, to…" Chloe searched for the words, "bridge the gap between the spirit world and our world."

Carrie let out a quick giggle but quickly tried to contain herself. "Sorry," she said with her hand over her mouth, trying to hold back the laugh.

Ignoring Carrie, Chloe continued. "A police detective that was in the house after the crimes reported seeing a pair of glowing red eyes."

"Very interesting," Sam said. "So we're here to act as mediums?"

"Is that a problem?" Chloe asked, suddenly concerned.

"No," Sam said after a moment. "Then what?" Chloe asked.

Sam paused. "I, we," he corrected, "have never dealt with malevolent spirits before. The hauntings we've worked have always been, for the most part, harmless. I've never been in a place where they claim ghosts have killed someone."

"Mr. Peters," Carrie cut in, "Are you backing out of our arrangement? Sam was taken aback by Carrie's statement.

"I seem to recall having to pay a large sum of money in advance to procure your services." She stared at Sam intently. "I would hate to have to ask for that payment back."

"No," Sam replied quickly. "I am definitely not backing out. I am just expressing a reservation of ours." He stopped for a moment to collect his thoughts. "We don't want *anyone* on this crew to be placed in harm's way."

"Personally," Jackson chimed in, "I hope the ghosts kill Rivers."

Chloe reached over and rapped Jackson on the back of the head with her open palm. "What's wrong with you?"

"The man is a pig," Jackson spat angrily.

"That may very well be," Chloe agreed, "but we don't have a show without him, and you are out of a job."

Jackson slumped back in his small wooden chair. He quickly crossed his arms across his chest, feeling like a child just scolded for stealing a cookie.

"Look," Chloe said after a moment, "This storm has got us all a little unnerved, but the shoot will continue." She looked over the solemn faces of her crew. "I think we all need a good night's sleep, and we'll all feel refreshed in the morning."

"Are you adjourning this meeting?" Jackson asked spitefully.

Chloe nodded. "Let's all meet down in the lobby at six tomorrow morning." Chloe watched as everyone but Sam and Morgan left the bar. She lifted her beverage off the dented wooden table and took a long drink of its alcoholic contents. After setting down the glass, she ran her hands over her face. "Can I tell you guys a secret?"

"Sure," Morgan replied.

114

"I don't think we're in any danger from ghosts. This crew is going to kill each other before any ghosts have the chance."

Morgan moved from her stool to a chair next to Chloe. "That's why we need to talk to you."

"Why?" Chloe said curiously.

"We're getting some really bad vibes here." Morgan said seriously. "Bad vibes?" Chloe echoed. "What are you, a Beach Boys song?"

"I'm not kidding," Morgan argued, slightly perturbed at the director's lack of seriousness.

"We've been sensing it since we arrived here in Stone Brook," Sam took up the conversation.

"Sensing what?" Chloe asked, sitting up in her chair.

"There's something," Sam looked over at Morgan, then back at Chloe, "evil here."

Morgan leaned close to Chloe and lowered her voice. "The shadows breathe."

"I don't understand," Chloe admitted. "Neither did we, until Morgan saw one."

Chloe looked at Morgan, who looked paler than the actor they had hired to play the vampire in the Highgate piece. "What did you see?"

"It was what I would best describe as a shadow." Morgan began to tap her black fingernails nervously against the table. "It had no visible features. It just looked like a mass of black with haunting red eyes."

"Oh, my God," Chloe said, "We need to get this on tape. Where's Trent?" She spun around in her seat to see if Trent had already left the bar. "Damn."

"Chloe," Morgan said sternly to get her

attention, "I think the crew is in harm's way here."

Chloe looked over at Sam. "What does the master psychic think?"

"I have to agree with my esteemed colleague. I don't feel safe here." Chloe stood up. "Well, what do you expect me to do? Scrap a live broadcast a day before it's airdate?" She walked around the small table nervously. "Do you realize how much money the network has already sunk into this project?" She ran her hands through her hair. "They would be very upset with me," she concluded.

"I realize the network would be out a chunk of cash," Sam admitted, "but they wouldn't have to worry about a murdered crew."

"Yeah," Morgan said after a minute, "Imagine the wrongful death suit that could be filed. The network could be sued for *millions*."

"Okay," Chloe said, "Now you're just bullying me." She leaned over and laid her hands on the table. "I assure both of you, this broadcast will happen. Now, are you in, or are you out?"

Morgan and Sam looked at each other for a long moment. Chloe could've sworn they were communicating telepathically with each other, but she had no way to prove that.

Sam nodded once, and turned his gaze back to Chloe. "In."

Chapter 10

Enbaugh stepped out of his cruiser followed closely by Montoya. He quickly pulled his jacket collar up around his ears and started to walk briskly toward the ambulance. The emergency room entrance of the Stone Brook General Hospital was built ten feet deeper than the outermost wall of the building and had a large overhang covering it. This provided a small measure of protection against Hurricane Katrina. The outside of the hospital was white stucco, with an almost southwestern paint scheme. Trim was painted a greenish blue and an almost pink shade of tan.

The ambulance he was approaching was one of three currently unloading patients. The vehicle was large and blocky, with the traditional white paint job, blue stripe down the side and the red and blue sirens on top. The dual back doors burst open and two EMTs dressed in blue shirts and black pants jumped out. The first, who had a stethoscope hanging around his neck, moved out of the way so his passengers could exit.

Enbaugh watched as Cane, Dawn and Bishop slowly exited. The EMTs pointed toward the emergency entrance and noted that all patients had to check in at the front desk. "I see your little outing went badly."

Cane looked up to see Enbaugh. "Detective," he said, acknowledging him. "To what do we owe the pleasure of this visit?"

Enbaugh shrugged. "I just heard over the radio the three people entrusted to me were heading to the hospital. I thought it would be best to come and check to make sure you weren't dead."

Bishop smiled. "That's very thoughtful of you, Detective."

Montoya stepped around Enbaugh and looked at the three. Cane was nursing a sore back, Dawn had a large white bandage taped to her forehead and one of Bishop's hands was completely wrapped in gauze. "What happened?"

"Occupational hazards," Cane replied. "Now if you don't mind, I need to get my team into the hospital," he looked up at the dark clouds looming overhead, "and out of this storm."

Enbaugh nodded. "Fine by me." He watched the three begin to head for the door. "Mr. Cane, can I have a word with you?"

Cane stopped and turned around. He nodded, then instructed Bishop and Dawn to head inside. Taking a few steps back across the cement, he stopped in front of Enbaugh. "What can I do for you, Detective?"

Enbaugh turned to Montoya. "Will you go make sure they get checked in correctly?"

Montoya nodded.

Enbaugh waited until his partner was well out of earshot to begin. "May I ask what happened at the Grant House?"

Cane thought for a moment. "We encountered some interesting phenomenon."

"Like?"

"Strange magnetic readings, and a hot spot in the middle of the room."

"Was that it?" Enbaugh asked curiously.

"No," Cane said after a moment, "we also found a human heart in the refrigerator."

118

"What?"

"It was embedded in the center of a birthday cake with the words 'you will not escape' scratched into the frosting," Cane reported grimly.

"Did you see any," Enbaugh looked around, then back at Cane, "glowing red eyes?"

Cane shook his head. "No."

"There's definitely something strange going on that house though, right?"

"It's too early to make a judgment call," Cane replied. "We need more investigation time, unfortunately, this storm is really hindering that."

"Are you planning to go back?" Enbaugh asked.

"Yes, first thing in the morning if we can."

"Where are you staying?"

Cane shrugged. "We haven't been to any hotels yet, and we were in such a rush to get here, we didn't have a chance to make reservations."

"There's a nice little place right around the corner from here," Enbaugh said. "While you guys are getting patched up, I'll run over and check you in on the department's tab."

"That's not necessary, Detective," Cane said. "We are able to pay our own way."

"I want to," Enbaugh said. "Look, I was a real ass to you and your group when we first met."

"Yes, you were," Cane agreed.

"I just want to apologize and try to make it up to you."

"Thank you, Detective," Cane replied. "That's most gracious of you." Enbaugh pulled his fedora down over his eyes and began to walk toward his car.

"Detective," Cane called out.

Enbaugh turned around to acknowledge Cane. "May I ask what brought on this change?"

Enbaugh thought for a moment, then looked at Cane thoughtfully. "I saw some really weird shit in that house, and I think you're the only ones who can tell me what it was."

Cane nodded. "We are."

Enbaugh turned and stepped into his car. He pulled the door closed and slid his key into the ignition. Turning it over, he heard the engine cough and sputter to life. Leaning back in the seat, he watched Cane turn and start to walk toward the emergency entrance. Leaning over onto the steering wheel, Enbaugh let out a long breath. He felt as if he had just unzipped his fly for the enemy. He watched the rain pelt the windshield for a moment before kicking on the windshield wipers and pulling away from the hospital. He couldn't help wondering if he had done the right thing.

***

The hospital was a mess. The wind was beating against the outer walls while the rain was quickly beginning to seep through the old roof and pool on the floor. The storm had knocked out power for most of the town, leaving the hospital running on generator power only. Most of the power was being routed to the emergency rooms and the ICU, while some was filtering into the rest of the place. Fluorescent lights in the ceiling flickered on and off, while some remained perpetually glowing an eerie blue light. The staff on hand was busy moving

120

patients from one side of the hospital to the other to take advantage of the power situation.

"You've been in the house, Detective Montoya, did you see anything strange?"

Montoya looked across the waiting room at Dawn, who was sitting with her hands clasped in her lap. "I see you are always the investigator."

Dawn nodded with a smile. "Can't help it."

"You should be resting. You may have a concussion," Montoya said seriously.

Dawn dismissed Montoya's worries with a wave of her hand, "I'm fine." She looked at the empty seat next to her. "I wonder how long Bishop's going to be back there?"

"I talked to one of the nurses when we arrived, and she said they were pretty backed up with the storm and all." Montoya leaned forward and adjusted her leather jacket, "Plus, I think they're a bit short-staffed at the moment. Some of the doctors and nurses couldn't make it in tonight—"

"Because of the road closures," Dawn finished.

Montoya nodded slowly. "This is our second major hurricane this year. We haven't even fully recovered from the last one yet."

"I can't imagine it ever feels like you get a break here in Florida." Montoya nodded, "It seems like just about the time we get cleaned up from the last hurricane season, another one hits us."

Dawn reached up and checked the bandage on her forehead. "You never answered my question, Detective."

"What was that?" Montoya asked coyly. "Did you see anything in the house?"

Montoya's mind instantly flashed back to the

baseball being hurled across the living room by an unseen hand. "I've never seen anything strange."

"What about Detective Enbaugh's claim that he saw a pair of glowing red eyes?"

Montoya shrugged. "I can't speak for the Detective, but I know he has been under a lot of stress lately."

"I don't—"

"I said, he's been under a lot of stress lately." Montoya reiterated.

An uncomfortable silence fell between the two. "Okay," Dawn said after a moment.

"Trick-or-treat!"

Dawn and Montoya both turned to see four small children standing in front of them. They were all dressed in Halloween costumes. One was dressed as a bumblebee with a yellow and black striped sweater, while another was swathed in brown fur looking like a teddy bear. Others were clothed in the blue hospital scrubs of the hospital.

Dawn inspected the group as a frown crossed her face. "I'm sorry, I don't have any candy."

Montoya reached into her jacket pocket and retrieved a handful of gold wrapped candies. "Here you go." She began dropping a few in each of the children's bags.

Dawn looked amazed. "Why are you carrying candy?"

Montoya smiled mischievously as she adjusted her black rimmed glasses. "It's All Hallow's Eve. You've got to have candy for the kids."

A large nurse charged around the corner to find the group of kids. "I told you not to wander off." She began corralling the kids like a cowboy bringing in the herd. She looked up at Dawn and Montoya, both sitting with a look of amusement on their faces. "I'm sorry if they were bothering you."

Montoya shook her head. "It's no problem at all."

"Who are these kids?" Dawn asked.

The nurse adjusted her light blue sweater, "These kids are residents here at the hospital. They're part of the children's ward."

"So these kids are," Dawn paused, "terminal cases?"

The nurse smiled sweetly. "We don't really like to talk about that in front of the children."

Dawn put her hand over her mouth, "Sorry."

"Don't worry about it," the nurse assured. She looked down at her group of trick-or-treaters. "Let's go, kids. I've heard Dr. Banner is passing out caramel apples."

The group cheered together and began to walk away from the waiting room.

"Bye, kids," Montoya called around the corner.

"Happy Halloween," the nurse said as she turned to leave. "Happy Halloween," Dawn repeated cheerfully.

Bishop charged around the corner, almost knocking the nurse to the ground. He wrapped his hands around her shoulders to stabilize her. "I'm sorry, are you all right?"

The nurse nodded. "Try to be more careful, okay?"

Bishop nodded quickly and walked around her. He spotted Dawn and Montoya and rushed toward them. His hand was tightly wrapped in white gauze and fastened with three silver pins. "Dawn,

Detective," he said out of breath.

"What's the matter, Bish?" Dawn asked. "Where's Cane?"

"He went to check us in."

Bishop spun around to see if he could spot Cane anywhere. "We need him right now."

"Why?" Montoya asked.

"There's someone we all need to talk to," Bishop said urgently.

***

Morgan sat up in her bed, although it wasn't right. She wasn't sleeping in her hotel room, but rather the large four-poster bed she had when she was a child. She looked down to see she was garbed in a long white silk and lace robe that seemed to be floating around her. She strained her eyes. The room was filled with light, but it seemed to be emanating from nowhere, yet at the same time, from everywhere. She clearly recognized the mural of a unicorn on her wall and the ever growing mountain of stuffed animals that lived beneath it. She turned and ran her hand along the white wallpaper behind her. She remembered the blue and white floral print. How many times had she stared at the flowers on the wall and let her imagination create new and unique shapes from them? she wondered. She ran her hand over the thick comforter on her bed. The feeling of the stitches and fabric were almost luxurious to her, a reminder of simpler times in her life.

It was home. She could taste the sweet smell of ginger snap cookies baking in the oven downstairs, and the familiar lingering scent of her father's aftershave. Everything was perfect, just as she remembered it, but this wasn't right. They had sold this home when she was fifteen and she hadn't been back since. She shouldn't be here. She should still be asleep in her hotel room in Stone Brook. Was this a dream? She instinctively reached over and took a drink from a tall glass of water sitting next to her bed. She always had one there. Just in case, as she liked to say.

Moving effortlessly through the hallway, she looked down at her feet. She was floating. She knew that wasn't right, but at the same time, she didn't care. It felt wonderful. She glanced into her parent's bedroom to the left. The room was in immaculate condition as always. Her mother, a full-time housewife, prided herself on her home. It was always clean. *Cleanliness is next to Godliness,* her mother often reminded her. Her mother was kind and beautiful as well. Morgan often wished she had been born with blonde hair like her mother, instead of dark like her father. The bouncy curls on her head made her feel at home, no matter where they were.

Once in the kitchen, she moved toward their tall white refrigerator and pulled open the door. A lone piece of apple pie and a glass of milk were sitting on the top shelf. Snatching the two items, she moved to the small wooden table that sat on the edge of the kitchen and sat down.

Where are the cookies?

Looking up, she could see her two brothers building a snowman outside the kitchen door. They couldn't have been more than eight and nine, respectively. They were busily rolling two large snowballs to place on top of the larger one they had already built. She likened the moment to a Normal Rockwell painting; her two brothers swathed in their winter clothes with bright red scarves wrapped around their necks that matched their rosy cheeks. Looking away, she took a bite of the pie with her fork. The pie was like heaven in her mouth. The warm flaky crust, even though it had been sitting in the refrigerator, and the gooey apple filling was everything she remembered. Looking back up at the door, she saw one of her brothers, now fully grown, standing in his green army fatigues with Mother and Father.

"No," Morgan said sternly, "I don't want to see this."

The image vanished and was quickly replaced by her two brothers putting the finishing touches on the snowman. They tapped the top hat firmly on his head and carefully inserted the old cob pipe into his coal mouth. *He's perfect,* Morgan thought as she took another bite of the ginger snap cookie.

"Are you going to sit there and eat cookies all day? We have work to do." Morgan polished off the remainder of the cookie. "Nope, sorry, I'm going to go help my brothers build a snowman," she said with a smile.

Standing up, Morgan rushed past the woman standing in her kitchen and ran toward the door. She paid no attention to who she was, only that the snow was waiting and her brothers would grow up so soon. She didn't want to miss a moment like she had before. She could see her brothers waving at her from the snow.

She stepped out the kitchen door and onto the soft summer grass. She took a deep breath and let the odors take her away. It smelled like fresh cut grass. She felt the individual blades poking up around her bare feet. Lifting up her silk robe, she ran across the lawn, almost giddy with pleasure. Across the street, she could see the Miller's house. Mrs. Miller always had a cookie for her, she wondered if she did now.

"We need to get to work, Morgan. People's lives are at stake."

Morgan looked up from her bed at the woman standing before her. "Who are you?"

"My name is Veranda," the woman replied. She was tall and slender wearing men's period clothing. A pair of baggy black pinstriped slacks hung around her waist, while a matching vest covered the white shirt she was wearing. She had the sleeves rolled up to her elbows and her long black hair was neatly tied behind her head with a red ribbon. Her eyes were haunting. They were sea foam green and seemed to go on forever. She was lovely, and somehow, very familiar.

Morgan wasn't quite sure where she knew this woman from, but she was just as sure she did. "Have we met before, Veranda?"

Veranda shook her head. "No, but we have work to do."

"Why should I listen to you?" Morgan turned and looked at the clock next to her bed. "Oh, God, I'm late for school. If I get a tardy slip one more time, I'll be in detention for a week."

Veranda sat down on the bed next to Morgan. She placed her hand on Morgan's shoulder and

127

softly caressed it. "Don't worry. That clock is completely wrong. What's important now is that we get to work."

"Doing what?" Morgan asked. "Saving lives."

"From what?"

Veranda slowly lifted her hand and pointed toward the open door. There, Morgan could see a dark form hovering silently. Its mass slowly changing into something vaguely human. It blinked its glowing red eyes once and let loose a horrible cackle from deep within the bowels of hell. Morgan recoiled slightly, but she wasn't scared, rather, more curious about the creature standing in her doorway. "What is it? Can I keep it?"

Veranda let out a soft laugh. "No, I'm afraid it's not housebroken." She turned back to Morgan. "This is what we need to save people from. I need your help."

"I don't understand," Morgan admitted.

"I am a seeker, like you," Veranda said from across the room. "A seeker of what?"

"The truth about a great many things," Veranda said with a crooked smile. "Together, we can stop the 'Ritual of Sevens'."

Morgan pounded her fists on her bed childishly. "I don't understand!" Veranda lifted her arms wide. She was now dressed in a flowing red silk robe like Morgan's. Her feet lifted off the floor and she began to slowly spin in place. "Just say that you will help me," her voice echoed as she vanished.

Morgan stood from the kitchen chair and glanced nervously around. Everything had changed. The house was now a broken shell of its former glory. The walls were charred black, all the windows were broken and remnants of furniture and appliances littered the scorched floor. The air had become still and cold, so much so that Morgan could see her breath in front of her. Wrapping her arms around her chest for warmth, she could feel the hard leather of her black jacket. She looked down to see she was now wearing a tattered black shirt, a pair of smooth leather pants and a high heeled pair of boots. Everything was hard and jagged now. Gone were the wonderful scents of her home and gone were her brothers playing in the snow outside. Only darkness remained. Snapping her head to the right, she could see a pair of red eyes slinking toward her from the hallway, and another pair just outside the kitchen window. Fear propelled her away from the burning pairs of eyes, but they drew ever closer. Closing her eyes tightly, she tried to think of a way out. Then it dawned on her. Lifting her face skyward, she shouted to no one and everyone at the same time, "I'll help you!"

Morgan sat straight up in her bed. Looking down, she breathed a long sigh of relief. She was back in her hotel room and safe. She fell back into her pillows and let her eyes close. *That was the strangest dream I've ever had,* she remarked. *Although a ginger snap cookie does sound good....*

Chapter 11

"I don't understand," Bishop admitted while walking into the darkened room, "the nurse told me that she was in here." He took another step into the room and stopped. The curtains on the far side were drawn tightly, and the two beds were completely empty. Both showed signs of recent use, the sheets on the bed nearest the window had been pushed haphazardly to the bottom, and they were completely missing on the second bed. Turning to his left, Bishop caught a glint of light off the saline inside an IV bottle. His eyes slowly followed the tubing down to the floor.

"Who?" Dawn asked quietly.

Ignoring her for the moment, Bishop walked further into the room, then suddenly stopped. He raised a hand to the group behind him to stop them from entering.

Dawn watched as he knelt down quietly near the foot of the bed. She could see he was trained intently on...something. "Bish?" she asked with a little more urgency spiking her tone.

"Hi," Bishop said sweetly. "My name's Nick."

He looked at the frightened girl cowering between the bed and the wooden nightstand. She had completely wrapped herself in the sheets while the IV chord dangled loosely next to her. Her eyes were wide.

"Is your name Kelley?" Bishop asked softly. "The nurse told me that your name is Kelley."

Dawn and Montoya began to enter the room. Kelley snapped her head around when she heard the soles of their shoes clicking against the hard floors of the hospital room. She frantically tried to skitter under the bed.

Bishop spun around and held up both hands this time. "Stop," he said quickly, "you're frightening her." Bishop turned back to the young woman in front of him. "No one's going to hurt you," he assured her. "We're here to help."

"What's going on, Bishop?" Dawn asked in a firmer tone.

Trying to keep one eye on the girl, Bishop slowly turned his head toward Dawn. "This girl's roommate was killed earlier this evening. The EMTs who brought her in told the nurses she kept mumbling something about glowing red eyes." A crooked smile crossed his face, "Sound familiar?"

"She wasn't my roommate," a weak voice corrected him. Bishop returned his attention to Kelley. "I'm sorry?"

"She wasn't my roommate, she was my girlfriend," Kelley reiterated, almost angrily. She began to slowly uncocoon herself from the blankets. She looked down at the trickle of blood that had dried on the top of her left hand. Two pieces of clear tape still clung to where she had ripped out the needle.

"We need you to help us, Kelley." Bishop lowered himself to the cold floor into a sitting position. "Can you tell us what happened?"

Dawn and Montoya, sensing Kelley's ease, slowly moved into the room. They stood silently behind Bishop looking down at the girl.

Kelley moved a shaky hand to her head and swiped aside her blonde bangs. Bishop could see two long scratches amidst a sea of bruises just

131

below her hairline. There were at least six or seven stitches in each cut. "We were attacked."

"By what?" Bishop was pushing. He knew that, but this woman might have the closest thing to an answer he'd gotten since he arrived.

Kelley began to tremble as she relived those horrible final minutes of Joanne's life in her mind. "Those eyes," she said as she began to weep softly, "all we could see were those eyes."

"What about the eyes?" Bishop wondered.

Kelley looked up at Bishop with a tear running down her cheek. She was biting her lower lip. "They're evil," she whispered with a hoarse voice. "Glowing, evil, red eyes." She let her gaze wander down to the floor.

"I don't understand," said Dawn for the first time.

Kelley looked up at Dawn while trying to fight back the tears. "They played with us," she said after a moment. "Have you ever seen a cat play with a wounded mouse? The mouse has no chance of escape. It knows it's going to die, but it can't get away. The cat is too powerful. Then the cat proceeds to play with it, batting it back and forth, biting it, then finally, after it gets bored with that game, it kills the mouse." Kelley could no longer contain the pain. She began to cry. "That's what we were. We were two wounded mice." Leaning over, she wrapped her hands around her sides. Her head felt like it was going to explode from her headache and the stitches in her forehead. She slipped her hands up to her temples and pressed firmly to try and stop the pain. "It played with us before it killed Joanne!"

132

Bishop lifted himself off the floor and moved toward Kelley. He opened his arms and she slid in next to him, burying her head in his chest. Bishop laid his hands softly on her back trying to comfort her, but he knew there was none to be had.

"Everything's going to be all right." He knew the words were hollow, but they were all he could think to say. She had watched a loved one die and could do nothing to help. He understood the feelings of helplessness she must be feeling. It must be excruciating.

He placed his hand on the back of her head, being careful not to hurt her. The soft blue fabric of her hospital gown was open in the rear, revealing her naked back. Bishop could see several long white patches of gauze held securely by strips of medical tape. He instantly winced at the sight. This girl had been to hell and back, and she had paid dearly on the return trip.

He slowly lifted her up from his chest and looked her in the eye. "Kelley, can you tell me what did this to you?"

Kelley sucked in a tear as she tried to clear her congested sinuses. Wiping the tears from her eyes and cheeks, she started to compose herself. "I don't know what they were."

"They?" Bishop repeated. "You mean there was more than one that attacked you?"

"Two," she answered between gasps.

Bishop processed the information for a second. "What did they look like?"

"They didn't look like anything, just…" Kelley searched for a word that would best describe what she saw, "shadows."

Bishop pressed her head back to his chest. He looked up at Dawn and Montoya, "Will you go retrieve the nurse?" The two women nodded.

"Kelley," Bishop said as he helped her off the ground, "I'm not going to let anything happen to you." He set her weak body on the edge of the bed. He lifted her legs and slid them up and carefully laid her head back. Grabbing the covers, he draped them over her, then slowly sat down on the edge of the bed. "We're going to find out what happened, and stop this."

"Who are you?" she wondered.

"I'm with the Office of Paranormal Investigation. We research phenomenon like this."

"You can't stop them," Kelley said grimly.

Bishop lifted himself off the bed and started to walk toward the door. "Get some rest," he said, leaning his hand against the doorframe, "the nurse will be in to check on you in a minute."

"Where are you going?"

"I need to talk to my colleagues, then I'll come back to check on you."

A slight smile crossed Kelley's face. She didn't know why, but she trusted this man. He had a good aura, she guessed. "Thank you, Nick."

Bishop nodded. "Anytime."

***

Cane paced the waiting room in front of the team. He slowly brought his hands around behind his back and clasped them together. His leather jacket was producing a satisfying swish with every step he took. Stopping, he turned to look at Bishop.

"That's incredible."

"I realize that, Cane," Bishop said, referring to the story he had just told him. "I don't think Kelley is making it up either."

Cane lifted a hand and rubbed the edge of his graying goatee. "Didn't you say the night nurse told you this woman was in shock when she was brought in?"

Bishop leaned forward in the curved green plastic chair and rested his elbows on his knees. He laced his fingers together. "Yes, but—"

"Don't you think that could account for her story?" Cane interjected. "Maybe," Bishop said with a sigh. He knew there were more plausible answers than killer shadows. Shock was one of them. "That doesn't explain the Enbaugh connection," he said after a moment. "The descriptions of what they saw are almost identical, Cane. You can't discount that."

Cane turned to Montoya. "How many people did the Detective tell his story to?"

"Just the captain and I," Montoya answered confidently. "No media?" Cane wondered.

Montoya shook her head. "That's not his style."

Cane leaned over and slid into a chair opposite Bishop. "That does lend some credibility to her story."

"In what way?" Montoya asked.

"If Detective Enbaugh didn't tell the media," Dawn started, "then his story wouldn't corrupt the public."

"Like what's been done with UFOs and alien abductions," Cane continued. "They've received so much media attention, anyone could tell you what

135

an alien looks like, or describe what the standard abduction scenario consists of."

"You don't think these are aliens, do you?" Montoya asked in shock. Cane shook his head with a smug smile on his face. "Don't be ridiculous.

That foolishness was concocted by some bored science fiction writer." Cane ran his hand through his hair. "We obviously need to take a look at this woman's apartment. Perhaps this phenomenon isn't just localized to the Grant House."

Bishop nodded. "I'll see if I can get her address from her charts."

"Good," Cane replied after a moment. "In the meantime, I suggest we all get some rest. They've set up a shelter downstairs."

"What about Detective Enbaugh?" Dawn asked, standing up. "Didn't you say he went to get us hotel rooms?"

"We can't wait for the Detective," Cane said quickly. "If he comes through, all the better for us. In the meantime, we all need to get some rest."

Montoya checked her watch. "Where is Enbaugh?"

***

Enbaugh rubbed his hand across the windshield of his car. It was bad enough that the wipers couldn't wipe away enough rain, now the inside was beginning to fog up. His meaty paw cut a great slash through the fog allowing him to see again. Reaching over to his left, he pressed his finger against the power window toggle. The window's motor groaned as it opened slightly. The wind whistled through the crack while the rain slipped inside.

Enbaugh leaned to his right in the seat to stop the rain from hitting him in the face. Through the windshield, Enbaugh could vaguely make out the red blinking of a traffic light. Slowing down, he brought his car to a stop near where he thought the intersection was.

The winds were incredible. His car began to rock back and forth from the force. Enbaugh knew they were threatening to tip it over. Peering out his window, he searched for familiar landmarks. The winds had already wreaked their havoc through town, and Enbaugh knew the worst was yet to come. The devastation so far was incredible. Trees had been completely uprooted and sent sailing into the fronts of stores. Windows were broken, while doors had been completely ripped off their hinges. Street signs were flailing wildly on their posts, as if they were made of rubber. A thick power pole ahead had been knocked over pulling the lines down with it. Showers of sparks jumped intermittently from the transformer onto the street.

Enbaugh began to worry about the fire hazard. Reaching to his right, he grabbed his radio and lifted it to his mouth. "Dispatch, this is Adam five-two."

The radio crackled with static for a moment. "Go ahead, fifty-two," a female voice instructed him.

"Dispatch, we have a downed power pole on the corner of Westchester and Spruce."

"We're contacting the power company right now, fifty-two," dispatch replied after a moment.

"Thanks, dispatch."

"Take care of yourself out there, fifty-two."

Enbaugh smiled. "Will do." He tossed the small black radio into the passenger seat.

Leaning forward onto the steering wheel, he tried to look both ways into the intersection. He couldn't see any traffic in either direction, so he cautiously pressed his foot on the accelerator. Glancing to his right, he saw a small coffee shop that still had partial power and so far, the front windows were intact. He instantly recognized it. Montoya and he often stopped there for a tall latte before starting a long shift. He now knew he was only two blocks from the Brenton Hotel in downtown Stone Brook.

Enbaugh returned his attention to the road in front of him. He became mesmerized by the rhythmic beating of the windshield wipers as they tried vainly to push the water from his window. The rain was at an almost torrential downfall right now. He was just glad it stopped hailing.

Looking down, he checked the clock on his radio. It was almost one-thirty in the morning, and he was exhausted. Sleep had been a luxury he hadn't afforded himself the past two days. Maybe he should stop, he thought. Try and wait out the storm. *No,* he told himself, *might as well press on. I'm almost there.* He saw a bolt of lightning shred the murky sky in front of him, followed closely by the clap of thunder.

"That was close," he said aloud.

The sky lit up again, but this time, he couldn't see the bolt. He hoped it was too far away to see; otherwise, it was right over him. He felt the hairs on the back of his neck and arms began to stand up.

138

"Shit."

He watched as a magnificent stream of bluish-white light broke through the clouds right in front of him. It attacked a tall palm tree just in front of his car. The lightning split the tree down the center, then arced up into a nearby lamppost. The bulb inside began to glow eerily from the electric discharge. The pole sparked once, then exploded, sending sparks raining down into the street. Enbaugh stood on the breaks trying to stop the car, but the wet roads were working against him. His vehicle began to hydroplane toward the crumbling light. The first bits of the post impacted his hood and shattered his windshield. Shards of glass shot inwards with the destructive capability of a bullet. His wheels completely lost their grip on the road and the car began to spin wildly toward the sidewalk. A third piece of the pole smashed into the roof of Enbaugh's car, denting it in.

Grabbing the wheel with both hands, Enbaugh tried to regain control of the car. He spun the wheel frantically against the spin, but it was no use. He had no traction. He felt the vehicle jump the curb. The jolt knocked him out of his seat, slamming his head against the now concave roof. Enbaugh's eyes rolled back into his head as he fell back into the seat unconscious.

The car rocketed into the brick side of the nearest building. It impacted with a sickening crunch of steel. The wall began to give way to the steel torpedo sending bricks showering down around it. The cruiser's momentum finally stopped as it came to a rest, partially embedded in the wall. The one remaining headlight shone intently in the interior of the shop and the mess that had been created.

Enbaugh flopped back into the seat, his body limp and wounded. A trickle of dark red blood ran down from his scalp onto his forehead and finally dripped off his chin. His right hand twitched, but suddenly stopped.

To his left, a pair of dark forms emerged from a shop across the street. They moved slowly, but deliberately, across the wet street toward the scene of the accident. Maybe they were attracted by the loud noise, or the carnage caused, but they were there. The two forms easily manipulated their shapes so they were each walking on two feet. Their footfalls made no sound, as if they weren't even touching the ground, rather floating just above it. They appeared to be wearing a large black cape that billowed in the wind. The two forms stopped in front of the car, their horrible red eyes appearing for the first time.

Enbaugh sucked in a deep breath as he slowly opened his eyes. Reaching up, he pressed the tender spot on his head, then quickly pulled his fingers away. He was bleeding badly. He needed immediate medical attention. Looking to his right, he searched for his small black radio, but then stopped. An odd sensation passed over him. At first, he thought there had been another lightning strike, but then he recognized the feeling. Spinning around in his seat, he came face to face with the two phantoms staring in his window. Enbaugh's eyes suddenly widened in horror.

"You will not escape," they assured him in unison.

Chapter 12

Rest wasn't coming readily to Bishop. Lying with his eyes closed, he laced his fingers behind his head. His mind was swimming with images from the past few days. His induction into the OPR had been brief and his first assignment had come even quicker. Was he ready? He wasn't sure. He was trying to rely on his academy training, but this was a completely different situation. He wondered if FBI agents, besides the ones you see on TV, ever chased after ghosts and what the protocol would be. A smile crossed his face for a moment, but then quickly vanished. He started to think about Kelley. For her, there would be no retribution. There was no human killer to find, no one to prosecute. There was no one to punish for this atrocious crime. How could he help her as he had so boldly promised?

Rolling over, he pounded his fist into the small pillow to try and fluff it up. The basement of the hospital could be best summed up in one word: dank. A dingy, light green tile had replaced the brightly lit walls and floors of the upper levels. Small wooden cots filled the area of what used to be, until tonight, a storage room. Large cardboard boxes and plastic containers were still stacked high in the far corner. Two lights hung in the middle of the bare ceiling, one working while the other blinked on and off as it buzzed like a hive of angry bees.

Each refugee from the storm had been given two tan linen blankets with the hospital's logo emblazoned on them and one small pillow. As Bishop adjusted on the cot, his feet broke through the bottom of the blanket. They were either too short, or he had been short-sheeted. *Not very damned funny either way,* he thought. Sitting up, Bishop let his bare feet fall to the cold tile floor. The sensation was quick like a bite as the cold surged over the bottom of his feet. He ripped them off the floor and stuffed them back beneath the blankets.

Bishop leaned over and scooped a small black flashlight off the floor. He had placed it there before going to bed. The storm was raging outside and he was sure the power would be knocked out before morning. Running his hand over the cool metallic shell, he pressed his thumb against the activation switch. A bright beam of light erupted from the bulb. Bishop quickly pressed his hand over the light and thumbed the switch again. He didn't realize it would be that bright and he didn't want to wake anyone up. He suddenly felt like a child hiding his flashlight from his parents so he could read at night.

Reaching over the side of the cot, he lifted his pair of white socks off his duffel bag and began to slip them on. Standing up, he began to make his way through the maze of beds toward the hallway, but stopped. He looked down at his attire. Wearing only a pair of blue boxers and a tight fitting white tank top, he decided he didn't want to go traipsing around the hospital in his underwear, so he walked back to his cot and pulled on a pair of jeans. Sitting back down on the edge of the cot, he slipped on his shoes.

Now fully dressed, Bishop slid the flashlight into his back pocket and walked toward the door. He stopped and looked back for a moment. There were nearly one hundred people camped out in this small room. He wondered how many more were stuck out in the storm. His heart was too big, he decided after a moment. He couldn't help everyone, no matter how much he wanted to.

Stepping into the hallway, he was met by the harsh white glare of fluorescent lights. He squinted his eyes as they struggled to become accustomed. He ran his hand through his short, messy hair. There wasn't much he could do about that now. The hallway was short, but wide. The green tile of the storeroom only worked its way halfway up the wall in here, replaced with white paint that had dulled to an awful tan. There were several large brown spots on the walls and ceiling, most of them caused by water damage. He wondered how people could stand to live in Florida. It was a Mecca for sun worshipers, but the devastation wreaked each year by tropical storms and hurricanes would be too much for him. It was a constant cycle of destruction and recovery. Just about the time you had your house of cards built up again, the wind would come and knock them over.

He glanced down at the silver watch on his wrist. It was almost two-thirty in the morning. He wasn't at all tired. *Damned insomnia,* Bishop cursed.

A noise startled him.

Spinning around, he scanned the hallway. It was completely empty, except for the occasional box or scrap of trash. Unconsciously, he tightened his grip on the small metal flashlight and clenched his teeth so hard, the small muscles in his jaw began to strain.

143

Silence.

He slowly began to relax his body. This was an old hospital. Occasionally, things creaked and moaned as the building settled. He knew he was acting irrationally but after what he had seen today, nothing seemed out of the realm of possibility. He slowly turned back and continued his journey down the hall. A few feet in front of him, it turned ninety degrees to the right. He felt like a mouse in a maze, searching for that tantalizing piece of cheese at the end, and hopefully, freedom.

Taking the turn, Bishop stopped dead in his tracks. Three feet inside, the hallway became dark. The lights had been knocked out by the storm. Two small rectangular windows near the top of the wall to his left were broken, allowing the wind and rain to whip inside. The tile floor was sopping wet. Looking through the darkness, he could see the opposite end of the hallway was still lit.

"The rain must've shorted out the lights," he said out loud reflexively. His mind was trying to push the fear away the only way he knew how. From his training at Quantico, he knew talking was a defense mechanism. "That's all, it's just a short."

He clicked the button on the flashlight and brought it up to his side. The white laser of light sliced through the darkness proving nothing was there. It was comforting to hold the light, perhaps as reassuring as a baby with its pacifier. Why was he so afraid? Swallowing hard, he took a step into the darkness, then another, followed by a third. His pace increased with each step while his focus remained on the light. There was nothing else to him at that moment except the light, and the feeling that....

He shook his head. He knew he was letting his fear get the best of him. He charged forward.

A loud cackle penetrated the darkness and echoed off the walls.

Bishop skidded to a stop dead in his tracks, almost slipping on the wet floor. His muscles suddenly became rigid and his senses went on full alert. As if fighting against his own body, he forced himself to turn around and look back. Bishop shined the flashlight down the tunnel as an acidy feeling erupted in his stomach. His light slowly moved from one side of the hall to the other. As he neared the right side, his beam disappeared, almost like it had been swallowed by the very darkness itself. He moved the flashlight past the dark spot and the beam reappeared. There was a black hole in the hallway.

He moved his light back to the hole. There was no reflection, and nothing to stop the beam of light. It was just blackness, almost the color and texture of black felt. A knot welled up in his throat and he found his breathing had become very shallow. He was in danger of hyperventilating. Looking down at the mass, he saw it was hovering above the floor. It was completely free-floating in space. He took a step forward, then stopped. *What the hell am I doing?* He assured himself this probably wasn't the best time to explore.

Slowly at first, he began to move away from the black hole. He couldn't even feel his feet. He just hoped they were doing what he told them to. He started to turn around—

The hole moved

—He stopped. Had he really seen that, or was his mind playing tricks on him? He almost wanted to laugh out loud at the absurd thought. It wasn't his mind playing tricks on him. A huge gust of wind tore into the hallway through the broken windows. It was powerful enough to push Bishop back a step. As he quickly regained his balance, he stared back into the darkened hallway. The hole was gone.

"What the—"

He was stopped in midsentence by a rustling noise behind him. It sounded like curtains flapping in the wind. Spinning around on the balls of his feet, he saw the hole floating in front of him. His reflexes threw him out of the way just as a clawed hand shot out of the form and tore across his chest. Bishop stumbled to the ground, but was quickly up again. He glanced momentarily down at his chest.

His white shirt had a long gash in it and three small scratches ran through the middle of it. They were quickly beginning to welt and bleed. Looking back up at the hole, Bishop was astonished to see it had taken human form and was almost an entire foot taller than him.

Bishop looked up and down the lanky phantom in front of him. It's arms and legs were long and slender, the hands ending in five sharp barbs at the end that almost resembled a hand. The creature's waist was no larger than Bishop's leg, and the entire thing appeared to be two-dimensional. It didn't look like it had any width at all.

The long slender head twisted back and forth as if it were a piece of paper blowing in the wind. When it finally came to rest, Bishop saw two red slits glowing in the darkness.

"Red eyes," Bishop uttered in horror.

The shadow swung its spindly arm toward Bishop with its talons extended. Dropping to the ground, Bishop narrowly avoided the hand. The being's power was very evident as the hand tore into the tiles on the wall, shattering them. Bishop stumbled off the floor and began to charge down the hallway. Glancing over his shoulder, he could see the shadow right behind him. It was gaining.

***

Morgan suddenly awoke from a dead sleep, her body lurching up into a sitting position. Her mind, still groggy with sleep, began to panic. She scanned her hotel room while she held her breath. Reaching up, she wiped the sweat off her forehead with the back of her hand. Slowly, her mind began to relax when she saw the empty room around her, but there was still something that wasn't right. An alarm was buzzing in the back of her brain, the same alarm that had sounded at the airport.

She reached over to her nightstand and clicked on the wooden lamp. A soft white light immediately filled the room. Pushing her legs over the edge of the bed, she cautiously stood up. Reaching down, she adjusted her short black nighty that barely hung over her hips. Her mind was still racing to understand what was happening. She walked quickly into the bathroom and splashed a handful of cool water on her face. Grabbing a towel from her right, she pressed it to her face and reveled for a moment in the softness of it. Dropping the towel on the counter, she instinctively reached for the crystal around her neck, then suddenly remembered she had lost it. She quickly cursed under her breath. It would take months to adjust another crystal to her body.

Turning, she walked out of the bathroom. Taking a right, she stopped in front of a large wooden chair and sank down into it. Morgan pressed her fingertips to her temples, aching for a moment of clarity. Leaning over, she rested her elbows on her knees as she continued to rub her head. The buzzing was still there.

***

Bishop arched his back to avoid a swing by the phantom. The creature's claws just missed his face, but reacted quickly. It swung again, this time, connecting. The long barbs on his hand ripped into Bishop's shirt, then into his chest. They cut like razors, slicing instead of tearing. Bishop stumbled back. He lifted his flashlight and swung hard toward the shadow. The light was met with no resistance as it went through the shadow. Bishop fell forward, but caught himself before he stumbled into the creature.

The shadow reacted quickly, wrapping its arms around Bishop. A terrible smile crossed its dark face, slowly exposing a toothy grin. Its large red eyes narrowed as it stared directly at Bishop. "You will not escape." Quickly, the being's arms began to grow around Bishop's body. It was engulfing him.

Bishop struggled against the folds of darkness surrounding him, but they were like coils of metal embracing him. The darkness was constricting his breathing as they tightened around his chest. His mind raced for a solution. He felt the metal of the flashlight in his right hand. Taking a chance, he lifted it up and pointed it toward the phantom. He clicked the button once, sending the bright beam of light directly into the creature's horrible red eyes.

The phantom suddenly recoiled as if it had been stung, the coils ripping away from Bishop in one fluid motion. A high-pitched scream erupted from the shadow's head.

Bishop glanced down at the flashlight. He had hurt it, but how? Looking up at the shadow, he decided this wasn't the time to determine that. Bishop turned on the balls of his feet and charged down the hallway. He pumped his legs hard until it felt like battery acid was coursing through his veins. The end of the hallway was less than three meters away now. The darkness was already beginning to transition into light. Bursting through the double doors, Bishop skidded to a stop. Turning around, he glanced back down the hall into the darkness. There was no sign of the phantom, but that didn't mean he was safe. Turning back, he ran the rest of the way. He didn't care where he was going; he just needed to be around other people.

***

Morgan leaned back in the plush wooden chair. The buzzing had finally stopped. Taking a deep breath of satisfaction, she stood and walked toward the small black mini-bar built into the cabinets adjacent to the large entertainment center. She pulled open the small door and looked across its contents. After a moment of deliberation, she settled on a small, clear bottle of vodka. Morgan stood and closed the bar with her foot. Turning around, she rested against the edge of the counter. She stared at the bottle in her hand, then unscrewed the top. Lifting it to her lips, she swallowed the harsh contents in one gulp.

She reached behind her and set the bottle with several of its cousins on the counter. She made a quick count. There were at least nine of the small, empty bottles standing quietly before her. It wasn't like her to drink this much. In fact, it wasn't like her to drink at all. She felt the warmth of the liquor sitting in her stomach. It was nice, but uncomfortable at the same time. Grabbing the bottles in her hands, she slid them off the counter and into the trash. The bottles made a satisfying clink as they hit the bottom. Looking up, she ran her hand through her long, dark hair sliding it over to the side and exposing her lovely neck. The alcohol was beginning to work its way through her blood stream. She was starting to feel wonderful.

Quickly turning away, she walked slowly across the carpeted floor toward the bed. Reaching down, she grabbed the bottom of her nighty and pulled it slowly over her head, revealing her supple naked body. Sliding back into bed, she cuddled up to the warm male body there. She began to kiss along the base of his neck as she ran her erect nipples along his back. The man slowly awoke from his slumber and rolled over. Morgan kissed him passionately on the lips.

Reaching his hand around her head, Sam kissed her back.

Chapter 13

Enbaugh finally came to. There was an odd tingling at the base of his spine, but it wasn't completely uncomfortable. A dull thud began to throb in the back of his head, obviously a repercussion of the accident.

His eyes shot open wide. He was in a car accident. He remembered that now. His mind went on full alert. *Where am I?* He began to look around. He was still strapped into his car. The frame was contorted and bent around him unnaturally. His legs and arms were pinned behind the dash, which had been shoved forward into his chest. Enbaugh tried to take a deep breath. To his horror, he couldn't. Leaning his head back, he looked up at a long gash in the roof. It had been partially torn back when it had crashed into the building.

Enbaugh wondered how long he had been out. He looked vainly over at the small digital clock mounted in his dashboard. The crash had all but annihilated the liquid crystal display. A large crack cut across its face allowing the black liquid to pool near the bottom. He shook his head to try and clear some of the cobwebs. He felt his metal watchband still wrapped around his wrist. If he could only pull his arm free, he could check the time, and call dispatch for help. That was assuming his radio survived the crash. Pulling hard on his left arm, he felt it budge but it was pinned tightly in a fold of the car door. He tugged again.

He realized it wasn't his arm that was pinned, rather his watch. "Figures," he said after a moment.

Pulling hard, he ripped his hand free of the

door. He felt his watch fall free of his arm. Enbaugh let out a long sigh as he looked at his bare wrist. Scanning the cab, he spotted his radio perched dangerously on the edge of the passenger seat. Any sudden movement would send it plummeting to the floor and well out of his reach. Moving his hand across his body, his fingertips brushed against the hard plastic shell of the radio. He tried to twist his body ever so slightly to increase his reach, but he was pinned firmly against the steering wheel. Enbaugh strained as hard as he could, but the radio was just beyond his grasp.

He leaned back in his seat in frustration as a trickle of fresh blood worked its way down his forehead through the maze of its crusty brethren. Or was it? Enbaugh felt another drop. Looking up through the gash, he felt a third drop hit his face. It was raining. Not as hard as it had been, but it was still raining. Enbaugh marveled at the dark clouds overhead. It was calm. There were no winds, only the light drizzle remained.

The town had passed into the eye of the hurricane. Enbaugh had always felt this was nature's way of teasing, because he knew it was fleeting. The winds would soon return when the opposite side of the storm hit the town. They were only being allowed a breather. It wasn't fair.

His mind suddenly recalled something it had seen last night before he had lost consciousness. He could see the eyes, the horrible red, glowing eyes. They had been right on top of him. If they had been human, he would've felt their breath on his face. Why was he still alive? He wondered about that one for some time. Whatever the reason was, he wasn't too keen on staying here to find out.

He began to push against the steering wheel with his chest. If he could push hard enough, maybe he could break the seat and slide out. He pushed harder, but it wasn't working. Even with his free hand, he couldn't generate enough force to accomplish his goal. He was stuck there until someone passed by. He knew the police and hospitals would be sending out rescue crews to try and locate trapped victims. This may be the only chance they had before the eye passed.

***

"It did what?" Cane asked.

"It ran away," Bishop said calmly.

"Because you shone your light in its eyes?" Cane asked again. Bishop nodded.

"Extraordinary," Cane said after a moment.

Cane was standing over an operating table in one of the first floor emergency rooms. Bishop was sitting quietly in the center with his feet dangling over the side. A dark blue had replaced the green tile of the basement, while the upper wall color remained the same. A lone nurse was putting the finishing touches on Bishop's chest. She had given him four stitches for the cut and was just now applying the bandages. She worked quickly as she ran the gauze around his bare chest.

"This is the second time I've had to patch you up, Mr. Bishop," the nurse announced as she pressed the final strip of adhesive into place. "Don't make me do it again."

Bishop smiled. "Yes, ma'am."

Cane waited until the nurse left to continue his line of questioning. He stood in front of Bishop, uneasily shifting his weight back and forth. "The only other case of extreme light sensitivity I can think of are vampires," Cane said rubbing his beard, "but even they aren't harmed by the beam generated from a flashlight."

"Maybe it's just light sensitive in general," Bishop theorized. "Maybe these things just can't be in light period."

"Yes," Cane said, "but does it hurt them to be in light, or just bother them?"

"I'm not following," Bishop interrupted with an "I'm sorry, I'm just a rookie" look on his face.

"Take vampires, for example. When they are exposed to direct sunlight, they burn and die. It can be used as a weapon against them," Cane essayed. "What we're trying to determine is if the light harms the creatures."

"Here's the odd part," Bishop started. He slipped off the exam table and slipped his torn shirt back on. "When I first saw the creature, I shined my light directly on it, and it didn't move. It didn't even twitch."

"Odd," Cane agreed.

"It has to be something about the eyes," Bishop said after a moment. "When the light hit its eyes, it screamed and bolted."

"Very good. We've got a working theory." Cane started to pace back and forth in front of the group. "Now what do we do with it?"

"We've got to stop these things," Bishop answered quickly. "They can't be allowed to go on killing."

"Yes, but how do we know where they are? We have several reports and all of them are from different points in the city," Cane pointed out.

"I think this all goes back to the Grant House," Bishop theorized. "Why?"

Bishop smiled. "Just playing a hunch."

The nurse popped her head back into the room. "We need you to clear out of here. We have a patient coming in."

"Another attack?" Cane probed.

"Sorry," the nurse said seriously, "this one's just a plain old car crash." The two quickly moved out of the room to the hallway where Dawn and Montoya joined them. They watched as an ambulance screeched to a stop in front of the open emergency doors and the back end was thrown open. Two men emerged quickly and began to pull out the gurney.

Montoya gasped when she saw the familiar form lying on top of it. "Jack." She rushed toward the men and began to accompany the gurney toward the ER. She reached down and grabbed his hand. "Jack, are you okay?"

Enbaugh looked up at her with bleary eyes. "I think so."

Montoya looked across at one of the EMTs, "What's his condition?"

The man looked up at Montoya. "He may have severe internal damage. We won't know for sure until we get him into the OR." The man spoke very seriously.

Montoya let out a gasp.

The gurney reached the doors to the ER and pushed through them. The same nurse that had asked them to leave was waiting for Montoya. "I'm sorry," she said, placing her hands on Montoya's shoulders, "you can't go in there."

"The hell I can't! That's my partner!"

"Detective, you need to let the doctors do their job," the nurse argued as she forcefully tried to restrain Montoya.

Montoya looked down at the smaller woman in front of her and wondered how she was stopping her. She let out a long sigh and stopped. "You're right." She placed a hand on the nurse's shoulder. "Please take care of him."

The nurse smiled sweetly. "We will," she said softly.

Bishop, Dawn, and Cane stood at the rear of the hall watching the events unfold. They were shocked, but they couldn't find the words to express it. Dawn took a step toward Montoya. She felt she had gotten to know her better than her two partners.

"He's going to be okay," Dawn reassured her.

Montoya looked over at Dawn. Her face was a mixture of horror and pain. "I think I need to be alone right now."

Dawn nodded once and patted Montoya softly on the back. She slowly turned around and walked back to the group.

"What now?" Bishop asked.

"We can't let this stop us," Cane said after a moment. "We have to find a way to stop these things."

Dawn nodded. "I have the sinking feeling they were involved with Detective Enbaugh somehow."

"Why is that?" Cane wondered.

"I don't know." Dawn shook her head, "I just

156

do."

Chapter 14

Chloe slowly lifted her head off the pillow as the alarm squawked next to her. Reaching over, she tapped the snooze button once. *The clock must be wrong,* she thought. *It's way too early to be five-thirty.* She lifted her gold wristwatch off the nightstand and stared intently at the dial. The numbers seemed to be written in gibberish for a moment, but then she felt her brain kick in. It was indeed five-thirty in the morning. She moaned and let her head fall back on the pillow. She needed coffee, or rather, she craved the caffeine, but she would happily settle for a few extra hours sleep. She was still suffering from jet lag and the time differential. It was only one-thirty in the morning back in California.

"Damned time zones," she cursed under her breath.

She slowly began to pull herself out of bed. Spreading her arms wide, she let out a gaping yawn. She had never been a morning person, and wasn't sure how she had survived this long. She had spent all night watching television in her room critiquing the local news coverage of the hurricane. After all, you never truly get away from work. They had done a fair job, in her opinion, but many of the cuts had been sloppy and a few of the reporters seemed downright ill prepared for the situation they had been thrust into.

She smiled for a moment. She had struggled with the decision to leave her position with her local news crew but now, in retrospect, almost six years later, things had worked out much better than she had hoped. She was the director for the Channel 2 evening news back in Pittsburgh. It was a great gig. While she was there, they were the most watched evening news in Pennsylvania. She had accepted an offer from the Ghost Chasers people after they saw a report she directed on a local UFO sighting. It had been a step down in position, but she would be based out of Hollywood. How could any director refuse that?

Of course, she had only planned to stay with Ghost Chasers until she could break into her true love of film. She wanted to be the youngest female to ever direct a big budget blockbuster for a major studio. She knew her rise to the top would be meteoric and she would become the toast of Tinsel Town. That had never happened. *At least, not yet,* she kept reminding herself. There was always hope. *Optimism,* she said to herself, *optimism.*

Standing up, Chloe walked casually toward the coffee pot sitting on the bar. She snatched a pack of complimentary coffee grounds from the counter and ripped open the pack. Flipping open the top of the brewer, she was pleasantly surprised to see a new filter already positioned for use. She tilted the paper package over and dumped its entire contents in. The shoot didn't start until nine, she had time to sit and drink a pot of coffee. Lifting the glass pot out of its base, she held it under the sink. She let her mind wander as it slowly filled with the crystal clear liquid.

Why is it Rivers always makes an ass of himself? She knew the answer as soon as she asked the question. He was a glory hound in every sense of the word. He needed the attention, good or bad,

159

to feel alive. She knew he would be a troublemaker from the first day she met him. He had been hired to replace the original host of the show who had left to pursue his—quote—"budding theater career". Everyone had tried to make him stay, but he wouldn't listen. He moved to New York City where he wrote, produced, directed and starred in his one-man show about his life. He was sure he would be the next sensation on Broadway. So sure, in fact, he spent hundreds of thousands of dollars producing and promoting the show. It was one of life's most unfair strokes. The show opened to abysmal reviews and closed two days later. After that, he found himself broke and alone. No director of producer in Hollywood would touch him with a ten foot pole. Life was harsh that way.

Chloe had been with Ghost Chasers for almost two years before Rivers was hired. She hated him. He was arrogant and egotistical from the beginning. He came in with an "I'm too good for this show" attitude that had really rubbed the cast and crew the wrong way. It seemed he and Chloe were always at each other's throats. Chloe had even found out later the crew was taking bets on which one would kill the other first. None of that stopped them from becoming sexually involved, though. The crew began referring to them as the "Sam and Dianne" of Ghost Chasers. That description wasn't too far off in reality. They loved to hate each other, but at the same time, they couldn't resist each other. At times during the relationship, she'd wished she could run off to the bar where everyone knew your name, or at the very least, just run away.

It was she who had ended the relationship. It

was close to five years now. She had discovered, to her dismay, Rivers was mounting one of the new interns. She was a happy, bouncy woman named Jennifer, who was intent on sleeping her way to the top. Unfortunately for her, she never realized Rivers was a dead end. Chloe had confronted him about it on the set one day in the middle of the shoot. Several of the grips had to forcefully restrain her. She didn't know why she was so angry. They had nothing together, but he was all she had. Chloe had been so focused on her career, she hadn't made many friends, let alone allowed any time to date. In hindsight, she realized she was just lonely, and a long way from home.

She watched the "on" light kick off on the coffee pot. The water and grounds had coagulated into a thick black liquid. Leaning close to the pot, she took a whiff of the contents. She loved that smell. Looking over the counter, she spotted a small white mug sitting next to the squat black microwave. She lifted the cup into one hand and the pot into the other. Pouring slowly, she watched the coffee fill the cup. This was the ambrosia of the gods, she told herself, cradling the mug in her small hands. She began to lift the cup to her mouth when the phone rang. Staring crossly at the tan device, she set down the mug and crossed the room.

Before the phone had a chance to ring a third time, she lifted it to her ear. "Hello?"

"Chloe," Carrie's voice was full of excitement on the end of the line. "What's up, Carrie?" Chloe said after a moment. It was never a good sign when your producer called you at five-forty in the morning. "Have you looked outside yet?"

161

"No I haven't. I just woke up a few minutes ago," Chloe admitted. "There's been a break in the storm," Carrie said fervently. "According to the local weatherman, Hurricane Katrina has moved off in a different direction."

"Really?" Chloe said, sharing Carrie's enthusiasm. "That's fantastic!"

"I'm going to call the others right now. I think we should meet at the Grant House in about an hour. That way, we can get a full day's shooting in before we go live tonight."

Chloe felt a little dismayed at Carrie's suggestion, but she knew she was right. "That's the plan." Chloe looked at her clock, "Let's all meet down in the lobby in say, forty-five minutes."

"We'll be there."

Chloe hung up the phone and looked across the room at her still steaming cup of coffee. She sighed. There was no time for that now. She had to get ready. Abandoning the cup, she grabbed her travel kit and walked into the bathroom.

***

Morgan reached over and snatched the phone from its base. She hauled it under the covers and to her ear. "Yeah?"

"Morgan?" The voice on the other end of the line sounded surprised. "This is Morgan," she said, still partially asleep.

"Morgan, this is Carrie, the producer."

Morgan's eyes widened. Her mind had suddenly become awake at the word "producer". "Yes, Carrie, what can I do for you?" She lifted herself onto her elbow as she threw the covers off her head.

"It seems we've been granted a break in the storm by the powers that be. We're all going to meet in the lobby in about a half an hour to take advantage of the good weather."

"Sounds great," Morgan said eagerly. "I'll be there."

"Morgan," Carrie said after a pause, "do you know where Sam is? I've been calling his room for ten minutes and I can't seem to get a hold of him."

A soft smile crossed her face. "Yeah, I know where he is. I'll bring him down with me."

Carrie chuckled politely. "I'll see the both of you in a half an hour then. You two behave yourselves."

Morgan laughed. "I wouldn't bet on it, but we'll be there on time." Morgan leaned over and hung up the phone. Laying back in bed, she turned her head to the right. Sam was facing away from her. All she could see was the back of his head and his shoulders. She reached over and shook his shoulder gently. "Sam?" She shook him a little more firmly. "Time to get up, Sam." *Maybe he's just a heavy sleeper,* she thought.

"Sam, we need to get going," she reiterated.

Grabbing his shoulder, she pulled him over onto his back. A scream welled up from deep in her throat as she jumped back off the bed. She stared in shock at the form in front of her. The sheets and comforter around Sam were stained a rusty red color. The blood had obviously been there for some time as it had completely oxidized. Morgan stared as the blank expression on Sam's face. His eyes were wide and staring off into space. There were no cuts of bruises on his head or neck, at least none that she could see. Only a small smattering of blood was visible.

Morgan took a deep breath and walked toward the corpse. "Sam?" she asked again, trying to hold back the tears. Slowly, she reached down and grabbed the covers. She didn't want to look. She began to pull them away. *Don't look*, she said again. *Please don't look*, she pleaded with herself. With one swift motion, she ripped the covers away and stumbled backward.

Sam had been completely eviscerated. A gaping hole ran from the top of his rib cage to between his legs. His organs had been mutilated and arranged messily inside his torso, while his intestines were partially wrapped around his waist. Morgan could see several of his ribs jutting out awkwardly from the wound.

She involuntarily doubled over and vomited on the floor. Her emotions were racing and her head was spinning wildly. Lifting herself up, she charged toward the door and threw it open. She screamed for help at the top of her lungs. She didn't have the clarity of thought to do anything else. She screamed again. Guests hastily began to run out of their rooms, some pulling on their bathrobes, others hastily wrapping a sheet or towel around their naked bodies. Morgan began to sob uncontrollably as she melted to the floor. Her legs were like rubber beneath her, and they would no longer support her weight. She crumpled into a heap. All she could see was Sam's dead body.

Trent emerged from his room, his white

bathrobe hanging off his shoulder, wearing only a pair of red boxer shorts. His frosted brown hair was a mess on top of his head. He scrambled toward Morgan and knelt down beside her. "What happened?" he asked frantically.

Morgan looked up with her tear choked eyes. "Why?" She repeated herself over and over. "Why?"

Trent spotted the blood on her fingertips. He slowly started to back away from her. "What did you do, Morgan?"

Morgan lurched forward and grabbed the ends of his bathrobe. "Why?" She screamed again.

Trent quickly pushed her away. He looked at the red smears on his robe in horror. Turning away from her, he walked briskly into the room and stopped.

From the door, he could see Sam's mutilated body. He held back the urge to vomit as he staggered out of the room. He had enough sense to close the door behind him. He turned quickly and threw his back to the wall for support. A large crowd had gathered around Morgan and the door. To his right, Trent could hear footsteps running up the hallway.

"What happened?" Chloe asked as she skidded to a stop in front of Trent. Her hair was wet and she had only a towel wrapped around herself.

Rivers was right behind her. "What the hell?" He dropped to the floor right next to Morgan.

Trent shook his head. "I wouldn't do that, Mr. Gallows." River looked up with anger in his eyes. "Why not?"

Trent glanced toward the door, then back to

165

Rivers. "Because she killed Sam Peters."

***

Montoya was sitting quietly in the waiting room of the hospital. Dawn and Bishop flanked her on both sides, while Cane sat directly across from her. It had been a long night. They had all taken turns sleeping in the hard plastic chairs while the other waited for word from the doctors. Montoya felt a sense of urgency every time a doctor or nurse walked past.

She took a deep breath, then bit off another chunk of the candy bar she had bought two hours ago. She was too nervous to eat, but she knew she needed the sustenance. *A woman can't survive on coffee alone,* she told herself as she took another gulp of the heavy black liquid. Setting the paper cup and candy bar on the chair next to her, she slid down into the seat and stretched her legs. Slowly standing up, she began to walk anxiously around the waiting area.

"You're going to wear out the tile," Cane joked.

"I can't just sit here. I feel so...." she struggled for words. "Useless?" Cane queried.

Montoya nodded. "We should've heard something by now. It's been hours."

"You can't do anything for him, Detective. He's in the hands of the doctors." He looked up into her worried eyes. "I'm sure he's fine."

Montoya heard her radio crackle to life. She quickly fished it out of her jacket pocket. "Go ahead, dispatch."

"We have an apparent homicide at the Brenton Hotel," a woman's voice reported unemotionally.

"Can't you get someone else to take a look?" Montoya asked.

"Sorry, Detective, captain requested you because you're the closest."

"On my way," she said angrily. Stuffing the radio into her pocket, she cursed under her breath. She turned around to see Cane, Dawn and Bishop standing behind her.

"Mind if we tag along?" Bishop asked innocently.

Montoya was about to refuse, but then sighed. "Why the hell not?" She turned and began to walk for the door. "Let's get a move on. We've got a dead body to take care of."

Chapter 15

Two large officers dressed in blue lifted Morgan off the floor. She had gone from sobbing insanely to being almost catatonic. Her dark mascara, which she had forgotten to take off the previous night, was streaked down her cheeks and her black nightie was barely covering her body. Her unblinking eyes were distant, as if she wasn't even there. She was a wreck with her long, black hair matted to her head. The two officers wrapped her slender arms behind her back and slipped the cuffs around her wrists. They made a horrid clicking noise as they locked shut. They began to lead her out of the building amidst gasps and muted whispers from the guests congregated in the hall.

Chloe had retreated to her room and slipped into a pair of jeans and a white sweater. She had hastily pulled her curly hair up behind her head before she had returned. She now stood shoulder to shoulder with Carrie, Trent and Rivers. The officers had already told them there was a detective on the way to question them, so they shouldn't stray very far.

Carrie was taking it the hardest. She wasn't upset at Sam's death, or Morgan's arrest, but rather that she was out two psychics and the live feed was less than fifteen hours away. She had been on her cell phone all morning trying to wrangle two replacements. She would be damned if she was letting this broadcast go down the tubes for a little thing like murder.

Rivers, on the other hand, was his traditional arrogant, pig-headed self. The first comment out of his mouth Chloe had heard was how he could see Morgan's "cute" ass. This wasn't fazing him at all, but then, no one expected it to. He would always be Rivers and somehow, at that moment, Chloe was thankful for that.

Trent was hard to read. Chloe had been trying to understand what was going through his twenty-two year old mind. It had shaken him, though. She could tell that. He had been chain-smoking ever since her return this morning. She could swear he had already been through a pack and a half just in the amount of time they had been waiting.

They had been standing in the hallway, just outside Morgan's room, for the better part of the morning. Chloe glanced down at her watch. It was closing in on seven am now. She didn't have time for this. She stopped. Had she really thought that? Did the value of human life mean nothing to her? She shook her head. It wasn't that way at all. She was just shaken. Her mind was reverting back to what she knew the best as a defense mechanism: work. She honestly couldn't see how they were going to finish this broadcast. She certainly didn't want to follow Rivers around in the house for an hour. He would be excruciatingly boring. Besides, he didn't know the material. They needed a psychic, or at least someone who was familiar with what happened in the house.

"I'm going back to my room," Rivers announced suddenly.

Chloe was pulled out of her thoughts by the comment. She spun to look at Rivers. "What did you say?"

"I said that I'm going back to my room," he

repeated. "I need to get ready for tonight and besides," a wicked smile crossed his face, "there's an awful stench coming from there."

Chloe looked at him angrily. How could he be so insensitive? "Are you actually a human being, Rivers, or some kind of mutated swine?"

Rivers started to walk away slowly. "You can come back to my room with me and check for yourself."

Chloe listened to him laugh at his own crude joke as he walked around the corner. "Jackass," she muttered under her breath.

***

Montoya, Bishop, Dawn and Cane had walked the few short blocks to the Brenton Hotel. Along the way, they had encountered Enbaugh's wrecked car. They had marveled at the fact that, with the extensive damage, Enbaugh had even survived the crash. Before they had left the hospital, Montoya had left her mobile number with the attending nurse. She had instructed them that she receive a call as soon as they knew Enbaugh's condition. She had spent most of the walk continually checking her phone. She would check to make sure it was on, then check if the batteries were good, and then five minutes later, repeat the process.

Dawn was worried about her. She didn't seem to be taking this very well. Dawn could tell Montoya would rather be at the hospital waiting for word on Enbaugh, and the wait was driving her crazy. She couldn't take it. None of them could. It was like water torture. Every doctor or nurse that walked in their direction could be the bearer of good or bad news, but then they would continue to walk by. It's funny how her mind associated things. "Sorry, not a winner, please try again" popped into Dawn's head.

"So, this is the Brenton?" Bishop asked.

Montoya looked up the face of the tall hotel, then over at Bishop, "Yep."

"Nice place," Bishop said as they began to walk inside.

The outside was littered with patrol cars. A lone ambulance sat near the door, its rear doors open and awaiting its precious cargo. Blockades had been set up around the entrance while yellow police tape hooked them together. Two officers, garbed in black rain slickers, stood at the front of the barricades holding people back. Several local news crews had parked their vans and were trying to break inside to get an exclusive.

Montoya stopped. She had to walk straight through the crowd to reach the entrance. She didn't want to be accosted this morning, but she knew some of the reporters would recognize her. In the past, she had held several press conferences for the media and she was generally the person they contacted inside the department for information. It wasn't part of her job description. Technically, that fell to the capable hands of the captain, but he didn't like doing it. She guessed at first it was the thrill of being on TV, then later it just became old hat. Everyone knew her, so they felt more comfortable contacting her.

One of the reporters, a tall woman with sleek brown hair, turned away from the barricade in defeat only to see Montoya approaching her. Her face suddenly brightened. Tapping her cameraman on the shoulder, she went charging through the group toward Montoya. "Detective Montoya," she said, sticking her microphone toward Montoya, "can you comment on the homicide this morning?"

Montoya pushed the microphone away. "No comment," she said firmly. The reporters smelled blood. They all began gathering around Montoya, each shouting their own question. "Does this have anything to do with the Grant murders?" one shouted. "Can you tell us about the rash of murders lately?" another screamed above the crowd.

Montoya was quickly losing her patience. "No comment," she repeated. "Detective," another reporter asked, "can you confirm your partner was a victim of this serial killer?"

Montoya stopped. Spinning around on her heels, she grabbed the reporter by the collar and yanked him toward her. "Detective Enbaugh is not dead," she hissed. "Why don't you vultures go find a different corpse to pick at and let us do our job?" She pushed the reporter back into his cameraman as she turned to walk away.

"What the fuck is her problem?" The reporter asked with a half-cocked smile on his face.

Bishop swept his leg under the reporter's, knocking him to the ground. Without saying a word, he continued behind Montoya.

The four reached the barricade and were immediately stopped by an officer. Montoya reached into her jacket and produced her badge. She pointed her thumb over her shoulder, "They're with me."

172

The officer nodded and lifted the tape. They quickly ducked under it and made their way toward the entrance. Montoya scolded herself. She had let them get to her and reacted badly. She knew she would hear about this from the captain. She returned her focus to the present. She had to have her wits about her. She was an officer of the law, she reminded herself. She was there to protect and serve, and she couldn't do that in the state she was in. A crime had been committed, a person had been killed, and it was her job to collect all the facts so a fair trial could be had. She steeled herself as they walked into the lobby.

Looking up, she spotted two officers bringing a woman down the stairs in handcuffs. Montoya stopped them at the bottom. "What have we here?" The woman refused to look up at Montoya.

"Morgan LeFay," one of the detectives responded. "She was in the room with the victim and she has his blood on her hands."

Montoya studied the woman for a moment. "Seems pretty open and shut, doesn't it?"

The officer nodded.

"On your way, then," Montoya instructed.

The two officers pushed Morgan forward. She stumbled and almost fell, but quickly regained her footing. For the first time, she lifted her head to get her bearings, and stopped. "You!" She broke free of the officer's grasp and rushed toward Bishop. "I know you."

Bishop took a step back with his hands raised. "I'm sorry, miss, I don't think we've ever met."

"You can tell them that I didn't do it! You

know the truth!" She struggled as the officers tried to restrain her. "Tell them!" she screamed.

"Tell them what?" Bishop asked, genuinely concerned. "I don't know what you're talking about."

"The shadows," Morgan shouted. "Tell them about the shadows!" Bishop felt as if a dagger had been plunged into the very center of his soul. "How do you know?"

"You've seen them," Morgan yelled as the officers pushed her toward the door. "I have seen you see them!"

"I don't understand," Bishop admitted, but it was too late. The officers had pulled her through the large double doors. Bishop spun around to face Cane and Dawn. "What the hell was that?"

"Very interesting," Cane said after a moment. "We shall have to talk to her, too."

Dawn pointed up the stairs at Montoya. "Come on, we'd better catch up."

***

"Right this way, Detective," said an officer as he motioned down the hall. Upon turning the corner, Montoya's senses were assaulted by the smell of smoke mingled with that of rotting flesh. She wondered if the body had been removed yet because this certainly wasn't the way a luxury hotel was supposed to smell. Montoya quickly stopped and turned to the officer she had just passed. "Has the body been removed?"

The officer frowned. He smelled it too. "No. The captain wanted us to leave it until the coroner's office could arrive. Unfortunately, the hurricane had a little fun with them last night."

"What happened?" Montoya asked.

"You know that big oak tree they have out front?"

"Yeah, I know the one."

The officer allowed himself a small chuckle, but then quickly regained his composure. "It's now inside the office."

"Holy Christ," Bishop muttered from behind Montoya. "Is everyone okay?" Montoya asked unemotionally.

The officer nodded. "There was no one there at the time. The only bad part is the trunk is blocking the parking garage. They can't haul out the meat wagon."

Montoya shook her head, then turned to the three behind her. "Take a deep breath now. We're not going to get any fresh air for a while." She paused, "I need you to stay out of my way, too. I'm here on official business."

Cane smiled as he turned Montoya around. "We won't even make a sound. Most of us are very accustomed to a crime scene. You won't have to worry about us at all."

Montoya couldn't tell if he was telling the truth, or bluffing her. Either way, she didn't care. She was here to get her business done. Nothing else. Fishing a small notepad out of her jacket pocket, she flipped it open and started down the hall. An officer just outside the crime scene was questioning a small group of people. She paid no attention to them for the moment. Her first priority was to examine the body. Slipping past the group, she made her way into the room.

***

Chloe looked up from the interview and smiled for the first time that morning. Perhaps her prayers had been answered. There, standing before her in all their scientific glory, were three members of the Office of Paranormal Investigation. She reached behind Trent and tapped Carrie on the shoulder.

Carrie glanced over at Chloe with a look of annoyance on her face. She said one last word into the phone then snapped it shut. "What?"

Chloe pointed down the hall. "OPR," she said cryptically.

Carrie's eyes suddenly widened. She raised her face toward the ceiling. "Thank you, God!" She looked back at Chloe, "When did they get here?"

"Just a moment ago. They walked in with a detective."

Carrie's face hardened for a moment, "Are you sure they're with the OPR?"

Chloe nodded. "That man in the back is Zachary Cane. We had him on the show during the first season."

"I don't remember having any members of the OPR on the show," Carrie admitted.

"It was before you started," Chloe clarified. "I think it was maybe our second or third episode."

Carrie began to size him up. "He seems very…."

"British?"

"No," Carrie said, "I was going to say stuffy."

Chloe let out a giggle. "Aren't they the same thing?"

"You're terrible," Carrie joked. "Do you think we should go introduce ourselves?"

"Why not? I wonder if he remembers me?"

The two women slipped past the officer, who was busy with Trent at the moment, and slunk down the hall toward Cane. Carrie slipped her small black cell phone into her pocket, while at the same time, retrieving a business card.

Chloe stopped right in front of the threesome. "Mr. Cane?" she asked gingerly.

Cane looked up at the woman almost startled. "Yes?"

"I don't know if you remember me," Chloe said as she extended her hand. "My name is Chloe Andrews. I'm with *Ghost Chasers, Inc.*"

Cane nodded. "Oh, yes. I remember you. What can I do for you, Ms. Andrews?"

"We were wondering if you were still with the Office of Paranormal Investigation," Carrie cut in. She slipped Cane her card. "I'm a producer of the show. My name's Carrie Lang."

Cane accepted the card and scanned it quickly. "It's nice to meet you, Ms. Lang." Cane stuffed the card into his jacket pocket. "Allow me to introduce my team. This is Dr. Dawn Lassiter and Nick Bishop."

Dawn and Bishop nodded accordingly.

"Do you have a moment to discuss business, Mr. Cane?" Carrie asked. "Of course."

Carrie smiled softly, but quickly returned to her game face. "As you know, today is Halloween, and we are planning a very special broadcast from right

177

here in Stone Brook."

Cane quickly pressed his hand to his forehead as if in revelation. "I had all but forgotten it was Halloween." He looked back up at Carrie. "I'm sorry, please continue."

"As I was saying, we are planning a very special episode of *Ghost Chasers, Inc.* tonight and we were wondering if you would like to be involved?" Cane smiled. "I appreciate the offer, but we're here on a case."

"From what I understand," Chloe interjected, "we're here for the same thing. Why can't we combine our efforts?"

"I'm sorry," Cane said gently, "but the OPR doesn't seek sensationalistic coverage of our work. We rely on scientific journals and quality news programs to relay our findings."

"I don't understand," Chloe admitted, dumbfounded. "You were on the show once."

Both Dawn and Bishop looked back at Cane with smiles on their faces. They now had blackmail material.

"That was a long time ago," Cane stuttered. "The OPR's policies have changed since then, mostly because of that appearance."

"Can you be a little more specific?" Carrie asked.

"The way you portrayed our organization was uncalled for. You referred to the OPR as a—and I quote—'bunch of hard-headed scientists who don't have the sense to look at the evidence in front of their pointed noses'. Did I hear that incorrectly?"

Chloe stepped in. "That was a long time ago, Mr. Cane. We have different executive producers now." She was lying through her teeth. "That won't happen again."

Cane smiled. "Do I detect a sense of urgency in your request?"

Chloe kicked at the floor like a child who was being punished. "We had two experts lined up," she admitted after a moment. "One of them is lying dead in that room over there, and the other is on her way to jail for his murder."

"Experts?" Bishop echoed. "I've seen your show. You don't use experts in the field, you hire half-assed psychics to go in and try and 'communicate' with the ghosts."

Carrie didn't like the direction this conversation was heading. "Then you can bring some credibility to our broadcast."

"Look at it this way," Cane countered, "your show is a like a tabloid. One day, you are reporting on the 'Bat-Boy' and the wolfman of Long Island. The next, your paper does a serious piece on an earthquake, or a terrorist attack but no one takes you seriously because you've already thrown your credibility as reporters out the window. There's no getting that back, no matter who you book on your show."

"I don't think you understand what we're offering you, Mr. Cane," Chloe said after an uncomfortable pause. "We will pay you for services rendered, and give you the chance to investigate this case on live national television. You don't get any more credible than that."

"I'm sorry, but the answer is still no," Cane replied. He turned and walked past the two women.

Bishop smiled at the two. "I like your show,"

he said with an almost fan boy zeal. He quickly caught up with Cane.

Dawn stood facing Carrie and Chloe. "Next time you want us on the show, you need to go through official channels."

"There *won't* be a next time," Carrie snorted and walked off. Chloe smiled. "Thanks anyway. You realize we had to try." Dawn nodded. "Do you mind if I ask you a question?"

"Go ahead."

"What is it exactly you're here to investigate?"

"A triple homicide that happened at 1658 Ontario Lane." Chloe leaned toward Dawn, "The officer that covered the crime reported seeing a pair of glowing red eyes."

Dawn's eyes widened. "You mean the Grant House? Dear God." She rushed past Chloe to catch up with Cane.

Chloe watched as Dawn grabbed Cane by the shoulder and whipped him around to face her. The two started talking frantically, almost arguing. After a moment, the entire team returned.

"Ms. Andrews, is there any way we can persuade you not to go into that house?" Cane asked.

Chloe smiled. She had just found her bargaining chip. "I'm afraid not. We go live in a little over twelve hours. It's much too late to scrap the show."

"You don't understand," argued Dawn. "There's something in that house."

"That's exactly what we were hoping for. If we actually find a ghost on national television, the ratings will skyrocket!"

"This is not some benevolent entity," Cane attempted to persuade her. "This..." he struggled for the word, "thing," he wasn't satisfied with that, but it was the best he could do, "is a killer. It's already taken the lives of four people here in Stone Brook and almost took one more last night."

"I'm sorry, Mr. Cane. There are hundreds of thousands of dollars riding on this broadcast in advertiser money. We can't pull out at the last moment." She leaned close, "Bad for business." Chloe began to walk away with a large smile on her face. Carrie would be proud. This level of deviousness almost rivaled her own.

"Ms. Andrews, we wouldn't have a problem having the local law enforcement bar you from the Grant House," Cane threatened.

Time for the trump card, Chloe gloated. "The mayor has already given our broadcast his blessing. Your efforts to stop us would be blocked."

"Damn," Cane muttered under his breath.

***

Montoya could instantly see where the smell was coming from. A curtain in the room had been pulled wide open allowing the sun directly onto the corpse. She hoped the occupants of the room had left it that way, or someone was about to get fired.

Montoya walked cautiously toward the corpse. She could see a mountain of blood soaked sheets piled up next to the body. As she took a few steps closer, she could tell the extent of the damage. His body had been split open from the base of his neck to the center of his groin and his vital organs had been rearranged inside the gaping cavity. If eviscerating him hadn't killed him, stuffing his heart into the area his stomach used to reside certainly did. She looked up at his face. There was an odd sense of calm on it. It wasn't frightened, or even in pain. It seemed very...serene. Odd.

That fact alone told her one thing: this man was dead before he was split open. Why had she decided to mutilate him after he was dead? She pondered this. Did she hate him so much she felt killing him wasn't enough? Nonetheless, it was a horrible, and senseless murder.

Leaning close to the body, she used her pen to push several of the organs out of the way. She examined the edge of the wound. It wasn't a clean cut as if a knife or razor had been used. It was jagged and messy. Sinew, tendons and muscle had been ripped away from bone. It looked as if, but it couldn't be, the wounds had been torn open with bare hands. Almost as if the flesh had been shredded. Montoya knew it would take much more than a one hundred and seventy pound woman to cause this kind of damage with her bare hands.

Montoya felt a tickle in her nose. She sucked it back once, but couldn't stop it. She let out a mighty sneeze. She clamped her hand over her nose to stifle a second sneeze. Looking up through blurry eyes, she saw her blast had awakened a fine spray of powder in the air. Wiping the dust from her eyes, she leaned over next to the body. It was covered with a fine black powder barely visible to the naked eye. Glancing past the body, she noticed the residue covered the sheets as well. Turning around, she pulled open the second curtain allowing the sunlight to spill completely into the room. She could see the black powder covering the entire floor and her footprints, as well as several others, preserved in the dust. Pulling a piece of paper out of her notebook, she scraped a small sample of the dust onto it with her pen. She stood and looked at the fine powder. Folding the paper in quarters, she tucked it neatly into her pocket.

She turned back toward the door. There were several pairs of odd footprints crossing the floor from the window to the bed, and then to the bathroom. She cursed herself for not noticing this earlier. She had inadvertently contaminated a crime scene. She needed to get a photographer on the scene as soon as possible before the prints were degraded even further. Being careful to step only in her own footprints, she made her way back across the floor. Once she was outside, she immediately dropped down to the floor and began to examine the carpet. There were no signs on the black powder. They seemed to stop dead at the edge of the room.

After a moment, Montoya stood and adjusted her clothing. She quickly wiped some of the dust off of her jacket. She wasn't sure what it was, but she knew she didn't want it on her.

Turning away from the door, she spotted her guests talking with two of the witnesses. She made her way down the hallway toward Cane and stopped just short of him. Tapping him on the shoulder, she waited for a response.

Cane slowly turned to face Montoya. "Detective."

"I need to run a sample I found down to the lab." She tapped the folded piece of paper in her pocket with satisfaction. "Are you coming?"

Cane shook his head. "I'd like you to meet Chloe Andrews." He looked back at Chloe, "Ms. Andrews, this is Detective Montoya." Cane turned back to Montoya. "She's the director for the television show, *Ghost Chasers, Inc.*"

Montoya extended her hand toward the younger woman and forced a smile. "Nice to meet you."

Chloe nodded. "Same here."

The group stood in an uncomfortable silence for a moment. Montoya found herself unconsciously sizing up Chloe and then Carrie.

Cane cleared his throat to grab everyone's attention. "Due to circumstances beyond our control," he announced gravely to Montoya, "we will be working with the Ghost Chasers Crew for the rest of our stay here in Stone Brook."

Chapter 16

Enbaugh snapped upright in bed. Tubes and wires were torn forcefully away from the tape that held them in place. His brow was sopping with sweat and the front of his hospital gown was soaked. A total sense of confusion set in. His last memory was of being in the car. His mind worked frantically to make sense of his surroundings, but he could tell he had been under heavy sedation. His motor skills had been affected as well as his mind. A thick haze had settled over his brain.

Glancing to his left, he slowly began to realize he was in a hospital room. The curtain divider between the two beds had been pulled completely shut, isolating Enbaugh from the rest of the room. He could hear and see the faint flicker of a television on the other side of the curtain, but he couldn't make out what program it was. Lifting his hand, he started to reach for his hair. He could feel the sweat sitting uncomfortably on his scalp. As his palm hit his forehead, he recoiled in pain. He became painfully aware of the large gash. Using his fingertips, he traced the edge of the bandage which ran around his head. It was being held in place by one small silver clasp that rested just above his left eyebrow. Lying slowly back down, he lifted his hands. There were several cuts and bruises along the back of one hand and a tube taped to the other. He hoped the rest of him didn't look as bad as his hands did.

Bringing his hands down next to his body, he looked over toward the large picture window that occupied the wall next to him. He could tell just by where the sun was sitting that it was morning. He didn't know exactly when, but he was sure. The dark clouds of the night before had given way to an eerily clear sky. On the horizon, he could see the dark clouds looming. They were coming back.

He must be in Stone Brook General Hospital, he reasoned. His eyes widened for a moment. Or maybe he had been life flighted to St. Petersburg.... He couldn't be sure. Looking out the window, he couldn't spot any familiar landmarks, but that was no indication of where he was, he reminded himself. His was still under the influence of a heavy anesthetic. His mind wasn't operating at peak efficiency.

He suddenly snapped to Montoya. The last time he had seen her, he had left her at the hospital with the OPR. He wondered if she was all right. His last memories before waking up here were of the violent storm raging outside his windshield. If the town had suffered that kind of damage, he wondered what condition the hospital was in. He tried not to think about it. He was just working himself into a fit and he didn't even know the truth. Isn't that the way it always is, though? Not having all the pieces of the puzzle present, but jumping to a conclusion. His ex-wife was like that. She would fly off on these wild tangents just because something set her off. He would always try and persuade her to look at the larger picture, to try and gather the rest of the information before making an assumption of guilt. She never did, though.

That's why he loved his work. Reason was his ally. He didn't have to spend his days second-guessing himself. It was his job to find the cold, hard facts. He would happily spend his morning examining a rug through a magnifying glass to collect stray fibers, or dusting for fingerprints. It was these clues that proved the truth; that pointed the way. No, he didn't have to deduce who the killer was while he played his violin, or smoked his pipe, he had facts on his side.

Despite what people thought, Enbaugh lived in a very orderly world. In his life, there was one truth: fact. Nothing else. If there were no hard evidence to support a thing, then it didn't exist. He didn't appear that way upon first inspection, always looking disheveled and messy. Even his apartment was a disaster. He had heard once that a messy desk was the mark of an orderly mind. It was only those with excruciatingly clean workspaces and homes that had cluttered minds. They were overcompensating for their self-proclaimed weakness. Outwardly, they would be a model of cleanliness and perfection, while on the inside, they were a tattered mess.

That was one of the things Enbaugh was most proud of: his ability to read people. It was a gift. He had always told Montoya that he could look a suspect in the eye and instantly know if they were guilty or not. He prided himself on being an excellent judge of character. He wasn't sure how he had read Cane so incorrectly....

"Good morning, Detective Enbaugh," a soft voice uttered from the edge of the curtain. A small face poked around the edge to smile at him. "How are we feeling this morning?"

Enbaugh lifted himself into a more dignified sitting position. "Fine," he croaked painfully. Reaching up, he felt his throat. There was a bandage around his neck, but he could feel the gash beneath it. He looked up at the nurse nervously.

"You should be talking normally in a few days," she said pleasantly. "Apparently, in the wreck, your throat was slashed. The cut was deep enough that it almost damaged your larynx, but luckily, the doctor was able to save it."

Enbaugh shook his head. He didn't remember his throat being cut. He knew he had the gash on his forehead, but when he passed out—

—the phantoms were there.

He was fine. His mind feverishly tried to recall the last images he could remember. It was difficult, like looking for the shore while socked in a patch of fog. Not knowing why, he reached down and ran his hand over his meaty chest. Pain shot in all directions as his fingers worked their way down. Acting without thought, he ripped at the light blue hospital gown and tore it down the middle exposing his battered chest. Long red gashes crisscrossed his chest in an awful pattern. Several rows of black stitches had to be added to close the wounds, as well as a few silver staples. He had the sudden flash of claws searing his chest.

The nurse became worried. "Detective Enbaugh, are you okay?"

"Mo..." Enbaugh finally managed to pass the words over his lips, "Montoya."

***

Morgan was cowering in the corner of her cell. The orange jumpsuit they had provided was much too large for her, but it was better than the black lacy number she had been wearing. She felt it was a tad inappropriate for jail. She brushed her dark hair out of her eyes and scanned the rest of the holding area slowly. She didn't want to give any of the other occupants the impression she was eyeing them. She had heard all the horror stories. Most of them she knew to be false, but still, it wasn't worth proving the skeptics wrong. She brought her knees up in front of her chest and wrapped her arms around them.

Her eyes were puffy from crying all morning. Her mind had finally settled down from its state of alarm to something resembling normal thought. She'd been replaying the morning's events over and over in her mind. Sam was dead and the truth of the matter was he was her hero. He was the one she aspired to be like in life, and now she was being blamed for his murder. *Why would I kill him? What would make them think I would do that to anyone, let alone Sam Peters?*

Morgan spied a heavy-set woman staring at her from across the cell. She was wearing the same orange suit and horrible plastic sandals, but she had removed the sleeves, probably to show off her multitude of tattoos. A long gothic cross ran down her right shoulder, apparently backlit by rays of sunshine. A long flowing ribbon crossed it and wrapped behind it. It had the words "in death we trust" emblazoned across it. Her other arm was a mixture of religious symbols and another woman's name. The image of a long black snake was coiled around her upper arm as it slithered down to her forearm. Her hair was short and cropped up slightly, allowing small dark wisps to fall onto her face. A lone streak of black ink ran from just above her right eyebrow to just below her eye. Morgan found herself wondering if it was actually a tattoo, or just a horrible scar.

"What are you looking at?" the woman asked coldly.

Morgan quickly diverted her attention to the floor. "Sorry, I didn't realize I was staring."

The large woman lifted herself off her perch and began to walk toward Morgan. Her footfalls against the cold concrete echoed loudly in Morgan's ears. Her heart was racing. She had been in jail less than a half an hour, and already she was going to get a shiv in her side. "I'm really sorry," Morgan pleaded. "I didn't mean to be rude."

The woman sat down on the bench next to Morgan. She stared quizzically at the young woman. "Hey," she said gruffly. "Look at me."

Morgan slowly lifted her eyes to meet the other woman's.

"I'm not going to hurt you," the woman assured her. "You just look scared out of your mind." The woman smiled as a look of confusion crossed Morgan's face. "My name's Jack."

"Jack?" Morgan echoed.

The woman smiled. "Short for Jackie," Jack leaned close, "but if you tell anyone, I'll kill you."

Morgan recoiled suddenly in terror. "I promise I won't—"

Jack laughed heartily. "You need to relax, kid." She slapped Morgan on the knee. "I was just kidding."

Morgan tried to muster a smile. "Sorry."

Jack shook her head. "You sure do apologize a lot." Her eyes wandered over the girl, then back to her face. "You don't strike me as the criminal type. What are you in for?"

"They think I murdered my hero," Morgan replied quietly. "Did you?"

"No," Morgan answered quickly. She looked at the hard face of Jack and began to relax. "What are you in for?"

Jack laughed again. "They think I killed my husband."

"Did you?"

Jack leaned close to Morgan. "You bet your sweet ass I did." Morgan felt her body tense again.

"I cleaved that fucker's head with a butcher knife," Jack announced proudly.

"What did he do to you?" Morgan stuttered. "He snored. A lot."

Morgan laughed involuntarily, but quickly forced herself to stop. It wasn't funny, but the way Jack had said it caught her off-guard. She wasn't sure how to reply.

"It's okay," A wave of Jack's thick hand dismissed Morgan's unease. "I'm usually not a violent person. Just don't snore around me."

Morgan found her humor to be in very bad taste, but what was she going to do? It wasn't like she could tell a killer her jokes were offending her. That didn't seem like the right course of action at the moment. Morgan forced a smile as if she had enjoyed Jack's humor.

Both women looked up as the heavy clink of steel bars echoed through the cell. A lone officer stood at the opened cell door. "Morgan LeFay?" he asked.

Morgan slipped into a sitting position as she lowered her feet to the ground. "Yes?"

"Warden wants to see you," the officer laughed at his own joke. "I always wanted to say that." He snickered again. "I need you to come with me."

Jack patted Morgan on the shoulder with her meaty paw. "Everything's going to be okay," she assured Morgan.

That was the first sensible thing anyone had said to Morgan all morning. She slowly stood up and walked toward the officer. Turning, she gave Jack one final glance. The officer grabbed her wrists and pulled them behind her back. She could feel the cold metal of the cuffs as he snapped them on. "Is this really necessary?" Morgan asked calmly.

"I'm afraid it is," the officer replied. "The captain doesn't like suspected killers roaming free."

"I didn't kill anyone," Morgan argued.

"Sure you didn't, honey," the officer said unemotionally. "Sure you didn't."

Chapter 17

Trent walked briskly past the front of the house with a large silver tripod slung over his shoulder. The crew had arrived on location about twenty minutes earlier, and set-up was progressing nicely. The white satellite van was parked in the driveway just behind what was left of the OPR's vehicle. A large yellow and red logo was painted on the left side of it, advertising the news station to which it belonged. One large dish rested quietly on its roof. Jackson had spooled out a large mess of cords onto the wet grass and was proceeding to attach them to a thick snake cable.

Meanwhile, Chris was busily attending to his various bits of sound equipment. "Shit," he muttered under his breath.

Jackson looked up and brushed his blonde hair out of his eyes. "What?" Chris was rifling through a dark green duffel bag. "I can't find the Shure."

"The what?" Jackson asked as he snapped another connecter into place. "The Shure," Chris repeated. Lifting the bag, he turned it over in his hands and dumped out the contents. "I can't find the microphone. I could've sworn I packed it."

"We can use the cordless lapel mics. It's no big deal," Jackson assured him.

"No," Chris said sternly. "The lapels will be fine for voice, but I like to have my Shure on a boom to pick up ambient noises. You can't really have a piece on ghosts and not have creepy noises."

"Won't the lapels pick that up?"

Chris sighed and nodded, "Yes, but only if it's loud enough. They'll completely miss the softer noises." He stood up and walked over to the van. He quickly rapped twice on the door with his knuckles.

A cloud of smoke rolled out of the van as the door popped open. "What is it?" the man asked. He was a grizzled veteran of the news business. Probably had been in it his entire life. His hair and goatee had completely gone gray, and his face read like a withered road map of his career. His left ear was pierced with a single gold stud and a short white scar lived over his right eye. He was wearing a dark red t-shirt with a tan fisherman's vest over it. Chris was sure he had every kind of video and audio connector stowed in the pockets of the vest. "If you want me to get the feed up, you need to leave me alone." He started to pull the door shut.

Chris grabbed the door before the man could close it completely and pushed it back open. "I need a favor."

The man lifted his cigarette and took a long drag while eyeing Chris. Flicking it out the door, he stepped out of the smokey den. "What kind of favor?"

"I forgot to pack my boom mic," Chris admitted uneasily. It made him sound like a first year rookie. "I need to know if you have a mic I can borrow."

The vet smiled. He loved doing favors. Everyone owed him something. Turning back to his van, he stepped inside. "What kind are you looking for?"

"I usually use a Shure SM81. It has a great low end, but I would also settle for an Audio Technica, or an AKG shotgun mic. Preferably the—" Chris was stopped in midsentence by a mic case hitting him square in the chest. His hands shot up to grab the plastic box before it could tumble to the ground. He shot the man in the van an angry glance. "Don't you know that can damage a mic's condenser?"

"That's all I have," the vet said, ignoring Chris' comments.

Chris popped open the case and lifted out the thin black microphone. "What the hell is this?" he asked while holding the plastic artifact in his hand. He rolled it over in his fingers and stared in awe at the brand name. "Who makes 'Uni-Zero'?"

"It's a little place I deal with just south of the border. It comes from the same factory that makes Nady Microphones."

"So this is some cheap Mexican knockoff?"

"What would you rather have? No boom mic, or a cheap Mexican knockoff?"

Chris weighed his options for a moment. Possibly having no mic was better than using the one in his hand, but then again…. Chris flipped it over in his hands. "What is this? It doesn't even use a standard XLR jack!"

"No, it has a permanent quarter inch adapter attached to it," The vet announced proudly. "Much less likely to be damaged after repeated use."

"Are you insane?" Chris shot at the vet. "This is a serious piece of shit!"

The vet smiled. "Take it or leave it, kid, but I'm sure your boss would be pretty unhappy if she found out her sound tech forgot some of his equipment on the day of the shoot."

Chris glared angrily at the man, but his face slowly softened into a smile. "You old son of a bitch."

The vet pulled a cigarette from the pack tucked into his vest. Removing a gold lighter from his pocket, he lit it and took a long drag. "Want a coffin nail, kid?" the vet asked, offering Chris a smoke.

"Pass."

The vet dug into another pocket on his vest and removed a small black cylinder. "Here," he said, tossing it to Chris, "you're probably going to need this adapter."

Chris smiled again. "Thanks, old man."

***

"Time?" Carrie called out.

A crewman snapped his head up from his work to look at the producer, "Eight-twenty-seven am."

Carrie nodded approvingly. *This was going to work*, she told herself. It was going to be a marvelous broadcast, maybe even change the face of television as they knew it. Turning slowly, she looked at the face of the Grant House before her. It was oddly menacing against the darkening sky behind it. Several windows on the second floor had been broken during the previous night's storm, giving it an almost dilapidated look. She smiled. That would most definitely add to the already eerie atmosphere.

She glanced across the front lawn. Her crew, in conjunction with the small news team that had brought the van, was working diligently on the shoot. They would begin to shoot backgrounds in about ten minutes, and move on to the actual re-enactment ten minutes after that. It was a very exciting morning. Carrie could almost feel electricity surging through the air. Which, in all actuality, was probably the case due to the downed power line in front of the house. She started to smile when she saw Chloe emerge from the house followed by Rivers and the three members of the OPR. She quickly strode across the wet lawn to meet them.

"How are we progressing?" she asked.

Chloe smiled. "Very nicely. They'll all be ready for the shoot tonight on schedule. We even have an added bonus."

Carrie cocked her head to the side. "What's that?"

"They've already been in the house and experienced some strange phenomenon." Chloe pointed to Bishop's bandaged hand. "He received first degree burns here yesterday."

"From what?"

Chloe smiled. "Nothing."

A wicked smile crossed Carrie's face. "Incredible."

"I don't think you all quite understand," Cane cut in. "This house isn't safe. Four people have died here recently and another was injured. I strongly suggest that you reconsider this broadcast."

"Too late for that, English," Carrie shot. "We go live tonight whether you like it or not."

"We're here to try and protect you idiots," Bishop shot out. He started to speak again, but Dawn quickly stopped him. She shook her head slowly at him.

Cane watched the outburst, then turned back to Carrie. "Ms. Lang," he said slowly, "do you want your talent to die on national television?"

Rivers eyes widened. "I thought you said it was completely safe in there, Carrie."

Carrie nodded. "It is, Rivers." She turned back to Cane. "It's going to happen, Mr. Cane. With or without you."

Cane spun quickly on his heels and ushered Dawn and Bishop away. "We'll see," he added menacingly.

Carrie lifted her hand and pressed her fingers firmly against the bridge of her nose. Closing her eyes, she took a deep breath. "Are they going to be like that all day?"

Chloe shrugged. "At least we have them."

Carrie nodded. "At least." She slowly removed her fingers and opened her eyes. "We have a slight problem."

"What?" Chloe asked.

"We don't have a child actor for the re-enactment."

Chloe shook her head. "No, we don't have any actors for the re- enactment. We were going to hire a few here in Florida, remember?"

"We can make do with what we have here for the adults," Carrie suggested, "but as for the child that died...."

"Maybe we'll just have to forgo the re-enactment," Chloe offered. "We have enough material to cover the entire hour as is. We can start with the house history, then move to the interviews with the OPR—"

What are we going to play over the history?" Carrie asked, slightly annoyed. "I don't think the audience really wants to sit and watch Rivers read the history for five minutes."

"Hey, wait a minute," Rivers shot out, realizing his character had been assaulted.

"If we had a re-enactment," Carrie continued, "we could run that over the top of River's voice-over."

"That still leaves the problem of where we're going to get the kid," Chloe reminded her.

Carrie lifted her cell phone out of her jacket pocket and began to dial a local number. "Let me make a few calls. We'll see what I can come up with."

"We have to have the raw feed to the studio in less than an hour so they can produce it," Chloe interjected.

Carrie nodded and turned away, cradling the phone to her ear.

Chloe looked over at Rivers. He was fidgeting with a lit cigarette in his hand. She watched him lift it shakily to his mouth and take a puff. "Are you okay?"

Rivers shook his head. "I don't think my insurance policy covers accidental death by a malevolent ghost."

Chloe couldn't help but laugh. "Nothing's going to happen, Rivers. You're just being paranoid."

Rivers dropped the cigarette and looked down at Chloe. "Am I?" He crushed the butt with his shoe and slowly exhaled his last puff in Chloe's face. "Four people have fucking died in this house! Not only died, but were horribly dismembered!"

"I think you're getting a little worked up over small potatoes," Chloe suggested.

"Oh, yeah? What if I fucking walk? You won't

have much of a show if I'm gone."

Chloe snickered. "Even when you're here, we don't have much of a show."

She knew that was the wrong thing to say as soon as it came out of her mouth.

Rivers glared at Chloe. "I don't have to put up with this shit," he announced. Turning, he started to walk away.

Chloe quickly grabbed his arm and spun him around. "I'm pretty sure you do have to put up with this shit, Rivers." She didn't want to pull her ace this early in the game, but he had left her no choice. "Stephen told me about the conversation you two had in his office. He told me if you fucked this up, you were gone, and he would blacklist you. Do you want that?"

Rivers started to speak, but stopped.

"Do you want that?" Chloe repeated with more anger in her voice. "I don't think you want to be one of those actors who shows up on Entertainment Tonight's 'Where are they now?' segment."

"The Biography Channel already said they wanted to do my life story," Rivers said like a spoiled brat.

Fire was burning in Chloe's eyes. "Fuck the Biography Channel. VH-1 wouldn't even do a show on you."

Rivers ripped his arm loose from Chloe's grip. "How dare you?" He spun and stomped away.

Chloe made no attempt to stop him this time. She knew he needed a little time to fume. *He'd be back*, she told herself. *He always came back.*

Chapter 18

"State your name."

"You know my name. It's right there on your damned report."

"I need you to state your name for the recording."

"You're recording this? You didn't say anything about a recording."

"Nervous?"

"Why should I be? I'm innocent."

"Then you'll have no problem stating your name."

Morgan sat back in her chair and stared across the small metal table at Montoya. "Morgan Lynn LeFay," she said finally. She leaned her elbows over on the table and began to run her fingers up her arm. She glanced about the small room. It had all the traditional trappings of any good crime movie. A lone table in the middle of a small room, a single light swaying from the ceiling, no windows, but one large mirror set into the wall behind Montoya. The walls were painted a bright white instead of the usual dingy gray or green. A solid blue stripe ran around the top of the wall, only broken in one place by a surveillance camera. Montoya was sitting quietly, jotting down notes in a small notepad.

"What are you writing?" Morgan asked.

"Notes," Montoya answered dryly without looking up. "About me?"

"No, I'm working on my grocery list." Montoya looked up at Morgan with a cross expression on her face.

"This is driving me out of my mind," Morgan

admitted after a moment. "Can we get started?"

"Oh, I'm sorry," Montoya said sarcastically, "am I keeping you from an appointment?" She slowly folded her notepad shut and crossed her hands on top of it. She looked Morgan up and down once, sizing her up. "Are you ready to begin?"

"That's what I've been saying for the past five minutes!" Morgan shouted.

"Calm down," Montoya said casually, almost friendly. "It's my job to gather all the facts. I just want to get to the bottom of this crime."

"Good," Morgan said. "That's what I want, too."

"Then we should have no problems," Montoya suggested. "What do you do for a living," she paused and flipped open her notepad. After cycling through a few pages, she finally returned her gaze to Morgan, "Ms. LeFay?"

Morgan was getting annoyed. She knew damn well Montoya knew her name. She was trying to break her. Morgan leaned back in her chair with a wide smile on her face. She was on to Montoya. It wasn't going to work. "I'm a paranormal investigator."

Montoya shook her head. "All the nuts roll downhill to Florida."

"What's that supposed to mean?"

Montoya shook her head. "Nothing. Just something I heard once." She lifted her pen from the table and began taking notes again. "What were you here investigating?"

"I was hired by *Ghost Chasers, Inc.* to help with this Halloween show of theirs. I was just supposed to go into the house, walk around for an hour, and tell them how I felt."

"Easy money."

Morgan nodded. "Bills start to pile up after a while."

Montoya laughed. "I hear that." Montoya lifted her pen from the pad. "Tell me about yourself."

"Why?"

"I want to know," Montoya answered quickly. "You don't have a very long paper trail."

"I don't think—"

Montoya shot up from her chair. "Answer the goddamned question!" She slammed her fist on the table. "This isn't an interview where you can pass on certain questions! If I ask you a question, you damned well better answer it! Do you understand, or do I have to throw your skinny ass back into your cell for another few hours?"

Morgan was shocked. She hadn't expected that kind of outburst. "I'm sorry," she said on the verge of tears. "I'm still just very upset."

"Then you better get your head screwed on right, or this is going to be a lot worse for you." Montoya slowly returned to her seat. "Now," she said, the rage completely absent from her voice, "tell me about yourself."

Morgan nodded. "Like I said, I'm a paranormal investigator. I work out of my home in New York, and I try to travel as much as possible."

"Why is that?"

"The ghosts don't come to me. I have to find them and I can't do that sitting in my office."

Montoya nodded. "Makes sense. Go on."

"I grew up just outside of Modesto, California. I guess I had a pretty normal childhood. My parents

203

were one of the few not divorced out of my friends.

I was fairly well adjusted, I guess as much as a Cali kid can be." Morgan adjusted uncomfortably in her seat. "I attended USC, where I attained a bachelor's degree in English. That's pretty much where I am."

"Why did you decide to become a paranormal investigator?"

Morgan was trying to avoid that question. She knew if she answered truthfully, Montoya would think she was insane. How could Morgan tell her? "I was just," Morgan struggled for the words, "interested in the supernatural and the occult." She looked nervously across the table at Montoya. Would Montoya realize she was lying?

"Okay," Montoya said as she exhaled deeply. She jotted a few quick notes in her pad. "Why didn't you go into teaching?"

"It just wasn't for me," Morgan admitted. At least that was the truth. "I remembered how I was in high school and I didn't want to deal with that on a daily basis."

"I thought you said you had a normal childhood."

Morgan nodded. "I did, but every kid gets a rebellious streak in high school. I wanted everything my way, or no way at all. I was very headstrong."

Montoya smiled. "What kid isn't?" She flipped to another page in her notebook, "Tell me about Sam Peters."

Morgan paused. She had been avoiding that memory. She had kept her mind in check, not allowing herself to dwell on the image she saw that morning. "He," Morgan swallowed hard, "was my

204

hero."

"Why?" Montoya asked softly.

"He was what young paranormal investigators look up to. He always stood by his statements. If Sam Peters told you he had seen and communicated with a ghost, then by God, he did. He was never one to back down from what he believed in." Morgan leaned forward on the table. "I saw him on television during my junior year at college. At first, I thought he was kind of spooky, but after I started reading his work and examining his findings, I found he was a genius."

"Why?" Montoya repeated.

"He kept meticulous field notes. He documented everything. I mean everything, from the color of the trim at a location, to the temperature and cloud cover. He let nothing slip through the cracks. That was very wise." Morgan sat back in her seat and flipped her black hair over her shoulder. "When you're in the profession we are, most people think you're a looney toon. They dismiss you out of hand without even listening to what you have to say. With Peter keeping the records he did, he was harder to dismiss. He had more proof than say the average person who says, 'I've seen a ghost'."

"I know exactly what you mean," Montoya said flashing back to her conversation with Enbaugh earlier in the week. She looked Morgan squarely in the eyes. "Why did you kill him then?"

Morgan recoiled in horror from the question. She knew this was coming, but she still wasn't ready for it. "I," she stuttered, "I didn't."

"Then who did?"

Morgan shook her head.

"Someone did," Montoya said, slowly raising her voice. "The man was gutted like a fish. That sort of thing just doesn't happen on its own!"

"I don't know," Morgan pleaded as a tear rolled down her cheek. She had hoped she would be stronger, that she wouldn't break, but it was too late for that now. "I didn't kill him."

"I have signed affidavits from guests at the hotel who said you had blood on your hands when you ran out of your room this morning."

"I touched the sheets. They were soaked with blood."

"We have photos of your hands, as well as samples of the blood. That alone will be enough to convict you." Montoya let the words sink in for a moment. She stood and walked to the far corner of the room. Turning around, she rested her back gently on the cool wall. "I need to know everything, Morgan." She pulled a piece of candy out of her pocket and popped it in her mouth. "Personally, I don't give a fuck if you get the chair for this. If I've done my job correctly, then my hands are clean, but I need to know the truth." She spit the candy out of her mouth. She hadn't realized she'd grabbed a sour one. Folding it back into its wrapper, she tucked it into her coat pocket. "What happened between the meeting last night and this morning?"

Morgan was visibly shaking. She had wrapped her arms around her midsection and had begun to rock in the chair. "We had sex, okay?"

"Is that all?"

The question surprised Morgan. "What do you mean?"

"Did your activities include any alcohol, or

206

possibly, drugs of any kind?"

"We had a few drinks, but that was all."

"That's odd," Montoya said. "I don't want to call you a liar, but I have evidence to the contrary."

Morgan sank in her chair. She had forgotten.

"We found a small amount of marijuana in one of your bags. There was also a pack of rolling papers in your purse, and," Montoya saved the best for last, "a partially smoked joint in an ashtray." She took a step toward Morgan. "You're lying to me."

"I'm not," Morgan argued. "I just forgot."

"Well, what else are you forgetting? Maybe that you eviscerated Sam Peters?"

"No," Morgan cried. "Why would I do that? I loved him."

"Like an obsessed fan?" Montoya shot back. "You realized you couldn't have him all to yourself and you killed him. I can see it all clearly now. You got him stoned, fucked him, then killed him in a fit of jealousy."

"That's not what happened at all," Morgan wailed. "Then what did happen?"

"We went back to my room after the meeting," Morgan sobbed, "and we had sex. We had a few drinks during and smoked the joint, but then we went to sleep."

"And?"

"I woke up a few hours later with a headache, had another drink, and we had sex again. Then we went back to sleep. Nothing else happened."

"Until you killed him, right?"

"No!"

"You're not going to tell me that you just woke up and found this bloody corpse lying next to you, are you?"

Morgan nodded. "That's exactly what happened. When I woke up, he was dead. I broke down and ran into the hall screaming. I needed someone to help me."

"To get rid of the body?"

Morgan shot up out of her seat and into Montoya's face. "What the fuck is wrong with you? The man was my hero. I didn't hurt a fucking hair on his head!"

"That's not the way I see it," Montoya smiled. "I think this is a pretty open and shut case. It's all a matter of a fanatical young woman who killed her hero. It's not completely unheard of. You'd rather he was dead than have to share him with the rest of the world."

"I idolized him."

Montoya nodded politely. "That's part of the problem, my dear." Moving away from Morgan, she swiped her notepad off the table and headed for the door. She stopped just short. "An officer will be in shortly to take you back to your cell." Montoya reached down and grabbed the door handle. "Don't take too much time getting used to that. You're going to be seeing bars for a long time."

Montoya left, leaving Morgan a shaking mess. Morgan ran her hand up to her face, then into her hair. She tried to choke back the sobs, but she couldn't. She was going down with the ship, and it looked like there was nothing she could do. Looking over at the mirror, she rushed toward it and began to pound on it with her fists. "Did you get all of that, you bastards?"

Turning away, she slowly sank down to the

floor and buried her head between her knees. She felt nauseous, and with good cause. Without looking up, she heard the door burst open and two officers enter. She could hear the jingling of their handcuffs as they approached her.

***

"All right," Carrie said quickly, "you're next, Mr. Bishop."

Bishop looked up at the redhead standing before him. She was shifting her weight impatiently from foot to foot. Lifting himself off the stoop in front of the house, he followed her inside. A maze of cables snaked across the hardwood floors into the living room. Several bright lights had been set up in front of the fireplace and were shining brightly on one of the leather couches. Two cameras were positioned strategically to capture a subject's every nuance as they recorded. Chloe sat in a small wooden chair in the middle of the room with her crew flanking her on either side. A small row of video equipment sat in front of her with two monitors showing what each of the cameras was recording.

Chloe was jotting down several notes on a clipboard as Trent and Jackson made their final adjustments. Chloe looked up from her notes. "Ready?"

Bishop nodded. "I've never done anything like this before. I'm a little nervous," he admitted.

"It's all right," Chloe assured him as she stood. "Don't even think about the cameras, just talk to me." She guided Bishop to the first couch and

209

began adjusting his attire. She quickly brushed a bit of dust off of his shoulders. Taking a step back, she assessed her work, then returned to her seat.

"What are you going to ask me?" Bishop asked.

"Just a few standard questions like name, qualifications, how long you've been doing this, and so on." Chloe looked over at Chris, "Sound?"

Chris nodded. "We were getting a really weird hum a minute ago, but I think I tracked it down."

"Camera?" she asked again.

Trent looked out from behind one of the large black cameras. "Ready."

"All right," Chloe said, making one final note. "Quiet on the set."

Jackson stepped out from behind the camera and repeated Chloe's order. He lifted the black and white clapperboard in front of Bishop's face and held it open.

"Sound?"

"Speed," Chris answered. "Camera?"

"Rolling," Trent barked. Chloe nodded at Jackson.

"*Ghost Chasers, Inc.*, Nick Bishop interview, mark." He snapped the clapperboard shut and quickly jumped out of the frame.

"Tell us a little about yourself," Chloe asked.

Bishop adjusted himself and then looked at Chloe. "Which camera am I supposed to be looking into?"

"Neither," Chloe said quickly. "Just look at me."

"Okay," Bishop said nervously. "You can edit that out, right?"

"Yes," Chloe replied impatiently. "Now tell us

about—"

"Because I don't want to look like an idiot on camera. I mean, I am a professional, after all." Bishop was babbling nervously. Even he knew it.

"Cut." Chloe said in frustration. She placed her clipboard on the floor next to her and glared at Bishop. "I realize you're nervous," she said sympathetically, "but the show must go on. If you make a mistake, don't dwell on it, just go on. We can edit it out."

"I'm sorry," Bishop started.

"It's okay," Chloe said with a sigh. "Let's try it again." She lifted her clipboard off of the floor and settled back into her chair. "Sound?"

"Speed," Chris said again. "Camera?"

"Rolling," Trent confirmed.

She nodded to Jackson again.

"*Ghost Chasers, Inc*., Nick Bishop interview, take 2, mark." He snapped the clapperboard again.

Chloe lifted her gaze to meet Bishop's. He was fidgeting uneasily in his seat. "Calm down," she instructed him.

Bishop nodded and took a deep breath. "Okay."

"Tell us a little about yourself."

Bishop drew in a second deep breath and slowly exhaled. "My name is Nick Bishop, and I am an investigator with the Office of Paranormal Research, or better known as the OPR."

"Talk to us about your first paranormal experience," Chloe prompted. "Well," a large smile crossed Bishop's face, "when I was a kid, probably around eleven or so, I lived in this house I was sure was haunted. It was my parent's place out in Arizona. A huge three story house that was probably older than the state itself." Bishop was slowly starting to loosen up. "I used to hear the strangest bumps and noises in the middle of the night, so I decided to try and get a photo of this supposed ghost." He had become completely animated, regaling the crew like a child talking about his first Christmas. "I spent weeks staying up with my little Polaroid camera, just waiting for it to walk by."

"Did you ever get a picture of your ghost?" Chloe asked.

"No," Bishop chuckled, "but I did scare the hell out of my parents quite a few times."

A subdued laugh ran over Chloe and the crew. Chloe scribbled a note on her pad, then returned her gaze to Bishop. "Why did you choose a career in the paranormal?"

"I want to prove these things are real," Bishop stated emotionally. "Have you ever seen something you just couldn't explain? You go talk to your mother or father, and they have no answers. You talk to your priest, or teacher, and they can't explain it." Bishop bit his lip, then continued. "I want to be the one who explains it. I want to tell people 'No, you're not crazy. You really did see something', and this is what it is."

"Why?" It was a deceptively simple question.

"There's too much finger pointing. Every time someone sees something they can't explain, their colleagues instantly label them as 'crazy', or 'unstable'. They are laughed at if they try and convey what they saw. I want to change that. I want to be the person that says, 'I believe you'." Bishop stopped, then smiled. "There are stranger things in

212

Heaven and Hell than even man can imagine."

Chloe smiled. "Great answer. Cut."

"That's it?" Bishop asked.

"That's it," Chloe said with a smile. "We just needed a little background on you."

"Great." Bishop stood up off the couch. "How was I?"

"You were fine," Chloe assured him.

"Thanks."

"Oh," Chloe called after Bishop as he walked toward the door, "can you send in Mr. Cane next?"

Bishop nodded. "Sure." Stepping outside, he was met with a small splatter of rain. Looking up, he could see the dark gray clouds had returned. It wasn't going to be long until the storm returned as well. It was barely sprinkling, but it was enough to be noticeable.

Glancing around the front of the house, Bishop spotted Cane and Dawn standing against the garage door on the far side of the house. They were being sheltered from the rain by a small overhang. Bishop quickly moved toward them. "Cane," he called out, "they're ready for you in there."

Cane glanced over at Dawn, "Into the fire."

Dawn laughed out loud. "Be brave, Cane." She patted him once on the back as he moved past her.

Stopping in front of Bishop, Cane adjusted his glasses. "I want you and Dawn to go talk to Ms. LeFay. I've already called ahead and cleared it with Detective Montoya."

Bishop nodded. "You just want her side of the story?"

"Basically," Cane agreed. "If you can get more, do so, but don't press her." Cane retrieved a small white cloth from his pocket and began to wipe his glasses. "Take the video camera. I want footage."

"Understood."

Cane started to move toward the front door of the house. "Good luck," Bishop said with a smile.

Cane nodded. "I think I'll need it."

Chapter 19

Enbaugh was lying on his back in the hospital bed. Several wires and tubes were running over and into his body, and he hurt. It wasn't a dull ache like muscle soreness, rather a constant throb from his head down. The nurse had given him a shot of painkillers, but over the past hour, they had started to wear off. The headache had returned. It ran from the base of his neck up through the back of his head. The pain seemed to branch off to the sides of his head near the top. The doctor said he had a mild case of whiplash. Enbaugh would hate to know what a severe case felt like. Looking over the blue hospital gown he was wearing, he felt so embarrassed. He hated wearing these things. He allowed a small smile to creep over his face. At least his dignity was intact. He tried to turn his head to look out the window, but a sharp pain shot up his neck. He stopped suddenly and held his head in place. It hurt too much to continue turning, but it was also too painful to turn back.

"I'm a freaking invalid," he croaked. He had never been exceptionally proud of his voice, but it was better than this squawk he had now. It was as if his voice died at the top of his throat and he was spitting out the carcass. Horrid.

His mind returned to the slashes on his chest. He was sure he didn't receive them in the accident. They were in all the wrong places, and his throat…. How could his throat have been slashed in the wreck? he wondered. Possibly a fragment of metal was dislodged during it and flew forward into the cab, but that didn't seem right. He had a clear recollection of the accident. He remembered the steering wheel had pinned him in his seat, but nothing had cut his chest or throat. His memories of the events after the accident were slowly beginning to resurface. Bits and fragments that didn't seem to make much sense were all jumbled in his brain. Knowing it was a jigsaw puzzle, he just needed to put the pieces together. His mind had been focusing on the eyes, but something more horrible had become clear, the claws. Tearing at him. Ripping at his flesh....

"How's our patient this morning?"

Enbaugh strained his eyes to see Montoya entering the room. "Montoya," he croaked.

"My, you have a lovely singing voice," she joked. She was carrying a large, yellow, smiley-face mug with a bouquet of flowers in it. She held it in front of his face for a moment. "I saw this in the gift shop and thought of you."

"Why?"

"Because you're idiotic, just like this stupid mug," Montoya ribbed. She set it on the table next to his bed. "Dear God," Montoya said, "you look like hell, Jack."

"Thanks," Enbaugh said with a frown on his face.

"At least you're ready for Halloween. I think you could win any costume contest with that get-up."

Enbaugh slowly raised his hand toward Montoya and extended his middle finger. His face cringed. Even that was painful. "Ouch."

"What happened out there?"

"You won't believe me."

216

Montoya grabbed a nearby chair and sat down. "Who says?"

Enbaugh slowly turned his head to face Montoya. He felt a twinge of pain and stopped. "I saw them again."

"Who?"

"The eyes," Enbaugh said with a cough. His entire body tightened up. Every time he coughed, he felt like he burst several stitches. He lifted his arm and wiped a bit of drool from his mouth. "Sorry, the body's not working real well at the moment."

"It's okay," Montoya said. Reaching over, she took his hand into her own. "Tell me what happened, if you can."

Enbaugh nodded and took a slow, deep, breath. Montoya could hear his lungs wheezing. "Lightning struck a nearby tree. I tried to swerve out of the way, but I lost control of my car. The paramedics told me they found me partially embedded in the side of a building."

Montoya nodded. "I've read the accident report." She had been skirting around the subject. It was time for the direct approach. "I want to know about the eyes, Jack. Tell me about the shadows."

Enbaugh slowly pulled open his gown revealing the lacerations on his chest. "They did this to me."

"The shadows?" Enbaugh nodded. "Why?"

"I don't think they had a reason."

Montoya was shocked at his answer. Sitting back in the chair, she let his statement sink in for a moment. It didn't make sense to her. It wasn't logical. These things didn't follow any kind of discernable pattern. "What are you trying to tell me?"

"Remember when you were a little kid and you used to rip the wings off bugs?"

Montoya nodded.

"It was like that. They had no compassion for me; I was just their plaything. They tortured me for no other reason than they could."

Montoya was horrified, but in some way, it made her feel better about Enbaugh. His story fit with the one Kelley had told Bishop last night. He wasn't insane. "What are they, Jack?"

Enbaugh tried to stifle a cough before continuing. Closing his eyes, he took a long, labored breath. It wasn't his lungs that hurt, rather the broken ribs around them. Every breath felt like a knife being plunged into his chest repeatedly. He needed another shot of morphine. "Will you summon the nurse?"

Montoya reached over to the table next to the bed and grabbed the small, white remote control. It had four buttons on it. One was labeled television, and the one directly above it had an arrow on it. She assumed that was to change the channel. The two below it were marked 'nurse' and 'panic'. She gently pressed the nurse button and returned the control to its original position. "You didn't answer my question, Jack. What are these shadow things?"

Enbaugh gripped Montoya's slender hand tightly. "Pure evil. They have no conscience to hinder them. They know only death and destruction."

"How do we stop them?"

Enbaugh shook his head, ever so slightly. "I don't think we can."

***

"You're very pasty," Carrie commented on Cane's complexion. "You don't see the sun very often, do you?"

Cane forced a laugh. "Ghosts don't usually come out during the day."

"I guess not." Carrie lifted a bit of powder and dabbed it on Cane's face. She repeated the process until she was happy with the results. "There," she said finally, "you look a little more human."

"Was that a compliment?" Cane asked. Carrie smiled. "Take it however you want."

Cane thought of a witty retort, but stopped himself. The working relationship between the OPR and *Ghost Chasers, Inc.* was already a bit strained. He didn't want to make it any worse. "Thank you."

"Are we ready?" Chloe asked from her seat in the living room. One by one, her crew signaled their readiness.

He quickly straightened his posture and folded his hands neatly in his lap. He didn't want to look like a slouch on television.

Chloe looked up and laughed. "You look like you have a stick up your ass. Loosen up a bit."

He let out a long sigh as he relaxed his posture. These people were wearing on Cane very quickly. His tolerance level had shrunk by a factor of ten as soon as his team had joined this broadcast. He had no patience for people like this; they weren't interested in actual scientific achievement or discovery. They just wanted ratings. It was rather sad in his opinion. They had no drive to better

219

themselves, or the world around them. Sure, they could claim some of their broadcasts actually taught viewers something, or piqued their interest in a given subject, but it wasn't very fulfilling in his opinion. They were controlled not by the search for knowledge, but by the almighty dollar. They were no more than another cog in the modern machine, but he digressed. He had volunteered to help them. He was here of his own volition.

"Mr. Cane," Chloe said, snapping him back to reality. "Are you ready to proceed?"

"Oh, yes, sorry," Cane said.

"I'm just going to ask you some very simple questions about who you are and what you do. This is just a quick bit piece we'll use to introduce the group."

"I understand."

Chloe smiled. "Answer as honestly as possible, and this will be better for all of us." She flipped a page on her clipboard and quickly scanned over her notes. "Shall we begin?"

Cane nodded.

Jackson stepped in front of Cane holding the clapperboard. "Quiet on the set," he announced. Holding the board in front of him, he looked into the camera, then snapped it shut.

"Tell us who Zachary Cane is," Chloe probed.

"I tend to think of myself as a scholar." He slipped off his glasses and began to clean them. "Not of traditional knowledge, but of the paranormal. It is always my goal on these kinds of outings to learn and record, rather than just find something."

"Okay," Chloe said after a brief pause, "but that

doesn't tell us who you are. What makes you tick? You're obviously from England, so what brought you to America?" Chloe realized this was going to be one of those interviews you really have to work for. She wasn't in the mood to fight for every word.

"I was born in London, England and moved here to America when I was very young. My family felt we could make a better life for ourselves here." He slipped his glasses back onto his face. "I realized early I had a fascination with the occult. It also helped that my parents were very open-minded. Which was odd. Especially for an English couple of their generation."

"So you began to follow the paranormal?" Chloe continued before Cane got off on a side-track.

"Yes. After graduating from school, I became a paranormal researcher full- time. It was then that I came upon a fellow traveler."

"Chairman Thomas Weiss?"

"Yes, Weiss." Cane shifted in his seat for a moment. "We scraped together what limited funds we had and formed the Office of Paranormal Research. We had lofty goals in those days. We were determined to prove to the world that this phenomenon really existed."

"What changed?"

"Weiss changed," Cane said angrily. "His focus shifted away from research, and more toward the business end of the company. He started his own empire from there. He became less and less of a scientist as the years passed."

Chloe smiled. This was great stuff. "It sounds as if there is quite a bit of animosity between you two. Did he steal the company from you?"

"In a sense," Cane admitted. "While it's true I still own half of the OPR, I don't really have any power in the company. Weiss created a board that controls all of the OPR's assets, and I don't have a seat on that."

"I don't follow," Chloe said. "You still own half of the company, but you have no say? How is that possible? You're the owner."

"It's not as black and white as it seems," Cane contradicted her.

"Holy shit!" Trent yelled from behind the camera. "Look behind Cane!" Cane spun around in his seat and his eyes widened. "You're getting this on film?"

"You bet your ass I am!" Trent acknowledged.

***

It had been several hours since Morgan had been questioned. She had been moved from general holding to her own cell inside the jail. She had no roommate this time, and actually found herself missing Jack's company. Her mind had slowly started to calm down. She was now occupying her time by reading some of the more obscene graffiti on the walls. A smile almost crossed her face when she saw the cliché scratches. She quickly counted up the pairs of five and came to an answer of eighty. She could barely conceive of eighty days in jail, but she knew she was facing many more than that. She would have to count her time in years instead of days.

Morgan suddenly sat straight up in her cell. "No." A cold sweat began to run down her forehead as the chills gripped her body. "Not again...."

***

A large blue mist had formed at the base of the staircase. It was hovering about three feet off the ground and was roughly two feet in diameter at any given moment. At its center, it appeared almost solid white, while the blue aura radiated out from around it. It was hovering motionlessly and silently in the air.

Cane leapt up from his seat and swung around the edge of the couch. He began barking orders at the crew like a drill sergeant. "Chloe, take notes. Write down the time, date, what it looks like and who's in the room. Trent, keep those cameras rolling. Chris, bring that boom mic closer to the phenomenon." He dug into his pocket and produced his small EMF Meter. Switching it on, he slowly approached the mist.

"Move to the left," Trent yelled. "You're blocking my shot."

Cane slowly strafed to the left, but continued moving forward. He glanced down at the needle on his meter. It was jumping wildly back and forth. At one point, it was off the scale. He glanced behind him. Chris was slowly bringing up the rear. His boom was extended to the fullest. "Are you hearing anything?"

"No, just the ambient sounds of the room," Chris said as he adjusted his headphones. "I need to get closer."

Cane stopped. "Go, get up there."

Chris glanced uneasily at Cane. "Are you

223

coming?"

"I'll be right behind you," he assured Chris. Digging into his opposite pocket, he produced a small digital thermometer. He wondered if it was the same phenomenon Bishop had encountered in the house yesterday. Moving the device forward, he saw a dramatic dip in temperature. "The thermometer just dropped from sixty-four degrees down to just thirty," Cane said with astonishment. He reached forward and patted Chris on the back. "Stop there. We don't know if this thing is dangerous."

"What?" Chris spun around to face Cane. "What do you mean dangerous? No one said anything about dangerous!"

"Shut up!" Cane twisted him back toward the mist.

***

Morgan jumped off her cot and charged the cell doors. Wrapping her hands around the bars, she began to scream wildly. She pulled with all her strength at the steel bars. "Let me out!" she screamed. "They're going to die!"

***

Cane slowly sidestepped Chris and moved a little closer to the mist. In one hand, he had his wildly gyrating EMF Meter, and in the other, his white digital thermometer. "Damn," he muttered to himself. "I need Dawn and Bishop here to take readings."

224

"It's doing something!" Chloe shouted from behind Cane.

Cane snapped his head up toward the mist. He was now less than a foot away from the event. He felt his heart sink into his chest.

The soft white and blue quickly mutated into solid black. Gone was the soft aura, replaced by hard black edges that seemed to swallow the light. The free-floating form slowly transformed from a noncorporeal shape into something vaguely human. It stood silently in front of Cane, dwarfing him by at least a foot.

Cane's EMF Meter began to squeal in his hand as the needle buried itself at the top. A thin wisp of smoke erupted from the meter as it quickly heated up in Cane's hand. The circuitry was melting inside the case. Tossing the box aside, Cane watched as it hit the floor and burst into flames. Cane glanced down at the thermometer. It looked like a stopwatch counting up time as the temperature rose. Dropping the device, Cane took a careful step back from the shadow. He shot a quick glance over his shoulder. Chris was frozen in terror.

"Chris! Get the fuck out of here!" Cane commanded.

Wasting no time, Chris quickly complied. Backpedaling away from the shadow, Chris' feet became entangled in the cords on the floor. He tumbled back toward the hardwood floor and hit with a crack. He instantly wrapped his hand around his left elbow and let out a slightly muffled yelp.

Cane knelt down and tried to help Chris off the floor. They were both in the direct line of the shadow, but it wasn't moving. Just observing. Cane

225

slowly stood up. "Everyone to the front door."

"The door is in front of that thing!" Chloe yelled. "I'm not going over there."

Cane shot an angry glance at Chloe, "Would you rather stay in here and die?"

"Good point," Chloe said.

Moving slowly around the couch, Trent, Chloe and Jackson walked toward Cane. Jackson was bringing up the rear of the group. Carefully, the group took the few remaining steps toward the door. Suddenly, the shadow's red eyes flashed, and it vanished without a trace.

"What the fuck?" Trent said quietly.

"At this point, I don't care." Chloe said quickly. "Open the door."

Cane reached down and grabbed the handle, but quickly snapped his hand away. "The handle is burning hot!"

"Shit!" Chloe cried out. "We can't get out this way!"

**

"What the hell are you wailing about?" The guard queried Morgan. Morgan had attached herself to the bars. She was standing on one of the connecting beams with her hands wrapped firmly around the bars. Her knuckles were white, she was squeezing so hard. "I need to get out of here!" Her hand shot through the bars. She swatted wildly at the guard. "Get me out of here or they're going to die!"

The guard reached down to his black belt and instinctively removed a small black bottle of pepper spray. Holding the bottle tightly in his hand, he took a step back from Morgan. "Settle down or I'll have to spray you!" He flipped the safety latch on the canister off. "I'm warning you!"

Morgan slowly slid down off the bars and took two steps away from them. Her eyes had shifted from green to a hollow black. Her hair and clothes were matted to her body in a sweaty mess. She lowered her gaze slightly and began to chant. Slowly at first, her body began to lift off the floor until her feet were dangling beneath her. She opened the palms of her hands as she raised her arms toward the guard, all the while still chanting. "I will not let another die," she warned. "Release me."

The guard began to panic. He stumbled back from Morgan with his spray still firmly in hand. Lifting his radio off his belt, he frantically keyed it. "I need back up, Goddamn it! Someone get down here and help me now!"

***

The group looked nervously around the living room of the Grant House. There was nothing. Only the electronic hum of the lights and equipment could be heard.

Cane looked down at his hand. His palm had turned a bright red from the burn, but it wasn't blistering. At least that was slightly comforting. He quickly surveyed the group. Aside from some heavy breathing, they appeared to be fine. He slowly adjusted his glasses. "Is everyone all right?"

"What the fuck was that, man?" Chris shouted.

"Damn, that was some weird shit."

"Yes," Cane agreed with Chris' guttural interpretation of the previous events. "That was strange, but why didn't it attack? It had us all cornered."

"At this point," Chloe said slowly as she caught her breath, "I don't care. We need to find a way out of here."

Jackson pointed over his shoulder. "There's a backdoor through the kitchen."

"Very good," Cane acknowledged. "Stay together and move toward the kitchen."

They quickly moved away from the front door and across the living room. A sudden sound caught the attention of the group. It was like a floorboard squeaking, but more distant. In turn, each of the crew's lights began to snap off. They stopped. Only silence again.

"It's toying with us," Trent speculated.

The two solid camera pods suddenly crashed to the floor, shattering one of the cameras.

"Ignore them," Cane said as the hairs on the back of his neck stood straight up. "Press on," he turned to look behind him, "quickly."

Chloe glanced back at Cane and her eyes widened. There were two shadows standing motionlessly in front of the door. "Jesus," she gasped. "Run!"

The crew took off in a dead run toward the kitchen just as the shadows attacked. Jackson was the first into the kitchen, followed closely by Chris and Trent. Chloe and Cane were just about in, when the kitchen door slammed shut in front of them.

Chloe slammed her hand against the door.

"No!"

"You will not escape," the shadows promised menacingly.

Cane spun around to see the first of two shadows almost on top of them, their red eyes glaring angrily as they approached. They were moving slowly and deliberately, as if they knew every step they took was torturing Chloe and Cane. Acting quickly, Cane pushed Chloe behind him and stood fast against the shadows. He dug into his jacket pocket and retrieved a small golden cross. Holding it between his thumb and forefinger, he thrust it toward the shadow.

The creature stopped less than a foot from Cane and examined the symbol. A horrible toothy grin crossed its black face. With a motion almost too quick to see, the shadow snatched the cross out of Cane's hand and held it up. "Your faith means nothing to me," it hissed as it crushed the cross in its hand. With the speed of a cobra, the shadow jutted toward Cane, his claws arched forward.

***

Morgan felt a surge of power flow over her body. Arching her back, she let out a long, low moan. With a sudden flip of her hands, the cell bars in front of her began to rattle violently. Screws and bolts began to dislodge themselves and fall helplessly to the floor. The bars groaned in protest as they began to lurch forward. Then the concrete surrounding them gave way, sending the door rocketing toward the deputy. Wrapping his arms around his head, the man felt the steel bars slam into him, knocking him to the floor. His head flipped back like a rag doll's and smacked into the concrete wall, rendering him unconscious.

Morgan watched as a solitary tickle of blood ran down from his scalp. She knew he wasn't dead. Floating out of the cell, she touched down just in front of the heap of steel in the hall, but she wasn't done yet. Grabbing a scrap of metal off the floor, she slowly drew it across her right palm and watched her blood well up around it. It didn't have to be a deep cut, just enough to make her bleed. Dropping the scrap, she knelt down and began to rub the blood in a small circle around her. Once the circle was complete, she stood tall inside it.

"Kemteh," she chanted. "Kemteh, soona, alipta. Kemteh, soona, alipta." Lifting her hands above her head, she repeated the chant a final time. A wave of power exploded from her body in all directions and knocked her to the ground. The very concrete walls of the jail rattled as the wave rumbled through them, then everything stopped. Lifting herself off the floor, she quickly wrapped her right hand inside her shirt to try and stop the bleeding. She glanced around the corridor. The world had become still. Dust from the explosion hung motionlessly in the air, and the trickle of blood on the guard's head had stopped in mid-drip. Taking a deep breath, she quickly made her way out of the jail.

***

The shadow stopped. Its claws were less than an inch from Cane's face. Cane looked over the being in front of him. Its very body seemed to be frozen in time. Carefully, Cane reached his hand toward the darkness, and to his amazement, went right through it. He waved his hand through the center of the shadow. It felt as if there were nothing there.

Chloe peeked out from behind Cane. "What the hell is going on?"

"I don't know," Cane answered inquisitively. "This is very odd. We should be dead by now."

"That's very comforting," Chloe reassured. "Can we leave now?"

"I'd like to get some readings."

"With what?" Chloe asked. "Your equipment exploded."

"Yes," Cane remembered the smoldering heap of electronic parts on the floor of the living room. "Damn."

"What if these things start moving again? I don't know about you, but I don't want to be here when it happens."

Cane nodded. "Agreed." Reaching over, he pressed his hand against the kitchen door. It swung open with minimal effort. Ignoring the possible ramifications for the moment, Cane and Chloe quickly stormed into the kitchen. Chris, Jackson and Trent were standing with the back door open. They all had the door grasped firmly. They weren't going to let this one close for anything until Chloe and Cane were through it. The two weaved around the center island and burst through the door.

Chapter 20

Bishop ran his hand along the steering wheel as he stared at the road ahead. He had never been in a hurricane, let alone been able to see the aftermath first-hand. It was heart-breaking. He saw small shops completely decimated by the storm. Their windows were broken, their goods looted by thieves in the night, and entire sections knocked over by the gale force winds. Owners stood outside trying to get a handle on the destruction as they swept up bits of broken glass and damaged merchandise. He wondered what they were going through. He knew some of them had probably worked their entire lives to build up their businesses, then just sat idly by as they were torn down by the vicious hand of mother nature.

As he brought the vehicle to a stop, he reached up and rubbed the bridge of his nose. He hadn't had much sleep in the past few days. First, it was the anxiety of a new job, then the storm, and finally last night, that *thing* that attacked him in the hospital. His mind flashed back to Kelley lying helplessly in her bed. She watched her lover die in front of her, then she was tortured, but not killed. Why? It just didn't add up in his mind. Why would they kill one, and not the other? For that matter, why was Morgan alive if it truly was the shadows that killed Sam Peters? There were too many questions, so many questions.

He glanced over at Dawn. She had her head propped up on the armrest. It didn't look exceedingly comfortable to him, but he wasn't going to be bothering her. She had closed her eyes and fallen asleep a few minutes ago. This trip was wearing on all of them. He wondered how Cane was holding up. He quickly perished the thought though. He realized he was an old pro at this. *Hell,* he thought, *the old man probably doesn't even sleep any more.* His mind turned to more grim explanations of Cane's sleeping patterns for a moment, but quickly returned to less lackadaisical thoughts.

She was beautiful, in every sense of the word. Dawn's body was long and slender, but not too much so. Bishop wasn't a big fan of the current "waif" trend in models. He thought it made them look like walking corpses. Something, in retrospect, he hoped he never truly encountered. That wasn't the extent of her beauty, though. She was also intelligent, and probably more so than many men she met, but not in the traditional sense of the word. She knew the paranormal, which Bishop found intoxicating. Most men would probably ask for the check as soon as she vaulted into stories of ghosts and goblins, but that was what he liked about her, far too much than he should. She was his co-worker, and so far, the only friend he had in the OPR. He quickly turned his attention back to the road. She had already shot him down once. He was sure he would get the same treatment again if the situation presented itself.

It was nice of the crew to let them borrow a car. After Bishop explained what had happened to the vehicle they had been driving, they were a little reluctant though. A smile flashed across Bishop's face. He reached over and tapped the power button on the stereo. Switching it over to the AM band, he began to scan for a news station. He hoped at least one of them had survived the storm. His hopes were met when a voice cut through the static.

"...Death toll still isn't in, and probably won't be available for several days, reports the National Guard. Residents are urged to seek shelter in their homes until Hurricane Katrina passes. We're not through it yet, ladies and gentlemen." The male broadcaster sounded frazzled. No doubt he had been at the station, and probably on the air, since the storm had been upgraded to a full-blown hurricane. *"Northern Florida has officially been declared a national disaster. The President is sending every man he can spare and has promised more federal aid to all counties affected. The National Weather Service expects Hurricane Katrina to begin dissipating in the early hours of November first as strong trade winds push the hurricane back out to sea. For more breaking news, keep your radios tuned to WH—"*

Bishop clicked off the radio. It was more than he wanted to hear. Glancing out through the windows, he could see the dark clouds moving in from the west.

It was just a matter of time before the outer edge of Katrina moved across Stone Brook. He checked his watch and cursed under his breath. That put it right about the time Ghost Chasers went live tonight.

***

"What the hell happened here?" Montoya shouted as she made her way through police

234

headquarters. Men were lifting themselves off the floor while rubbing their heads amidst a sea of destruction. Desks had been flipped over, filing cabinets were bent in half and half a coffee mug was embedded about six inches into one of the walls.

"She escaped," an officer moaned as he regained his balance. A large purple bruise was forming on his left cheek and a crusty drop of blood was hanging off his lower lip. "She tore the fucking place up."

Montoya looked around in awe. "Who did this?"

"The murder suspect," the officer said with a cough. "The LeFay woman." Montoya's eyes suddenly widened. "How could one woman do all this?"

She glanced to her right to see two more officers lifting themselves out from under a large metal desk. "It looks like Hurricane Katrina hit us."

The officer mustered a laugh. "I don't think that's too far from the truth."

"Has anyone checked the jail? Did any other prisoners escape?"

The officer shook his head. He was still too groggy from his encounter to be of any use, so Montoya quickly left him behind. Her long leather coat made an almost comforting swishing sound as she traversed the destroyed lobby. Reaching into her pocket, she removed a small beret and pinned her hair quickly to the top of her head. Sliding her hand beneath her coat, she wrapped her fingers around the cold metallic grip of her pistol. Stopping just in front of the access door, she peered into the hallway. Debris littered the floor while a thick cloud of dust hung in the air. It was a mess. Montoya could barely see the fluorescent lights on the ceiling through the cloud, but she could tell the hallway was empty. There were no dark forms moving about. She hoped to God none of the other prisoners had escaped. They didn't have the manpower to round them all back up, especially during this storm.

Taking a deep breath, she walked cautiously into what looked like a war zone. Bits of concrete crunched under her feet as she walked. The dust was getting into her eyes and making them water. She began to unconsciously blink to try and clear her vision. Scanning the floor, she could see parts of the cell bars bent and scattered about. She stopped and turned to her right. A small gasp escaped her lips.

The entire front of the third cell had been torn off. Montoya took a step closer to examine the wreckage. It looked like the hinges that held the bars in place had been ripped or blown out of the wall. The concrete around the door had shredded as the long anchor bolts ripped away. The light fixture above the cell had been torn from the roof, probably when the bars ejected. A live wire was hanging exposed from the wound in the roof spitting sparks toward the ground. She took a step back to avoid them. She had never seen anything like this before. It was almost unimaginable that one person could do this.

"Detective...."

A voice behind her caught her attention. Spinning around, she squeezed her weapon tightly in her sweaty hands. She glanced nervously around, but could find nothing. There was no one in the hall with her. She felt something graze her ankle. Jumping back, she glanced down into the pile of rubble that stood at the mouth of the cell. She quickly made out a hand reaching out of the heap.

"Jesus," she muttered under her breath. "Hold on, I'll get you out of there." Using all her strength, she began to push the rubble away with her hands.

Piece by piece, she became more frantic. She knew the man underneath was dying and his time was running out. Pushing hard, she slid a large section of the cell out of the way revealing the guard's upper body. He was a mess, but he was alive.

She reached down and grabbed his hand. She held it tightly for a long moment. "I'm going to get help."

"Don't leave me," he pleaded. "I'm cold."

"It's going to be all right, I promise." She squeezed his hand again. "I'll be right back. Hold on, okay?"

The guard nodded bravely and let go. Montoya's heart was pounding. She could see that far off look in the guard's eyes; that look a person got just before they died. Recklessly standing up, she skittered through the rubble as she made her way out of the hallway. Grabbing the nearest phone, she quickly dialed 911.

"911," the operator answered unemotionally.

"This is Detective Caroline Montoya. I need paramedics to Police Headquarters. We have an officer down!"

237

***

"Jesus Christ!" Chris yelled as he slammed the door shut behind him. "What the fuck was that?"

The group had exited into a small garden at the rear of the Grant House. A tall wooden fence with no visible gate ran the length of the area. Tall green bushes sat around various willow trees and hordes of colorful flowers littered the area. A small stone path wound its way through the center of the garden toward a small stone rest and water fountain. The area was in disarray. Trees had been blown over from last night's storm, and it appeared as if some kind of projectile had damaged the ceramic fountain. Pieces were scattered about the ground near the bench as a stream of water flowed from its cracked bowl.

The group quickly made their way toward the shattered fountain, as it was the furthest they could get from the house without actually climbing the fence. They were all still terrified, but slowly starting to come down from their adrenaline rush. Their hearts were beating wildly to try and satisfy their bodies' need for oxygen.

Cane dropped down onto the rest and laced his fingers behind his head. Looking up at the house, his fear began to slowly be replaced with his natural inquisitiveness. "Why didn't it attack?"

"Who cares?" Chris said between deep breaths. "All I know is I'm alive and I am not going to question that." He held up his hand next to his face. "See that?

It's a gift horse." He turned his head away from his hand. "Notice how I'm not looking it in the

238

mouth?"

"That's all very well," Cane said slowly, "but we need answers."

"Mr. Cane's right," Chloe spoke up. "These things are killing people."

"Thank you," Cane said as he rubbed his beard.

"Yeah?" Jackson said with disdain. "Well, I don't give a rat's ass. I am not going back into that house, and as soon as I get out of this fucking garden, I'm getting back on the first plane to Los Angeles."

"We can't quit," Trent interjected.

"Oh no?" Jackson said with a smirk on his face. "Watch me." Trent stepped up to Jackson. "Quitter," he growled.

Jackson brushed a piece of his blonde hair out of his eyes. "I don't think I like your attitude." He pushed Trent away from him and took a step back.

Trent immediately rushed forward and pushed Jackson back. Jackson reacted quickly by throwing a quick jab into Trent's nose. Fighting off the pain, Trent wiped off a trickle of blood and prepared his retaliation.

Chloe intervened. "Stop it!"

"Bickering won't get us anywhere," Cane admonished. "We need to keep our heads about us."

"I didn't sign up to fucking die down here. I don't know about the rest of you, but I don't think this is covered by hazard pay." He took another step away from the group. "We almost died in there!"

"We didn't though," Cane reminded him.

"Next time, we might not be so lucky," Jackson added.

"Look," Chloe said impatiently, "we're here to

do a job. Like it or not, we go live in less than twelve hours." She crossed her arms—a standard defensive posture for her—and looked angrily at the group. "If any of you want to walk, be my guest, but don't expect to be welcomed back in L.A. with open arms. If you go, you're fired." She let her words sink in. "Any takers?"

Jackson was scared, but he wasn't stupid. For the most part, this was a good, steady job. In the film industry, those weren't always easy to find. He looked over at Trent and Chris. They were standing firmly behind Chloe. He swallowed hard. "I'm staying."

Chloe's face softened, "Good."

"I want my objections noted," he added quickly.

Chloe nodded. "Noted. Now can we get back to work?"

"What's the plan?" Chris asked.

Chloe thought for a moment. "We need to see how much of our equipment we can salvage from inside. If we have any footage of the activity that's usable, we have to get it. Then we need to find Rivers."

"Where did he run off to?" Cane asked.

Chloe shook her head. "I don't know. He was pretty pissed off when he stomped out of here earlier. My first guess would be to check all the bars in the area. He has a propensity to drown his feelings in alcohol." She looked over her team. "Jackson, why don't you go look for Rivers? Trent and I will try and salvage our equipment. Cane, you and Chris can tell Carrie what happened, and then I think you should round up the rest of your team."

Chapter 21

Bishop leaned over and nudged Dawn. Her eyes shot wide open as she sat up in the seat. They had arrived at the Stone Brook Police Department only moments ago, but were stopped by several officers. The area was littered with police cars and ambulances, their red and blue lights glancing menacingly off the sides of the surrounding buildings. Several men and women were being carried out of the station on stretchers, while others were limping clear under their own power. Something about this scene seemed horribly familiar to both.

"What the hell happened here?" Dawn asked. Bishop shrugged, "It looks like a damn war zone."

The two slowly stepped out of the car and began to walk toward the station. They easily avoided the officers on the perimeter, as they were too busy holding out members of the local media. Weaving through the maze of police cruisers, the two stopped in front of a large white ambulance. They watched as one of the officers was wheeled out of the building and into the back of the vehicle. His head looked like a sack of doorknobs, and his arm was clearly broken. He was mumbling something almost incoherently to the technicians. Bishop pressed close to the ambulance and cupped his ear. The officer mumbled again. Bishop drew back from the emergency vehicle and shot a strange glance at Dawn.

"What did he say?" Dawn asked.

Bishop shook his head. "I probably didn't hear him correctly and from his condition, I would say he's probably in shock and incoherent, but—"

"What did he say?" Dawn pressed.

"He said she floated," Bishop said with a worried look on his face. "Who floated?" Dawn wondered.

"I don't know, but I plan to find out." He started to push his way through a crowd of officers toward the entrance. Reaching back, he grabbed Dawn by the hand and led her through. Before anyone knew it, the two were up the stairs and through the front doors.

Bishop and Dawn skidded to a halt just inside the door. "Christ," Bishop said in awe.

"Maybe you were right," Dawn said as she looked at the devastation in front of her. "It looks like there was a war in here."

Bishop suddenly spotted a familiar black coat among the EMTs and work crews. "Detective Montoya!"

Montoya spun around and began to scan the lobby for the source of her page. Her eyes finally settled on Bishop and Dawn standing just inside the entrance. She returned her attention to the officer in front of her. "Get that done, okay?"

The younger officer nodded, then went about completing Montoya's orders.

Montoya worked her way across to Dawn and Bishop. "What can I do for you two?"

"What happened here?" Dawn immediately asked.

"One of our prisoners escaped and tore up the place," Montoya said with shame in her voice.

"One prisoner?" Dawn echoed in awe. "One person did all this?"

"Who was it?" Bishop probed.

"I'm really not at liberty to say," Montoya said loudly as she glanced around. Bishop instantly realized she was trying to cover her tracks. "Come with me," she instructed them quietly.

The three moved through the destruction toward a connecting hallway in the rear of the room. Montoya took a quick left at the end of the hall and stopped in front of the first door on the right. Reaching down, she twisted the handle and pushed the door open. "This is Detective Enbaugh's office," she said as she moved inside. "I don't think he would mind if we used it."

"How is the detective?" Bishop wondered.

"He's going to be okay," Montoya assured them. "He suffered some pretty bad injuries from the accident, but the doctors are sure he'll make a full recovery." Her expression darkened. "He saw them again."

"The phantoms?" Bishop asked.

Montoya nodded. "He thinks they tortured him and," she took a deep breath, "that we can't stop them."

"Did he say if he found out anything else about them?" Dawn wondered. "Only that they are pure evil," Montoya said gravely. She walked around Enbaugh's desk and slipped into his chair. She let out a long sigh, then propped her elbows on his desk. She motioned for Bishop and Dawn to sit down.

"Tell us what happened here," Dawn asked after a moment.

"I'm not really sure," Montoya confessed. "From what fragments I can piece together, this was all done by one woman."

"I knew it," Bishop said with a crooked smile. "Women are evil!"

Dawn reached over and smacked him on the back of his head. "Now is not the time," she warned him. "I'm sorry, Detective, please continue."

"The girl we picked up this morning at the hotel, Morgan LeFay, she escaped and did this. I'm getting a lot of conflicting reports from eyewitnesses, but they all say she did this by herself."

"And that she floated," Bishop added. Montoya nodded. "I've heard that myself."

"How did she get out of her cell?" Dawn queried. Montoya paused. "She blew the door off."

"What?" Bishop exclaimed. "She literally blew off the cell door?"

"Plus most of the wall around it," Montoya admitted. "We don't know how. Forensics has been in there ever since it happened, and they can't find any trace of any kind of explosives used."

"Jesus," Bishop said after a moment, "who is this lady? Wonder Woman?"

"I put out an APB on her. I consider her extremely dangerous." Montoya shifted uneasily in her chair. "We have to find her. Several of our best officers are fighting for their lives right now because of her."

"But no one's dead?" Dawn asked.

"No," Montoya said, "but I don't see what that has to do with anything. She probably just didn't have the opportunity to kill anyone."

"With that kind of power?" Bishop said, understanding where Dawn was heading with her line of questions. "How could she not have killed anyone?"

"It looks like a bomb went off out there," Dawn continued; "yet all the officers are alive. She blew off her cell door, for God's sake. I don't think it would've been a problem to kill all the officers out there."

"She didn't though," Bishop added. "She just roughed a few of them up to escape. I don't think she really wanted to hurt anyone."

Montoya slammed her fist on Enbaugh's desk. "We can sit here and speculate on her motives all day, but the fact of the matter is that she escaped from police custody, resisted arrest and almost killed several of my men. That means she's a fugitive, and a dangerous one at that."

Bishop held up his hands in a surrendering gesture. "Whoa, hold up, Detective. We were just advancing a theory. We didn't mean to imply she was any less guilty of her crimes."

Montoya slowly unclenched her fist and relaxed. "I'm sorry, with all that's happened in the past few days, I guess I'm burning on a short fuse."

Dawn nodded. "That's completely understandable."

Slipping back into Enbaugh's high-backed chair, Montoya looked over the two figures in front of her. "What do we do now?"

"I think we only have one course of action," Bishop conceded. Dawn waited for a moment, "And that is?"

"We need to stop these shadows." Bishop stood and walked around the desk toward Montoya. "It's obvious now that these things, whatever they happen to be, are at the root of all this. It seems, at least to me, that Morgan was a nice, normal girl before she arrived here in Stone Brook. Something's changed her."

"You're speculating," Montoya pointed out. "You have no idea who Morgan LeFay was, or is," she quickly corrected him. "She may have been a nut from the get-go."

"I can't subscribe to that theory," Bishop argued. "From what I've learned from the *Ghost Chasers, Inc.* crew, she was a nice, normal girl when they first met her."

"They all say that, Bishop. Have you ever seen a reporter interview the neighbor of a serial killer?" Dawn's expression went blank. "He was the nicest guy," she started in a stilted, monotone voice, "always very quiet. Even helped me build my doghouse. They don't say 'I was in fear for my life every minute'!"

Her tone quickly changed. "I was just waiting for the day that whacko would come blazing through my door with a chainsaw!" She smiled. "See where I'm going with this?"

"Yeah, that's all fine and great," Bishop said, dismissing her poor attempt at humor, "but that's just a stereotypical view of a killer. That doesn't help us at all."

"So what *are* we talking about here?" Montoya asked, hoping this conversation would come to a conclusion.

"Spirit possession," Bishop said firmly.

Dawn laughed out loud, "You aren't serious?"

"Haven't you guys ever seen 'Exorcist'?"

Montoya shook her head. "I can't believe I'm

listening to this." She looked Bishop in the eyes. "I don't think I saw Morgan's head spinning around, or her vomiting pea soup on everyone."

"That's not exactly what I'm talking about," Bishop argued. He was digging a hole. "I—"

"Let it go, kid," Dawn finally said. "There are supernatural answers here, but that isn't one of them." She leaned back in her chair and briefly collected her thoughts. "What I think we need to do here is let Detective Montoya do her job. She needs to get a dangerous element off the street before it hurts someone." She bit her lip for a moment, then stopped, realizing what she was doing. "Bishop and I will head down to the country clerk's office and see if we can dig up anything on the Grant House. Maybe it has some kind of paranormal history." Montoya nodded. "If you need anything from me, you have my number." Dawn nodded.

"I'll check back with you in about an hour to see what you've got," Montoya said as she stood up. She pushed past Bishop and headed for the door.

Once she was gone, Bishop slid into her vacant chair. "You didn't really think I was talking about her head spinning around, did you?"

Dawn shook her head. "Shut up, Bishop."

***

Morgan stopped. *I can't let them find me. I have to stop them.*

She ducked into an alley just as a black and white cruised by. Getting as far back as she could, she finally allowed herself to rest. She pressed her body against the cool brick wall in front of her. The cold felt good against her hot flesh. She had been ducking in and out of alleys and buildings ever since she'd escaped the police station. She wouldn't stop, but now, she needed to. Her body cried out for rest as her heart thumped wildly in her chest. She slowed her breathing. She was now taking long, deep breaths instead of the short, shallow ones that were hyperventilating her. She looked up to see a small stream of water running off a drainage pipe. Stepping under it, she let the cool rainwater run over her face and down onto her body. She needed to focus. There was a task at hand.

What the hell am I doing? She asked herself out of the blue. *Why am I running from the police? I'm only making my situation worse—because you have to.*

Her mind wandered back to earlier when she was incarcerated. *Where did that power come from?* She had never displayed that kind of power before, nor had she ever wanted to. She considered herself a good person. Her heart was true and just, but what she did today bordered on....

She didn't want to admit it.

Evil.

She had conducted a spell or two in her life. A Glamour, or a cleansing spell, but nothing like this. She didn't even know she was capable of those kinds of feats. Her world was spinning around her now. Her life had changed in ways that even she had yet to comprehend, and it was still evolving. She wondered if she would recognize herself in a mirror now. How had she gone from working with her hero on a television show one minute, to being accused of his murder the next? How did these two points connect? Where was the strand of logic that bound them?

It was almost *too* much. That fact alone was strange. It *should* be too much. She knew herself very well, as self-exploration was a favorite pastime of hers, but this wasn't right. She didn't have the constitution for this. She hated to say it, but the Morgan she knew would have crumbled by now. How was she holding on? What force was driving her on, and why?

Letting the water run over her head and through her black hair, Morgan leaned forward and let it spill onto the back of her neck. She gasped once as a shiver ran down her spine. Stepping away from the stream, she ran her hands over her hair to wring out some of the wetness, then back over her face. She didn't know why or how, but she had a moment of clarity. A single instant where it seemed like everything in the universe made sense.

I am not Morgan LeFay.

She shook her head. The clarity had unfortunately, past. *What did that mean*? *I am Morgan LeFay and have been all my life.* She was too confused, and her head was throbbing.

She raised her face to the sky and looked at the dark gray clouds gathering. The storm would return soon, and with it, the shadows would be free to roam. How she knew that, she wasn't sure, but she didn't doubt it. She and the storm were the keys to this, but why?

***

The neighborhood was quiet. Most of the

windows and doors had been boarded up because of the storm. Jackson wondered if the people of this town kept a supply of plywood and nails at the ready at all times. A person would make a killing in the lumber industry here. Of course, that would be benefiting from someone else's loss, but that idea really didn't seem to bother him. Looking up, he could see the dark clouds overhead, and then he felt the first raindrop. He buttoned up his jacket and began to walk a little more briskly toward his destination. He didn't want to be caught in the storm, but then again, was that as bad as the other option he was facing?

Jackson stopped dead in his tracks. Chloe had told him to go and find Rivers, then bring him back. He didn't want to go back to that house. He knew what lived there. He had seen them with his own eyes. He looked down at his watch and winced. It was less than seven hours from the live broadcast. Their host was missing, the crew was almost killed earlier and the psychic they had hired had been murdered. They were batting a thousand.

He looked around. He didn't even know where he was. How was he supposed to find a man in a city he wasn't familiar with? Chloe had just told him to check all the bars, but that didn't do him a lot of good. He had no idea how many bars this town had, let alone where they were.

He felt another raindrop hit his forehead. He held out his hand, palm up, waiting for the next drop to fall. He could see them all around him, small, dark spots on the sidewalk and road. It was spitting. Not quite raining, but almost. Jackson hated Florida. That much he was sure of. Why couldn't he be on some comfy sound stage back in California? Jackson slowly began to walk again. His only way out of here, he knew, was to find Rivers and get back to the Grant House. Then that was it. He was quitting right after that. There was no way anyone on that crew was dragging him back into that house. He would rather be struck by lightning than go back inside.

He looked up at the sky with a wry smile on his face. "Just kidding about the lightning remark."

He wasn't an overly religious man, but he knew better than to tempt fate so openly like that. All you were doing was sticking your neck down on the chopping block.

Rounding a corner, he spotted a bar nestled between two squat buildings just past the residential section. The sign out front was lit, so he assumed they were open. The bar was built much like a sea shanty, but Jackson knew it was probably much studier. A fisherman's net and anchor were hanging on the front of the bar just next to the front door and one small window. He glanced up at the sign. "'The Wharf'," he said out loud.

Pushing the door to the tiny bar open, his senses were immediately assaulted by the smoke and the smell. The instantly recognizable odors of vomit and urine burned his nose as he walked in. This was a high quality establishment all right. The door slammed shut behind him as he moved further inside. It took a moment for his eyes to adjust to the low light levels, but quickly, the dingy interior appeared out of the blackness. It was much as he expected. Two round tables sat in the middle of the floor and a short bar ran along the back wall. Two

251

small lights hung from the ceiling above the tables, sending two conical shafts of brightness to the floor. Jackson could see one man passed out in the corner, his clothes tattered, and probably the source of some of the smells. Three more men were gathered around one of the tables drinking mugs of beer and exchanging old stories, while still two other man sat at the bar. Jackson slowly made his way through the smoke. He spotted the bartender sitting near the rear searching through the local want ads.

"Excuse me, barkeep?" Jackson asked as he slid onto an empty stool.

The scruffy man slowly lowered his newspaper and looked at Jackson. No doubt, his mind was assessing if it was worth it to get out of his seat or not. After a minute, he finally stood up and walked toward Jackson. "What?"

Jackson was a little taken aback by the bartender's tone, but he quickly recomposed himself. "Just have a quick question for you."

"Piss off, kid. If you ain't drinkin', then I don't give a shit." The man started to turn around and return to his seat.

"Wait," Jackson said. He dug his hand into his pocket and produced a small wad of bills. Flipping off two fives, he laid them on the bar. "I'll have a draft." The bartender nodded. After selecting what was probably his cleanest mug, he filled it to the brim with the golden liquid. Setting it on the bar in front of Jackson, he snatched the money and turned toward the cash register. He eventually returned with what he considered was the correct change.

Jackson didn't question. At this point, he really didn't care. "Can I ask you a question now?"

The bartender shot Jackson an angry glance. "Can't you see I'm busy? Drink your beer and shut up."

Jackson let out a quick sigh. "Seven bucks for a mug of beer," he muttered to himself. He lifted the glass to his lips and took a quick sip of the fluid inside but quickly stopped as it hit his taste buds. Dropping the mug back to the bar, Jackson leaned over and spit the nauseating liquid onto the floor. "Jesus!" He wiped his arm across his mouth. "It tastes like warm piss!"

The bartender, in spite of himself, started to laugh out loud. "Best beer in Florida, kid."

Jackson pushed the mug away and stood up. As he turned from the bar, he just happened to glance down at the man curled up in the corner. At first, it didn't register, but he quickly did a double take. "Rivers?" He knelt down next to Rivers and looked him over. He had passed out in a pool of his own vomit. Jackson quickly filed the information away in his blackmail folder then proceeded to try and wake him. He shook his shoulder. "Rivers?" he asked again, this time a little more firmly. "Rivers!" he finally shouted.

"Damn." Fishing his cell phone out of his pocket, Jackson hit his speed dial. He listened impatiently as the phone rang. "Come on, pick up all ready."

"This is Chloe."

"It's Jackson. I found Rivers."

"I needed some good news," she said excitedly amidst the crackle and hiss of the cellular connection. "Where are you guys?"

"In a bar about a mile from the Grant House,"

Jackson responded. "You're going to have to send a car."

"Why?"

"Rivers is passed out, and it looks like he chummed on himself a couple of times." He wasn't sure why, but Jackson was getting a real delight out of telling Chloe this.

Chloe let out an audible sigh. "All right, I'll send the car. Just stay put."

Chapter 22

The storm had returned. The brief pause, which was the eye of the hurricane, had past. The wall of wind and weather tore through Stone Brook, destroying any attempts the citizens had made that day to repair or protect their belongings. Some of the older residents likened it to the bomb scares in the '50's. At the drop of a hat, they were to abandon whatever they were doing and seek shelter, as if that would actually help. The only thing missing now were the sirens, and the old-timers really didn't miss them.

Palm trees that had bent in submission against the winds the night before were now being completely uprooted and hurled from their resting places. The pelting rain pounded buildings and howling winds whipped around the streets. It was almost as if it wasn't enough. The storm had gotten a taste for blood and apparently liked it. Of course, that's vilifying an act of nature as if it had a conscience or emotions. That was giving it too much credit. It was a mindless machine of destruction. It had no other purpose. It would swoop in from the ocean on the warm trade winds, annihilate whatever it touched, then whisk away like a ghost in the night, never to be heard from again.

It wasn't fair. People spend their whole lives saving and building up their dreams. They scrape every penny and dime together in a meager savings account just so they could pay the bills that month and work toward their future. Slowly, their dreams become reality. They feel fulfilled. They can finally sit back, relax, and enjoy the things they never could.

Then *it* comes.

With one fell swoop, it wipes a lifetime of work away. No thought of what it's doing to the people. It's just business as usual for the hurricane. It really isn't fair.

Cane shook his head. He was letting his mind wander. He was perched inside the small white satellite van outside the Grant House. It was almost empty, except for a few consoles and a ragged baseball cap that had long since been forgotten. He looked out the sliding door at the weather. It was dark on the horizon, almost black. *A portent of things to come?* He ran his fingers up to his goatee and began to work them through the hairs. He found he often did this when he was overly worried about something, and right now, he was really worried.

He had no answers. To his, or the company's, knowledge, something like this had never happened before. Never had they recorded or heard of an instance where spirits, or beings, terrorized an entire town. This was completely unprecedented. It was almost if the very gates of hell had been opened....

Paranormal phenomenon, in his experience, was often generalized to one location. The sites of old, unmarked cemeteries were often the home of restless spirits, as were sacred places. Sometimes, if a person died violently, or by their own hand in a place, they appeared to be doomed to roam the halls of where they died. That was punishment, Cane was sure. The spirit was exiled from heaven, never to know rest. *That's probably why they're so angry*, Cane joked.

Stepping out of the van, Cane ducked into the garage to escape the storm. He had been helping move equipment from the van to the garage most of the afternoon. The crew had decided it would be easier, and safer, if they were inside. They really didn't want to be sitting in a tiny, cramped van while the storm raged.

"We still need to get the cameras out of the house," Carrie announced. She was sitting in the rear of the garage, slowly smoking a cigarette. Dropping the butt to the ground, she crushed it with her foot. "Any volunteers?"

The crew was silent.

Carrie looked angry. This shoot was turning out to be the biggest disaster of her career. "Look," she said after a moment, "if no one volunteers, I'm just going to choose someone to go."

There were still no takers.

"Fine," Carrie said with a grunt. She scanned over the crew before her, finally allowing her eyes to settle on one man. "Trent," she hissed, "since you're the camera man, you go get the equipment."

Trent swallowed hard. He had almost been hiding behind a stack of equipment, hoping not to get picked. He looked at Carrie, his eyes pleading with her not to make him go. After a moment, the stark reality of the situation set in. He had no choice.

"I'll go."

The entire crew spun around to see Cane raising his hand. An audible wave of relief passed over the crew. Someone else was going to do it.

"Mr. Cane," Carrie addressed, "are you that anxious to get back into the house?"

257

"No," Cane admitted, "but I don't think we should be sending one of them," he said, pointing to the crew. "I am a trained professional and capable of handling a situation like this." He almost believed himself. "It's only right that I go."

"Wow," Carrie drew the word out sarcastically. "I didn't know I was asking for the five dollar speech. I was just curious." She looked over Cane with a smile, then motioned to the door much like a stewardess would as she pointed out the exits on an airplane. "Be my guest."

Winding his way through the stacks of equipment, Cane eventually found his way to the door that connected the garage to the house. Pausing, he finally reached down and wrapped his hand around the knob. He hadn't been back in the house since earlier in the day. None of them had. He was actually surprised they wanted to set up in the garage, as it was technically part of the house. Looking behind him, he noticed the entire crew had stopped what they were doing and had turned their complete attention to him. It was a bit unnerving.

He took a deep breath and opened the door. A rush of warm air came out of the house. It was in stark comparison to the cool, damp air of the garage. Taking a step inside, Cane slowly looked around. He was standing inside a small hallway. Peering down to the end, he could see that it led into the dining room. It was no more than five feet wide. It felt like it was an afterthought. Something squeezed into the house by the architect after the owners asked for revisions. He ran his fingers along the plain, white walls. He expected, that at any moment, a creature was going to burst through the wall and devour him. This house rattled him. Something he hadn't felt since his very first investigation all those years ago. It was crawling under his skin.

Thud.

Cane jerked his head up toward the ceiling. That sound had definitely come from the second floor. He slowly turned around and surveyed the faces of the crew. From their pale expressions, he knew they had heard it as well. He quickly returned his attention to the end of the hallway.

Thud...thud.

His instincts were screaming at him to run, but he didn't. He held his position. He listened again for the muffled thump from the second floor. He began to wonder what it could be. The image of a dead body being tossed on the floor suddenly came to mind. *Focus! Have to stay sharp,* he scolded himself. He took a step forward. Then another. He wasn't sure if he was consciously moving, or just willing himself forward. His hands braced firmly against the walls, he slowly arrived at the mouth of the hall.

The dining room and living room were quiet. Bits of gear still littered the floor and the acrid smell of burnt electrical equipment filled his nose. It was probably from his fried EMF Meter. At least he hoped so. His goals were the two cameras. He needed to know if any of the footage had survived. One had been completely knocked over, but the other was still standing.

Mustering all his courage, he let go of the hallway walls and moved into the living room. He visually scanned the area, looking for any trace of

259

something out of the ordinary. A drop of sweat ran down his forehead. He felt it run into his eyebrow, then drip off. He hadn't realized he had broken out in a cold sweat. *Dear God,* he said shamefully. *I'm terrified.*

Thud.

Flipping around, Cane dashed across the living room and pressed his back against the wall. At least that way, he would be able to see what was coming...he hoped. His heart was racing. Glancing up at the ceiling, he tried to glean some kind of information out of it as to what was causing the noises, but he knew it was futile. His mind was just racing out of fear. Suddenly, an odd sensation passed over him. It was a cold chill that ran down his back, but it was strange. It was external. Cane slowly pulled himself away from the wall and turned around. To his horror, a viscous red fluid was bleeding from the top of it. It was oozing down toward the floor, where it was starting to pool on the carpet. Cane reached around and ran his hand over the back of his jacket, only to find the fluid on it.

Ripping off his leather jacket, he tossed it on the floor and stepped away. He didn't know what the red liquid was, but he knew he didn't want it on him. He noticed a small wisp of smoke flitting up from his coat. Kneeling down next to it, he was astonished to see the fluid eating through the leather like an acid. Cane stood up and glanced around. The wall was bleeding faster now. The pool was slowly approaching his position.

Thud.

That was all Cane could take. Spinning around, he started to make his way toward the hall, but stopped. The entrance was gone. There was no sign of the hallway he had entered through. In a panic, Cane ran his hands over the wall in front of him.

"This is where it was," he assured himself. "I know it."

Pounding on the wall in frustration, Cane heard a crack. Looking closely, he could see a small break where he had hit it. Finding a spark of hope, he reared back and threw his full weight into his fist. It connected solidly with the wall, and it gave under the stress. Cane peered in, only to find another wall behind it. He cursed under his breath. He wasn't losing it, he kept telling himself. This was some kind of trick.

He turned and looked back into the living room. The red fluid had engulfed most of the floor and was working its way over the furniture. Cane was transfixed for a moment. He had never seen a liquid run up before. He watched for several seconds as the red fluid charged up the side of one of the leather couches. It slowly began to disintegrate before his eyes.

Thud.

"What the hell is that?" he shouted to no one.

Snapping his head to his left, he remembered the kitchen entrance in the dining room. To Cane's surprise, the door was partially open. Moving quickly around the dining table, he pushed it open. The kitchen seemed normal except for...he wasn't sure. Something seemed a bit off, but he couldn't place it. He ran his eyes over the counters, then to the stove and refrigerator. Everything seemed to be in place. His eyes wandered down to the black floor. There was no glare on the surface. That's probably

261

because there's no sunlight hitting it, Cane reasoned. All in all, it seemed normal.

Cane took a step forward...and connected with nothing. No floor. Nothing. He tried to catch himself on the doorframe, but he missed. He tumbled into the blackness that was the kitchen's floor. Flailing his arms wildly, he somehow snagged the edge of the island with his fingertips. Reaching his other hand up, he tried to get a better grip on the lip. He looked across the kitchen. He was hanging below where the floor would have been. It seemed very surreal to him. The island and the counters seemed to be floating in mid-air. There was nothing supporting them from below, only more darkness.

His mind tried to reason through the strangeness, but logic was failing him. He tried to focus, tried to bring out the scientist to examine the subject, but there was no sense to be made. He looked down again. There were no walls, no visible end, nothing. Just darkness. His mind began to put together a working theory.

He looked at his hand, the same one he touched the fluid with on the back of his jacket, there was nothing on it. No burns, and no red fluid. "If that substance can melt furniture and eat through leather, it surely would've gone through my hand like it was nothing." He was losing his grip. His fingers slowly began to slip off the lip of the island, but he held fast. "The hallway," he said to himself as he tried not to panic. "I came in through a hallway, but then it was gone...." A wry smile suddenly crossed his face. "I understand now."

He let go.

***

Enbaugh carefully poked his head out of his room. He felt like hell, but there was someone he wanted to meet. He had overheard the doctors talking about her earlier, and it had piqued his curiosity. Someone else had survived. That, in his opinion, was a miraculous thing. The hallway was clear, and the night nurse was away from her station. Enbaugh walked slowly out his door, IV in tow, his feet pattering against the cold floor.

He slowly ran his hand over his sore neck. The muscle relaxer the nurse had given him earlier had relieved some of the pain. At least he was able to turn his head more than an inch now. That was a relief. With every step he took, the pain worsened. He could feel every stitch in his body acutely as if they were tugging at his very flesh. This was important, though. He needed to speak with this woman, if only to reclaim his sanity.

He paused at the end of the corridor. He knew she was on this floor, but wasn't sure what room she was in. Enbaugh just knew her name was Kelley and she had survived. That was enough for him. He slowly turned the corner after making sure it was free of doctors and nurses. He knew he would have to call on his detective skills to find this woman. It wasn't going to be easy—

He stopped. Looking to his left, he peered into a darkened room. Glancing up at the chart hanging on the wall, he quickly read the name. Amazingly, it was her room. *Or,* he thought, *I could just rely on dumb luck.*

263

Taking a step into the room, he quickly pulled back. Maybe this woman wasn't ready for visitors, he reasoned. *She's been through a traumatic experience.* Enbaugh pondered his course of action for a moment. *Maybe I should knock.* Reaching up, he tapped his knuckles on the open wooden door.

"You can come in," came a voice from the darkness. "I mean you're halfway there already."

"I'm sorry," croaked Enbaugh, "I didn't mean to disturb you."

"It's okay. I think I could use some company right now. I don't really want to be alone."

Walking into the room, Enbaugh reached for the light switch. "I prefer it dark," Kelley warned him.

He pulled his hand away from the switch. "Sorry." Moving around her bed, Enbaugh slowly sank down into a small plastic chair. His body groaned in protest as he moved in ways he hadn't for days. He reached out a hand toward Kelley. "My name's Jack."

Kelley was sitting Indian style in the center of her bed. She had the covers partially pulled over one knee and two pillows propped up behind her back. Her blonde hair was partially matted to her head from sleep, and she didn't care. The light blue hospital gown was hanging lazily off her left shoulder, exposing the edges of several cuts on her chest. "Mine's Kelley." She slowly reached out and shook his hand.

"Are you okay?" Enbaugh asked carefully. Kelley shook her head. "No. You?"

Enbaugh smiled. "I've been better." He wasn't sure if he should just jump straight into his

264

questions, or try and gain her trust with small talk. He scolded himself, *again with the detective shtick. This is not a criminal you're interrogating,* he reminded himself. *This is a scared young woman who just needs a friend at the moment.* "Have you tried the food here yet? Horrible."

Kelley smiled. "That lovely piece of meatloaf we had today looked more like cardboard than meat."

"So what do you do for a living, Kelley?"

"I work here," she replied calmly. "I'm a nurse at this hospital."

"Is it strange being on the other side of the stethoscope?" Enbaugh wondered.

"A bit," Kelley admitted. "I understand a little more what the patients are going through." She looked over the wounded man in front of her. His injuries were as extensive as hers. "What happened?"

"What do you mean?"

Kelley pointed at the bandage around his throat. "How did you end up here?"

"I was in a car accident during the hurricane."

"How did it happen?"

"It was just a mess," Enbaugh admitted. "The storm was really bad and I wasn't paying as much attention to the road as I should have been."

"I'm sorry," Kelley said sympathetically. "I hate to see bad things happen to good people."

Enbaugh wasn't sure if she was talking about his accident, or reflecting on her situation. "How do you know I'm a good person?"

Kelley smiled softly. "I can just tell."

Enbaugh let that one slide. He had seen enough voodoo creepy shit these last few days to last him another lifetime. He really didn't want to find out this girl was a witch or something. He didn't think he could handle it. "So, what happened to you?"

Kelley paused.

Enbaugh pulled back. He realized he had pressed the panic button. "I shouldn't ask. I'm sorry."

"No," Kelley retorted after a moment, "It's okay. It's fair. I asked you what happened, so you have the right to ask me."

"If you don't want to talk about it, I will understand. It's no big deal."

"I need to deal," she admitted, "and the best way to do that is to talk about it."

"With an experienced grief counselor," Enbaugh added. "We don't have to talk about anything that will make you uncomfortable."

"I was brutally tortured and made to watch while my girlfriend was killed." Enbaugh forgot to take a breath. The sheer rawness of her statement had both startled him and sent shivers down his spine. "Dear God."

Kelley shook her head. "It's okay, I think I'm in denial right now. I keep expecting her to walk through that door bringing me flowers or balloons and a big card that says, 'get well soon'. I realize she's dead," Kelley admitted, "but my brain, or rather my heart, won't accept that." She adjusted uncomfortably in bed.

She had been in the same position for most of the day and her feet and ankles had fallen asleep.

"Who did this to you?" Enbaugh asked

266

tentatively.

The eyes.

Kelley gasped. She had been trying not to think about them, but now the memories came flooding back. "I don't know what they were," she said with a slight tremor in her voice. "This is going to sound crazy, but I know they weren't human." She reached around and grabbed a pillow. Holding it tightly in her arms, she buried her face in it for a moment. "I heard the police talking about me yesterday after they took my statement. They think I did it," Kelley said frantically. She looked up at Enbaugh. "They think I just snapped and killed my girlfriend. They want to give me a complete psych evaluation to make sure I'm not crazy."

"Did you do it?" Enbaugh said with a level voice. Kelley looked him straight in the eye. "No." Enbaugh nodded. "I believe you."

"Thank you. I think you're only the second person who does."

"Who was the first?"

"Nick Bishop."

Enbaugh smiled. "I was working with him before my accident. He's a nice guy." He let the smile quickly fade from his face. There were more important matters at stake. "We're not insane."

Kelley's eyes widened. "You?"

Enbaugh nodded. "I've seen them too." He pulled down the neck of his gown to reveal the scratches on his chest. "They did this to me."

Kelley stared in awe at the wounds. "Did you see the eyes? Those awful red eyes?"

Enbaugh nodded. "That's one of the last things I remember before I lost consciousness after my

267

accident. Those eyes moving toward me."

"What are they, Jack?"

"I don't have any idea," Enbaugh admitted with a huff, "but I think we've got the right people working on it."

"Bishop will find out," Kelley agreed. "Are you going to be all right?"

Kelley nodded. "Eventually. It's going to take time, but I'll be okay."

"You're very brave," Enbaugh said with a smile.

"Thank you." She sat up and arched her back to stretch. "By the way, you never told me what you do."

"I'm a cop."

"Oh," Kelley said quietly. "They sent you into question me, didn't they?"

"No, I—"

She was quickly becoming agitated. "You do think I killed her! You think I went fucking insane and hacked my girlfriend to pieces. Then I just started carving on myself to create an alibi!"

"Just calm down, Kelley," Enbaugh said as he stood. "You're slime." She looked at Enbaugh angrily. "Get out."

"Now wait just a damned minute," Enbaugh shot back. "Let me explain."

"Get lo—"

"Shut up," Enbaugh said forcefully, hurting his throat. He had to stop for a minute to hold back the wave of coughing about to erupt from his chest. He leaned over and rested a hand on the bed. "I overheard the doctors talking about you this morning. I didn't come here to question you, but I did come for answers." He straightened up and took a slow, deep breath. "I needed to know that I wasn't losing my mind. It seems like I was the only person that kept seeing these damned things and living. Everyone else who saw one is now dead. You were my best shot at an answer. You saw one and survived!"

Kelley's rage vanished after realizing he had also helped her. "I'm sorry. I'm just a little on edge right now."

"It's okay," Enbaugh said quietly. "You're allowed."

"Thanks, Officer Jack," she said with a smile. "That's Detective Jack to you, missy."

She patted Enbaugh on the shoulder. "My mistake." Turning, Enbaugh started toward the door.

"Would you like to stay?" Kelley asked quickly. "We could just talk."

"Maybe tomorrow," Enbaugh offered. "Right now, I need to get back to bed. I think my painkillers are starting to wear off, and if the nurse finds me out of bed, she's going to have a tizzy."

"How do you think this is going to turn out?" Kelley asked finally. Enbaugh shook his head. "I wish I knew."

Chapter 23

They were each taking turns hitting the door with their shoulder. Each man took a full running start and focused all their energy on what looked to be fragile. At one point, they had even used a hammer they found in the garage to knock off the knob in hopes they could gain access into the house. After numerous tries, Trent and Chris finally forced their way inside. The wooden doorjamb shattered as the knob ripped through it. The two of them went skittering to the floor as all their weight was on the door when it finally gave. Like frightened kittens, the two leapt to their feet and glanced around nervously. Everything seemed quiet. Cane had been inside for well over half an hour now, and they were starting to get worried.

"That was weird," Trent said as he dusted himself off. "It was like something was holding the door closed—"

"And then just let go," Chris finished.

Trent nodded. "Maybe that something doesn't want us in here."

"Well it's a little late now," Chris said, looking down the hall into the house. "We're already here, and the door's...." Chris stopped. "Turn around slowly," he instructed Trent.

Trent carefully spun on his heels. His mouth fell agape. "What the hell?" The door was closed.

Trent reached over and grabbed the handle. It shook loosely in his hand, but wouldn't turn. Suddenly, it hit him. "There shouldn't be a handle here. We took it off." He let go and took a step back.

"Look at the frame."

Trent quickly scanned it. "It's completely intact."

"We broke it when we came in," Chris assured. "I saw the pieces of wood on the floor." He looked down and slowly muttered his favorite swear word. "The wood is gone," he said without any surprise. "This house is fucked up."

"I knew we shouldn't have let Mr. Cane come in here by himself," Trent said in a scolding tone.

"I didn't see you raising your hand when Carrie asked for volunteers. Besides, he was acting all 'I'm British and I know everything about ghosts'."

"He was not. He was saving our ass."

"She-it," Chris said slowly. "I would've been all up in here in a minute. I would've been all capital g, and busted a cap in some ghost's ass."

"Okay, Martin," Trent said sarcastically. "Can we focus here? I am officially freaked out."

"Sorry, man, defense mechanism."

Trent nodded. "Should we try the door, or should we look for Cane?" Chris looked down the hallway, then back at the door. "My first instinct is the door, but I'm pretty sure we aren't getting through it. We probably better look for Cane. Since we're here."

"Since we're here," Trent agreed.

The two cautiously made their way down the narrow hallway toward the dining room. The house was much darker than it was this afternoon, probably due to the storm outside. Chris felt with his hand along the wall for a light switch. Fumbling onto a set of four switches, he flipped them all on, then off again.

271

"Figures. No power," he said.

The two peeked around the edge of the hallway. The house was silent. Even the air seemed stale. Trent spotted his camera equipment still lying in the living room.

"I think I can salvage most of that," he said under his breath. "I need to try and get it out of here."

Chris nodded. "I'll help."

The two slowly made their way out of the dining room. Everything seemed to be as it was when they left earlier in the day. Nothing had been disturbed. Stepping into the great room, the two quickly surveyed their surroundings. The shattered pieces of Cane's ghost hunting equipment still lay heaped in the corner, and the shimmering shards of glass from the mirror were still scattered about at the foot of the stairs. A wisp of cool air suddenly flowed over them.

Trent stopped. "Did you feel that?"

Chris nodded. "Let's get the equipment, and get out of here."

The two turned toward the living room and the equipment. Moving quickly and quietly, they began to round up the bits and pieces of the cameras. Trent worked diligently to check both cameras and hurriedly decided only one was salvageable. He was in too much of a hurry to take both, although he was sure he could fix the broken one. Meanwhile, Chris was rounding up the majority of his sound equipment. He lifted his boom and headphones off the floor as well as his DAT recorder. If they had the footage of the earlier interviews, then they would need the sound, he reasoned. Besides, audiotape often revealed things video didn't. He had been reading about a field of study known as Electronic Voice Phenomenon. This was when a stray voice or sound was recorded that couldn't be made by a human or a machine. It was very fascinating to him, and it concreted his position. Everyone always needed a soundman.

Chris....

Chris stood straight up and looked at Trent. "Did you say something?" Trent shook his head without looking away from his work. "No."

Chris looked around the house. There was nothing, only the house. He felt a cold chill run down his neck.

Chrisss....

"Did you just hear that?"

Trent looked up at his colleague. "Hear what?"

"It sounded like...." He strained his ears in the silence. "Something called...." He shook his head. This place was getting to him. He realized it was his subconscious working against him. With good reason, he reminded himself. Several people had died in this house. He just needed to get out of here. Scooping the last of his equipment up, he quickly started toward the hallway.

"Hold on," Trent called after him. "This is more than I can carry. I need an extra pair of hands."

Chris spun around and glared at Trent. A general feeling of uneasiness was quickly growing in him every extra moment he stood in the house. "Take what you can carry. We're not coming back."

"What about tonight?"

Chris was growing visibly agitated. "To hell

273

with tonight. I'm walking out that door and not stopping. I'll walk back to California if I have to. As long as I'm not here."

Chrisss....

Chris let his equipment fall out of his hands and onto the floor. He turned away from the living room. "You had to have heard that," he said almost frantically.

"I didn't hear anything," Trent assured him as he lifted his camera and stood.

Chrisssss....

"What the fuck are you?" Chris yelled at the house. He stumbled blindly back into the dining room, almost tripping over one of the chairs. He quickly caught his balance against the table. "Leave me alone!" He pressed the heels of his hands against his temples as if to stifle a headache.

Chrissssssss....

Chris snapped his head toward the open kitchen door. His heart began to race uncontrollably when he saw it. It was motionless. Just watching him with those burning red eyes. They weren't human shaped either. They had more of an almond shape to them. Much like the images of the little gray aliens with the wraparound black eyes, but this was much more horrible. The creature had no definition. It was there, and yet not. It was just staring at him through the kitchen door.

"You will not escape, Chris," the creature moaned with pleasure.

Chris tried to call out for Trent, but found the words stuck in the pit of his throat. He pushed with all his might to scream, or at least move, but nothing happened. A sort of paralysis settled over his limbs. He felt a tear run down his cheek. He knew, in that instant, he was going to die.

The shadow lashed out with a swiftness too quick for the human eye to catch. All at once, it was upon Chris. Its rolling darkness beginning to envelop him, all the while, the red eyes stared unblinkingly at him. At that moment, Chris snapped. His mind shut down and his body went into automatic defense mode. Balling up his fists, he swung wildly at the darkness, but connected with nothing. He reached up and clawed at the shadow's eyes, only to have a similar effect. The whole time, the creature seemed to be enjoying Chris' struggle, as if taking pleasure from it. The shadow's laughter echoed through the folds of darkness. In his final act of desperation, Chris began to swing his arms wildly in all directions, but it was useless. It was as if there was nothing there. With one fluid motion, the shadow plunged a clawed hand into Chris' chest. It slowly wrapped its fingers around his beating heart and began to squeeze. Chris felt his heart straining to beat against the fingers, but it was failing. They were like steel bands constricting ever tighter.

Chris watched the shadow's eyes harden as they narrowed into thin, burning, red slits. His mind was frantic, but he focused on one thought. "Though I walk through the valley of the shadow of death," he gasped, "I shall fear no evil. I shall fear no evil," he spat at the creature in front of him.

The shadow ripped its hand out of Chris' chest, and with it, his heart. Chris slowly looked down at the gaping, bloody hole in his torso, then his body fell limply to the carpeted floor in a pool of his own blood. The shadow stood mockingly above him, marveling at his work.

Trent looked up. "Chris?" He searched the living and dining rooms for his friend. He couldn't understand. He had only looked away for a moment, and then…. "Chris? Where the hell are you?" He walked slowly out of the living room, his camera equipment in tow. Turning, he glanced down the hallway to see the door still closed. "What the hell?" A wave of nausea passed over him and settled in the pit of his stomach. This wasn't good.

Turning back, he noticed a dark mist hovering at the foot of the stairs. It quickly transfigured into a more menacing form, that of a large, snarling dog with glowing red eyes. The beast charged.

"Oh shit." Holding the camera firmly against his chest the way a running back cradled the football, he pumped his legs hard and dashed down the hallway. Not even taking the time to look back, Trent reached the door at the end and quickly mumbled a prayer. He could hear the thud of the beast's footfalls behind him. They were rapidly growing louder. It was almost on top of him.

Reaching down, his hand passed effortlessly though the doorknob. "Fuck," he said in desperation.

He reached forward. There was nothing there. No door. Jumping through what appeared to him as a solid door, he landed awkwardly on the bottom step and tumbled onto the concrete floor of the garage. His ankle hit first and immediately buckled. His knee followed closely and he felt something pop as it impacted. Rolling onto his back in agony, he stared at the gaping hole behind him. There *was* no door. He and Chris had broken through it when they went in.

It was all an illusion. He jumped to his feet, despite the protest from his knee and ankle. There was nothing in the hallway but the broken door and wooden splinters from the doorjamb. There was no sign of the beast. "What the fuck is going on here?" he muttered as he tried to catch his breath.

***

"What exactly are we looking for?" Bishop asked as he sorted through another stack of folders.

"We want to find out if anything else has happened like this at the Grant House," Dawn replied through a pile of paperwork. "Or anything significant that would tie these events together."

They had gained unlimited access to the country clerk's files after a quick call to Detective Montoya to confirm their identity. The county clerk's office was a lot smaller than either of them had expected for a city of Stone Brook's population. It was a small, three room building built adjacent to the city courthouse. One of the rooms had been designated a break room, while the other held the office of the county clerk, a one F. Liam Simms (a somewhat greasy, little weasel of a man neither Dawn or Bishop cared for very much), and the last held all the records. Dawn had laughed at the layout of the County Clerk's office. It took real bureaucracy, with the obvious limited space of this office, to designate one entire room, the largest of the three, a break room.

The records room was wall-to-wall filing

cabinets. All the cabinets looked as if they were pre-1960 as they were painted a dingy mustard yellow. The filing system was completely antiquated, and most of the files contained a large amount of dust, along with the paperwork. A lone ceiling fanned churned noisily above them.

Dawn and Bishop were both camped out on the floor amidst a sea of folders and papers dealing with the area the Grant House was built on and the actual house itself. They had spent almost an hour in the tiny, cramped room, staring mind numbingly at the reams of double and triple filed forms.

"Why does the government need everything in triplicate?" Dawn wondered.

"It's supposed to make file keeping easier," Bishop replied. "One copy goes to the person, another goes to the county clerk, while the final copy is usually sent off to the county or state government."

"Then why do I keep finding all three copies in these files?"

"Somebody messed up."

"Obviously," Dawn said as she pushed another stack of files away from her. "This is getting monotonous and we haven't found anything that even remotely looks promising."

"We did find that one dump certificate," Bishop reminded.

"Ooh," Dawn said sarcastically, "be still my beating heart." She ran her hand through her hair and let out a long sigh. "I don't think that building a neighborhood over an old dump site is in the least significant."

"Just being thorough," Bishop said with a

smile. He tossed his folder on the floor and grabbed the next one in the stack. Flipping it open, he stopped. "Do you think this would count as significant?" He passed the folder over to Dawn.

She quickly scanned the pages inside and nodded. "I would definitely say this counts." She lifted a page out and read it again. "Seven mysterious deaths were recorded in Stone Brook over seventy years ago. This is a coroner's report." She read further down the page. "Their bodies were mutilated. Police theorized this is some kind of cult activity, but it could never be proven."

"Where were the bodies found?"

Dawn read further down the page. "It says all three were recovered from the dump just outside of town. Each person killed was last seen working at the landfill."

"How long did these killings go on?"

"I'm not sure," Dawn admitted, "but I've got all six of the coroner's reports, and they're all dated within a day of each other."

"So either they found all the bodies at once at a later date, or all the killings happened at once," Bishop theorized. "Does it say why the police thought it was occult activity?"

"Everything was occult back then," Dawn said with a frown. "If it was something they couldn't explain, then it was witches or the devil." She flipped the piece of paper over in her hand. "Wait a minute," her eyes widened as she ran her finger over several lines of messily scrawled writing, "it says along with each victim's heart being removed, something was stolen from each of the victims, something that held personal importance to them. It would either be taken off their person, or stolen from their homes the same day as their death. We know at least two of our victims' hearts have been removed."

"That's how they connected the killings to the occult?" Bishop wondered. "That seems very circumstantial to me. Often murders are just botched robberies anyway, and it could be purely coincidental that our victims' hearts were removed. Remember, they didn't take the boy's heart."

"Let's not be too hasty," Dawn said quickly. "Let's look at this for a moment." She sat the piece of paper aside while she pondered the clues. "In some occult rituals, it is important to have the heart and personal objects to complete the dark magic, but what kind of ritual would they be performing?"

"Hold on. You're basing your theories on ideas police had over seventy years ago. You said it yourself, whenever they couldn't explain something, it was automatically labeled occult."

"Yes," Dawn agreed, "but this seems different."

"We don't even know if the shadows were involved with the murders back then, and besides, do we know if the hearts were taken from the current victims?"

Dawn smiled. "There's one way to find out." Reaching into her pocket, Dawn produced a small silver, rectangular cell phone. She tapped in a number on the luminescent pad and pressed the 'talk' button.

"Who are you calling?" Bishop wondered.

Dawn held up one finger to silence Bishop as she listened to the ring. She smiled when she heard a familiar click. "Maria? This is Dawn." She waited for a moment as she listened to the response. "That's great. I'm glad your boy is doing so well."

Bishop looked on inquisitively as he silently voiced the name 'Maria'. Dawn help up her hand again. "Yeah...yeah," she agreed to an unheard question. "Listen, I need some quick information. I need you to dig up everything you can find on six murders that took place seventy-seven years ago here in Stone Brook. That's right." She listened for a moment, "Oh yeah, one more thing: I need you to reference any occult rituals that use human hearts. Specifically, six of them." Dawn nodded her head. "I know that's a very broad query, but I think it's important. Thanks, Maria." Dawn pulled the phone away from her ear and tapped the 'end' button.

"Who's Maria?"

Dawn smiled. "She's the Head Records Keeper back at the OPR. She can find out anything about anything," Dawn bragged. "She won't let us down."

"Great." Bishop paused, "Why are you having her look up occult rituals?"

"I just have a hunch," Dawn said with a wry smile. "Let's get out of here."

***

"Jesus," Chloe muttered as she looked over the lump (that was the best word she could think of to describe him. He was humanoid in shape, but not quite appearing as if he was from this planet.) in front of her. Jackson had returned only moments ago with Rivers in tow. He was a complete and utter mess. His clothes were stained the color of his vomit and his eyes were glossed over the same color as a dirty fish tank. He couldn't even stand. The only way he was remaining upright was with Jackson's help.

The three were standing just outside the Grant House on the driveway. Large raindrops were falling to the ground around them, occasionally being whipped up by the winds into their faces. Chloe quickly wished the storm would change its course. Sometimes they did that, Chloe argued with herself. She prayed this was one of those times. The last thing she needed now was a hurricane destroying her broadcast. It seemed like everything else was doing a good job of that already. She brushed her long, windswept bangs out of her face. She wondered if there was some higher power working against her, almost as if she wasn't supposed to finish this show. It certainly seemed that way from her point of view. A quick recap: one of her original experts was dead and the other was in jail being accused of the crime. Half her equipment had been destroyed by some kind of ghost thing, one of her replacement experts had vanished inside the house, and now her host was drunk off his ass. *Perfect,* she thought. *This is exactly how I learned to do it in film school.*

"Will you get this smelly fucker off me?" Jackson yelped. "I think flies are starting to gather." Jackson slipped out from beneath Rivers' arm, sending him toppling to the ground.

Chloe knelt down to examine the heap of man. "Rivers," she said calmly much to her own surprise, "how are you feeling?"

Rivers jerked his head up toward Chloe and smiled broadly. He was completely shit-faced and he knew it. By this point, though, he was way past the point of giving a shit. "I feel great," he slurred. "Never better." He stifled a beer burp that was threatening to turn into a full-blown dry heave.

"You look like shit," Chloe assessed. "Do you realize we go on the air in," she glanced down at her watch, "four hours? I need you to be at one hundred percent by then. If not better."

Rivers clumsily lifted his hand and made the 'okay' gesture. "You got it, boss woman."

"I'm not fucking kidding around, you piece of shit. We're going live coast- to-coast and you're tanked!" Chloe's voice was quickly escalating beyond calm. "You sober up right now or," she didn't have a threat. The broadcast either went with him, or not at all. She tried frantically to think of something that might snap him out of his stupor. "Or I'm going to call Stephen."

Rivers' eyes widened. That one name sliced through the alcohol induced haze like a laser beam. "No," he gasped. Channeling all his focus, Rivers tried to lift his soggy carcass off the ground. Once on his feet, he began to stumble back down. His arms shot straight out like a tightrope walker's trying to stay on the wire. He harnessed every fiber of muscle in his body, every ounce of concentration, to stay upright. This was important. Chloe had just pulled the net out from beneath him. If he were to fail…. "Wait," Rivers gasped, out of breath. "I can do it."

Chloe quickly tried to conceal her smile. Her threat had been a success. She wondered in hindsight if she would've actually done it, maybe if Rivers had called her bluff, but luckily, he hadn't.

"All right," she said coolly. "We'll try this, but if you aren't completely sober by air time," she reached out and grabbed Rivers by the chin, "I'm calling Stephen." She dug into her pocket and produced her compact, black cell phone. "I have his number on speed dial." She almost cringed. She was pushing it too far and she knew it.

"Okay," Rivers conceded, "okay. I'll be ready." He slowly ran his hand through his dingy red hair.

Chloe quickly slipped her phone back into her pocket and gave Rivers the once over. She turned to Jackson, "Go get him cleaned up."

"Since when did I become his keeper?" Jackson protested. "Since I said so," Chloe said sternly.

Jackson opened his mouth to argue, but a quick glance from Chloe warned him off. "I'll take him back to the hotel."

Chloe nodded and looked up into the darkened sky. "Better hurry. The storm's back."

Jackson wrapped an arm around Rivers' shoulder and began to lead him back to the car. "Come on, you stinky bastard."

"Hey," Rivers shot back.

Deep down, Jackson was enjoying this. He had always hated Rivers, and now he was being allowed a chance at redemption, or vengeance in this case. "Get in the car and shut up," Jackson instructed him forcefully.

Chloe leaned her head back and let the drops fall on her face. She knew that in an hour or so, the storm would be at full strength and venturing out would be completely impossible. As the two pulled out of the driveway in their rented maroon sedan, she allowed a smile to creep across her face and finally erupt into a complete toothy grin. The power she held over Rivers right now was intoxicating. She wished she had this power all those years ago when they were together. Things would've been different, she assured herself. Things would have been much different. *I should call Stephen anyway, she thought spitefully, just to teach Rivers a lesson. No, that's just being vindictive.*

"So what?" Chloe said with a grin. Reaching into her pocket, she quickly retrieved her cell phone and began to dial. "It's time for some payback." Lifting the cell phone to her ear, she listened intently as it rang. This time, she was going to do it. There needed to be ramifications for Rivers' actions. After all, she had been bailing him out for years.

Suddenly, a hand grabbed her by the shoulder and spun her around. Chloe wobbled uneasily to see Carrie standing before her. Her face was almost as white as the blouse she was wearing. "Chloe," she barely mouthed her name as tears streamed down her cheeks.

Chloe snapped her cell phone shut and deposited it back into her pocket. "What happened, Carrie?"

Carrie shook her head. "I...."

"You can tell me," Chloe said comfortingly.

Taking a deep breath, Carrie tried to calm down. "It's my fault. I'm so sorry. I could've stopped them, but I didn't. I could've—"

"Stop," Chloe said firmly. "You're babbling. Tell me what happened." Carrie bit her lip. "Chris is dead."

"Oh God."

Carrie fell forward into Chloe's arms and began to sob uncontrollably against her shoulder. Chloe wrapped an arm around Carrie and used the other to caress her hair. She wanted to cry as well, but who would be there to hold her? She had known Chris longer than Carrie, so it should be...she stopped. She was being petty. Someone was dead. Everyone had to deal with their grief in their own way. Right now, she had to be strong. She was the leader of this team, and if this broadcast was going to succeed, then it would be up to her to reach deep down inside herself and find the strength.

Listen to yourself, she said spitefully. *A member of your crew is dead, and you're still worried about the show. What kind of monster are you?*

Probably not as bad as the ones inside that house, she decided. At least, she hoped not.

Chapter 24

They already have six, Morgan worried. *I pray they don't get the seventh. I don't know if I'll be able to stop them if they do.*

Morgan was standing on the roof of a two story building that overlooked the small neighborhood where the Grant House was. The rain had been pelting her for hours while the wind whipped her hair around her face, but she was beyond being cold and wet. She realized that now. She had more power than they did. She was beginning to understand. The dream had shown her the way. It had explained everything to her in intricate detail. She had only needed to look inside herself to find the answers. There *was* work to be done, and she and Veranda were going to finish it.

She silenced her mind for a moment to hear the wind whispering to her. The hour was drawing near. Her and Veranda had to stop them. Morgan snapped her head down in the direction of the Grant House as electricity crackled from her hands. *I will not allow them to complete the Ritual of the Sevens. I will die before I let that happen.* Summoning her power, she lifted her nimble body into the wind and let it carry her toward her destination. She needed to bide her time, but it wouldn't be long now. Not long at all....

***

"Check, check, can you hear me?"

"We've got you, Chloe," Daniels replied. "There's about a four second delay on the video

287

feed, though. Trying to correct now." He reached down and punched several keys on the pad in front of him. His nimble fingers worked quickly over the controls as he twisted knobs and pulled down several small levers. He turned to the operator to his left, "Hey, Mike, can you boost the signal a bit?"

Mike shook his head. "I'm giving' ya all she's got, Captain," he replied with a butchered Scottish accent and a smile.

"Very funny, jackass. Like I haven't heard that one a million times before," Daniels replied. He keyed his mic. "Can't correct, we're just going to have to go with the delay." Daniels looked up at the two monitors in front of him. One showed an image of Chloe standing in the garage of the Grant House in Stone Brook, Florida, while the other had the ever-present color bars. He was glad he was here instead of in Florida. Chloe had a jacket wrapped tightly around her body, and he was wearing a pair of khaki shorts and sandals. *Sometimes being the board op wasn't all that bad*, Daniels thought.

"How does the feed look?" Chloe asked into her headset.

"There's a little static every now and again, but otherwise, the feed is exceptionally clear. Are you sure you're in the middle of a hurricane down there?" Daniels asked with a chuckle.

"Pretty damned sure," Chloe snapped, then the audio channel went dead. Daniels looked up at the monitor. Chloe had ripped the headset off and was quickly walking out of the frame. "Some people just can't take a joke."

***

Running her hand through her hair, Chloe made her way across the garage. It was quiet now, not the bustling scene it had been an hour ago. Equipment sat unchecked on the floor next to coils of large black cable, and only two members of her crew were present. Carrie had turned into a full-blown chain smoker, lighting one cigarette off the end of the one before it. She was sitting alone in the far corner of the garage, as far away from the house as she could get and still be out of the storm. Her usually well-kept hair was a mess atop her head from her continuously running her fingers through it as she fidgeted. Her hands were visibly shaking, and she was still at least two shades paler than usual. Trent, on the other hand, had barely moved in an hour. He had refused to be taken to the hospital this close to broadcast time for fear he wouldn't make it back in time. He was being the consummate professional, but also an idiot in Chloe's opinion. He had, at the very least, sprained his ankle and that required medical attention.

Chloe knelt down next to Trent. He was sprawled out on the cold cement floor of the garage with his sore knee and ankle stretched out. He was slowly rubbing his hands over his swollen knee. She gently placed her hand on his shoulder. "Are you okay?" she asked sweetly. He looked in bad shape.

Trent looked up at his boss. She could see the pain in his eyes. It wasn't just the pain of his injuries, but of losing a friend. It had been horrible news to her as well, but Chris' death hadn't affected her the same way it had Trent. They were the two closest members of the crew, and they had been there the longest. She had always envied their unique bond. It was forged in the early, lean years of the show, and had developed into a mutual respect for each other's work and an unwavering loyalty to each other. It was to be respected, but it was also so unique, Trent would never feel that again. Chloe's heart sank.

"Yeah," Trent said slowly. "I'll make it."

"I still think you should go and at least get checked out at the hospital. You may have broken something," Chloe warned him.

"I'll be fine, besides, we're less than two hours from airtime. What if I don't make it back in time? It's not like there's a lot of crew left to cover for me."

That was harsh, but she knew he was just angry. "Okay. Just sit back and rest up." She stood up and turned away. There was no use talking to him at the moment. He was seeing the world through angry red eyes, and there was nothing she could do about that. She certainly wished she could alter time and bring everyone back, but that just wasn't possible. Or at least, she thought it wasn't. Wishful thinking, she told herself. No sense dwelling on the past. There's too much work to be done. *Does that make me sound ghoulish?*

She stopped near the front of the garage and reached toward the wall. There she felt a small black button and pressed it. The automatic garage door creaked in protest as it began to rise. Once outside, Chloe reached through the door and tapped the button, again closing the door behind her. She had one of the Grant's automatic garage door openers in her pocket. There was no way in hell she was going back into that house alone, and when the garage door was closed, the house was the only entrance. She would not be stuck in there, not even for a minute.

She lifted her face skyward and let the raindrops fall over her. This seemed to be the only thing that brought her peace at the moment. Her mind was cluttered with details of the broadcast, and guilt. She hated to admit it, but she felt guilty about Chris' death. And why shouldn't she? He was killed while under her watch. Aren't bosses supposed to have some kind of liability for things like that? At the moment, she truly hoped so. It would be far better to be punished now, than have to live with his death on her conscience for the rest of her life. She didn't understand how military men coped. How could generals sit in secure offices in another country and draw up plans that would surely send young men to their deaths? Did they feel no guilt or remorse? Or were the men simple numbers on a piece of paper handed to them at the end of the day? There were no faces, only numbers.

Chris was dead. Sam was dead. Cane was missing and presumed dead. Things were going great. She wondered if she got another member of her crew killed if she would be eligible for a set of steak knives. At least her wicked sense of humor hadn't abandoned her completely.

She was wrapped up in the storm. The wind was howling around her and the rain was beating against her exposed flesh. It was what she needed right now. It made her feel alive (for what that was worth at the moment). Slowly, she sank down into the wet grass around her. Balling up her fists, she pressed them against her eyes and started to cry. It was not a soft sob, nor just a quiet tear running down her cheek, rather a deep belly cry. She was letting out everything pent up inside her. She was a failure and one of her friends was dead. Why had she been chosen for this godforsaken assignment? Did the fates have it in for her? Lifting up to her knees, she vomited on the grass. Her insides felt as if they were being turned inside out. She heaved again. Everything was coming up. The pain, the guilt, even that penny she swallowed in elementary school. Everything. She wrapped her hands around her aching stomach muscles as she threw up again. Taking a deep, forced breath, she rocked back and sobbed again. Her face showed the pain and agony she had been feeling since this morning.

She had been lying to herself and everyone around her. She wasn't the strong-willed director she envisioned herself as, not at all. She was a frightened little girl who was hiding behind the mask she had created for herself. Now two men, and possibly a third, were dead because of her vanity. She slowly drew her hand across her mouth to wipe away the excess vomit. It was all over. Her crew was in shambles, and her broadcast a total disaster.

She saw a flicker of lightning arc across the sky. She found herself secretly wishing a bolt would split the heavens and strike her where she stood. It would be easier than dealing with the pain.

STOP.

She looked down at the mess she had made in front of her as she caught her breath. She was completely soaked to the bone. Her clothes were sticking to her thin frame, and her hair hung messily around her face. What was she doing? Slowly standing up, she coughed once to clear her lungs, then took a deep breath. She wasn't going to allow herself to wallow in self-pity. After all, that's what it really was. She wasn't mourning the death of a friend, she was mourning herself, and she wasn't dead yet. How could she have let herself sink so low so fast? She was actually thinking of dying, for God's sake. She balled her fists again, this time, not in pain, but rather in protest. She wasn't going to allow herself to sink into regret and depression. There was too much work to be done, and she had to do it. This live broadcast would be the best fucking hour of television anyone had ever seen, she assured herself. She would do it not only for herself, but also for those who had fallen trying to bring it to fruition. It was what they would have wanted. She knew that now. No amount of wallowing around in the muck would bring them back. She would have to honor their memory the only way she knew how, and by God, she would do a damned good job of it.

She dug into her pocket and pulled out the garage door opener. Clicking the large button once, she waited as the door slowly creaked open. Once inside, she tossed the remote and stood in front of Carrie and Trent like Patton addressing the troops.

"We are two hours from airtime," she said, "let's get our ass in gear, people. We have a show to do," Chloe stated boldly.

***

Dawn had both hands firmly on the steering wheel as she tried to keep the car from blowing off the road. Her knuckles were white from the amount of pressure she was using. The car was being tossed about by the storm. The winds would change direction from moment to moment and sweep her across the rain soaked pavement, then immediately toss her back in the other direction. She had the windshield wipers on high, but it wasn't helping much. Visibility had been greatly reduced by the blowing debris and rain. Her shortened field of vision kept her nerves on edge.

"I take it you haven't driven in this kind of weather before," Bishop stated as he swallowed hard. Dawn's driving was scaring the hell out of him, but he was too much of a man to admit it. He had both feet pressed firmly to the floor and one hand wrapped tightly around the "oh shit" handle above him. His vision was transfixed on the road ahead of them in fear. "Maybe we should pull over and—"

"And what?" Dawn bated him, "let *you* drive?"

Bishop shook his head. "I was going to say, 'maybe we should pull over and wait out the storm'." He smiled, "And they think men are egotistical about their driving."

Dawn exhaled slowly. "Sorry. This whole mess has just got me a little on edge."

"I know what you mean," Bishop agreed. "Killer ghosts that seem to be following some kind of pattern. It's just too wild."

"That's the part that strikes me as odd," Dawn admitted. "We read the killings happened seventy-seven years ago, right?"

Bishop nodded.

"Why would the ghosts come back to complete

a ritual seventy-seven years later?" She slowly brought the car to a stop in an intersection and flipped on her blinker (although she really didn't know why, it wasn't like any cars could actually see it). "The police files stated they never captured any of the killers."

"Yeah, we read that," Bishop followed. "So?"

"Hauntings are usually the result of unfinished business," Dawn said from experience. "When a spirit is unable to complete their tasks during their mortal lives, they spend the rest of eternity stuck in a kind of infinite loop."

"I'm not following."

"From what Cane and I have found on previous cases involving ghosts, or paranormal activity, is that they are doomed to repeat the past, but aren't able to change it."

"Or willing to change it," Bishop theorized.

"No," Dawn said thoughtfully, "if that were the case, then they would finish whatever they had to do and move on. I don't think they are able to complete their task. They can follow the exact same path they did before, but just before they finish, they are forced to go back to their starting point."

"Do not pass go, do not collect two hundred dollars," Bishop said dryly. "Exactly," Dawn snapped. "So if these people were never captured by the police, what stopped them from finishing?"

"Some kind of outside interference," Bishop said finally. "That's the only logical answer."

"So," Dawn said as she bit her lip, "we have two forgone conclusions: something stopped these men from completing their task, but they found a way back to finish it."

Bishop nodded, "But to finish what?"

"I wish I knew," Dawn said with exasperation. "It must be the key; the one piece of information that will reveal everything to us."

"The ever-elusive 'x' marks the spot theory," Bishop interjected.

"You know, you could help figure this thing out instead of just coming up with interesting quips," Dawn spat. "I need some help."

"Sorry," Bishop said as he sank down into his seat. "I just don't have very much experience with this stuff yet. I'm kind of 'flying by wire' here."

"You obviously have some kind of interest in the supernatural, or you wouldn't have joined the OPR," Dawn retorted quickly. "That means you must have read books on the subject, or watched documentaries, or soaked up some kind of knowledge on the paranormal and the occult." Dawn reached over and patted Bishop on the knee. "All I'm trying to say here is that anything you can think of, no matter how insignificant you may think it is, you need to share it."

Bishop smiled, "You're right. I just feel a bit out of my league talking to you and Cane most of the time. It's like being a Star Wars fan all your life, then finally getting a chance to sit down with George Lucas. I mean, what would you ask in that situation?"

"Don't tell me you're some kind of Trekkie," Dawn laughed.

"Wrong series. Trekkies watch Star Trek." Bishop adjusted his coat, "I watch Star Wars."

"Enough said," Dawn said with a chuckle. "I think I understand. You shouldn't feel dumb around

Cane and me. We both had to start somewhere as well, and to tell you the truth, Cane's knowledge of subjects still intimidates me a little as well."

"Good to know I'm not the only one in this boat."

The two were startled by Dawn's cell phone. Dawn quickly dug into her coat pocket and retrieved the small phone. Clicking it on, she pressed it to her ear. "Hello? Oh, hi, Maria."

Bishop became hopeful. It had been less than half an hour since Dawn had contacted the Records Department at the OPR. This could mean good news, possibly even a much needed break.

Dawn nodded once, then hung up the phone. "We have our 'why'."

"Well, are you going to tell me, or just keep me hanging?" Bishop asked excitedly.

"Maria cross-referenced all the information we gave her and came up with some very interesting, and somewhat disturbing facts." Dawn stuffed the phone back in her pocket and returned her hand to the wheel. "It seems that our killers seventy-seven years ago did have a record."

"Tell," Bishop instructed her excitedly.

"They were some kind of unholy trinity that had formed a group known as the 'Dark Moon' cult. Apparently, their cult was formed around Revelations 8:12."

Bishop snapped his fingers, "I know that one. It talks about the apocalypse." He thought for a moment, then cleared his throat, "And the fourth angel sounded, and the third part of the sun was smitten, and the third part of the moon, and the third part of the stars; so as the third part of them was

297

darkened, and the day shone not for a third part of it, and the night likewise."

"I'm impressed."

"Bible school," Bishop smiled. "These cultists have the same rudimentary knowledge of the Bible every religious nut seems to have. That passage isn't actually talking about the moon going dark. It's more of a reference to things that will happen and the moon and sun are just symbols of that."

"Interesting," Dawn agreed, "but it's still a passage about the end of time."

"Yes, part of the seven trumpets."

"There's that number again," Dawn said eagerly. "It seems that things come in sevens for our cultists. Seven trumpets, seventy-seven years and seven hearts," Dawn said grimly.

"Seven hearts?"

"They were performing what is known as the 'Ritual of Sevens'. If they complete it, it would basically give them unlimited power and make them, for all intents and purposes, immortal."

"Did Maria tell you that?"

Dawn nodded. "She said the ritual could only be performed every seventy- seven years on Halloween. It requires seven human hearts and seven personal effects from the victims."

"Why seven?"

"Unknown," Dawn replied. "Seven seems to have some kind of cosmic importance."

"Tell me more about the ritual," Bishop said.

"The 'Ritual of Sevens', if performed correctly, gives one the 'essence' of the people killed, thereby giving a person seven extra lifetimes and all the power they had."

298

"So there's a pattern we didn't see," Bishop theorized. "These murders are connected. Each of them had to have some kind of developed or latent paranormal abilities."

Dawn snapped her fingers. "Like Sam Peters, the world renowned psychic."

"Exactly," Bishop grinned unevenly as if he were the sole keeper of the world's biggest secret. Knowledge is power, and he knew that well. "So that means the Grants all had some kind of psychic ability, as well as Kelley's girlfriend."

"But counting all the Grants and the girlfriend, that's only four hearts. They need seven."

"There may be more we don't know about yet."

"God, I hope not. Today is Halloween and we're heading back into the lion's den."

Bishop nodded. "We need to talk to Cane. He can tell us what to do."

***

Cane awoke in a dark place. There was only the faint flicker of light on the far side of this place. He could see a small, tapered candle burning close to the nub. A quick estimation proved to him that he wouldn't have light much longer.

He reached up and felt his forehead. There was a large goose egg forming just below his hairline. At least that was a good sign. He knew he didn't have a concussion. He couldn't remember how he arrived in this place. The last thing he remembered was falling....

He slowly began to feel the floor around him. It was cold and hard, but not exactly level. It could be rock, he theorized, some kind of cave. He stretched out his arm in the darkness to see if he could find the wall, and was surprised when he did. It felt similar to the floor, but damp, as if a trickle of water was running down it. He knew he was in a cave, or some kind of structure built into the rock. He wasn't sure which, but he was determined to find out.

Maybe he didn't understand after all. He had thought he understood the shadow's games, but things hadn't turned out the way he expected. What, really, did he expect? To be standing in the middle of the Grant's living room as if nothing happened? He realized now he may've been asking a little too much. He had thought it was all an illusion, but this certainly felt real. Therein lies the rub, it all felt real. The vertigo he experienced while hanging above the bottomless pit, the smell of the chemicals the red fluid was kicking up as it ate through the couch, it was all so real. Could he be in another illusion created by the shadows?

He slowly stood up. A rattling sound rang off the walls of the cave as he shuffled his feet forward. It was very familiar. He had heard it before. Kneeling down, Cane ran his hand down his pant leg until he reached his ankle. He suddenly realized what the sound was, and it was very real. A metal cuff had been attached to his legs with a heavy chain leading from them. Spinning around, he traced the chain's winding path along the floor until he reached the wall. There he found a large steel plate bolted to it that the chains were attached to. He tugged once on the chain to check for weaknesses, but wasn't surprised to find the plates were solid.

"Bloody hell," he muttered under his breath.

The light flickered around him. Glancing up, he watched the candle's flame dance at the end of the wick. *That was odd,* he thought. *I didn't stir up the air enough to disturb the candle.* He watched as the flame settled back down, then flittered again. *There's a breeze in here. That means this room is connected to the outside somehow.* He scanned the darkness for any traces of an egress or a stairwell that led out of the cave, but found only inky blackness. Then an idea struck him.

"My cell phone," he said quickly. Reaching for his jacket pocket…he stopped. He had jettisoned his jacket in the living room. He let his head fall forward in exasperation. It had his cell phone and a small flashlight he kept for emergencies. "Score one for the British," he said angrily.

Standing up, he decided to test the length of the chains. Taking baby steps away from the wall, he slowly crept forward with his arms feeling blindly in front of him. He stopped when he felt the chains become taut. Reaching around, he felt a wall in front of him and one to his right. Glancing to his left, he realized he could make it to the candle. At least he could have light to navigate, he decided. He had taken one step toward the light, when it flickered once and went out.

"Should've seen that one coming."

Then it struck him. He could feel no breeze. Not even the slightest trickle of air. The air in this room was completely still. Then came another horrible realization; he was not alone. Skittering back across the floor, he pressed his back up against the wall and became silent. His breathing became slow and deep, but it was all he could hear. The cave was now completely dark, and he was utterly immersed in its murkiness. He slowly sank down the wall until he was crouching next to his chains. His heart was thumping in his ears.

"He has no power."

Cane heard the voice like a gunshot. It was everywhere all at once, and nowhere at the same time. He frantically swung his head around to try and locate the source of the voice, but there was nothing but blackness.

"We can still use him," came another voice. The voice sounded coarse, as if it were being filtered through sandpaper, or as if it died at the bottom of the creature's throat and was being propelled forward by sheer will. The very wavelengths had been deconstructed, and piled on top of each other incorrectly as it echoed into itself. All the voices sounded like this, but each had a distinctly different pitch. They were grotesque in their inhumanness.

An acidy feeling began to burn at the pit of Cane's stomach. He was completely at the mercy of his unknown captors. He could do nothing but wait. This was killing him.

"He is useless to use," a third voice stated with a hiss, as if said through clenched teeth.

Three sets of red eyes blinked into existence in front of Cane. They were all at the same height, at least seven feet off the ground, and completely unwavering. They neither blinked, nor turned away. Their horrible gaze remained focused on Cane. He felt his heart sink.

"We need two more," the first shadow protested.

If Cane weren't frightened out of his wits, he might've found this conversation completely fascinating. The only thing that anyone had reported the shadows saying was "You will not escape". This proved they were intelligent, instead of the mindless killing machines that everyone else perceived them as. He listened to the conversation become heated between the creatures. His fear was slowly beginning to quell, replaced by a scientist's interest. He had never been witness to a discussion between, Cane quickly searched for a fitting term, ghosts. This completely disproved Dawn's theory of the afterlife. They were not stuck in a loop as she suggested. They were completely free to go and do what they wanted. It was apparently the ghost's own personality and drive that kept them repeating past mistakes over again. They weren't being forced to relive their experiences, rather change what had originally happened. *Interesting concept*, he thought. He just hoped he would be able to eventually share it with someone.

"This is not one of the chosen," the third shadow argued.

"We can't let this one go. The ritual is tonight. We may need him yet," the first voice concluded.

It sounded as though they were squabbling over what to do with Cane, and that the first shadow had just put his proverbial foot down. *Incredible,* he repeated to himself. *If only these were controlled circumstances, I—*

A hand clamped around Cane's throat and ripped him out of his thoughts. Cane's hands instantly shot toward the hand and tried to pull it away. He was surprised when he made contact with

303

something. It was cold, almost freezing to the touch. He recalled the sensation of handling dry ice, how it was so cold, it burned flesh on contact. His neck was beginning to burn.

"We may need you," the shadow growled. "You will not escape."

Cane suddenly laughed out loud. He wasn't sure why, but that struck him as extraordinarily funny. It was like the shadow had added that just to sound menacing (which, of course, it was). The hand suddenly retracted and left Cane giggling on the floor. He ran his hand over his neck. His flesh was cold to the touch, but he didn't think any serious damage had been done. He laughed again, then let out a long breath.

"Why don't they just ask me for my bloomin' lunch money next time?" Dusting himself off, Cane slid back to the wall and sat down. It appeared he wasn't going anywhere for a while. He began to wonder where this cave was.

It could be anywhere as the phantoms had struck all over the small town of Stone Brook, but they seemed to keep coming back to the Grant House. Maybe this cave was located near the house, Cane theorized. *Then again,* he thought grimly, *this may just be the place they are going to perform the ritual they were talking about. A nice, secluded location away from prying eyes.* He wished he knew what ritual they were talking about. Scratch that. He wished he had a hacksaw. Scratch that one too. He really wished he were back in his apartment in Washington watching "I Love Lucy" reruns.

Chapter 25

Enbaugh snapped his head up. He had fallen asleep in the chair next to Kelley's bed. They had been watching a rerun of "Hogan's Hero's" on television, and he guessed he'd just nodded off. Glancing over at Kelley, he realized she had too. The bluish light of the television was casting a serene glow across the blankets she had wrapped around her body. She had almost curled into a fetal position in the middle of the hospital bed. The head was elevated just a bit, so she had slid down to the middle. He wasn't sure why, but she reminded him of a child sleeping in the back seat of a car on a long trip home. Perhaps because he and his brother had always done so on the way back from Grandmother's. He smiled involuntarily at the thought. Even if he weren't asleep on the trip, he would always fake it so his father would have to carry him to bed.

He wished his father were here now. They had always been close, and Enbaugh had always felt his father was one of the few people he could actually talk to in his life. His mother had died when he was ten, so his father and brother were all he had. After her death, they had become what his father referred to as a "fighting unit". He had served in the Vietnam War, so there was always a military slant on everything he did. While other kids his age were out playing, Enbaugh often pulled K-P. His father was very strict, but he was also the kindest man Enbaugh ever knew. When his father would take Enbaugh into his large, hard hands, Enbaugh knew nothing in the world could hurt him.

He died three years ago from cancer, more specifically, a tumor in the right temporal lobe of his brain. The last six months before his death were hard on the family. Because the tumor was buried in his brain, it had caused him to almost go insane. Enbaugh frowned at the memory. On a trip to see his father one afternoon, he found him naked on the floor in a puddle of his own vomit. It wasn't befitting for a man of his stature. After all, he was supposed to be the warrior that came to his kid's rescue, not the other way around. His disease, even through the treatments and many surgeries, had progressed to such an extreme state, he didn't even remember his family. Often, toward the end, when Enbaugh came to visit, he had to remind his father of who he was, and more than once, he had to explain what happened to his mother. Each time, his father would take the news like a train wreck, sobbing uncontrollably because he couldn't deal properly with his emotions. When he finally did die, a cold Tuesday morning in January, there was relief in all their hearts. The man who had been their protector, their warrior, was finally getting some long deserved peace. Enbaugh truly hoped there was a heaven so his mother and father could be reunited.

Enbaugh tried to shake the thoughts from his head. He couldn't help it. His father had died in a hospital, and these places always reeked of death to him. He wondered how many thousands of people had finally given up their battles and died in this place. If any place in this world was truly haunted, he was sure it would be a hospital.

His mind wandered to the members of the OPR.

He wondered how they were faring. Not liking to admit it in mixed company, he had always had a fascination with the supernatural. He had spent many a happy childhood day watching black and white monster movies wondering if the stories presented were even remotely possible. He would've liked to find out, but like so many others, he had no idea on where to begin, or what to do to seek that knowledge. When the time came, his father had urged him to seek a military career, but that hadn't been the path Enbaugh wanted to follow. He instead chose a career in the police force, and convinced his father he was still doing good, but on the home front.

Enbaugh glanced up at the clock. It was nearing five p.m. He thought about reaching for the television remote. The *Ghost Chaser's, Inc.* program would be on in about an hour and he was wondering if they were running any specials beforehand. After all, it was Halloween. Enbaugh smiled again. He was almost glad he wasn't out on the streets tonight. Strange shit happened on Halloween. Average, ordinary people transformed into outlaws on this night. He wasn't sure what the psychology was behind it, but wearing a cheap rubber mask, or a new set of clothes, allowed people to release their inner desires. He knew the boys in blue would have a tough go of it tonight, so he was content to stay right here next to Kelley and watch television. He needed a break anyway, and this was an all-expense paid vacation. He didn't like the fact that the doctors were pumping drugs into his system, but he could live with it as long as those cute nurses kept coming back to check on him.

"Speaking of checking on me," Enbaugh said quickly, "I think I'm late for my medication. They're probably looking for me right now." He glanced over at Kelley again. She was sleeping quietly for the moment. Maybe he should go and at least check in.

Enbaugh glanced out through the large window next to Kelley's bed. Twilight should just be starting to set, but due to the storm, it was already dark outside. He wondered if the hurricane would intrude on anyone's Halloween plans. He shook his head with a grin. Even a hurricane wouldn't stop them.

Placing both hands firmly on the arms of the chair, he lifted himself out of it. His body was sore from sitting so long, but at least he hadn't been lying uselessly in bed. He yawned once, then stretched modestly, hoping he wouldn't pop any stitches. He suddenly felt the scratches in his chest throb slightly. He wondered why he and Kelley were marked up by the phantoms, yet not killed. They had ample opportunity to do so. Maybe they were just not to the phantom's liking. Enbaugh chuckled to himself. Wasn't that the story of his life, though?

He turned and began to walk toward the door, when something caught his attention. He slowly turned back into the room and scanned it, his eyes making a note of everything in the room. *Maybe it's just my imagination,* he thought, *or the drugs they keep dumping into me. They've got me so on edge. Now you're just making excuses,* he scolded himself. *You know what's got you all jumpy.* He looked back at Kelley. She was still dead asleep. He cringed at the word "dead". After the last few days, he decided he should re-examine some of his descriptive phrases. Enbaugh breathed a sigh of relief.

Turning back toward the door, he was startled to see a black shape whip in front of him. He quickly stumbled back toward Kelley. Reaching behind him, he grabbed her leg and started to shake it.

"Kelley, wake up! They're back!" He shook her leg again, then he felt his heart in his throat. Slowly turning around, he felt all his fears become realized.

A shadow was standing next to the bed with Kelley's head cradled in one of its clawed hands. Its other hand was poised at her throat, while a delicious smile hung just below its eyes. Kelley's eyes were wild with fear as she lay in the creature's arm. From the expression on her face, Enbaugh was sure she felt like she was about to die. She pleaded silently with Enbaugh to do something.

Enbaugh made a quick motion toward the shadow. The shadow's smile broadened as it shook its head. It used its free hand to point over Enbaugh's shoulder. Slowly turning, Enbaugh cursed under his breath when he saw the two other phantoms standing just behind him. They were both in human form, and both had a large, toothy grin covering their dark faces. Their large almond-shaped eyes had hardened to burning red slits in their heads as they stared at him.

Enbaugh returned his gaze to the first shadow. "What do you want?" he asked slowly. Unwilling to provoke an attack, he had to know what was going on. He felt he was due at least that much.

The shadow ran its razor sharp claw down Kelley's hospital gown, slicing it open as it went, exposing the young girl's chest. Just above her left breast, the creature carved the picture of a heart in her skin. Kelley shrieked in terror and pain as blood poured from wound.

Enbaugh took a step toward the creature, but was quickly restrained by the other two shadows. They reached around and tore open his hospital gown revealing the similar scratches on his chest. The first shadow pointed his finger at Enbaugh's chest. Enbaugh slowly looked down. His eyes widened. He had a similar cut on the upper left-hand side of his chest. He hadn't noticed it was heart-shaped before. Angrily, he looked up at the phantom. It was just playing with Kelley and him. It had been from the start. Enbaugh had enough.

"Well, are you going to fucking kill us?" he shouted.

Kelley began to shake her head frantically in quiet protest. This was not the course of action she wanted Enbaugh to take.

The shadow slowly looked down at Kelley, then up to his two minions. He slowly nodded once.

All at once, one of the dark hands burst through Enbaugh's chest from behind. He blinked once in shock, then looked down at the black arm. In its hand was Enbaugh's still beating heart, dark red blood still spurting from the torn arteries and veins. Enbaugh gasped for breath as the shadow ripped its hand from his chest. He fell helplessly to his knees, his eyes still on the first phantom's face. Almost like a faraway echo, he could hear the shadow's laughter and see the pleasure in the creature's burning red eyes. He tilted his head back and a solemn laugh escaped his lips. *I'm coming, Dad.*

Kelley looked on in horror as Enbaugh's massive frame toppled lifelessly to the ground. She knew the same fate was waiting for her. The two shadows quickly moved across the room toward Kelley, their eyes transfixed on her healthy, pink flesh. She wasn't sure, but it was almost as if they were staring at her breasts with pleasure. One of the shadows started to reach down toward Kelley's chest, but was quickly stopped by the first.

"This one has power," he hissed. "We want her alive." He looked down at her face lovingly and caressed her cheek with its jagged fingers, "At least until tonight."

Kelley glanced up into the being's eyes. Then came the startling realization. "I know who you are."

***

Bishop was finally glad to be out of the car. Dawn's driving scared him. Dawn had rushed ahead to the house, but he was still a bit apprehensive about entering, even if it was only the garage. It was, after all, still part of the house, and these phantoms didn't seem to respect boundary lines. The whole idea of a ghost performing a mystical ritual just made his flesh crawl, and if it was to increase their power...he shuddered to think about the consequences. Then a memory flashed in his mind of the night in the hospital. *They have a weakness, and I know it. I have to tell Cane.*

Bishop picked up his pace as he strode toward

the garage. He passed the empty satellite van and stopped in front of the large, white metal door. He rapped quickly three times until he heard the mechanism start to grind. He stood impatiently in front of the massive door as it slowly worked open. It seemed like an eternity that he stood there. He had vital information and this couldn't wait. Ducking down, he slid under the door as it continued to rise. Taking a few steps inside, he stopped and looked at the diminished crew standing before him. He quickly glanced over their faces and instantly knew something was wrong. It didn't take a detective to figure it out. This room had the air of a funeral parlor, rather than a television set. He could see a thick cloud of death looming over each head.

He moved quickly past the piles of equipment to Dawn's side. She was standing with Chloe and Carrie, and each had their heads bowed. "What's going on?" he asked quietly. One by one, each woman looked up at Bishop, then quickly returned their gaze to the floor. "What happened?" he asked again, this time with more force behind his voice.

Dawn turned to look at Bishop. Tears were hanging on the bottom of her eyelids threatening to stream down her face at any moment. She opened her mouth, but no sound came out. She slowly took a deep breath to collect herself, then tried again. "There's been…." she stuttered, then started again, "there's been a death."

Bishop took a step back from the group as his eyes widened. He snapped his head around and began to frantically search the garage. It was Cane. Dawn didn't have to say a word. He glimpsed the broken door leading into the house and quickly made up his mind. Spinning on his heels, he started for the door. "I'm going in after him."

Dawn raced after him. Reaching out, she grabbed him by the hand and by an act of sheer will, stopped him. "You can't."

Bishop's eyes were full of anger as he glared at Dawn. She was betraying him. "I'm going in that house right now," he said through clenched teeth, "and I'm going to bring back Cane."

"They already tried that," Dawn pleaded. She didn't want to lose her entire team in one day. "Don't you think they tried that?"

"They're not me," Bishop shouted egotistically.

He wasn't rational at the moment, and Dawn knew that. Her first instinct was to charge into the house as well, but that was before Carrie told her what happened to Cane's rescue team. "They lost a member of their crew, Bishop. They sent in Trent and Chris to look for Cane and they lost Chris." She paused, "He's dead, Bish."

"I don't care," Bishop said, wrenching his arm free. "I'm going in." Dawn quickly grabbed Bishop again. This time, she wasn't letting go.

"Stop," she implored quietly. "Please listen to me."

Bishop started forward again, then stopped. "How can you do this? You claimed this man was your best friend, and now you just want me to let go? Am I understanding you correctly?" he asked angrily. "If it were one of us in there, do you think he would waste a moment standing out here and discussing it?" Bishop waited a moment for a response, but was too impatient to listen to it. "No.

He would be charging in with guns blazing, looking for us."

"I know he would," Dawn said softly as the tears erupted from their perch on her eyelids and streaked down her cheeks, "but we can't." She lifted her hand and quickly wiped away the tears, trying to salvage her mascara before it was too late. Taking a deep breath, she cleared her throat. She could feel an involuntary spasm of crying tugging at her insides. It was all she could do to stop it.

"I don't understand," Bishop exhaled deeply and tried to calm down. He felt like a dog trying to understand the concept of death. "I have to do something," he added calmly.

"We will," pledged Dawn, "but right now, we need to look at the bigger picture. If Cane is dead, they have six hearts now, counting Chris'. If you go charging in there, you'll be an easy target, and they'll have all seven hearts. We can't let that happen, Bishop. They can't complete the ritual."

"You have to let me go," Bishop argued. "Why?"

It was only one word, yet an extremely complicated question. His motives were at the very heart of the matter. Why did he so desperately need to rush in there? Had he grown so attached to Cane that he was willing to give up his own life, or was it for another reason? Had he grown that attached to Dawn? He mulled over the thoughts in his brain. Perhaps the simplest answer was that he was loyal. No matter what his true feelings were for the individuals he worked with, they were a team now. They relied on each other, gave each other strength, and were each other's courage. He knew that being part of a team was being part of a family, and loyalty was the tie that bound them together. He was willing to risk his life for his teammate, his brother. The answer came succinctly to him.

"I know what can hurt them," Bishop stated boldly.

"What?" Dawn asked curiously. As far as she knew, these creatures had no weaknesses.

Bishop smiled. "A direct burst of light directly into their eyes repels them," he said honestly. "Not just sunlight, but any light," he reiterated.

Dawn thought for a moment. "I'm not sure that proves anything. I think at best," she considered her words carefully with a sigh, "we can say we have a working theory here."

"That's exactly what Cain said."

"What?"

Bishop quickly remembered that Dawn wasn't in the emergency room when he had first discussed his findings. "When I told Cane what happened, he said the same thing. Only that we had a working theory."

Dawn was at once flattered by Bishop's remarks and saddened by them. It was nice to know that after all that time together, they were starting to rub off on each other, but just hearing his name was difficult. She returned her attention to Bishop and started to search for alternatives to his train of thought. "Maybe you just startled it," she offered as a possibility.

"I think I was the startled one," Bishop admitted sheepishly. "I didn't do it purposely, it just kind of happened by accident." He studied Dawn's facial expression and knew she wasn't buying it. He kicked at the ground and dug his hands deep into his jeans' pockets. "I know what I saw," he defended. "I *know* it will work."

"I'm sure you do, Bish, but that's a pretty flimsy concept to be holding on to when one of those killers comes rushing for your heart."

Her words hit like a ton of bricks. He couldn't defy her logic; rather, he was beaten down by it. He subtly returned to his previous argument. "I can't just stand here," he said quietly.

"Oh yes we can," Chloe interrupted.

Dawn and Bishop suddenly had the feeling everyone in the garage had been listening the entire time. Dawn turned around to face Chloe. "Why is that?" she asked quickly, trying not to be angry she had been eavesdropped upon.

Chloe tapped her watch. "We go live in forty minutes." She tried to muster a smile, "Then we *all* go into the house."

"Cane might be dead by then," Bishop said under his breath.

Dawn spun and looked at her partner angrily. "He's probably already dead." She stopped. She hadn't meant for that to come out that way. She was just angry and tired, and she had just lost her best friend. She wished Bishop could step into her shoes for just a moment, to see how this was truly affecting her, how it was ripping her insides to shreds. She lifted her hand and started to talk, but quickly bit her lip. She wasn't sure what she should say. "We need to focus our energy on helping these people, and if what you say is true, we may just have a way of doing it." She reached over and pressed her hand gently to Bishop's shoulder.

"You're a good man," she paused again, "and I'm truly glad you're on our side." She could see the pain in his eyes. She wasn't sure if he had dealt with death like this before. She hadn't. She wanted desperately to reach out, to know what he was feeling, so he would open his arms and let her cry on his shoulder. She needed to know she wasn't alone now, but she was. *Alone in a crowd of people,* she stated. *How's that for irony?* She finally said the only thing that she could. It was the only thing that made sense at the moment. "Let's get to work. We have a job to do."

"What do you need me to do?" Bishop asked warily.

"I need you to rig up some 'ghost zappers'," Dawn said with her best— *forced*—smile. "Find all the flashlights you can, and make sure everyone on the crew has one before we go into the house." She patted Bishop on the back, "Go now." Turning back to Chloe and the rest of the crew, she quickly assessed the situation. "Get your crew ready," she instructed Chloe evenly. "We're going to bring you the story of the century live from coast-to-coast."

Chloe smiled broadly. That was exactly what she wanted to hear. Turning to Carrie and Trent, she clapped her hands in front of her, "You heard the lady. Let's mount up, people. We're live in," she checked her watch again, "thirty- seven minutes."

Chapter 26

"Come on, Rivers," Jackson said impatiently, "it's twenty 'til nine. We have to get back."

"Perfection takes time, you dildo," River's announced egotistically from the bathroom in his "broadcasting" voice. "Someday you'll realize that, and then you'll be a real boy."

Jackson sighed. He hated when Rivers talked like that outside the studio. His voice dropped down to the back of his throat and boomed in that kind of "I'm a superhero here to save the world" kind of way. Jackson was seated in a thick green chair just outside the kitchen in River's room. He was running the silver blade of his small pocketknife under his fingernails to remove a few stray particles of dirt and grime that had settled there. Pulling the blade away, he studied his just off-white fingernails. They still weren't clean, but it was as close as he was going to get. Looking around quickly, he wiped the grime off his blade on the arm of the chair, then snapped the knife shut. He stood up as he slipped it back into his pocket. Walking into the small kitchen, he spotted a small bottle of alcohol sitting open on the counter. The lid was lying helplessly next to it, with a half empty malt glass as company. Jackson lifted the bottle and sniffed the contents. Immediately, he pulled back from the bottle and took a deep breath to clear his pallet. Whatever Rivers was drinking, it was strong. He tilted the bottle down and read the label, "Tennessee whiskey. Nice." Setting the bottle back down on the counter, Jackson made his way to the bathroom door.

"Come on, Rivers. We need to hit the road. It's

going to take us ten minutes to get back to the Grant House."

"I don't know about you," Rivers boomed from the bathroom, "but I'm not all that eager to get back there."

Jackson had a sinking feeling. *Maybe Rivers is trying to sabotage the broadcast....* "We go live coast-to-coast in fifteen minutes. We can't be late," Jackson paused, "and we *have* to do it."

"I know," Rivers replied quickly. "That places just gives me the heebie- jeebies."

Jackson laughed under his breath. That just didn't sound right coming from Rivers. "I can't imagine why," Jackson said sarcastically.

Rivers poked his head out of the bathroom door. His lower face was covered with a thick white lather, while a lit cigarette hung awkwardly out of his mouth. The ash, which was now about an inch long, was dangling perilously off the end of the smoke, threatening every second to dive into the shaving cream. Rivers' hair was slicked back against his head, apparently in its prequaffed state. At least it was an improvement from the way he'd looked like earlier. Rivers grabbed the cigarette from his mouth and flicked the ash toward Jackson. "It's because all those people died there, you moron."

Jackson rolled his eyes back. "It was a joke, Rivers."

"Oh," he said as he exhaled a long trail of smoke from his pursed lips. "I knew that." He pulled his head back into the bathroom. "We're down to ten minutes," Jackson announced. "Thank you, Big Ben. I know. Just let me finish shaving."

"Hurry," Jackson advised for the millionth time. "Chloe expected us to be there a half an hour ago."

"Chloe's got her panties on too tight," Rivers said with a giggle. "I should know. I've been in 'em. Everything's going to work out just fine. I'll make it there in time, just like I always do."

Jackson glanced down at his watch nervously. He knew if Rivers didn't make it, it would be his fault. It wasn't fair, but that was the truth of the matter. He had been charged with babysitting Rivers, and he didn't want to fail. Stephen wouldn't fire Rivers, but he would have no problem firing a grunt like Jackson, and he knew that. Jackson tapped on the door with his knuckles. "Come on," he said with exasperation in his voice. He waited. "Rivers?"

Slowly Jackson reached down and slid his fingers around the gold doorknob. Twisting it to the right, he began to open the door. He didn't want to see Rivers naked. It would probably scar his mind permanently. He wondered quickly how Chloe lived with herself after seeing him au naturel. Jackson shuddered at the thought. Peeking his head through the crack of the door, he spotted Rivers, fully clothed, standing motionlessly with his back against the wall. Jackson confidently pushed the door the remainder of the way open.

"What in the hell are you doing?" Jackson asked impatiently. Rivers slowly lifted a hand and pointed one finger over Jackson's shoulder.

Jackson stopped. He could see a partial reflection in the large mirror in front of him of something large and dark. He snapped his head to the left allowing the dark form to come into full view.

"Oh shit."

Planting his feet like a line-backer to get leverage, he shot out his hand and wrapped his hands around Rivers' arms. Throwing all his weight to his right, he pulled both himself and Rivers quickly out of the bathroom just as the phantom lashed out with one of its clawed hands. Quickly grabbing a towel off the floor, Jackson pushed Rivers frantically toward the door. He tossed the towel to him as they moved through the exit. "Clean up. We're getting the fuck out of here."

Rivers slapped the towel to his face and began to remove the last of the shaving cream as they moved down the hallway toward the bank of elevators. "That was quick thinking, boy," he complimented Trent.

Jackson was scanning the hall with his eyes as they went. "Be quiet."

"I just gave you a compliment," Rivers said angrily. "I demand a 'thank you'."

"Shut up, Rivers," Jackson growled.

Rivers tossed the towel loosely into the hall and stopped. "You listen to me—"

"No, you listen to me." Jackson spun around and faced Rivers with anger in his eyes. "You have a job to do, and I'll be damned if I don't get you there. I'm not letting you die on my watch...." Jackson's eyes widened.

"What?" Rivers asked with a timbre of fear in his voice.

Without speaking, Jackson leapt forward and pushed Rivers to the ground, narrowly avoiding a phantom that had just appeared out of the wall. The shadow stopped above Jackson and lashed out with his hands. Rolling to his left, he saw the phantom's hands dig into the carpeted floor where he was just positioned. Performing a reverse somersault, Jackson vaulted to his feet with a nimbleness even he didn't know he possessed. Ducking another one of the shadow's lunges, Jackson ripped Rivers from the floor and began a mad dash for the elevator.

"It's right behind us!" Rivers shouted frantically. "I know," Jackson replied coolly.

Turning left down the hallway, Jackson could see the elevators just ahead. He glanced up at the lights above them and smiled. Luck was on his side. The elevator was only three floors below and counting toward them. Reaching out, he hit the down button with his thumb and spun around. He knew until the elevator arrived, he would be on the offensive. He pulled Rivers behind him and stared down the hallway…at nothing. It was gone.

"Where the hell did it go?" Jackson muttered. "Did you see?"

Rivers shook his head. "It was right behind us when we got up. That's all I know."

Jackson tensed every muscle in his body. Until the elevator arrived, they were completely vulnerable. It could come from anywhere. Then a thought occurred to him. Even in the elevator, they would be vulnerable. "Damn," Jackson hissed. "I didn't think of that."

"What?" Rivers asked nervously just as a dark form loomed out of the wall behind them.

Jackson caught it out of the corner of his eye. Reaching behind him, he pulled Rivers around and pushed him forward. The phantom lashed out, its claws ripping into the small of Jackson's back. Jackson cried out in pain, but didn't let his focus slip. Dropping down, he spun on his heels and brought the butt of his hand up into the shadow's face, and to his amazement, connected. The phantom reeled back. It hadn't expected a counterattack. Seizing the moment, Jackson grabbed Rivers and dashed madly away from the elevator just as the door slid open.

An elderly man began to step off the elevator when he caught sight of the phantom. "Sweet mother of Mary," he muttered in a weak voice. He tried to step back onto the elevator, but his hip was apparently bad and he was fumbling with his silver cane.

The phantom jerked its head toward the man, its red eyes burning with hatred. "You have no power," it growled. It slowly began to move away from the man in the direction of Rivers and Jackson.

The elderly man fell back into the elevator to the sickening crunch of his other hip. He shrieked once as he wrapped his hands around it. At least he was alive.

Jackson skittered, with Rivers in tow, around another corner. He slowed slightly when he spotted the door to the stairs. Pushing through the door, he heard an alarm start to sound. He knew it was an emergency exit, but he didn't care. The two traversed the stairwell haphazardly as they made their way down. Jackson glanced behind them. "I think we lost it."

"How can you be sure?" Rivers asked, still moving quickly down the stairs. "It's not behind us." Jackson was losing momentum. He could feel the wounds on his back bleeding profusely as they throbbed. It wasn't bad, but he knew it would need some kind of medical attention. He could hear Rivers wheezing as he took a breath. "Are you okay?"

Rivers nodded. "Been smoking too long. We need to keep going." Jackson stopped. "It's okay," he assured. "You can stop and catch your breath."

Rivers nodded and slowed to a stop. He looked up at the floor marker on the wall. They were just below the fifth floor. "We're almost there. We're going to make it."

Jackson swallowed hard. "No, I don't think so."

Rivers looked up to see the phantom standing on the landing just above them. "We can run."

Jackson shook his head. "Look below us."

Rivers complied. He felt his heart sink at the sight of a second phantom standing below them on the stairs. "We're trapped."

Jackson extended his open hand to Rivers. "It's been nice working with you."

Rivers reached up and shook Jackson's hand. "Same here."

The two fast friends looked at the shadows approaching them. They were moving, slowly, deliberately, as if they knew this was torturing Rivers and Jackson. One by one, they took the stairs, their red eyes glowing brightly in the dim light of the stairwell. Jackson and Rivers pressed themselves into the corner of the stairwell, their muscles tensed and their hearts throbbing in their throats. They didn't want to go out like this. They had come so far, only to be stopped.

324

Jackson stepped forward and shook his fist at the phantoms. "If you're going to kill us, then just get fucking on with it!"

Rivers shook his head quickly. "Let's not be rash here, Jackson."

"You will not escape," the shadow above them moaned with pleasure. "Yes they will," a female voice boomed from above them.

Rivers and Jackson snapped their heads up to see Morgan floating down the center of the stairwell toward them. Electricity was pulsing over her body and her black hair was flowing in waves around her. Her feet were pressed together with her toes pointed toward the ground, her arms were spread wide with palms open. A sinister grin was spread across her face and her eyes had gone completely black. Rivers wasn't sure who he should be more afraid of, the phantoms, or Morgan.

The two phantoms locked on Morgan and hissed. "Veranda," they said in unison. "You will not stop us this time."

"Veranda?" Jackson asked Rivers quietly. "I thought her name was Morgan."

Rivers shrugged. He was completely enthralled with the events unfolding before them.

The two phantoms leapt from their positions on the stairs toward Morgan, their claws fully extended. They latched onto her body like cats attacking a dog, ripping and shredding as they hung on. Yet Morgan's facial expression remained unchanged, in fact, it seemed like her smile had widened slightly. The dark forms began to merge around her, engulfing her body in a swell of darkness.

"Sweet Jesus," Rivers gasped. "They're killing her."

Before the last syllable had left Rivers' lips, the blackness around Morgan erupted in white light. The two phantoms were thrown against the wall opposite Morgan. Their black bodies hit hard and slowly slid down to the stairs. Before they had a chance to move, Morgan was on them both. Wrapping her hands around their faces, she created another blast of white light in her palms. The shadows shrieked in pain as the light assaulted their eyes. She squeezed harder and the shrieking became worse. It was inhuman, a high-pitched squeal entangled horribly with a low frequency rumble. No human was capable of that sound. Jackson and Rivers cupped their hands over their ears and pressed themselves against the concrete walls of the stairwell. At any moment, they both expected their eardrums to burst and blood to begin pouring from their ear canals.

Morgan squeezed again and hit the phantoms with another burst of white light. Her fingertips were beginning to dig into the darkness of their heads. The two creatures were thrashing wildly below her, trying to break free. Their claws were shearing holes in the concrete around them, and yet Morgan continued to punish them. Jackson could swear he could see pure, unadulterated pleasure on Morgan's face as she tortured the two beings. One of the shadows fell limp on the ground, its body solely supported by Morgan's grasp. She turned her head slightly to enjoy her victory. She squeezed one last time and felt the phantom's head deflate in her hand like a broken balloon. It was dead...again. The second phantom took the opportunity and lashed its claws toward Morgan's face. The blow caught her off-guard as the creature's fingers sliced into the flesh of her cheek. She lost her grip on the phantom as she stumbled back, allowing it time to flee. She turned quickly and shot a blast of white energy toward the creature, but it was too late. It had already vanished into the wall and her attack impacted harmlessly against the concrete. She returned her attention to the black mass lying at her feet.

Jackson and Rivers were slowly making their way up the stairs toward Morgan. "What the hell are those things?" Rivers asked bravely.

Morgan spun around and looked at the duo nervously. "Stay back," she warned. "I don't want to hurt you."

"Who?" Jackson asked, holding up his hands. "We're on your side." Morgan looked up into the empty stairwell and suddenly, was gone. Her body rocketed off into the darkness in front of Rivers and Jackson.

Rivers slammed his fist against the rail. "What in the hell is going on around here?"

Jackson was staring at the motionless black figure in front of them. Its form had quickly begun to decay, melting into the ground around it. Its red eyes became hollow openings in its head, then disappeared altogether. It was fascinating, yet horrible at the same time. "That's the exact same thing I would like to know," Jackson said slowly. Leaning over, he ran his finger through the black mess on the floor and examined it. "It's like," he searched for the word, "goo."

"What do you think it is?" Rivers asked while taking a step forward. "Could it be ghost blood or something like that?"

He brought the substance close to his face and took a sniff. It smelled of burnt rubber. He immediately pushed the pungent substance away. "I don't think so." Jackson wiped the tarlike substance off on the step, "But that's because I don't think this was a ghost." He quickly glanced down at his watch. "Shit," he muttered, "we need to get going. Chloe's going to have our asses."

***

"Where in the fuck are those two?" Chloe asked impatiently. "If they're not here in fifteen seconds, I'm going to have both their asses." She paced back and forth inside her small makeshift director's booth. With the help of the local television crew, they had erected the tiny ten by ten foot booth in the middle of the garage. Small cubical walls had been placed on three sides to keep the distractions to a minimum, while a bank of three televisions stood against the back wall with a desk and mixing console in front of them. One monitor had the live feed from Trent's camera, the second was a video link to the broadcast booth back in California, and the third was the actual live television feed so she could monitor the show. Two men stood in the booth with her, one was a meek young man from the local station who assured her that he would be able to run things, and the other was the station's grisly technician, still tweaking a few last minute connections.

328

Chloe was wearing a headset with a microphone on it so she could keep in constant contact with Trent and the team inside. She was pacing across the small booth—which was no more than three steps either way. Her arms were crossed warily across her chest and she was playing with her fingers nervously. She checked her watch. It was three minutes until show time. She hadn't had time to prep Rivers on the way the show was going to flow. He was just going to have to wing it. She wasn't sure he was capable, but she had to keep a positive outlook on the broadcast. After all, this was her major directorial debut. Sure, she had directed hundreds of segments over the course of her years at *Ghost Chasers, Inc.*, but she had never been in charge of an entire broadcast. What was she worried about Rivers for? It was herself that she should be concerned about. *I'm digging a hole,* she cautioned. *Not a good way to begin a live coast-to- coast broadcast.*

She glanced down at the monitor showing Trent's video feed. She could see Dawn and Bishop standing uncomfortably inside the house being attended to by Carrie. Each was taking turns glancing behind them as Carrie straightened up their wardrobe. She couldn't blame them. She was glad she was out in the garage rather than in the house itself. Several bars of static ran down Trent's feed. She reached up and cued her mic. "We've got a little interference, Trent. See if you can't lock it down."

"Check," came Trent's reply over her headset. His voice sounded confident, strong. She wondered what must be going through his mind. Not only was he stuck in the house, but he also had to look at everything through the narrow lens of the camera. If something were sneaking up behind him, he would never know until it was too late. She shuddered. Maybe it was better that way. She had seen those…things in the house. Best to die quickly. She mentally scolded herself for thinking that.

She watched the snow clear up from the monitor. "That's better. What was wrong?"

"I think this camera got a little damaged earlier. Just had to jiggle some wires."

Chloe took a deep breath. "Okay. Keep an eye on it."

"You got it, boss lady," Trent replied cheerfully. "Dawn, Bishop?" Chloe asked.

She watched Dawn and Bishop both reach a hand up to their individual headsets and look into the camera. "What's up, Chloe?" Bishop asked.

"Just checking the connection," she said after a moment. She took another deep breath. "Are you two alright?"

They nodded and smiled. Bishop quickly gave the camera the thumbs up. "Good as gold, Chloe."

"Good," she said with relief. "Stay focused and have a good show. We're live in one minute." She glanced over at the third monitor to see the credits rolling on the previous program. It was just a matter of seconds now. She heard the garage door begin to rise. Poking her head out of the booth, she watched Rivers and Jackson charge in out of the storm. She rushed angrily to meet them.

"You're late," she accused.

"I know," Rivers said with his trademark smile. "We have a good excuse though." He reached over

330

to Jackson and spun him around.

Chloe looked in horror at the four deep scratches in his back. "What happened?"

"No time for the whole story," Rivers said as he walked confidently toward the house. "Short version: phantoms attacked, we ran, Morgan saved the day."

"What?" Chloe asked in shock. "*Our* Morgan?"

Rivers nodded as he walked up the steps to the house. "One and the same."

"I don't—"

"No time," Rivers said, glancing down at his watch, "gotta show to do." Chloe nodded, then glanced over at Jackson. "Are you okay?"

Jackson nodded. "I'll be fine."

"Good," Chloe said with a smile. "You're on sound tonight."

"Where's Chris?"

Chloe shook her head. She didn't have time, or the heart, to tell him. She pointed to a small pile of equipment in the corner. "There's his stuff. Get moving."

Jackson, without hearing a word, understood. He bent down and scooped Chris' equipment off the floor. Slipping the black headphones over his ears, he nodded at Chloe, then made his way into the house.

Chloe quickly rushed back to her booth. "You ready, Jimmy?" she asked her board op.

The man nodded. His fingers were already poised at the controls and his brow was glistening with nervous sweat.

She patted the grizzled tech on the back. "Everything check out?"

He looked up at Chloe with a cigarette butt dangling from his lower lip. "It's as good as it's going to get," he said with his "four pack a day" voice.

"Stay close," she advised. "We may need a quick fix."

The tech nodded as he moved out of the booth. Pulling out the small folding chair, Chloe slid down behind the table. She placed both hands flat on the table and closed her eyes for a moment. She quickly ran a prayer through her head, then slowly exhaled. It was going to be a long night, she just knew it. She reached over and angled a small microphone toward herself. "What's the time, Daniels?" she asked, addressing the second monitor.

Daniels' face appeared in the small television screen. "We are twenty-two seconds from go time. Everything good on your end?"

Chloe nodded. "Give me the signal," she said. Daniel held up five fingers in front of the camera.

Chloe quickly hit her headset mic. "We are go in," she waited for Daniels to start counting down, "five seconds. Four...three...." she continued the count silently in her head. Turning to the first monitor, she watched the show's opening graphics spill onto the screen with footage they had shot earlier in the day edited together. The music swelled and it rolled into the opening credits. She keyed her mic again. "We are going to Rivers in four seconds." She watched Trent's monitor quickly swing around the living room to focus on Rivers and just barely catching Carrie dashing out of the way. He was standing motionlessly in the center of the living room with one hand in his pant pocket and the other bent slightly in front of him. That stance always reminded Chloe of Rod Serling coming out to introduce the weekly episode of the "Twilight Zone" with a cigarette in his hand. "Camera one," she said with a deep breath, "we're live."

Trent hit the switch on his camera, flipping the red light on the top of it. It was the universal signal actors and newsmen used to determine what camera to look at, and if they were on the air.

Rivers straightened up and smiled broadly. While on the way over, he had time to fix his mussed hair slightly and straighten the black suit he was wearing. His dark red tie was cinched up tightly around his neck and his enunciation was impeccable. He was ready. He counted two seconds silently in his head, then launched into his opening.

"Good evening and welcome to a special Halloween edition of *Ghost Chasers, Incorporated*," he said in his full-blown broadcaster voice.

***

"Overlay the graphic," Chloe said slowly. She glanced over at the first monitor to see an orange and purple Halloween computer graphic roll onto the screen with a glowing jack-o'-lantern and Rivers' name on it. "Give him six seconds, then peel off the graphic."

***

"I'm Rivers Gallows and we're bringing you

333

this episode live from a supposedly haunted residence in Stone Brook, Florida," he said matter-of-factly. Rivers slowly started to walk around the living room with Trent panning with him. He wanted to give the viewers a look at the house. "A usually sleepy town near St. Petersburg, recently this town has had a rash of strange occurrences, and several murders in the midst of the especially violent Hurricane Katrina."

Chloe hit the mic on the desk. "Cue the first segment," she instructed Daniels. Turning to the first monitor, she watched as Rivers' image faded into the pretaped first segment. It was a short history of Stone Brook they had cobbled together that morning. Dominic Jameson, a fantastic radioman back in L.A., had done all the voice-over work for the episode. Chloe tapped her headset, "We're back in two minutes. Good work, Rivers."

She watched as Rivers bowed into the camera. "Did you expect anything less?"

Chloe smiled. It was good to know he was in full broadcast mode tonight.

"When we come back from this segment, talk about what we're going to be doing tonight, introduce Bishop and Dawn, and then send us to commercial break."

Rivers nodded. "Time?"

"You have a minute twenty remaining," Jimmy replied from his position at the board. In front of him, he had the master clock—a list of what time everything started, including commercial breaks—and a stopwatch. He was anxiously watching the seconds tick away on the first segment.

Chloe looked up to see Stephen's face appear

on the second monitor. "Chloe?"

"Yeah, Stephen?"

"Good stuff," he said with a smile. "Looks great so far. Keep up the good work."

"Thanks, Stephen," Chloe said modestly.

"I'll get out of Daniels' way so he can work."

"Thanks again, Stephen." It was good to know he was checking in on the broadcast. At least that was a good sign. She knew, however, his mood would be somewhat darker when she returned to Hollywood with part of her crew dead.

She quickly ran her hand through her hair. What was she thinking? *Major movie productions are completely shut down if one person is accidentally killed, and here we are with three deaths, and we're still on the air....*

"Thirty seconds, Ms. Andrews," Jimmy said. She tapped her headset. "Did you hear that?"

Rivers pressed his finger against the small clear speaker in his ear and nodded at the camera. Turning to Dawn and Bishop, he made sure he knew their last names. There was nothing more unprofessional than forgetting someone's name on the air. He might look like a bit of a dork asking before he went on the air, but he was better safe than sorry. He nodded at their reply and said their full names silently three times. He had a pretty good memory for terms and technique, but when it came to names, he was horrible. He often wondered how he remembered his own name most days.

Chloe watched the first monitor go black for a second, then the special live Ghost Chasers logo appeared on the screen with more of Dominic Jameson's voiceover work. "I love that man's voice," Chloe said to Jimmy. She pressed a button on her headset. "We're back in five, Rivers."

Rivers watched the red light appear above the camera. "This town has seen its share of experts in the last few days, and we're privileged to have two of them here. He walked slowly toward his guests. "It's my pleasure to introduce Dawn Lassiter and Nick Bishop of the Office of Paranormal Research, better known as the OPR. Dawn, Nick, welcome to *Ghost Chasers, Inc.*"

Dawn and Bishop nodded at Rivers. They had been instructed not to look directly into the camera as Rivers did. It was only acceptable for the host to do so when directly addressing the home audience. They were to talk to Rivers only while on the air.

"Thank you, Rivers," Dawn said cordially.

"Tell me a little about the Office of Paranormal Investigation," Rivers prompted.

"Certainly," Dawn said with a smile. "The OPR is a privately funded organization based out of Washington D.C. with the one goal of meticulously researching paranormal phenomenon. We're trying to take the 'super' out of 'supernatural'." She smiled broadly at her own cleverness.

"What sort of thing does the OPR investigate?" Rivers wondered. "Anything that can't be easily explained by mainstream science," Dawn explained. "Ghosts, lake monsters, UFOs, that sort of thing."

Rivers nodded and turned to the camera. "A little later in the program, Dawn and Nick will be taking us through the house as we search for the source of the haunting, but right now, we have to take a commercial break. Stay tuned, there's more of this special live Halloween edition of *Ghost*

Chasers, Incorporated coming up." Rivers ended with a very serious look on his face that remained until the red light blinked off. It was then that Rivers' posture slumped over and he dug into his suit pocket for his pack of cigarettes. "How long do we have, Chloe?"

"Three and a half minutes in the commercial break, then another seven minutes for the second recorded segment."

"Good," Rivers said as he lit his cigarette. "I'm getting out of this house for a minute. What's the second segment?"

"It's," Chloe paused, looking for the information, "a segment about the previous haunted houses we've investigated."

"And then?" Rivers asked.

"We have the 'Highgate Vampire' story we taped about two weeks ago."

"Why did we wait so long to air the vampire segment?" Rivers wondered as he took a puff from his cigarette.

"Stephen felt it would be perfect for the Halloween episode."

"Okay," Rivers said as he exhaled the gray smoke from his lungs. "I'm coming out there for a minute."

Carrie stepped out from behind Trent and Jackson and tapped Rivers' coat pocket. "Can I bum a smoke?"

Rivers nodded. He didn't usually share his cigarettes (the fact of the matter was that Rivers *never* shared his "precious" cigarettes), but this was a special occasion. He lifted his black, metal lighter out of his pocket and lit it. Carrie leaned over and

337

took a long drag off the flame, sucking the thick smoke into her lungs. A look of relief passed over her face as the nicotine hit her blood stream. "Let's get out of here." He turned to look at Dawn and Bishop. "You coming?"

The two nodded and followed the crew into the garage. "So far so good," Bishop said with a smile.

Dawn nodded. "It seems oddly quiet at the moment."

They failed to notice the two pairs of red eyes watching them silently from the staircase.

Chapter 27

"So far so good," Chloe addressed her crew. They had all gathered in front of her during the short break to get away from the house, although most of them realized, none better than Bishop, Rivers and Jackson, the phantoms could strike anywhere, let alone in the house. Jackson had seated himself on a small stack of milk crates and was doing his best to nurse his back while Rivers and Carrie were busy chain-smoking. Trent, Bishop and Dawn were all standing in front of Chloe listening to every word. "I'm very happy with the show so far." She glanced down at her stopwatch. They had almost five minutes remaining in the break. "Let's get back into the house and get ready."

"Where do want us to start?" Dawn asked.

"I'm really not sure," Chloe admitted. "I was thinking the upstairs, because that's where the Grants were killed, but then I thought that might be a little to grisly. Opinions?"

Dawn nodded. "I think we should work our way up to the second floor, after all, no one's been up there since the coroner had to collect the Grants' bodies. We have no idea of what we'll find."

"I—"

All heads snapped to the right to see the garage door slowly lifting up. A general wave of anxiety passed over the group as they watched.

"That's it," a feminine voice yelled from under the door. Montoya finally revealed herself after the door was up. Stepping inside, she shook the rain off her coat and hair and walked quickly toward Chloe. The group could see several squad cars positioned outside with their lights flashing through the storm.

"What's going on?" Dawn asked, intercepting Montoya. "He's dead."

"Who?"

Montoya stopped and looked Dawn in the eye. "Jack." Dawn gasped.

"We found him dead at the hospital twenty minutes ago. His heart had been ripped out of his chest," Montoya said gravely. Everyone could tell this was killing her, but she was determined to stay strong. "He was found in Kelley's room, but she was missing."

Bishop stepped forward. "Kelley's gone?"

Montoya nodded. "We found traces of her blood on the bed, but that could be from previous injuries. The lab boys are checking it out right now." Montoya stepped around Dawn and faced Chloe. "I'm shutting you down."

Chloe tore off her headset. "You can't do that. We have permission from the mayor to film here. Plus, we're in the middle of our live broadcast. You can't take us off now."

Montoya's face remained unchanged. "Watch me." She pulled a yellow envelope from beneath her arm and tore it open. Pulling out three white documents, she cleared her throat and began to read. "As of October thirty-first, Stone Brook hereby rescinds all filming licenses granted locally or by the state, by orders of the Chief of Police, and the Mayor." Montoya handed the papers to Chloe. "Read them if you want to. It's all there in black ink."

Chloe stared angrily at the pages. "Son of a bitch!" she shouted angrily. Tossing the papers to

340

the ground, she stepped into Montoya's face. "I will not pull the plug on this broadcast. We're going live on the air in one minute."

"No you're not," Montoya countered. Grabbing Chloe by the shoulder, she spun her around and pinned her arms behind her back. Reaching into her pocket, she pulled out a heavy silver pair of handcuffs and snapped them tightly around Chloe's wrists. "I am placing you under arrest."

"Now hold on just a damned minute," Carrie cut in. "You can't just bust in here and arrest our director. We have a show to do. Millions of dollars in sponsorships are on the line here. We can't just stop in the middle and say 'oops, sorry. We're bad'."

"I'm afraid that's exactly what you're going to have to do," Montoya said solemnly. "This is for your own good. I'm advising everyone to get the hell away from this house and find a nice, safe place to hide for the night. I don't want to see your bodies in the morgue tomorrow morning." Montoya turned and started to push Chloe toward the open garage door. "You all have five minutes to clear out. If you're not out in that time, my men will come in here and arrest every single one of you."

"Caroline," Dawn said as she stepped forward, "wait a minute. Why are you doing this?"

Montoya stopped then turned to face Dawn. She kept one of her hands firmly around Chloe's handcuffs. "This is not open for debate, Dawn."

"I realize that," Dawn conceded. "I just want to talk. Friend to friend."

"Not now," Montoya said with a forced smile.

"I'm sorry about Detective Enbaugh. He was a

good man, but I lost one of my closest friends here today as well. Cane died earlier in the house."

"Doesn't that make you want to get as far away from this place as you can?"

Dawn nodded. "Yes it does, but I have a job to do."

"To film this television program?" Montoya asked cynically.

"No, to stop the killings." Dawn leaned close to Montoya. "We know why they're here, and we know how to stop them."

Montoya's hopes began to rise, but she quickly beat them back down into her chest. She would love to have revenge on those bastards, but that wasn't the point. "At what cost, Dawn? The lives of the crew? Bishop? When is it going to end?"

"Tonight," Dawn stated, "at midnight. That's when this all ends if we can stop it. Otherwise, get used to living with evil demons that kill randomly and without remorse."

"I'm not following."

"The phantoms are performing a ritual tonight. It's called 'The Ritual of Sevens' and it can only happen every seventy-seven years on Halloween. To complete the ritual, they need seven hearts. They have that now, counting Enbaugh's. If they are allowed to continue unabated, they will become almost omnipotent in their powers. Right now, they have weaknesses, but if they finish...." she let Montoya's imagination fill in the blank. It was far more efficient in her opinion. "Look, I'm not saying stopping them will be easy, but we have no other choice. We can't let these things finish the ritual. It would mean the end of not only Stone Brook, but all

342

of us."

Montoya looked away from Dawn and back at Chloe. "We'll die, just like he did."

"No," Dawn said compassionately, "if we stop them, we *all* have a fighting chance."

"Please, Detective," Chloe pleaded. "Let us finish."

Montoya shook her head. "I'm sorry. I can't. I have orders to follow, and that means this production is officially shut down, and your two minutes are up. Everyone out."

"Goddamn it, Caroline," Dawn shouted, to the amazement of the entire crew. "You may be saving the lives of a dozen people, but you are throwing away tens of thousands. I hope you can live with that on your conscience." Dawn took a deep breath to try and get her rage under control. "Listen," she said after a moment, "I'm sorry Jack is dead, but you can't punish the rest of us for that."

"I'm not punishing anyone!" Montoya shouted. "I'm saving lives!"

"Like you couldn't do for Enbaugh."

Montoya nodded as a tear appeared in her right eye. "Like I couldn't do for Jack." The tear jerked loose of her eyelid and rolled down her cheek. "He was my family," Montoya said quietly. "I'm not going to let those damned things hurt anyone else I care about."

"Then help us," Bishop jumped in. "We can stop the phantoms tonight, once and for all."

"I can't," Montoya said with a deep regret. "I have to follow orders and get you people out of here. It's my job."

"And we're just trying to do our jobs,

343

Caroline." Dawn took a step closer to Montoya. "Let us work. We *can* stop this. Then no one else will be hurt. We promise."

"I'm sorry—" Montoya started, but was cut off by the slam of the garage door.

Everyone jumped back, almost falling over each other. They hadn't realized they were that unnerved just by being there.

"Jesus Christ," Rivers shouted from the back of the garage. "That about gave me a fucking heart attack!"

Bishop looked up at the motor hanging from the roof. The chain had been disengaged from the motor, allowing the door to fall freely down. He wondered if the emergency pin had been pulled. Grabbing a nearby milk crate, he stepped on top and started to examine the door. Every automatic garage door came with a safety release pin, so that in case a pet or a child got trapped under the door and the sensors didn't detect them, someone could pull the pin and open the door manually. Bishop glanced over the rigging. The pin was still firmly in place, but the chain was broken. He lifted up the edge of the thin chain. It was smooth, appearing more as if it had been cut rather than broken. "I think it's been sabotaged."

"By whom?" Montoya asked. "Who would want to stay in this Godforsaken house with those things?" She realized she had just answered her own question.

"They must've been listening to us," Dawn said with just a touch of paranoia. "They realize we're on to them."

"That means they're here in the house," Bishop

continued. "That also means the ritual will probably be performed here in the house." He thought about the implications for a moment. "They're going to kill us all."

Montoya shook her head. "I won't accept that. It's just some kind of freak mechanical failure. If the chain is really cut, then the garage door should just lift right up." She let go of Chloe and reached down for the small silver handle at the base of the door. Tugging with all her might, she couldn't get the door to move. "Want to give me a hand here, Bishop?"

Bishop nodded and knelt down next to Montoya. Sliding the edges of his fingers under the door, he lifted with his arms and knees, but couldn't get the door to budge. He fell back on the floor and tried to catch his breath. "Freak mechanical failure, huh?"

"All right," Montoya said with determination. "I'll just go use the front door. There's got to be a way out of this place." She turned and started to charge, with Chloe in tow, toward the door leading into the house.

"Wait," Carrie said, stepping in front of Montoya, "you can't go in there alone."

"The hell I can't." Montoya pulled her pistol from its holster and cradled it in her hand. Taking a step forward, she peered into the darkened house and stopped. Mustering up all her courage, she stepped into the long hallway and followed it into the house. She stood quietly with her weapon drawn at the mouth of the living room, scanning the darkness. Digging deep, she relied on her police training and instincts to guide her across the living room. Spinning around, she checked the room behind her. Once satisfied, she reached behind and slowly wrapped her long fingers around the doorknob. She twisted it hard to the right, and was surprised when it smoothly answered. Pulling gently on the door, it didn't budge. Turning around, she applied more force to the door. Still nothing. "Fuck it," she finally said. "Take a step back," she warned Chloe. Aiming her weapon at the door, she fired several rounds into the metal handle until it was hanging loosely from its cradle. Sliding the gun between her belt and pants, she reached with both hands for the door and tugged again to no avail. "Fuck!" She turned back to Chloe. "Is there a back way out of here?"

Chloe nodded. "Through the kitchen."

Montoya grabbed the small chain between the handcuffs and led Chloe toward the kitchen through the dining room. Stepping in front of her prisoner, she lifted her weapon from her belt and held it tightly between both hands and pressed her back to the kitchen door. Taking a deep breath, she burst through it and quickly scanned the kitchen. It was completely empty. Glancing out the large windows, she could see Hurricane Katrina raging outside. She knew this wasn't the best place to be for long. Those windows would surely give before the night was over. She could already hear the branches of the oak trees tapping against them, soon, they would be banging against them, and then they would be inside. Step by step, she made her way quickly and quietly across the kitchen until she was standing in front of the back door. It had four panels of stained glass inset into it, creating an eerie light pattern across the floor around her.

Reaching down, Montoya tested the knob. This one wouldn't turn at all. Flipping her gun around so she was holding it by the barrel, she swung it hard toward the glass, knowing it would break. The butt of the gun hit the glass and stopped. Nothing. She swung again with the same result. "What the hell is going on in this house?" she muttered to herself.

Taking three steps back, she aimed her weapon at the glass and fired two rounds. No effect. That should've shattered the glass instantly. There was something definitely wrong here. Reversing her course, Montoya found Chloe standing right where she left her. Grabbing her by the arm, she led her back into the garage with the others.

Dawn and Bishop were the first to look up. "How did it go?" Montoya shook her head. "We're stuck in this damned place."

Bishop looked over to Dawn and voiced a silent 'I told you so'. "What now, Detective?"

"I don't know."

"I do," Carrie cut in. "Let us do our jobs. We're back on the air in forty seconds."

Montoya rolled the thought around for a moment. "All right," she said finally. "We're going to do this my way, though."

"Fine," Chloe agreed. "Unlock the cuffs so I can work."

Reaching into her pocket, Montoya produced a small, silver key. Sliding it into the locks, she removed the cuffs and returned them to her pocket.

Chloe rubbed her wrists for a moment. "Okay, people, places. We're on in ten." She quickly moved back to the booth and took her seat next to

Jimmy. Trent and Jackson rounded up their equipment and made their way back into the house. Rivers and Carrie immediately followed them.

Dawn and Bishop moved to Montoya's side. "What's the plan, Detective?" Bishop asked.

Montoya smiled. "I thought you guys had the plan."

Dawn and Bishop looked at each other with a smile. "You're with us then. We have to get in there. We're on in five seconds."

The red light blinked on and Trent pointed his finger at Rivers.

"Coming up in the next segment," Rivers billboarded, "we'll be talking with the members of the OPR as they take us through the house and show us the scene of the murders of an entire family. It should be fascinating," Rivers said with a smile. "For *Ghost Chasers, Incorporated,* I'm Rivers Gallows, and we'll be right back after these commercial messages."

Chapter 28

Cane had company. He wasn't sure who it was at first, but at least he knew it was human. Reaching out in the darkness, he felt a shaking, frightened body cowering in the corner. He had no idea when she had arrived, but she was alive. He could tell by the shallow, frantic breathing echoing off the cave walls. He placed his hand firmly in the center of her back to try and comfort her. "It's going to be okay," he said softly.

The woman shrieked and pulled away from his touch. "Don't kill me! Please don't kill me! I'm too young to die," she beseeched.

"I'm not going to hurt you," Cane eased in his soft British accent. "I'm stuck down here, just like you are." He thought for a moment. "I'm one of the good guys," he added, using the tired American cliché.

"Who are you?"

"My name is Cane. I'm from the Office of Paranormal Investigation." The woman perked up. "You work with Nick Bishop?"

"Yes," Cane said with a smile. "How did you know that?"

"I'm Kelley. Kelley Windel. Nick came and talked to me while I was in the hospital."

"Oh yes, I remember. You were one of the girls who was—" he quickly bit his tongue. Shouldn't be dredging up painful memories like that. "I know who you are, Kelley," he corrected himself.

"Where are we, Mr. Cane?" Kelley asked in a meager voice.

"I'm not really sure," Cane admitted. "Some

349

kind of cave as far as I can tell."

Silence ensued between the two. They were both glad to have someone with them, but they didn't know what to say. The sound of them adjusting on the cold rock floor echoed off the hard walls of the cave and amplified it. Each scuff, each movement became a roar of sound in their cramped prison cell. It was too much to bear. With each noise, they both worried it would bring the phantoms down on them. They both resolved themselves to sitting motionlessly in silence.

What do you say to someone you're going to die with? Cane wondered.

The same thing you'd say to anyone else, Kelley answered.

He could hear her clearly speaking in his mind, but he knew she hadn't spoken a word. "How did you do that?" Cane asked out loud.

I've been able to do it since I was a child. Not really sure why, Kelley replied with her mind.

You're telepathic, Cane thought.

Yes.

"That's most incredible." A thought formed in his mind. He leaned forward to ask, but he realized Kelley was already answering it.

I have read their minds.

"What did you see?"

Kelley shuddered. *It's horrible in there. Just darkness with an occasional thought surfacing. I looked into one of the phantom's mind earlier and thought I was going to get trapped in it. The darkness is completely pervasive. It swallowed me whole and I got lost in the madness that is their minds. It's like swimming in dark water, where I*

350

couldn't touch the bottom and couldn't see the shore. It's a feeling of complete and total hopelessness.

Did it reveal anything to you? Cane found himself asking questions mentally. He had worked with telepaths before and found it much faster than speaking. You just had to watch what you thought around a telepath. A stray thought could get you in a heap of trouble.

Yes, Kelley said quickly. *I know who they are, and what they want.*

Cane's eyes widened. *What?*

Us, she answered gravely, *but more specifically, our hearts. Why?*

Their minds are almost unfathomable in their darkness, Kelley stated as a precursor to her following statements, *I couldn't find everything, but I did hit upon a few strange thoughts. They're after people with special gifts, like mine. They plan to perform a ritual that involves transferring our power to them.*

For what purpose? Cane asked.

From what I could gather, they think this ritual will make them almost godlike. They will become unstoppable.

The three horseman of the apocalypse, Cane thought with disdain. *How does the ritual work?*

Kelley shook her head. *I'm not clear on that one. I just know it involves our hearts and it has to be completed tonight. The window of opportunity only comes around every so often.*

What are they? Ghosts? Dead cultists brought back to life?

They aren't ghosts. They can be stopped,

351

Kelley answered. *Apparently, they all died performing this ritual seventy-seven years ago. They then, somehow, escaped hell and returned to finish their work. They are more like a demon than ghost,* Kelley essayed, *but are kind of a hybrid of the two. They have the weaknesses of a demon and the abilities of ghosts.* She started to adjust her body, but quickly stopped when she heard a scraping noise. *That wasn't me.*

We're not alone, Cane agreed.

"Stop wasting it!" A raspy voice boomed from the darkness, then two red eyes blinked into existence. "Stop wasting the girl's power!" The phantom lashed out and drew his claws across Cane's face.

Cane recoiled in pain, warm blood spilling from his new wounds. He watched with a mixture of terror and amazement as the two red eyes disappeared into the blackness. "That was interesting," Cane spat cynically.

"Are you all right?"

"Yeah," Cane said as he tried to stop the bleeding, "but I don't think the warranty is valid on me anymore. We need to stop this ritual."

"I know," Kelley replied seriously, "but how?"

"How far can your telepathic powers reach?"

"I'm not sure," Kelley replied. "Why?"

"Do you think you can get a message to Dawn and Bishop and lead them to us?"

"I don't even know where we are. How am I going to lead them to us? It's not like they can follow the sound of my voice. It'll be in their heads."

"At least let them know we're still alive," Cane

countered. "Okay," Kelley said slowly. "Give me a minute."

Pressing her hands to the sides of her head, she began to focus her energy. Clearing her mind, she retained only the names of Dawn and Bishop. *Hear me. Cane is alive.*

***

Bishop glanced down at his black metallic flashlight. Clicking the button, he watched as the bright beam of light sliced through the murky darkness of the Grant House. Tapping the button again, he slid the flashlight into his back pocket. He just wanted to make sure everything was in working order before they went upstairs. He didn't know what to expect. He glanced over at Dawn. The two were standing at the rear of the living room, their backs to the staircase. She was fidgeting nervously with her flashlight, waiting to go on the air. Then it hit him like the last fragments of an echo at the bottom of a canyon. He strained his ears in the silence for a moment.

"Did you just say something?" Bishop asked Dawn.

Dawn turned to her partner and shook her head, "No, but I just heard something, too."

"What was it?" Bishop wondered.

"I don't know. Maybe a phantom's trick."

"I don't think so," Bishop said. "It sounded feminine. It said Cane was alive."

Dawn nodded. "We'll find him."

Rivers was about to bring them back from the third recorded segment of the program and take the

353

crew upstairs. Carrie was standing behind Trent with a coil of cables in her hand, while Jackson was steadying his boom above Rivers' head. Rivers was sucking the last drag of nicotine out of a demolished cigarette as he waited.

"We're back in fifteen seconds," Chloe announced over the headsets.

Dawn pointed to a black box sitting just beyond Rivers. "Our equipment. I forgot it was in here."

Bishop slowly made his way to the box and knelt down in front of it. Popping the latches, he flipped open the top of the hard plastic case. There wasn't much equipment left inside from their earlier venture, but some of it would do nicely. He lifted out another Electromagnetic Field Meter and a slick, white Air Ion Counter. Closing the lid of the box, Bishop returned to Dawn's side. He quickly handed her the Air Ion Counter and the notepad. Slipping the tape measure into his jacket pocket, he flipped the switch on the EMF Meter. The needle jumped to life and he heard the familiar crackling noise from an internal speaker.

"I'm already getting high readings," Bishop warned them.

"I'm surprised with all the paranormal activity in this house you can actually get a distinct reading. The needle should be buried as soon as you turn it on," Dawn said. Lifting her Air Ion Counter, she tapped a series of buttons on its face. "I'm seeing a high concentration of positive ions in this part of the house," she said, deciphering the digital readout on the counter. "It could be from the television equipment though." She snapped the counter off and slid it into her pocket. "I don't think these are

354

going to do us any good."

"Any little edge will help," Bishop said positively. He looked up to see the red light flicker on.

"Welcome back to our special live Halloween edition of *Ghost Chasers, Incorporated.* I'm Rivers Gallows. We're coming to you live from Stone Brook, Florida from the scene of a grisly triple murder. Local law enforcement officials reported seeing a pair of glowing red eyes in the house, leading us to believe this case was supernatural in origin. As we told you at the top of the show, we have two very special experts joining us tonight from the Office of Paranormal Research, Dawn Lassiter and Nick Bishop." Rivers turned to greet Dawn and Bishop. "Can you tell us your theories on this case?"

Dawn nodded, "Certainly. We believe these murders were part of an occult ritual. All their hearts, with the exception of the young boy's, were removed and taken from the scene."

"Sounds horrific," Rivers commented in a completely inappropriate voice. "Do you know what the ritual is?"

"As yet, we are unsure," she said, omitting details, "but we hope to find out tonight, Rivers."

"Nick," Rivers said slowly, "what interested you in this case?"

Bishop smiled. "I'm just tagging along with my partners." He knew that wasn't the answer Rivers wanted, and that was exactly why he gave it. "Seriously though, this is an incredible chance to study supernatural phenomenon."

"Very good," said a slightly perturbed Rivers.

355

"Are we ready to head upstairs?"

Dawn nodded.

"I'll let you two take the lead, and guide us through the house," Rivers said almost cowardly.

"Okay," Dawn said directly to the camera, "if you'll accompany us upstairs, we'll begin the investigation."

***

"Keep a wide angle on Dawn and Bishop," Chloe whispered into her mic while watching the third monitor. "If anything should rear its ugly head, we want to catch it on tape."

Montoya had taken up a position directly behind Chloe in the booth. She was overseeing the operation, but didn't claim to understand it. Clasping her hands behind her back, she watched the third monitor with a worried feeling in the pit of her stomach. *This isn't good,* was her only thought. Leaning forward, she pressed her hands to the back of Chloe's chair. "You can communicate directly with the crew?"

Chloe nodded while keeping her vision trained on the three monitors. "They all have a small ear bud they can hear my commands on. If I see something on the monitor they don't, I can alert them immediately."

Montoya let out a long sigh. "Doesn't this make you feel powerless? I mean, looking at these monitors, you could watch the entire crew die and you wouldn't be able to help them."

"That part of the job just comes with the territory," Chloe replied. "They're on their own. I can tell them what I want to see, but it's up to them to follow through."

"I hate this," Montoya said as she stood up.

***

Dawn stood at the base of the staircase staring up into the darkness. She had no desire to go up there, let alone take a television crew with her. She felt Bishop standing just behind her and took the first step. Lifting the Air Ion Counter, she slowly made her way up the stairs. Her pulse was racing. "What do you have on the EMF Meter, Bishop?"

Bishop tapped the square plastic housing of the needle. It was dancing wildly back and forth; jumping from zero to maximum, then back again. "Either this thing is shot, or we've got a reading off the scale."

"Keep an eye on it," Dawn said, trying to sound as professional as possible.

The silence was deafening. Outside, they could hear Katrina's winds pounding against the side of the house. It, and the fact their lives were in danger, was making them all feel uncomfortable.

Rivers had fallen back to the rear of the group behind Carrie and had unconsciously pulled a cigarette out of his pocket. Lighting it, he took a long drag and exhaled slowly. He kept glancing nervously behind him. He didn't want to be in the lead, but he wasn't sure he wanted to be bringing up the rear either.

Carrie was slowly unwinding the thick, black cable as they made their way toward the second floor. Their remote unit had been damaged earlier necessitating the use of snake cable to the director's booth. Her slender fingers were working over the cable slowly so as not to let out too much, but just enough to keep Trent unhindered. She knew she had enough cable to run over this entire house. She hoped she wouldn't have to. Acid was churning in her stomach as it ate away at her lining. She needed an antacid tablet. Glancing down at her watch, she saw there was well over a half an hour left in the broadcast and muttered several profanities under her breath.

Jackson pressed one of his hands against the black headphones and listened to the ambient noises of the house. He could hear the storm howling outside and every creaking step the group took up the stairs. Someone was even scraping his or her feet. He wasn't sure whom. Reaching down to the DAT recorder slung over his shoulder, he inched the volume knob forward. He wasn't familiar with all the workings of Chris' equipment, but he was trying to learn fast. Damn fast.

Bishop pulled his flashlight from his back pocket and gripped it tightly in his sweaty palm. *Aim for the eyes,* he reminded himself. *Anything else, and it's your ass.* He clicked on the light and focused it at the top of the stairs. There was only emptiness there, to his relief. He had half expected all the phantoms to be standing there with evil grins on their faces just waiting to kill the entire crew. He glanced down at his EMF Meter. The needle was now firmly buried. "Dawn...."

"Yeah, Bish," she acknowledged quietly. "I think we're in trouble."

Dawn stopped and turned to face her partner.

"What is it?"

Bishop lifted the EMF Meter so Dawn could read the display. "I've never seen a constant reading this high before."

"Neither have I," Dawn said quietly. She looked down to address the camera. "We just had a spike on the Electromagnetic Field Meter. From our research, we know ghosts generate large electromagnetic fields, so we can read them with this device. It's like following a ghost's footsteps," she added. "Neither Nick nor myself have ever seen a reading this high before."

"What does that mean?" Rivers asked from the rear.

"It could mean one of two things. Either we're sensing that ghosts were here recently, or that they are here right now."

The crew shuddered in unison.

Dawn could sense their unease, but knew she needed to continue. Cane was here...somewhere. "We'll continue upstairs."

A pool of red fluid began to gather on the roof above the crew.

Dawn took the last step to the second floor and stopped dead in her tracks. There was a wide central hall with doors on each side, but at the end, a large hole had been carved into the wall. It looked like an optical illusion. She could see a portion of the window still remaining, so the storm was visible through it, yet the hole was completely dark and seemed to stretch on forever. "Bishop, take a look at that."

"Wow," he breathed. "That's incredible."

Trent made his way up the last few steps and

took a position behind Dawn and Bishop. He focused his camera tightly on the hole, trying to see inside. "Are you getting this, Chloe?" He asked into his headset.

"That's the weirdest fucking thing I've ever seen," Chloe answered back as she stared at the third monitor.

Dawn felt something wet fall on the back of her neck. Reaching up, she wiped it onto her hand. "Shine your light over here, Bish."

Bishop quickly complied and shone his flashlight on her hand. "What the hell is that?" he asked as he looked at the thick red fluid.

Dawn shook her head. "It almost looks like—"

"Blood," Rivers cut in. He was standing just behind Dawn, looking over her shoulder. "Where did it come from?"

Bishop flipped his flashlight up toward the ceiling and let out a gasp. Trent quickly followed suit with his camera. "It's hanging on the roof," he said quickly.

A sea of viscous red fluid had gathered on the roof above them. It looked like an upside down swimming pool as the fluid lapped at the walls around it. The crew could clearly see waves in the fluid and what appeared to be faces. They looked as if they were in pain as they were continually ripped apart, then reformed in other parts of the wave. Their silent screams unnerved the crew.

"What's keeping it up there?" Rivers asked.

"I don't have the first clue," Bishop replied. He watched as another drop broke free of the mass and fell to the floor. Stepping out of its way, he saw it hit the thick carpeting just in front of him. Bishop

360

dropped to his knees and examined the fluid. To his amazement, the carpet below the drop began to smoke as if being burnt. "Dear Lord," he said quietly as he rose to his feet. Glancing around, he could see drops beginning to fall around the crew. "It's an acid," Bishop said quickly. Turning back to the crew, he could see the fluid starting to separate from the ceiling in an upside down tsunami. It was falling down on *them*.

"Run!"

***

Cane and Kelley were sitting quietly against the wall of the cave. They hadn't spoken for what seemed like an eternity, but was probably closer to twenty minutes. They were each taking turns picking small pebbles off the ground and tossing them at the opposite wall. They had discovered, shortly after Kelley had sent the message, that she was also chained to the wall. Neither of them could get very far.

"What time do you think it is?" Kelley asked.

"I'm not sure," Cane answered honestly. "We're in kind of a sensory deprivation chamber here. Day and night have no bearing on us."

"Look."

Cane spun his head around. "What am I looking at?"

"Behind you," Kelley instructed him.

Cane slowly turned to see behind him. There was a dull bluish light filtering into the cavern from places, or persons, unknown. For the first time, he could see a long tunnel that led into the cave. The light was strange. It seemed to be crawling along the floors and walls as if it was alive. It kept creeping steadily toward them.

"What do you think it is?"

"I don't have any idea."

"Any thoughts?"

Kelley quieted her mind. "What I'm sensing doesn't make much sense. I can read two completely different personalities inhabiting one body. There seems to be a struggle for dominance between the two personalities as well."

"But it's a person?" Cane asked. "A woman."

They both looked up at the light as it grew brighter. Whoever it was, it was getting closer.

You have no reason to fear me, boomed a voice in their heads. *I have come to stop them.*

Cane looked over at Kelley. "Another telepath?"

Kelley shook her head quickly. There was a twinge of fear in her voice when she answered, "I don't think so. Whatever it is, it's *very* powerful."

Cane lifted himself off the floor and quickly configured his body into a defensive posture. "I won't let it hurt you, Kelley."

"I feel very reassured by that," Kelley said cynically. "Thanks."

The two watched the light grow in intensity. There was no doubt it was heading toward them. Kelley and Cane waited with bated breath for whomever it was to show. They could tell there was a bend in the tunnel that led into the cave as the bluish white light spilled further into it.

"Who's there?" Cane yelled. He couldn't take it anymore. "I am Veranda Till," a female voice answered steadily.

Cane and Kelley watched as a female form floated around the corner and came into full view. The light that seemed to be emanating from her body engulfed her. Cane recognized her as Morgan LeFay.

"What do you want, Morgan?" Cane asked, still believing she had murdered Sam Peters.

"Morgan is the vessel I am inhabiting," the woman replied. She stared at Cane with her black eyes. "My name is Veranda."

"Veranda," Cane said uneasily, "what do you want?"

"I have come to help you and Kelley."

Kelley was shocked Veranda knew her name. "How do you know—?"

"Your name?" Veranda asked. "I know all," she answered cryptically. "You are what the phantoms seek to contain. You are what must escape."

"They want my power," Kelley agreed.

"It's more than that," Veranda countered. "They want your very essence."

"What is this ritual that they are about to perform?" Cane queried.

"It is known as the 'Ritual of Sevens'," Veranda answered evenly as she gradually floated to the floor. "They need seven hearts, seven personal effects, and it must be completed by midnight tonight. All seven hearts must be from people who have psychic powers. The phantoms believe through this ritual, they will gain the power of all seven people and their lives, making them almost immortal."

"How do you know all of this?" Cane asked.

"I stopped them from performing this same ritual seventy-seven years ago tonight ."

Cane took a moment to examine Veranda-Morgan's statement. "How have they, and you for that matter, returned?"

"There are things you cannot understand as humans. Once you have passed over the threshold into the afterlife, you will understand." Veranda continued, "I killed the original three priests who tried to perform the ritual, but in doing so, I lost my own life as well. I am now forever tied to them and the ritual."

"Interesting," Cane exhaled. "Why have you chosen Morgan's body?"

"I took the strongest person who was going to be directly involved with the ritual."

"But why—"

Veranda waived her hand in front of Cane's face, stopping him. "There is no more time for questions. The hour of the ritual looms near. We must hurry."

"Hurry to where?" Cane asked.

"To meet some friends."

Cane pointed down at the shackles around his and Kelley's ankles. "Unless you brought a hacksaw, we're not going anywhere."

Veranda-Morgan glanced down at the chains and laughed. Snapping her fingers, the chains and shackles turned into dust and fell away. Looking back at Kelley and Cane, she smiled. "Follow me."

Chapter 29

Diving through the mouth of the cave, Bishop stopped to look back. The fluid had vanished. He had entered the cave last, after making sure the entire crew was safe. One by one, they had charged into the cave to avoid the acidy red liquid, but where was it? Bishop slowly turned around to see the rest of the crew picking themselves off the ground and starting to dust off. Trent was the next up, his camera still firmly fastened to his shoulder, the red light still blazing in the darkness. Bishop moved over to Dawn and then to Rivers, helping them up. He patted Rivers firmly on the back and pointed to the camera, "We're still on the air."

Rivers could hear Chloe shouting frantically in her earpiece. Lifting up his hand, he tore the small clear bud from his ear and let it hang loosely over his shoulder. Trying to quickly gather his thoughts, he addressed the camera. "Ladies and gentlemen," he said warily as he searched for the words to describe what had just happened. "I don't know if I can even begin to give justice to what just happened with words. This was the most incredible sight this man has ever beheld." He turned and glanced out the mouth of the cave. "We were chased in here by some kind of acid that seemed to be falling from the roof, and by here, I mean a cave that has somehow appeared in an outer wall of the house. Can we get a shot of the mouth of the cave?"

Trent quickly complied and spun the camera toward the mouth. His usually steady hold on the camera was now shaking slightly, and he could tell the camera had taken a hard fall. A few stray lines of static were rolling over the image in his eyepiece. With his steadying hand, he reached up and rapped the camera once with his knuckles, then again. The static momentarily faded, leaving him with a clear shot of the hallway through the cave. It was completely empty.

No signs of the acid existed. He rolled the fader with his fingers, zooming in on the ceiling. He expected to at least see a few black scorch marks on the roof from the acid. He panned down to the floor. Nothing. No burns, no ragged edges on the thick gray carpet, nothing.

"As you can see," Rivers continued his narration; "there is no evidence of the red acid that chased us in here."

Trent quickly returned his focus to Rivers.

"Now we're standing in this cave that leads to who knows where, but hopefully, to the root of this haunting. I don't think I can say this enough, what we just encountered was truly phenomenal in nature." He reached down and grabbed the ear bud and pressed it firmly back into his ear. "Through this speaker," Rivers began to explain, "I can hear the director." He waited for a moment. "She's telling me that we need to take a commercial break." Rivers nodded to the unheard words of Chloe. "For *Ghost Chasers, Incorporated*, I'm Rivers Gallows. We'll be right back." Rivers held still until the red light vanished from the camera. Once gone, he collapsed to the floor with a moan.

Carrie quickly rushed to his side. "What is it, Rivers?" She placed her hand on his shoulder.

"I was just chased by red acid and forced to dive into a cave. What the fuck do you think is the matter?" Rivers asked angrily. "Plus, I think I banged up my knee really good." He reached down and placed his hands gently on his knee. His pants were torn around the knee, exposing the bleeding red scrape over the cap.

"We need to get out of here," Carrie said to everyone. "I don't like this at all."

"I don't think that's an option," Bishop said from the back of the group. Carrie glanced up at the younger man with anger in her eyes. "You're not going to give me some bullshit scientific reason we have to stay, are you?"

"No," Bishop said slowly. He was standing just inside the cave. He reached his hand out into the empty air. As it was about to pass through the mouth, it was suddenly stopped and forced back. A ripple crossed over the air in front of the cave. "There's something here stopping us."

Dawn stepped forward. "That's amazing. Does it hurt to touch?" Bishop shook his head.

Dawn gingerly reached forward, her fingers stretching the invisible membrane that held them in. "It's like the skin on fresh milk."

"Thank you for that wonderful analogy," Jackson said. "I think my stomach just turned."

Dawn smiled. "Sorry."

Bishop turned to face the group. "Well, what's the plan?"

The crew looked at Bishop, then at each other, then back at Bishop again. None of them wanted to be there, but there didn't seem like they were being presented with much of a choice.

Trent stepped forward. "I think we should investigate," he said boldly. "That's what we're

367

here for, after all."

Rivers shook his head. "We should stay put," he argued. "The last thing we want to do is get lost in this damned cave. We may never see daylight again."

"I tend to agree with Rivers," Carrie stated. "I don't want to die in here."

"Jackson?" Bishop asked.

Jackson shrugged. "I don't really know, man. We don't have a lot of choices here."

Bishop nodded, then looked at Dawn. "What do you think?"

Dawn bit her lip. "I say explore. Like Jackson said, we don't have many other choices."

"I concur," Bishop said quickly. He pressed two fingers to the monitor in his ear. "Let's see how our fearless leader votes," he said, referring to Chloe.

***

Chloe stared at the second monitor. Stephen's face was plastered across the center of the screen. He was yelling something excitedly, but she had the sound muted in her headset. Apparently, he loved this. Looking over at the third monitor, she could see the frightened faces of her crew. She began nervously twisting her hair between her thumb and forefinger. This was her decision alone and time was running out. She knew how cliché that sounded, but it really was. In the panic, the network had gone to a ninety-second commercial break that consisted of two of their promos, and a thirty second national spot, commonly known as "filler" in the industry. She didn't know what to do. She wanted to pull her crew out of there, but there was still almost fifteen minutes left in the show. She knew she could fill that with pre-recorded segments and one or two live breaks with Rivers saying "hi" and "goodbye", but she didn't want to do that, and apparently, from looking at the second monitor again, Stephen didn't want her to either. Chloe also knew the audience wouldn't accept that either, not after what they had just seen.

"Chloe?" Bishop's voice interrupted her thoughts. "Go ahead, Bishop," she responded in a whisper. "We need a decision."

His statement was cold and hard, like being blindsided by a runaway bus. Chloe knew she held all their fates in her hand, and like those three sirens from Greek mythology, she threatened to sever the strings with her golden scissors.

She turned and cast a worried glance at Montoya, who was standing behind her. Montoya nodded once as if to say it was her call, but it was also a warning. Montoya's face was quietly threatening Chloe. She would not let another die on her watch. Not again.

"Okay," she said with an exasperated breath, "let's do it."

Snip.

"Let's explore the cave." She glanced down at her watch. "We have a little less than twenty seconds left in this commercial break," she thought out loud. "Here's what we're going to do. We're going to drop the rest of the pre-recorded segments for the remainder of the show and stay exclusively with you while you explore the cave."

"What if we find nothing?" Rivers asked. "We don't want another 'Al Capone's Vault' on our hands here."

"Well, then at least we gave it our best shot," Chloe answered seriously, but after what she had seen on that third monitor, she was sure they would find something. There was no doubt of that in her mind. "We're back in ten seconds, Rivers."

***

Rivers stood up and quickly dusted himself off the best he could. He then straightened the lapels of his jacket and straightened his tie. *This is going to be a long fifteen minutes,* he told himself. Looking up at the camera, he waited for the red light to wink on.

"You're watching a special live Halloween edition of *Ghost Chasers, Incorporated.* I'm Rivers Gallows," he said in his "announcer" voice. "If you're just joining us, you've missed a hell of a ride so far and it promises to get wilder from here. We're standing inside a cave that was cut into the second floor of a house in Stone Brook, Florida the *second* floor," he added seriously. "With the remaining time in this broadcast, we are going to explore this strange structure and see what happens. We expect some pretty spectacular finds along the way." He looked over at Dawn and Bishop and smiled, "Leading the way will be our resident experts from the Office of Paranormal Investigation, Dawn Lassiter and Nick Bishop."

Trent quickly panned to Dawn and Bishop. They were both completely surprised by the introduction.

Bishop cleared his throat and tried to think of what to say. He didn't have the built-in broadcaster tools Rivers had and he could feel every set of the millions of eyes watching him from home. He swallowed hard, then remembered his equipment. Lifting his EMF Meter, he held it up to the camera. "Because this structure is supernatural in appearance, it will be nearly impossible for us to get reliable readings in here." He pointed to the buried needle on the device. "The same goes for Dawn's Air Ion Counter. These have become almost virtually useless in here. The only thing we have to rely on now is our wits, and our trusty flashlights."

Bishop moved past Trent further into the cave. He stopped briefly to look back, but then pressed on. Trent was right behind him, followed by Jackson, Carrie, Rivers and Dawn bringing up the rear. The pungent smell of must was quickly filling their nostrils, almost to the point of nausea. About four meters into the cave, it started down at a gentle slope, then turned left. The ground was stable, and to their luck, there were no small pebbles or debris lying on the floor that could trip them. Bishop moved his flashlight across the structures in front of him. They roof appeared to almost be ribbed, and he suddenly found himself feeling like Jonas swallowed by the whale. He could almost make out the shapes of ribs running down the walls from a central spine. He wondered if this is what it felt like to be eaten.

Moving his light along the floor, he stopped when he saw something reflect the light. Kneeling down, he ran his light over the floor until he spotted it again. Reaching down, he lifted it up to the camera. It was a gold necklace with a heart-shaped charm on the end.

"It looks like a locket." Setting his flashlight down, he pried open the two halves and stared at the pictures inside. They were of Kelley and Joanne. This was Joanne's locket. "This belonged to a girl who was murdered yesterday here in Stone Brook."

"What is it doing here?" Rivers asked.

"I don't really know...." Bishop suddenly remembered. "It must be part of the 'Ritual of Sevens'," he surmised. "They need seven hearts and a personal effect from each of the victims. This must be what it's for."

"Then why is it here in the middle of this place?" Dawn wondered aloud. "I'm assuming they dropped it," Bishop sighed, "and they will come looking for it. They absolutely need it to complete the ritual." He looked down at the ground and muttered a silent curse. *It wasn't as if we were in enough trouble*...Bishop stood up and slipped the locket into his pocket. "This may buy us some time," he said after a moment. Looking up into the cave, he shined his light straight down the center. There was nothing but darkness for as far as the eye could see. "We should keep going."

***

Cane and Kelley walked slowly behind the hovering Veranda-Morgan. It was ludicrous to even think that, Cane laughed to himself. She was *hovering*. If that wasn't enough to sober anyone, he didn't know what would. They had been moving in

372

the cave, guided by Veranda-Morgan and her self-emanating light, for what felt like an eternity. The cave, no more than five feet tall in places, was a winding mess. He felt like they had been walking in circles because every part of the cave looked the same. He guessed it was a dull brown, but he couldn't really tell in the glare of Veranda-Morgan's bluish light. He glanced back at Kelley. She was walking slowly on bare feet with her hospital gown wrapped tightly around her. She was a mess. He could see a small trickle of blood on her left hand from where the IV needle had been ripped out and her face was still red and bruised. He needed to get her out of here, but he still wasn't sure about Veranda-Morgan. Was she a friend or foe? It was true she had released them, but that may have been just to lead them back to the phantoms and the ritual.

They turned another corner and stopped. Veranda-Morgan bobbed up and down slightly as if a current of wind was destabilizing her float. Cane could see the faint traces of a yellowish light bleeding into the cave. Peeking around Veranda-Morgan, he saw a wide-open area inside it. The ceiling must've been at least twenty feet high, and the diameter of the circular room stretched to almost thirty feet across. A white pentagram was carved into the middle of the room with a tall, white candle burning at each point of the star. Several bizarre symbols, none of which Cane recognized, were painted inside the star with what looked like blood. He counted at least a hundred tapered, white candles sitting on outcroppings of the rock around the room and the faint smell of incense tickled his nose. This was definitely a place of evil.

"Is this where the ritual is going to be held?" Cane asked.

Veranda-Morgan looked down at Cane and nodded. Her eyes had changed from eerie, pure black to an almost milky white. "This is where the ritual is already being held." She raised her hand and pointed to two dark forms hovering near the pentagram. "They have sacrificed six hearts so far."

Cane watched as the two black forms undulated and transformed into human form. They walked toward the circle, each with an item in their hands. Cane strained to see what they had, but couldn't quite make it out. He saw them stop just outside the circle and drop to their knees, then each one placed their object in the center of the circle. Cane's eyes widened. It was a human heart along with a personal item from the victim. He could tell it was a small black wallet. The shadow flipped it open revealing a badge and a photo ID. *Detective Enbaugh,* Cane mourned silently.

The two shadows hardened their red eyes into slits and tossed their heads back. Lifting up their bodies while still in the kneeling position, each floated slightly around the circle. A crack appeared in the center of the star, red light seeping from it. As the two creatures floated faster, the crack opened wider and engulfed the heart and item. A beam of red light shot up from the opening and began to engulf the entire cave. It struck the two phantoms first, sending them screaming to the ground.

Cane watched in horror as the phantoms writhed on the ground in what looked to him like agony. They tore at their own mass with their claws, exposing pools of black liquid below them. "What's happening?"

"No power is without its price," Veranda-Morgan replied stoically.

Cane looked back at the phantoms. They had abandoned their human form in favor of a black mass. Each was slowly pulling away from the circle. Cane took a nervous step back. "Should we move?"

"Why?"

He pointed to the red light, still moving outward from the pentagram. "Won't that hurt us?"

Veranda-Morgan laughed softly. "Don't be foolish. The light will fade before it reaches us."

Cane took another step back, and pulled Kelley with him. "I don't think so."

The red light began to wash over the edges of the cave and into the passageway. It wasn't dissipating. Cane spun around and took Kelley by the hand. The two retreated the way they had come, leaving Veranda-Morgan alone. Catching sight of a connecting tunnel, Cane cut left and pulled Kelley along with him.

Veranda-Morgan faced the red light head on. She wasn't frightened of a little light display like the phantoms were. Steeling herself, she let the light wash over her. As it went, an odd sensation passed over her. The light was supernatural in origin, as was a part of her. The two supernatural elements began to merge. Morgan felt Veranda being ripped from her. She screamed in pain as it felt like a limb being torn off. Morgan spun around in mid-air to see the blue light leaving her with the red. In the blue light, she could see a young woman, not much older than she was with light, curly brown hair and stark green eyes. Her mouth was wide open in a scream, but no sound could be heard. Her long, frail, hand was reaching out for Morgan. In response, Morgan grasped for the almost translucent hand, but felt her own hand swing right through it. She watched as the final blue strands were cleaved from her abdomen and Veranda was washed away with the red light. Morgan felt her body become heavy as it fell to the ground. Her head slammed against a small outcropping of rocks and wrenched into an unnatural position.

The world was growing dark around her. Veranda was gone. At once, she was relieved and worried, but all that didn't matter anymore. She moved her eyes up into the ritual area and saw the phantoms recovering from their ordeal. It wouldn't be long until they had all the hearts.

Chapter 30

"Did you see that?" Bishop asked. "It looked like a red flash of light just ahead of us."

"What do you think it was?" Rivers queried.

"To be honest, I'm not sure." Bishop turned and looked back at Trent. "Did you get that?"

Trent pushed his hand in front of the camera lens and gave the thumbs up.

Bishop stopped and strained his ears. "Did you...?" he let his question trail off as the noise sounded again. This time, it was more distinct, almost like footfalls. Holding his flashlight tightly in his hand, he pointed the beam into the darkness. With his free hand, he signaled for the group to move away. He wasn't sure what was heading their direction, but he wanted the crew well out of harm's way. He glanced back to see the crew quickly following his non-verbal instructions. He knew they weren't exactly raring to meet one of the phantoms in this confined space. His mind was awash in fear. Should he call out, or would that further attract what was coming? *Something wicked this way comes,* he found himself silently quoting. Taking a nervous step forward, he tried to steady himself. The noise was growing louder. It was definitely heading toward the crew. He turned and focused on Jackson, "Are you picking up that sound?"

Jackson nodded. He had his free hand pressed firmly to his headphones, while the other balanced the boom in front of him. Moving his free hand, he moved it down to the recorder slung over his shoulder and toggled the volume knob with his thumb. "I can't quite make it out," he whispered, "but it sounds like footsteps."

Bishop agreed. "That was my guess as well. "

A sudden shriek cut through the silence like a switchblade. Jackson ripped the headphones off his head to try and protect his hearing as Bishop and Trent whipped around. Bishop caught sight of a black form breaking free of the wall just above Carrie, while several long tentacles of darkness were already beginning to wind around her. Trent stumbled back in fear as Rivers and Jackson fell to the ground. The camera hit with a crack of plastic and metal, but continued to send signals to the booth.

Bishop could hear Chloe screaming in his earpiece. Tearing it from his ear, he made a quick decision and charged the phantom. Wrapping his arms around Carrie, he tried to rip her free of the shadow's grasp. Lifting up his flashlight, he aimed the beam directly into the dark mass. The light seemed to be swallowed by the darkness now fully emerged from the wall. Bishop knew he had to hit the eyes, but he didn't see them. He quickly uttered a silent prayer that they had not wised up to his scheme. Another arm of darkness shot out from the mass and wrapped around Carrie's throat. She began to gasp for air as it slowly crushed her windpipe. Lashing out with the metal flashlight, Bishop tried to hit the phantom, but it was like swinging at thin air. He swung again, this time, passing the flashlight through the center of the creature. Still nothing.

"Please," Carrie whispered through forced breaths. Tears were streaming down her face and her arms were thrashing wildly in an effort to free

378

herself. Her eyes were already starting to glass over from lack of oxygen.

The shadow suddenly cackled ominously. "You will not escape," it assured them. Whipping another arm around, it sent Bishop's flashlight skittering to the stone floor. Then, in a move that was much too quick to see, it shot two separate arms out that knocked Bishop to the ground.

Bishop felt his head hit the wall with a sickening crunch. A trickle of blood rolled down his forehead and onto his upper lip. Wiping the blood away with his sleeve, he tried to make it to his feet, but instead, fell hard to the ground.

Dawn braced herself and rushed the phantom. Holding her flashlight tightly in her hands, she swung forcefully down at the black mass. The phantom cackled again as the handle went straight through it. Trying to regain her balance, Dawn swung again, this time, somehow connecting with the creature. The black mass let out a shriek of pain as the cold metal of the flashlight slammed against it. "It can't keep that state permanently," Dawn ventured. "It has to become solid." Dawn took an uncomfortable step back and from the corner of her eye, she could see Jackson moving to her aid. "Get Carrie," Dawn instructed him.

Jackson nodded. Fixing his eyes on the creature, he dumped the last of his equipment on the ground. He felt the cuts on his back throbbing from his last encounter with the phantoms, a not so subtle warning about the danger of this being. Taking a step back, he pressed his arm to the wall, then exploded in one fluent motion toward the creature. Wrapping his arms around the mass, the two

379

impacted the wall and crumbled to the floor. The phantom's tentacles were torn free of Carrie, sending her spilling to the floor and gasping for air.

"Jackson!" Dawn screamed. "No!"

The phantom clawed brutally at Jackson's flesh trying to break free. It was like a caged animal, its only thought of freedom. "Is that all you've got?" Jackson asked as he reared back, blood spilling from the gashes on his chest. Balling up his fist, he sent it sailing toward the shadow's mass. He felt little resistance as his hand plunged into the darkness…and through. He felt his knuckles crack against the hard stone ground, breaking several of them. Jackson ripped his crushed hand free of the darkness and cradled it in his other hand as a yelp escaped his lips.

Seizing the opportunity, the phantom quickly changed into human form and stood up over Jackson. "I remember you," it hissed. "You will not escape…this time." Its red eyes flashed wickedly at its opponent. At once, a wave of darkness spilled out from the shadow and engulfed Jackson. He writhed inside the blackness, trying to break free. Kicking and punching, he tried to find a way out of the complete darkness. He felt himself screaming out, but there was no sound, only darkness.

While the phantom's attention was on Jackson, Dawn crept quietly around it, her flashlight tightly in her hand. Stopping only a foot away from the creature, she took a deep breath and lashed out with the light. The metal of the flashlight hit the being squarely in the back of the head. It stumbled forward, but before it could retaliate, Dawn was on it. Wrapping her hands around its neck, she squeezed as tightly as she could.

Finally regaining his balance, Bishop looked up at the melee that had ensued. He watched Dawn holding onto the back of the phantom with all her might, then he spotted the eyes. Reaching down, he snatched his flashlight from the floor and charged.

Dawn pushed her hand up to what would've been considered the creature's chin and twisted hard. That move would've broken anyone else's neck, but instead, the phantom's head spun one hundred and eighty degrees to face her, its eyes glaring brightly at her. An evil grin crossed the shadow's face as two tentacles shot out from its head and snaked around Dawn's face. Lifting her up, the creature waited for her neck to separate.

Throwing a punch across the phantom's face, Bishop lifted the flashlight up to the creature's eyes. It shrieked in terror as all the darkness instantly retracted. The creature moved away from the light, its arms swinging madly as it tried to knock away the beam. Holding the light steadily on the phantom's eyes, Bishop led it into one of the ribs of the cave. The creature clawed at the rock walls trying to escape. "You don't like that much, do you?" Bishop asked with a grin. His head was still pounding, but this was giving him a small measure of satisfaction. He glanced back at the crew. "Go! Now!"

Taking the cue, the crew, including Carrie and Jackson, retreated from the creature. Turning back around, Bishop swallowed hard. It was gone. The white beam of his flashlight was now focused on the wall of the cave. Taking a nervous step back, Bishop turned to look at Dawn. "Where did it go?"

Dawn shook her head. "I was looking at you."

The two slowly began to backpedal. Spinning around, they both charged deeper into the cave.

"We can't stop these things, can we?" Dawn asked.

Bishop didn't even respond to the question. She knew the answer, and so did he. He just didn't want to admit it out loud. Bishop glanced behind him. They weren't being followed, but how could they be sure? These things can obviously travel through walls, so they could be anywhere. Bishop returned his gaze forward, but not in time to see the figure running toward him. He hit hard, knocking them both to the ground. Quickly recovering, Bishop skittered backwards on his hands and feet to put some distance between the two. He pushed frantically on the rocks without even glancing back at what he hit.

"Bishop," Dawn said with an air of excitement in her voice. "Look." Bishop stopped. Slowly, he turned his head back to the person he hit. A smile flashed across his face. "Cane!" He leapt to his feet and ran to his partner. Over Cane's shoulder, he could see Trent and Rivers snickering quietly at his spill. Extending a hand to the elder man, Bishop helped him off the ground. "Are you okay?"

"I was," Cane said with a wink, "until you plowed me over."

Dawn rushed forward and wrapped her arms around Cane's neck. "Oh my God!" She shouted enthusiastically, "I'm so glad to see you!"

Cane returned the hug, but at the same time tried to loosen Dawn's grip. "It's good to see you too, but you're choking me," he gasped.

Dawn immediately let go and stood staring at her best friend. "What happened?"

"It's a long story," Cane dismissed the question by waiving his hand. "Right now, we have bigger things to worry about."

"'The Ritual of Sevens'," Dawn said.

Cane nodded. "I see you've been doing some research."

"We don't know where it's being held," Bishop said hastily. "We do," Cane said, pointing at Kelley.

Bishop noticed Kelley for the first time. A worried look of concern crossed his face. "Are you alright?"

Kelley stepped forward and smiled sheepishly at Bishop. "Yeah, now that I'm with you."

Dawn rolled her eyes. *I thought she was a lesbian.* Kelley turned and shot a dirty glance toward Dawn. "What's she doing here?" Bishop asked.

"The phantoms brought her here. She was to be part of their ritual." Bishop returned his gaze to Kelley. "That would mean that you—"

Have power, Kelley answered mentally.

A peculiar smile crossed Bishop's face. "That's wild."

Cane turned away from Bishop and back to Dawn. "Morgan's down there," he said, pointing deeper into the cave. "She may be hurt. We need to get her and Kelley out of here."

"And stop the ritual," Dawn added.

Along with the crew, the members of the OPR and Kelley turned into the darkness of the cave and headed down. From here, there was no turning back.

Chapter 31

Morgan was dying. She could feel her very essence slipping out of her the way Veranda had only moments earlier. She felt somewhat stupid. As a witch, she knew death was but a part of life. Neither the end nor the beginning, instead, it was just a stop made between the passages of time. She knew her time would come as everyone's would, but not this way. She had fallen and broken her neck. *At least,* she thought, *I could've been killed by the phantoms.* It was not hers to question, though. Her fate was already sealed. All she could do was hope for a better ending in the next life. *Probably,* she sneered, *I'll return as a slug, or an aardvark. That would be fitting.*

She carefully opened her eyes. The world around her was dark, but she could make out faint shapes in the haze. The flicker of candles and a trace of burning red…the shadows were here, but she couldn't be concerned about that right now. She tried to lift up her head to take a better look around, but found herself unable. The muscles in her neck were trying to respond, but there was nothing there to push against. She could feel that several vertebrae in her neck had been severed; at least one had been crushed. She could feel that she was vertical, but that was the extent of it. Below her neck, everything was numb. Her body may as well have been gone as it was useless to her.

A thought manifested in her mind of a healing spell. She had done it several years ago to her roommate's puppy when he broke his leg. She had actually healed the dog's leg, but not perfectly. It still required being in a cast for several weeks, but she had hastened its recovery. Perhaps she could accomplish the same with her neck. If not be completely healed, at least give herself a little more time. The human body, especially the nervous system, was a very fragile piece of equipment. Healing spells were notoriously difficult to perform correctly, and she wasn't exactly in the best of conditions right now. She weighed her options. She was dying anyway, might as well take a crack at it. *Crack, very funny. Death has made me giddy....*

She closed her eyes and cleared her thoughts. An image of her wounded neck appeared very clearly in her mind's eye. It was kind of like looking at a three dimensional x-ray. She could clearly see the separated bones and the one that was partially broken. It wasn't as bad as she had first feared. Channeling all her focus on the image, she began to see bright flashes of orange and green around the damaged areas. Slowly, the bones began to mend together, the nerves and blood vessels even repairing themselves. She watched as the muscles around the bones knitted together, forming an almost normal structure. She focused on the broken vertebrae. It wasn't darning. It had, however, returned to its normal position in her neck. Concentrating, she tried to heal the broken bone. Muscles and nerves wound their way around and through the bone, but she could not repair it.

She opened her eyes and lifted her head up. A sound like cereal crunching came from her neck, but at least she was able to move it. She twitched her fingers and toes and amazingly, could feel them. It had almost completely worked. She slowly turned and looked around. Her body was pinned to the wall of the cave with her arms spread wide like a crucifix. Her clothes were ripped open exposing her bare chest. A heart-shaped figure had been carved into it. She knew they meant to take her heart. Looking down, she could clearly see the pentagram and candles. Two shadows in human form were lurking just below her with wide smiles on their faces.

She was to be the seventh heart in their ritual….

Morgan uttered a silent prayer. She knew more people were down here, she could feel their presence. She just hoped they would arrive in time.

***

Cane led the crew down the winding passage. Ahead of him, he could see the soft golden glow of candles in the darkness. Stopping, he pressed against the wall of the passage and turned back to the crew. "This is it," he whispered cautiously. "The ritual is being performed in the chamber at the bottom of this tunnel."

"What's the plan?" Dawn asked.

Cane looked over the group. "I don't want any civilian casualties. The crew should stay back here."

"It's a little too late for that," Carrie said from the back of the group. Several large black bruises had formed on her throat. "We've already lost our sound tech to these fuckers."

"All the more reason you should stay here," Cane warned them. "Dawn, you and Bishop come with me. Kelley, you stay back with the crew."

386

"We're live on the air, Mr. Cane," Rivers reminded him from the back of the group. "We need to film this."

Cane mulled the idea around in his head for a moment. "All right," he said finally, "but it's your ass. I don't want any of you to enter the ritual chamber. Stay back where you'll be safe."

Rivers nodded.

Cane turned back into the tunnel and started down. Dawn and Bishop moved from the middle of the group to join him. Each had a flashlight in their hands as they crept soundlessly down the passage.

Rivers moved to the front of the crew and began to lead them down. Pausing only momentarily to address the camera, he started his narration. "We're now entering one of the lower chambers in this maze of passageways. From eyewitness accounts, a dark ritual is being performed there and our experts from the OPR have vowed to stop it. This reporter isn't exactly sure what the ritual entails, but I'm sure it's bad news." Rivers could hear Chloe groaning in his earpiece. Even he knew it was a lame statement. "Let me assure you, the viewer at home, that this is completely real. We are standing in the middle of what is sure to become a volatile situation. Our cameras will continually roll in order to bring you every detail of what is sure to be a chilling encounter. I have to warn you, ladies and gentlemen, what you are about to see may be gruesome. Our younger viewers and the squeamish may want to turn away from the television."

Rivers stepped away from the camera so Trent could get complete, uninterrupted shots of the action.

***

"This is great," Chloe heard Stephen say from the second monitor. "The top brass here at the network are already talking video and DVD sales."

Chloe let her head fall into her hands. *Great,* she thought, *a DVD of my crew dying.*

***

Cane poked his head around the corner and immediately scanned for Morgan. "I can't see her," he reported.

"What can you see?" Dawn asked, placing a hand on his back.

"It looks like the chamber is empty. The pentagram is still there, and all the candles are still burning, but there's no sign of the phantoms."

"What's the game plan, chief?" Bishop asked.

"We need to disrupt the circle. That will buy us some time. Then we need to find the last heart and destroy it." Cane paused, "Dear Lord, I hope they haven't already finished."

"We better get in there," Dawn said.

"Who are you, John Wayne?" Bishop laughed. "If we go charging in there, they'll kick our ass no questions asked. We need to have a better plan than that."

Everyone perked up at the sound of a woman's scream, then silence. They immediately turned back to the crew. "Who was that?" Cane asked.

The crew shrugged.

388

"It wasn't us," Rivers said with a cigarette hanging out of his mouth.

The three turned back to the chamber. "Looks like our plan just got thrown out," Dawn said quickly.

"Agreed," Cane said. "We go in on three."

He held up three fingers with his free hand and silently mouthed the word three. Flipping one down, he mouthed two. Laying down the last finger, the three stood up from their positions and charged blindly into the chamber. They all skidded to a stop when they found the source of the scream. They saw two shadows standing on the wall next to the lifeless body of Morgan. The first shadow had just ripped out her heart and still held it in his hand. The other was rummaging over her body looking for a personal item.

"That's the seventh heart," Cane yelled.

The two shadows snapped their heads around to see the three trespassers in their chamber. A loud hiss escaped their lips as they leapt off the wall and crouched on the floor. The first shadow lifted the heart to his chest and slipped it into the darkness. The heart was quickly absorbed for safekeeping. The second shadow's form quickly mutated into that of a large, sleek dog. It's red eyes slanted back on its head as it growled at the intruders. "You will die," they voiced together.

"That's a new one," Bishop said nervously.

The shadows charged. The first one slammed head first into Cane, knocking him to the ground, while the second careened into Dawn and Bishop.

Cane quickly recovered, lifting himself off the ground. Clicking the power button on his flashlight, he swung it around to face the shadow and hit it squarely in the eyes. The creature screamed in pain as it tried to back away. Moving forward, Cane swung his free hand back across the phantom's head connecting solidly. Dropping down, he kicked the legs out from under the phantom, sending it hard to the floor. Jumping back, Cane narrowly avoided a wild swing from a dark tentacle. It whipped just past his chest and cracked like a bullwhip. A second tentacle caught the elder man off-guard, ripping through his shoulder like a torpedo. Cane fell to the ground in agony, blood pouring from his wound. To his dismay, his flashlight fell to the floor next to him, just out of his grasp.

Bishop rolled onto his back and pushed Dawn out of the way. The second shadow—the shadow dog—was charging. Clicking the button on his flashlight, he sent the white beam of light arcing out across the darkness, just missing the dog's eyes. Without time to correct, the dog was upon him, its long white fangs and claws ripping at Bishop's clothes. Lifting herself off the floor, Dawn bent down into a three point stance. Digging in the balls of her feet, she rocketed toward the dog and checked it with her shoulder. The shadow dog yelped as it hit the floor, but was quickly back up on its feet. Lifting her flashlight, Dawn swung hard and caught the dog on the side of the head, giving Bishop just enough time to scoot out of the way.

The first shadow knelt down next to Cane and sneered. Lifting its arm, it formed it into a long, pointed tentacle and shot it into the wound on Cane's shoulder. Cane gritted his teeth and held back the scream. He wouldn't give the creature the satisfaction. The phantom twisted the tentacle and slowly started to increase its girth. Cane bit down onto his lip to try and stifle the pain. He looked up into the creature's eyes. It was enjoying his pain and was in no rush to end it.

Using its free hand, the creature reached into its chest and retrieved Morgan's heart, along with what looked like a button from her shirt. "Do you see these?" it hissed. "This is the end of history." Lifting it up, it tossed them lazily into the center of the pentagram. It twisted the tentacle again, then smiled with delight. It had a better idea. Cane watched as a ripple of spikes began to form on the arm and move quickly toward the end. Three spikes jutted out into Cane's shoulder, ripping muscles and flesh. Cane couldn't hold it any longer. He let out a bellowing scream. Striking out with his free hand, Cane watched his hand slice right through the shadow with no effect. The shadow cackled with glee. Moving his hand down into his pocket, Cane felt a silver pen in his pocket. Grabbing it firmly, he quickly slid it out of his pocket.

Dawn surged left just as the dog lunged at her, its claws barely missing her head. Glancing up, she saw a large crack forming in the middle of the pentagram around the heart. "Bishop!"

Bishop snapped his head around to see the heart. He jumped off the floor and sprinted toward the circle. Dropping his flashlight, he dove forward with both hands reaching for the heart, but was stopped short. He hit the rock floor hard with his chin. Looking back, he could see the dog holding one of his ankles firmly in its mouth. "Fuck," he muttered. Kicking back, he hit the dog in the teeth, but it held fast. He kicked again, but this time, he felt the dog's teeth break the flesh of his ankle. Bishop let out a muffled cry. "I can't get it, Dawn!"

She was already on it. As soon as she saw the dog grab Bishop's foot, she had charged toward the pentagram. Dropping down to her knees, she reached toward the crack for the heart. The red light burned her flesh. Ripping her hand back, she cradled her burnt hand. She couldn't let the heart be swallowed. Reaching back into the red light, she tried to ignore the searing red light as she rummaged around for the heart. Suddenly, she felt it. Like a baby touching a hot stove, she ripped the heart and her hand free of the light. To her amazement, the rift quickly sealed. Snapping her head back, she spotted the dog eyeing her. "Oh shit."

The first shadow's head flipped toward the pentagram and sneered at Dawn. It pulled the tentacle free from Cane's shoulder and began to stand up. Seizing the moment, Cane sat up and grabbed the shadow by the throat. *They can only be transparent when they're happy,* he thought as his fingers connected. The phantom's head snapped around to face Cane with its red eyes burning with hatred. Quickly, Cane lifted the silver ballpoint pen and plunged it forward into the creature's eye. The shadow fell back, black liquid spurting from the wound. It writhed in agony on the floor as it tried to free the pen. Cane leapt forward onto the creature and forced the pen further into the being's eye. The creature shrieked in pain as a pool of the black fluid was forming around it.

Reaching back, Cane retrieved his flashlight,

and using the blunt end, smashed it into the shadow's opposite eye. Standing back, Cane watched as the phantom slowed to a stop and its body began to decompose.

Holding Morgan's heart in her hand, Dawn took several steps away from the dog. "You want this?" she teased. "You're going to have to come and get it."

Dawn could see Bishop slowly lifting himself off the floor and moving toward the dog on his injured ankle. The dog had crouched down on his front paws, while its back legs looked ready to spring. It was snarling loudly and its red eyes had narrowed into small slits of evil.

Bishop glanced back at Cane, who was standing triumphantly over a pool of black liquid. Cane turned to look at Bishop.

"The eyes." Bishop nodded.

Dawn took another uncomfortable step back from the dog. She didn't want to run because then the creature would charge and she knew it could easily take her. She watched the dog creep forward. It's every move a calculated adjustment. It knew she wanted to run. It was just trying to catch her off-guard. Dawn spotted Cane and Bishop moving toward the dog and started forming a plan. Rearing back, she tossed the heart toward Cane. "Catch!"

Cane quickly moved under the heart and caught it with his good arm. Spinning around, he ran toward the back of the cave holding the heart like a football. "What now?" he yelled frantically.

Bishop already knew what to do. As the dog spun around to chase Cane, he threw himself on top of it, knocking them both to the ground. Moving quickly, Bishop wrapped his palms around the dog's head and pressed his thumbs into its eyes. The shadow dog yelped in pain as Bishop felt his thumbs burst through the red membranes of the dog's eyes. A black fluid sprayed out of the eyes, washing over everything, including Bishop. Moving his hands, Bishop dug his thumbs further into the phantom's eyes. It was writhing in pain below him. With one final act of evil, a stray tentacle shot off the dog's chest and burst through Bishop's right thigh. Bishop held steady as he pushed his thumbs harder. He heard one final whimper from the phantom, then its body went limp. Taking a deep breath, Bishop fell backward off the dog and onto the cold floor.

"Good work," Cane's familiar accent said from across the cave. "Can you walk?"

Bishop nodded, "I don't want to, but I can."

Dawn stepped in front of Bishop and extended a hand down. "Come on." Bishop grabbed Dawn's hand and forced himself up. He felt a burst of pain in his legs as he stood up. "I think I need a doctor." He looked over at Cane nursing his bloody shoulder, "And so do you. Let's get out of here."

"Agreed," Dawn said as she wrapped an arm around Bishop.

The three slowly walked across the cave, but stopped in the center of the pentagram.

"We shouldn't leave this here," Dawn said.

Cane smiled and lifted a small lighter out of his pocket. "I wholeheartedly agree." Flicking the lighter, he watched the small blue butane flame jump from the top. Kneeling down, he touched the flame to the edge of the circle and stepped back.

The pentagram erupted into a circle of green flames, but then quickly burnt out, leaving nothing but a bare stone floor.

"You've done that before, haven't you?" Bishop asked with a smile. "No," Cane admitted, "but I've always wanted to."

The three walked out of the cave and into the arms of the waiting crew. Rivers stepped forward and stopped the three before they could move past. "Can you tell me what it was like in there?"

"Incredible," Bishop said with a deep breath.

"Please," Dawn said, pushing past Rivers, "we need to get these two to a hospital."

Rivers turned back to the camera and smiled broadly. He heard Chloe in his ear telling him to wrap it up. "What you have seen here tonight is real. This was actual phenomenon in this house. There were no special effects used, and no camera tricks involved. We hope what you have seen has chilled you, but also deepened your understanding of the events that *do* happen in real life. For *Ghost Chasers, Incorporated*, I'm Rivers Gallows. Happy Halloween."

He watched the red light blink off and could see the smiles on the faces of the crew behind it.

Chloe's voice cut across their earphones, "And we're clear."

Chapter 32

Bishop and Cane sat together in the back of an ambulance while two EMTs patched them up. One was wrapping gauze around Cane's shoulder, while the other was applying an ointment to Bishop's ankle. The red and blue lights were casting an almost serene glow across the Grant House. Hurricane Katrina had let up about an hour ago and was moving back out to sea where she would become nothing more than a tropical storm, then return to the point she was spawned. Several police cruisers were sitting around the house working diligently under Detective Montoya's direction to clean up the scene. Dawn and Kelley were standing just outside the ambulance looking in.

Cane looked up and smiled at Bishop. "Not bad for a first assignment?" Bishop laughed. "Not bad at all."

"Still want to be a part of the team?"

Bishop nodded without hesitation. "You bet. Somebody's going to have to watch after you."

Cane extended his hand. "Partners?"

Bishop grabbed Cane's hand and shook it firmly. "Partners."

The EMT working on Cane patted him on the shoulder and stood up. "You still need to go to the hospital, but you're patched up for the time being."

Cane nodded. "Thanks."

The EMT moved to the back of the ambulance and helped Kelley inside. "We need to get all of you down to General as soon as possible."

Dawn followed Kelley into the truck and sat down on the edge next to Cane, while Kelley was

396

laid on the stretcher in the middle. Dawn, Cane and Bishop looked at each other, then at Kelley.

"Where are you going to go after this, Kelley?" Bishop asked. "I don't know," she replied as the EMT worked on her.

Bishop looked up at Cane with a smile. "How about a foursome?" Cane shook his head with a smile. "Not another rookie partner."

Bishop looked back down at Kelley. "How would you like to come work for the Office of Paranormal Investigation?"

Kelley smiled. "I thought you'd never ask."

***

The back doors of the ambulance were slammed shut and the vehicle made its way out of the driveway and onto the street. A light rain was still falling over Stone Brook, but it was soft and cleansing.

A pair of red eyes appeared in the second floor window of the Grant House. It was half past midnight. It would have to wait another seventy-seven years to complete the ritual. It was so close this time, but it would be patient. It had to be. After all, it had almost eighty years to wait. Turning away from the window, it walked out into the hallway and took a left. Moving briskly down the hall, it stopped in front of a mirror and smiled. This would do nicely. It was everything it needed to seek its revenge. It was *perfect*.

Moving down the stairs, it walked past several uniformed officers on the way to the door. One officer took notice. "Can I help you, miss?"

Morgan looked at the officer with a smile, "No thank you." Turning away, she walked out the front door and into the night.